The Uncollected Stories of Mary Wilkins Freeman

The Uncollected Stories of Mary Wilkins Freeman

MARY R. REICHARDT

University Press of Mississippi
Jackson & London

95 94 93 92   4 3 2 1

The paper in this book meets the guidelines for permanence and durability of the
Committee on Production Guidelines for Book Longevity of the Council on Library
Resources.

Library of Congress Cataloging-in-Publication Data

Freeman, Mary Eleanor Wilkins, 1852–1930.
  [Short stories. Selections]
  The uncollected stories of Mary Wilkins Freeman / [compiled by]
Mary R. Reichardt.
    p.   cm.
  Includes bibliographical references.
  ISBN 0-87805-564-9 (cloth). — ISBN 0-87805-565-7 (paper)
  I. Reichardt, Mary R.   II. Title.
PS1711.R45   1992
813'.54—dc20   91-48011
                                                                 CIP

British Library Cataloging-in-Publication data available

CONTENTS

v

CHRONOLOGY

1852   Born in Randolph, Massachusetts
1867   Moves with family to Brattleboro, Vermont
1870   Graduates from high school and enters Mt. Holyoke
1871   Leaves Mt. Holyoke because of ill health
1876   Anna Wilkins, Mary's only sister, dies.
1880   Mother dies.
1881   Publishes several poems in children's magazines *Wide Awake* and *St. Nicholas*
1882   Receives fifty dollars from the *Boston Sunday Budget* for her first adult story, "The Shadow Family"
1883   Father dies; "Two Old Lovers" published in *Harper's Bazar*; returns to Randolph to live.
1887   Publication of *A Humble Romance and Other Stories*
1891   *A New England Nun and Other Stories*
1893   *Jane Field; Giles Corey, Yeoman*
1894   *Pembroke*
1896   *Madelon*
1897   *Jerome, A Poor Man*; becomes engaged to Charles Freeman.
1898   *Silence and Other Stories; The People of Our Neighborhood*
1899   *The Jamesons*
1900   *The Love of Parson Lord and Other Stories; The Heart's Highway*
1901   *Understudies; The Portion of Labor*
1902   Marries Charles Freeman on January 1
1903   *Six Trees; The Wind in the Rose-Bush and Other Stories of the Supernatural*
1904   *The Givers*

1905 *The Debtor*
1906 *"Doc" Gordon*
1907 *The Fair Lavinia and Others; By the Light of the Soul*
1908 *The Shoulders of Atlas;* chapter in Howells' "cooperative" novel *The Whole Family*
1909 *The Winning Lady and Others*
1912 *The Yates Pride: A Romance; The Butterfly House*
1914 *The Copy-Cat and Other Stories*
1917 *An Alabaster Box*
1918 *Edgewater People*
1921 Charles Freeman committed to New Jersey State Hospital for the Insane at Trenton
1922 Mary Freeman is legally separated from Charles Freeman.
1923 Charles Freeman dies.
1926 Receives the William Dean Howells Gold Medal for Fiction from the American Academy of Arts and Letters; is elected to membership in the National Institute of Arts and Letters.
1927 *The Best Stories of Mary E. Wilkins,* edited by Henry W. Lanier
1930 Dies in Metuchen, New Jersey

INTRODUCTION

Interest in the works of Mary Wilkins Freeman has grown steadily since Edward Foster published what remains the standard biography, *Mary E. Wilkins Freeman,* in 1956. In particular, feminist scholarship of the last twenty years has reintroduced Freeman to a modern audience and drawn attention to her women's themes. Although Freeman was lauded in her day primarily for her realism in chronicling the decline of New England, this resurgence of interest in recent years has focused on what is now seen as her most compelling and characteristic theme: women's struggles for self-assertion and self-identity in often repressive and impoverished circumstances.

Few today would question Freeman's important position in turn-of-the-century American fiction or her significant contributions to the development of the American short story. Not merely an exceptional regional writer intent on careful delineation of local characters and customs and exact transcription of indigenous dialect, Freeman participated as well in the rise of modern, psychological literature. Skilled at revealing deep-seated emotions and concealed attitudes with a line or two of apparently inconsequential dialogue or gesture, Freeman employed her dramatic style to express the inner lives—the frustrations, struggles, fears, and hopes—of a wide variety of New England women. She is, of course, best known for her superb portraits of women who attempt to rebel against the norms of a patriarchal society and the strictures of conservative religion; such stories as "The Revolt of 'Mother'," "A Village Singer," and "A New England Nun" are now regularly anthologized. But Freeman's rebel figures, while important, constitute only one image in her overall portrait of women and womanhood. Equally important are those women who accept the Victorian ideal of mother and wife; those without marriage prospects who face both a financially insecure and socially crippled future; those frustrated with, yet submissive to, the confines of marriage; and those who must daily deal with advancing age, poverty, and loneliness. Looked at collectively, therefore, Freeman's writings constitute a detailed and elaborate study of late nineteenth- and early twentieth-century New England women.

A dedicated professional writer, Freeman devoted nearly fifty years of her life to her craft. During this long career, her daily habits rarely varied; she once half-jokingly told a visitor that her companion of many years, Mary John Wales, "shuts me in my study each morning and won't let me out till I have written at least fifteen hundred words" (Garland, 128). After her marriage in 1902, her husband Charles Freeman similarly helped her arrange her schedule so that she could concentrate on her writing. Her disciplined habits resulted in a prolific output: fourteen novels, nearly 250 adult short stories, several plays, and numerous poems, children's works, and nonfiction essays. Though plagued by various illnesses and a deteriorating marriage in her later years, Freeman wrote steadily up to her death in 1930. "I feel [my writing] is all I came into the world for," she wrote poignantly toward the end of her life, "and [that I] have failed dismally if it is not a success" (Kendrick, 424).

Success came quickly for Freeman. Not many years after publication of her first extant short story for adults, "Two Old Lovers," in an 1883 edition of *Harper's Bazar*, Freeman's fiction was producing "something like a craze" both in this country and abroad ("Notes," 101). Her popularity soared with the publication of the two collections *A Humble Romance* (1887) and *A New England Nun* (1891) and continued to remain high until around the turn of the century. Indeed, for several years, a number of the era's most prominent magazines, such as *Harper's*, *Lippincott's*, *Century*, and *Woman's Home Companion*, regularly solicited stories from Mary Wilkins; she herself once marveled at the "ridiculous prices" her work commanded (Kendrick, 321).

For personal and professional reasons, however, after 1895 Freeman increasingly turned her attention to writing novels. As early as 1885 she had expressed the desire to attempt longer works, describing the "little melody" of the short story as a prelude to the "grand opera" of

the novel (Kendrick, 382). With the relative success of her New England novels *Jane Field* (1893) and *Pembroke* (1894), she evidently
felt that her "natural growth" as an author had rendered her equal
to the task (Kendrick, 63). Over the next two decades, therefore,
she experimented with a variety of genres ranging from historical romance to broad farce. The majority of these longer works, some running to nearly 500 pages, being at times implausibly plotted and halt-
ingly developed, failed in the eyes of her critics. Attempting in her
novel-writing to accomplish the dual aims of expanding her personal
repertoire and satisfying an unpredictable popular market, Freeman
sacrificed in this latter period some of the spontaneity and powerful
originality that consistently characterized her early short fiction. As
she increasingly abandoned her New England themes and her sparse,
compressed style, the subsequent loss of realism resulted at times in
artificiality, and the terse, direct dialogue became labored, overwritten
prose. Thus her concentration on novels in this stage of her career
inadvertently contributed to her reputation's decline.

Equally responsible for the waning of Freeman's popularity in the
first decades of this century were larger cultural and literary shifts.
Among other factors, the reading public's new taste for the exotic and
the adventure story began to render her rural settings and feminine
subject matter passé. Keenly aware of the diminishing "market for
[her] own wares," Freeman frankly admitted her perplexity to an as-
piring young writer in 1926: "Everything is different since the War
and since even the pre-war days for I think the change antedated the
War. As nearly as I can understand the situation, there is in arts and
letters a sort of frantic impulse for something erratic, out of the common. . . . I am about as bewildered by the whole situation as you are"
(Kendrick, 401–2).

Although never again as popular as she had been after the appearance of her first two collections, Freeman continued to produce short
fiction throughout her career, successfully publishing nearly 130 stories between 1900 and 1930. Inevitably, some of these later works
suffer from the same unfortunate characteristics as the novels she was
concurrently composing: forced prose, implausible plots, weak endings. Yet despite frequent suggestions to the contrary, it is important
to note that Freeman did not lose her talent in these years, nor did

her marriage at the age of forty-nine adversely affect her writing. Although her later work became increasingly uneven, many of Freeman's post-1900 stories rival her earlier tales, evincing the same careful attention to craft and insightful unfolding of theme.

Currently, Freeman's readers have at their disposal nearly all of her 146 originally collected stories. However, nearly 100 of her short stories were not collected during her lifetime, and most were, therefore, never reprinted after their initial appearance in various magazines and newspapers. Astute in the management of her business affairs, Freeman habitually worked with her publishers, primarily the Harper and Brothers firm, to select the stories making up her various collections. Those stories, however, were not picked with an eye to their intrinsic aesthetic or technical merit alone; rather, Freeman's editors most often chose works consistent with a pre-established theme or "hook" around which the collection was to be organized. The collection *Silence and Other Stories* (1898), for example, consists of works set in the Puritan past; *Understudies* (1901), of symbolic animal and flower tales; *The Givers* (1904), of stories contrasting the effects of generosity versus selfishness; and *Edgewater People* (1918), of interrelated tales centering on individuals in a small village. A number of skillfully written and powerfully conceived stories, therefore, were set aside merely because they did not fit into the editors' plan at the time.

This volume of Freeman's short fiction brings together for the first time twenty of the best of Freeman's uncollected tales, thus contributing to our growing reevaluation of a remarkable author. Arranged chronologically, the stories span much of Freeman's career, beginning with "Emmy," written at the height of her success in 1891 and coinciding with the publication of *A New England Nun*, and concluding with both "The Jester," her last published story, and "The White Shawl," one of several undated and unfinished manuscripts left at the time of her death. Within these pages, we discover Freeman once again delving into the inner lives of women, exploring their relationships with parents, with other women, and with men. We see women contemplate, accept, or reject marriage, an institution yet a social and, often, economic necessity in Freeman's New England. We witness some women attempting to adjust to their new roles within marriage and others who, alone and lonely, face with unspoken dread the prospect of a monotonous and impoverished future. We also encounter subject matter less common in Freeman's work. Five stories ("A Guest in Sodom," "The Cloak Also," "The Slip of the Leash," "The Jester," and "The Hall Bedroom") involve male protagonists. Three stories ("The Hall Bedroom," "The White Shawl," and "Sweet-Flowering Perennial") are mystery tales, and three ("Juliza," "The Blue Butterfly," and "The Prism") feature various kinds of women artists. In addition, several late stories show Freeman's attempt to incorporate modern themes into her fiction: for example, an automobile figures prominently in "A Guest in Sodom" and "Mother-Wings." Each of the stories in this volume continues to give witness to Freeman's wide-ranging subject matter, dramatic style, and skillful use of dialogue. Many of them serve as well to broaden our understanding of her women's themes, challenging at times the perception that the rebel figure is necessarily at the core of her most characteristic fiction. Although Freeman's women protagonists are frequently strong, decisive, and self-determining, they are usually also practical, choosing to exert or suppress their wills according to the very real and often extremely limiting circumstances of their lives.

Of the eighty-odd uncollected stories that do not appear in this volume, the majority are holiday tales, as titles such as "A Christmas Lady," "Mrs. Sackett's Easter Bonnet," "Susan Jane's Valentine," and "A Thanksgiving Thief" indicate. Once her name became a household word, Freeman was regularly commissioned to produce such works and, always practical, generally did not hesitate to tailor her writing to the specifications of individual editors, so that the quality of these stories is extremely uneven. Many end disappointingly with a platitude appropriate to the season despite development of otherwise realistic situations and themes; others, poorly plotted from the outset, seem forced. A few, however, including those reprinted in this volume ("For the Love of One's Self," "The Horn of Plenty," and "Friend of My Heart"), achieve internal power and tension in spite of the overt holiday intent.

Another large group of uncollected stories straddles the border between children's and adult fiction or involves child protagonists; these stories include "The Cautious King and the All-Round Wise Woman," "Honorable Tommy," "How Charlotte Ellen Went Visiting," and "A

War-Time Dress." Freeman began her career as a writer of children's poetry and tales and continued to achieve success in that field for many years. It is sometimes difficult to determine whether a story was originally intended for children or for adults. Others, although notable for their sensitive depictions of magnified childhood fears, in general hold little appeal for a modern audience because of their sentimental subject matter. A complete listing of Freeman's stories written for adults, both collected and uncollected, can be found in the appendix to this volume.

The following brief observations may help to provide a context for the stories the reader is about to encounter. We first note those involving the subject Freeman examined from nearly every angle during her long literary career: women and marriage. Not married until her late forties, Freeman had for much of her life doubted the value of marriage and used her fiction to explore the personal, familial, and social ramifications of the married and the single conditions. A large group of her stories, for example, portrays family tension resulting from a young woman in conflict with her mother over the question of marriage. Intent, for her own purposes, on having her daughter marry well, a mother in Freeman's world not only nags the daughter but may even use extreme measures—including deceit and witchcraft—to procure such a marriage. Feeling trapped between the demands of filial obedience and a desire to choose her mate freely, the daughter grows increasingly frustrated over her mother's interference. Such suppressed aggression and hostility often lead to the figure of the "bad" or "villain" mother in the daughter's mind, an image appearing frequently in Freeman's stories about women and marriage. The well-known tale "Louisa" is one of many illustrating this type of struggle.

Two stories in this collection portray such conflict. In "Mother-Wings," Mrs. Bodley resorts to a series of ridiculous actions to convince her neighbors that her "old-fashioned" and "backward" daughter Ann is about to wed a wealthy widower. Her subterfuge succeeds; to her consternation, Ann is greeted by congratulations wherever she goes. However, when the young man Ann loves backs away because of the rumor of her impending marriage, Ann confronts her mother angrily: "You have tried and tried to push me into everything else, and I have submitted. . . . But to try to push me into marriage!" As do a number of Freeman's mothers, Mrs. Bodley must eventually humble herself before her daughter, painfully confessing her wrongdoing.

In "The Witch's Daughter," a well-meaning mother takes drastic measures to secure a suitor for her daughter. One of a number of witch-like or vampire-like mothers in Freeman's fiction, old Elma Franklin turns to witchcraft to "compel" love for her daughter, Daphne. Ann Douglas Wood, writing perceptively about the recurring image of witchcraft in women's regional writing, attributes Freeman's use of it not only to her lifelong feeling of being an "outcast," but also to the fact that she may have felt responsible for "sapping" the life out of her parents and sister, all of whom died while she was still a young woman (Wood, 27). In this story, the daughter's failure to attract a suitor is associated with the powerful mother, who must first be annihilated before the daughter can hope to marry. To her horror, Daphne soon realizes that the price of obtaining a lover is nothing less than her mother's life. Elma's incantation succeeds; as she sinks to the ground, her self-sacrifice is grossly ennobled by the young couple: ". . . they stooped over her and they knew that she had been no witch, but a great lover."

A number of characteristic Freeman stories initiate a seemingly conventional love plot only to interrupt that plot and subordinate the romantic concern, focusing attention instead on the internal struggles of the female protagonist. Borrowing a technique used by writers of sentimental/domestic fiction, Freeman often contrasts a conventional heroine—a fair, dependent, and weak female—with a stronger, more practical, and decidedly unromantic one. The romantic woman succeeds in coming between a pair of lovers; the stronger woman, who can retain the man if she so chooses, eventually and after much deliberation "gives" him to her weaker counterpart. Her motives are rarely altruistic; rather, on some level she realizes that the male, usually described as effeminate, vacillating, or passive, is much more the romantic ingénue's equal. The stronger woman knows that marriage with such a partner would be ultimately unsatisfactory; on the other hand, she is also fully cognizant of the social and personal stigma of spinsterhood. She will most likely have no other chances. Relegating the conventional pair of lovers to the subplot, Freeman concentrates in the remainder of the story on the inner dilemma of the woman left alone. "A New England Nun" is one of many Freeman stories that ironically upsets a conventional love plot in such a manner.

In "Emmy," the female protagonist's concern for the welfare of Jim Parsons, an attractive yet reckless young man, leads her to importune her rival Flora Marsh to restrain him from undertaking a dangerous sea voyage. Emmy realizes that, in doing so, she will lose Jim to Flora, and that she will have to contend with both her own loneliness and the disappointed hopes of her family. "With a monotone of life behind her and one stretching before," Emmy nevertheless remains resolute as the couple is wed; her deep affection for the young man is, the narrator tells us, "greater than marriage."

In "Juliza," heavy-set, unromantic, yet talented Juliza Peck learns that her lover of many years, Frank Williams, no longer wishes to marry her. "Like a bashful child, blushing, and half-smiling," Frank admits he has fallen in love with another woman. Astonished, Juliza nevertheless remains in full control, even offering to care for Frank's ailing mother as he goes to court his new love. Called on to exercise her gift for oration at Frank's wedding, Juliza triumphs in her ability to hold the wedding party so spellbound with her recital that they virtually forget the bridal couple itself. A well-crafted tale, "Juliza" also makes a strong statement about artistic sublimation, much like the one made in "A Village Singer." Juliza's art, an acceptable way of channeling her emotions, consists of repeating what others have written, just as her life is, in effect, bound up by what others decide. She does resist, yet only within the limits of her options.

Finally, in "Friend of My Heart," Catherine Dexter eventually chooses to give up Lucius Converse, a middle-aged man searching only for a warm home and appetizing meals, to her weaker and unstable friend, Elvira Meredith. Freeman notes Catherine's painful dilemma closely. A practical and perceptive woman, Catherine understands both Lucius's and her own needs; she carefully weighs the consequences of marrying him or not. She is, moreover, fully aware that if she rejects him, she will have no other opportunities for marriage. Although this holiday story ends sentimentally, Freeman nevertheless makes the conflicting emotions of Catherine's decision clear: "A great loneliness was over her. . . . a high courage, as of one who leads herself to battle." Although in the end alone and often lonely,

Freeman's protagonists who forego marriage reveal an inner strength that at times amounts to heroism.

In another group of stories, Freeman portrays women struggling with self-acceptance and self-assertion in affairs of the heart. In "Criss-Cross," two impoverished and elderly women, frustrated with the monotony of their lives, agree to exchange households for a week. During that time, each relives a memory of a lost love and is thereby refreshed, able to continue to face the long stretch of days ahead. In "The Doll Lady," the young woman Minnie, angry at overhearing the minister assert that she is nothing but a mindless "doll," slyly rewrites his sermon to center on the text "Judge not, that ye be not judged." Her boldness consequently succeeds in teaching the proud young man a much-needed lesson in humility. Lastly, in "For the Love of One's Self," the lonely and unattractive factory worker Amanda Dearborn refuses to believe that another could love her even when she is courted by a co-worker, Frank Ayres. Embittered by her hard life and torn between her own selfishness and the memory of her dead mother's generosity, Amanda seethes inwardly as she toils: ". . . her thoughts were anarchistic, almost blasphemous. . . . she realized with a subtle defiance and rebellion that she was not in a spiritual sense a good woman." At first rejecting the gifts she receives from Frank, Amanda gradually begins to accept herself as lovable and thus becomes capable of acknowledging his hesitant advances. "For the Love of One's Self" is one of many Freeman stories, including the previously collected "A Mistaken Charity," that examines the art of giving and receiving with grace, the intimate psychological connection between self-love and generosity.

Often weak-willed and unresponsive, Freeman's male characters pale in contrast to her strong and self-determining female protagonists. In two stories collected here, however, proud young women learn to accept their young men's inadequacies precisely because they are able, for the first time, to see their own. In these tales as elsewhere, Freeman examines women who must temper their ideals with both the shortcomings of their own personalities and the limited circumstances of their lives. Such women come to realize that marriage with what seem to them weak, passive, or dull men requires much compromise. Lucilla Childs, in "The Horn of Plenty," is despondent because she is unable to find a mate suitable for someone with her many advantages and accomplishments. Through the counsel of her relative Abby Armstrong, who herself has courageously faced a difficult marriage, Lucilla eventually agrees to reconsider the attentions of Sammy, her unexciting, but stalwart, beau. In "Humble Pie," schoolteacher Maria Gorham, "quietly poised . . . in her own self-esteem," scorns her faithful and kind, yet dull-seeming, suitor, Dexter Ray. But when she herself is forced to endure ridicule for the first time, Maria emerges from her self-centeredness and recognizes Dexter's inner worth. Such Freeman protagonists enter marriage with eyes open, fully aware of what they stand to gain or lose by their decision.

In two stories in this volume, as she does in "The Revolt of 'Mother,'" Freeman takes a candid look at a woman's lot after marriage. Contemplating her own imminent union with Charles Freeman, Mary Wilkins expressed on occasion the fear that marriage might not only limit her artistic development, but also, and even more disturbingly, violate the essential "self." In a telling letter written to a friend who was herself about to marry, Freeman voiced the concern that marriage might "swallow" a woman up, absorbing her identity completely: "I am to be married myself before long," she wrote. "If *you* don't see the old *me*, I shall run and run until I find her. And as for you, no man shall ever swallow you up entirely . . ." (Kendrick, 243).

Written shortly before Freeman's marriage, "The Prism" explores the potential toll marriage might exact from a woman's creative life. A lonely and introspective child, Diantha Fielding discovers reflected in a prism a mystical world of beauty lacking from her own mundane existence. Later, as a young woman, she attempts to confide her precious secret in her fiancé but encounters only his scornful laughter: "What a child you are, dear! . . . Don't talk such nonsense." When Diantha risks losing the young man, however, she buries the prism, insisting she saw nothing in it at all; subsequently, the two marry. At the end, conceding that Diantha now enjoys a certain "earthly bliss," the narrator nevertheless ironically questions whether or not she has also forfeited her "birthright" in her willing suppression of her imaginative capabilities. Also composed just prior to Freeman's marriage, "A Tragedy from the Trivial" examines emotional cruelty in marriage.

Incapable of pleasing her selfish, tight-fisted husband, Charlotte May leaves him to return to her job in a department store. Once there, however, she devotes herself to scraping together enough money to pay her husband back for what she considers her extravagance within the marriage. The emotional strain of the effort soon overcomes her, and she falls ill. Upon her death, the narrator bitterly concludes that "At the last she had learned her little lesson of obedience and thrift . . . and all her waste of life was over."

Although numerous Freeman stories involve women and marriage, several of her female protagonists live for quite other ideals. The well-known tales "A Village Singer" and "A Poetess" concern female artists, as do "Juliza" and "The Prism." But perhaps the consummate artist story in Freeman's canon is "The Blue Butterfly." Marcia Keyes is passionately involved in her dressmaking. When a wealthy socialite solicits her services for her daughter's coming-out dress, Marcia expends all her energy and even her own meager savings in the effort. The result so far exceeds the expectations of all involved that Marcia, "like an artist who sees for the first time upon the canvas the realization of his ideal," experiences utter fulfillment.

Intent on portraying the lives of women, Freeman rarely wrote stories with male protagonists. In fact, the theme in several stories ostensibly revolving around a male may be seen as the effect of the male's often reckless or improvident behavior on his wife and children. In "The Cloak Also," a work perhaps stemming from Freeman's memory of her own father's failure at shopkeeping, good-hearted but naive Joel Rice cherishes the dream of owning a dry-goods store. He lacks, however, the most fundamental business sense. Borrowing his wife Susan's savings, he succeeds in opening his store, only to go bankrupt quickly through poor management. In despair, and to his wife's humiliation, Joel publicly rails against the community he believes has cheated him; soon thereafter, he commits suicide. Ironically, his death leaves his bereft family better off than they had been while he was alive.

"The Slip of the Leash," a story similar to Hawthorne's "Wakefield," concerns the plight of Adam Andersen, who one day "went wild," abruptly deserting his wife and children. His trip to the West is short-lived, however; soon returning, he hides himself for years in a clump of bushes within sight of his home. During that time, he watches his family come and go, witnessing their increasingly futile attempts to support themselves. He returns to the household only when he can no longer endure their desperation.

A third story with a male protagonist, "A Guest in Sodom," is also related by a man, one of Freeman's many gossiping first-person narrators. He recounts the comic tale of Benjamin Rice, a meek and trusting man who, despite others' warnings, insists on purchasing an automobile from a disreputable company. Patiently repairing the car after each of its many breakdowns, Benjamin only gradually realizes that he has been duped. So shocked is he to discover dishonesty in the world that he is driven insane, declaring his own righteousness to the village before succumbing to his fate: "I have never wronged my fellowman. . . . Oh, if I could have died before I lost my faith in my fellowmen, and seen the wickedness of the world!"

Freeman's last published story, "The Jester," is one of a handful of her works, including the previously collected "The Balking of Christopher," that sensitively probes the inner life of a male protagonist. Jonathan Clapp is "handicapped" with, we are told, a deformity of the soul. Overshadowed by his selfish and histrionic mother, he quickly learns that the remedy for his loneliness lies in his ability to make others laugh. Invited to enact the jester in a town play, Jonathan gives a stellar performance. But his skill at role-playing has, tragically, rendered him incapable of accepting human love. The story's cynical commentary on the inconstancy of love coupled with its pessimistic tone makes it among the darkest of Freeman tales.

In a final category are the three mystery tales reprinted here. Freeman's dramatic style, her careful unfolding of events through dialogue and encounter, and her keen sense of the uncanny make her a noteworthy writer of stories of the supernatural. In 1903, six of these tales were collected in *The Wind in the Rose-Bush and Other Stories of the Supernatural*, a volume recently republished by Academy Chicago Press. The murder mystery "The Long Arm," written in conjunction with Joseph Edgar Chamberlin and based on a sensational 1892 case in which a Tennessee woman murdered her female lover, was issued separately in *The Long Arm and Other Detective Stories* (1895). That story, which won its authors a substantial monetary prize in the Bach-eller Syndicate Short Story contest, is not collected here because of its excessive length.

The mystery tales in this volume each postulate a dimension beyond those we experience through physical sense. In "Sweet-Flowering Per-ennial," middle-aged Clara, invited to spend time at the wealthy home of her school friend Selma, is mystified at the sight of a young, beautiful girl coming and going from the house. Learning that Selma has felt cheated of her youth by her family's preoccupation with an invalid sister, Clara attempts to understand the strange "power of per-ennial bloom" she enviously observes in Selma. The fountain-of-youth theme in this tale is one that Freeman, who expressed fears of her own aging, explores in other works, such as the previously col-lected "The Three Old Sisters and the Old Beau."

Left in manuscript form with two endings at Freeman's death, "The White Shawl" is developed almost entirely through dialogue. Willy, the keeper of the town's railroad crossing gates, lies dying on a stormy night, attended by his elderly wife, Susy. Though restless, he derives comfort from his certainty that the tower guard is switching the trains safely through the gates in his stead. Susy, however, conceals the truth from the ailing man: no one is operating the switches. During the long, tense night of her agonized vigil, the desperate woman relies on prayer. The morning light brings not only her old husband's death, but also the news of the odd circumstances that have prevented a tragic crash: in some mysterious way, Susy, a woman of great faith and unselfish love, has guided the trains that fateful night. As the doctor attending the couple the next day comments in one of the story's endings, "Maybe there is a thinner wall and a door into the next dimension for loving women that men never find."

Lastly, in "The Hall Bedroom," a cramped, boardinghouse room reveals to its down-on-their-luck residents irresistible secrets of a sen-sual world beyond that of mere time and space. A framed tale, the story is unfolded through the diary entries of a man who, possessing "the soul of an explorer," is frustrated by the poverty and ill health that have sharply curtailed his ambitions. Gradually, he is drawn to escape his demeaning circumstances by entering a fascinating dimension that offers fulfillment to all of his physical senses. Initially appearing in a 1903 edition of *Collier's*, "The Hall Bedroom" was republished in the 1905 volume, *Short Story Classics (American)*, edited by William Patten. It is collected here not only because of the relative obscurity of that volume, but also because its unusual theme and singular narrative style make it unique among Freeman's stories.

Over the last several decades, critics of Mary Wilkins Freeman have routinely called for further scholarly work on this prolific author, and certainly her novels, plays, and children's writings still need attention. However, as Freeman's expertise clearly lay in the short story, we must also continue to examine that genre, refining the work undertaken by critics in the last twenty years. Most readers who are familiar with her anthologized stories consider Freeman to be a portrayer of rebel figures such as Louisa Ellis in "A New England Nun," who refuses marriage; Sarah Penn in "The Revolt of 'Mother'," who openly defies her husband; and Candace Whitcomb in "A Village Singer," who scandalizes an entire community. These stories are central to Freeman's canon and rightly deserve the praise they have received.

However, readers who investigate further will find in Freeman's work a rich and varied landscape, peopled with New England women of every age and type. They will discover that Freeman's female protagonists, rarely openly rebellious, are inwardly torn between their own desires and the demands of their roles and relationships within the family and the community. Freeman brings such women as Juliza in "Juliza," Diantha in "The Prism," Catherine in "Friend of My Heart," and Lucilla in "The Horn of Plenty," to the moment when social and psychological factors converge to force a decision, often in the matter of marriage. She probes deeply and perceptively into the motives, fears, and aspirations making up that decision.

When Freeman's female characters are stripped of external support, the stories achieve great power. Struggling for meaning, identity, and union with others, these women must come to terms with their private consciences, their deepest longings, societal and religious proscriptions on their behavior, and the needs and demands of others. Such an interior struggle is, ultimately, a spiritual and lonely one—no more and no less than the human condition. This concentration on the interior battles of women lends to Freeman's work a universality that has often been overlooked and establishes her as far more than a mere regional writer.

Although far less frequent in her canon of short fiction, Freeman's stories involving male protagonists further our understanding of her major themes. Sons, husbands, and parents, males in Freeman's world are closely bound in relation to others; their actions influence the family and are affected by it. Like Freeman's female protagonists, characters such as Joel in "The Cloak Also," Jonathan in "The Jester," and Adam in "The Slip of the Leash" must reconcile individual desires with social roles. Failure to do so results in both personal and familial tragedy.

Freeman's imagination was fertile and her art wide-ranging. Sharply individualized, her characters linger in our memories. Her skill at manipulating conventional plots for ironic purposes and her mastery of suspense in her stories of the supernatural mark her as an innovative and compelling stylist. Her greatest achievement, however, lies in the suggestive power of her terse dialogue and objective, flat descriptions. Though little happens in the external world in a Freeman story, great interior adventures are undertaken and great battles won. The publication of this volume of her uncollected stories is a significant step in the effort to bring Freeman's best works, stories long neglected, before readers. My hope is that it will contribute to our ongoing evaluation of and appreciation for a talented and determined artist.

The Freeman stories reprinted here were originally published in a variety of magazines, both British and American. Hence, shifts in style, spelling, and punctuation are the result of our efforts to be faithful to each text as it was originally published. Only obvious typographical errors have been corrected.

Over the last two decades, three volumes in particular have been instrumental in acquainting modern readers with the best of Freeman's previously collected short fiction. Michele Clark's *The Revolt of Mother and Other Stories* (Feminist Press, 1974); Barbara Solomon's *Short Fiction of Sarah Orne Jewett and Mary Wilkins Freeman* (New American Library, 1979); and Marjorie Pryse's *Selected Stories of Mary E. Wilkins Freeman* (Norton, 1983) brought together twenty-seven stories from several of Freeman's fourteen original collections. Other collections such as *Six Trees, Understudies,* and *The Copy-Cat and Other Stories* are currently available through reprint services, as are several of Freeman's novels, such as *Pembroke* and *The Shoulders of Atlas*. Freeman's original volumes can still be found on the shelves of most major libraries.

Works Cited

Garland, Hamlin. *Hamlin Garland's Diaries.* Edited by Donald Pizer. San Marino, Cal.: Huntington Library, 1968.

Kendrick, Brent L., ed. *The Infant Sphinx: Collected Letters of Mary E. Wilkins Freeman.* Metuchen, N.J.: Scarecrow Press, 1985.

"Notes." *The Critic* 14 (23 Aug. 1890): 101.

Wood, Ann Douglas. "The Literature of Impoverishment: The Women Local Colorists in America 1865–1914." *Women's Studies* I (1972): 3–40.

The Uncollected Stories of Mary Wilkins Freeman

Emmy

"I don't see how you can stand this awful wind."

"Oh, you get used to it. After you'd lived here forty year, an' seen ev'rythin' slantendicular in the wind the whole 'durin' time, you'd get so you wouldn't think much about it. You'd feel slantendicular yourself."

"I do b'lieve you have grown kind of sideways, Lucy Ann. Don't you think she has, Emmeline?"

Mrs. Elkins asked the question of her sister, Mrs. Emmeline Cares. Mrs. Cares kept her fair, large face intent upon her sewing. "I've said she had, time an' time again; but you ain't paid no attention to it," she replied, scarcely opening her fine lips.

"Well, I dunno but you have," Mrs. Elkins said apologetically; "but I ain't realized it till just now. Can't you stand up straighter, Lucy Ann? You hadn't ought to get to loppin' over so."

Mrs. Sands stood at the kitchen table rolling out biscuits for tea. She smiled the shrewdly reflective smile of a philosopher. "Well, mebbe I hadn't ought to," said she; "but I dunno as it makes much difference. I ain't so young as I was once, an' mebbe if I don't lay out any extry strength in holdin' of myself up straight I'll last the longer for 't."

"I should think you'd have a little more regard for your own looks," said Mrs. Cares in a calm, indignant voice. She took strong, even stitches in her white seam.

"Land! I dunno as I'd know myself if I met myself out a-walkin' on the bluff," returned Mrs. Sands; "I don't think five minutes a day about how I look."

3

"If you jest tried to think of it, an' stood up straight, an' didn't allow yourself to lean over so, it wouldn't take long," said Mrs. Elkins.

"If folks won't listen to what folks say, an' don't have no regard to how they look, there ain't no use talkin'. I'll give it up," said Mrs. Cares.

Mrs. Sands said no more; she put the pans of biscuit into the oven with a sober air. Her two sisters sat sewing with their nice, voluminous black skirts gathered carefully up from contact with the kitchen floor. They had followed Mrs. Sands into the kitchen when she went out to prepare tea. They came from a town ten miles inland, and were spending the day with her. Their horse and buggy were out in the shed behind the house. The two visiting sisters were trussed up tightly in their fine black gowns, there were gleams of jet upon their high bosoms, there were nice ruffles in their necks and sleeves, their faded light hair was arranged in snugly braided little coronals, and their front locks were crimped.

Mrs. Sands, beside them, showed plainly the marks of the sea upon her; since she had been exposed to the buffetings of its strong salt winds she had changed as much as the coast. Her complexion had been similar to her sisters', fair, although not blonde; now all the fresh tints were gone out of it, and it could well assimilate with the grays and browns of the rocks and seaweeds down on the shore. She was tall and lean, and leaned sideways, as her sister claimed; she wore a loose, limp, brown dress, and her hair had a rough stringiness over her temples.

After she had put the biscuits into the stove oven she sat down for a minute. She could not fry the fish until Emmy returned; she had gone down to the store after some salt pork. The kitchen had a small, dark interior; it was plastered, and the plaster and unpainted woodwork were brown with smoke. All the color in the room was in a row of tomatoes ripening on the window-sill. The one window looked upon a stretch of wind-swept yard. The edge of the bluff and the sea were upon the other side of the house. The wind was from landward: it beat upon the house in great gusts; now and then a window rattled. The visiting sisters sewed: Mrs. Elkins was using red worsted in some fancy work; Mrs. Cares took nice stiches in some fine white cloth and embroidery. Her daughter was getting ready to be married, and she was doing some needlework for her.

Mrs. Sands kept her eyes fixed upon the work of her sister Mrs. Cares; finally she spoke. "I s'pose you an' Susy have got about all you want to do, with her sewin'?" she said.

"I guess we have," Mrs. Cares assented; "all we can spring to. Susy's about wore out."

"It's a good deal of a strain on a girl, gettin' ready to be married. I dunno how Emmy'd stand it." Mrs. Sands fixed her sober eyes upon the wild sky visible through the window, the corners of her thin mouth curved in a sly smile, but her sisters did not notice it.

Mrs. Cares shook out her work, and took a dainty stitch with a jerk. "I ruther guess it's a strain."

"I guess it would come pretty hard on Emmy."

"It ain't the sewin' alone, neither. She's up pretty late two nights a week, too, an' that tells on her."

"Yes; I dunno of anythin' that tells on anybody's looks quicker than bein' up late nights. Emmy's been up considerable late along back, an' I can see that she shows it."

"Don't you think this is handsome edging on this skirt?" inquired Mrs. Cares.

"Yes, it is real handsome. How much do you get for Susy's skirts, Emmeline? I s'pose I've got to buy some for Emmy before long, most likely."

"Three yards."

"Well, that's about what I thought. Emmy's got to have some new skirts, I s'pose, by an' by."

"Susy's havin' six made," said Mrs. Cares with subdued loftiness, "an' they is all trimmed to death. I tell her it's kind of silly."

"Let me see, how much of that gray cashmere did you say you got for Susy's dress? I s'pose Emmy'll be wantin' one by an' by."

"I b'lieve I got twelve yards."

"I s'pose Emmy'd take about the same."

"I guess she would. Susy's is most done."

"It's one of the handsomest dresses for a bride to come out in that I ever see," Mrs. Elkins chimed in enthusiastically.

Mrs. Sands took her eyes from the window. She turned them towards her sisters, a dark blush crept over her face, her smile dispersed.

"I don't s'pose you've heard about Emmy," said she.

The sisters stared at her. "Why, no," said Mrs. Cares. "What is it about her?"

"Well—I—expect she's got—somebody waitin' on her."

"Why, you don't say so, Lucy Ann!" cried Mrs. Elkins.

"Well, I must say I never thought Emmy 'd get anybody," said Mrs. Cares. "Not that she ain't a real good girl, but she ain't never seemed to me like one that would get married. Who is it, Lucy Ann?"

"He's a real likely young man. He owns a boat; got in yesterday. I s'pose he'll be up to-night."

"Got anythin' laid by?"

"I shouldn't wonder if he had. He's done pretty well, they say, an' he's stiddy as a clock."

"What's his name?" Mrs. Cares asked the question with a frown between her eyes. Mrs. Elkins bent forward, smiling curiously.

"Jim Parsons."

"One of Sam Parsons's boys?"

"Yes; the others are dead, you know. He's all the one left of the family. He sold the house last year; now he boards over to Capen's."

"How much did he sell the house for?"

"About nine hundred."

"I s'pose he's got that laid up."

"I rather guess he has."

"Well, that'll set 'em up housekeepin'. When are they goin' to be married?"

Mrs. Sands's face twitched a little. "Well, I dunno," she said. "I dunno as they've got quite so fur as that yet."

"Then it ain't settled?"

"Well, no—I guess not. I guess they ain't quite settled it betwixt 'em yet."

Mrs. Cares's eyes, fastened upon her sister's, grew sharper. "How long has he been comin' here?"

"Well, I dunno. He's been away a spell now. He come here awhile before he went."

"Three months?"

"No, I guess it wasn't—hardly three."

"Two?"

"No; I guess not quite."

"Well, he must have been comin' a month if he's been courtin' at all—if he meant anythin' serious."

"Well, I dunno but 'twas about a month in all; he's been comin' an' goin' with his boat. It's kinder hard to reckon," said Mrs. Sands, feebly.

"Has he ever took her anywhere?"

"He took her ridin' over to Denbury."

"More'n once?"

Mrs. Sands shook her head.

"Has he give her anythin'?"

"No—not as I know of. He's brought mack'ral an' perch in sev'ral times."

"Well," said Mrs. Cares, "you take my advice, Lucy Ann, an' don't you be too sure. You can't tell about these young fellers. They're more'n likely not to mean anythin', an' Emmy's a real good girl; but she ain't one of the kind that young fellers take to, I shouldn't think. Who's comin'?"

"Emmy," said Mrs. Sands, with an attempt at dignity.

The door opened then, and Emmy entered. She had a brown paper parcel, and she handed it at once to her mother.

"Here's the pork, mother," said she.

"I'd like to know where you have been all this time."

"I had to wait. I couldn't help it. The store was full of folks."

Emmy was not as tall as her mother; she was very thin, and there was a little stoop in her slight shoulders. Her young face looked darkly and gravely from under her wind-beaten hat; a draggled plume trailed over the brim, two loops of ribbon stood up grotesquely.

"Do look at Emmy's hat!" said Mrs. Elkins, laughing.

"It's all blown to pieces in this wind," remarked Mrs. Sands. She was slicing the pork.

Emmy removed her hat soberly, and straightened the plume and the ribbon. She had a complexion like her mother's, and the winds had beaten all the brightness out of it. Her blue eyes looked as strange in her sallow face as blue violets would have looked in sand. She had tried to curl her front hair, but the wind had taken out all the curls, and the straight locks hung over her temples. She wore a cheap, blue gingham dress; she and her mother had tried to fashion it after the style of some of the cottagers' costumes. There were plaitings and drapery, but it was poor and homely, and beginning to fade.

Emmy's aunts surveyed her sharply; finally Mrs. Elkins spoke with a titter: "Well, Emmy, is he comin' up to-night?"

Emmy gave a great start. She looked scared and pitiful, but she answered rather shortly, "I don't know of anybody that's comin'." Then she went quickly into the sitting-room. Presently her mother followed, and found her smoothing her hair before the looking-glass.

Mrs. Sands walked around, and looked at her with a kind of sharp tenderness. "What is it?" she asked; "what's the matter with you?"

"Nothin'."

"Yes, there is, too. You needn't tell me. I saw the minute you come in somethin' had come across you. What is it?"

"Nothin' has come across me. I wish you wouldn't act so silly, mother."

"Did you see anything of him?" Mrs. Sands's voice dropped to a whisper. Emmy nodded as if she were forced to.

"Where—"

"In the road. Don't, mother!"

"Walkin'?"

"No."

"Ridin'?"

"Yes."

"Anybody with him?"

"Flora Marsh."

Mrs. Sands stood looking at Emmy. "He'd ought to be ashamed of himself," said she. "Don't you mind nothin' about it, Emmy. He ain't worth it."

Emmy strained back her straggling front hair and pinned it tightly; her full forehead showed, and her face, no longer shaded by the straying locks, had a severe cast.

"I don't know why he ain't worth it," said she. "I don't know why he'd ought to be ashamed of himself goin' to ride with Flora Marsh. I can't hold a candle to her."

"Well, I should think after the way he's been comin' here—"

"He ain't been here long. He ain't never asked me to have him. He ain't beholden to go with me if he don't want to."

"Emmy Sands, ain't he set up with you?"

"That don't make it out he's got to marry me."

"Well, you can stick up for him if you want to. I ruther guess—"

"Somebody's comin'," said Emmy; and Mrs. Cares opened the door.

"The pork's burnin'," said she, "an' I guess you'll have to turn it over, Lucy Ann; I'm afraid of its spatterin' on my dress if I try it. What's the matter?"

"Nothin'," answered Mrs. Sands; and she went out and turned the pork and fried the fish. Emmy set the table; her aunts questioned her about her "beau," but got little satisfaction.

"I ain't got any beau," she said; and that was all she would say.

Pretty soon her father came, a large man lumbering wearily across the yard with a wheel-barrow load of potatoes. He was a small farmer. He had a nervous face although it was so fleshy, and he looked at his wife and Emmy with an anxious frown between his eyes. He did not say much to his sisters-in-law: he had been as cordial to them as he was able at noon; company disturbed him.

As soon as he could he beckoned his wife into the sitting-room. "Come in here a minute, Lucy Ann," said he. When he had shut the door he looked at her impressively. "What do ye think I see?" he whispered mysteriously; "young Parsons out ridin' with the Marsh girl."

Mrs. Sands held the knife with which she turned the fish. "I know it," said she, impatiently. "Emmy see 'em."

"She didn't!"

"Yes; she met 'em when she was comin' home from the store. I've got to go an' turn the fish; I can smell 'em burnin' now."

"Did she act as if she minded it much?"

"I couldn't see as she did. She acted kind of touchy. I can't stan' here, or them fish will be burnt to a cinder. You'd better get you out a clean pocket-handkerchief before you come to the table."

Supper, with its company-fare of fried fish, hot biscuits, and a frosted cake, was quite late. The guests had to take their leave directly afterward, as they had a long drive. Mr. Sands brought the horse and buggy around, and Mrs. Sands got our her sisters' bonnets and wraps. She watched them as they put on their little flower-topped bonnets and adjusted their lace veils over their crimps. She had not had a bonnet so fine for years, but she felt no envy. She seldom looked in the glass, and never except to see if she were tidy. The sea had seemed to cultivate a certain objectiveness in her since she had lived near it. It was as if the relative smallness of her personality beside the infinite had come home to her.

When the sisters were in the buggy they walked the horse across the yard to the road, and Mrs. Sands walked at the side, talking. When she reached the road Mrs. Cares, who was driving, reined in the horse. A young man and woman were passing in a buggy.

"Who's that?" called Mrs. Elkins, after they had passed.

Mrs. Cares turned sharply on her sister: "Ain't that Jim Parsons?"

"Yes, I ruther think 'twas him."

"Who was that with him?"

"I guess 'twas the Marsh girl."

Mrs. Cares tightened the reins. "Well," said she, "I guess you'll find out there's somethin' in what I told you, Lucy Ann. It ain't best to be too sure. Well, mebbe she'll find somebody else, now that the ice is broke. Good-by."

Mrs. Sands stood beside a great wild rose bush and watched her sisters drive down the wood. The twilight was coming fast, but the full moon was rising, and it would be light in spite of the clouds, so there would be no difficulty about the two women driving home.

Mrs. Sands returned to the house, the sweep of the wind strong at her back. Emmy was washing the dishes. "Ain't you goin' to change your dress?" asked her mother.

"No, I guess not."

"Hadn't you better? We might have somebody in, an' that don't look hardly fit."

"I guess we sha'n't have anybody in."

"Well, it ain't best to be too sure."

Emmy said nothing more. She kept on washing and wiping the tea-things. The corners of her mouth dropped, but nerve and resolution were in the motion of her elbows. After the dishes were put away she sat down with some sewing. Her mother sat opposite with her knitting-work. Mrs. Sands knitted fast, pursing her lips tightly and wrinkling her forehead. She and Emmy scarcely spoke during the evening. At nine o'clock there was a step at the door, and a sudden red flamed over Emmy's face; her mother started. "There, I told you to change your dress," she whispered. But the door opened and it was only Isaac Sands. He stepped in cautiously, looked anxiously around the room, and then sat down.

"Well, how are you gettin' along?" he said.

"Pretty well," replied Emmy.

"Anybody been in?" he inquired in a casual voice.

Mrs. Sands shook her head. Pretty soon Emmy laid aside her work and went upstairs to bed in her plain little room. After she was in bed she lay listening to the murmur of her parents' voices in the room below. She knew they were talking about her. She felt intense shame that they should be discussing her love matters. It seemed sometimes to this little soul, setting forth for the first time out of her harbor of youth, as if the friendly watchers on the pier caused her more discomfort than the roughness of the voyage. It seemed to Emmy that her parents talked all night; she was not conscious of any cessation.

When she went down in the morning her mother looked sharply at her. "You don't look as if you'd slept a wink; great hollers under your eyes," said she.

"I've slept enough," replied Emmy.

That morning she went about as usual helping her mother; she was always very quiet. When her father came home at noon he had the news that Jim Parsons was going to stay in town a week. Whether Emmy watched or not, her father and mother watched every day for her recreant lover to come, but he did not. He was seen walking and riding with the other girl. Isaac kept a sharp watch upon him, then came home and reported to his wife. They said little about it to Emmy. Emmy, meek and small and quiet, had little dignity about her, but there was a certain reserve which produced the same effect. Her parents were somewhat shy of imposing upon it.

In the mean time Jim Parsons, a young fellow with eyes as blue and bold as the sea, with a rough, hard grace in his sinewy figure, and a rude, merry way, had troubled himself about Emmy more than people knew. Once or twice he had met her on the bluff, his brown face had blushed darkly, and he had stammered forth some greeting. But Emmy had looked quite soberly and calmly at him and returned his greeting, and he had said to himself that she did not care. If he had been charged with offense he would have believed in his own freedom from guilt; left to himself he was not quite sure, and disliked to meet Emmy on the bluff. He was a strange person to have thought twice of Emmy Sands, but she had had her attraction for him, and she had it now. Many a night Jim Parsons was upon the verge of forsaking his new love and returning to his old, but the beauty and the imperious ways of the new one held him. If Flora Marsh had not been in the village within sight and hearing, Emmy would at any time have regained her lover. Simple and uncritical as she was, she had an intuition of the fact herself.

"It's because Flora came in his way, and she's pretty; if he were only away from her he wouldn't think so much more of her," she used to think to herself when she sat sewing so busily and nobody could tell that she was thinking at all. Emmy had even discovered how Jim's first deflection came about. When he came in from his cruise Flora and some other girls had been down at the landing. There had been joking, and she had as good as asked him in her way, whose prettiness disguised its boldness, to take her to ride. Thus it had gone on.

Jim was to leave on a Thursday, sailing over to Rockland for some stores and a part of his crew, then off the next morning on his fishing cruise. The night before Emmy said to herself, "This is the last night she'll have him."

On Thursday all the sky was red at sunset, the northeast wind blew, and the sea looked beaten flat beneath it; outside the surf it had a metallic calmness. Gulls were flying over a long rock that jutted out into the water a little distance down the coast. Isaac Sands, out early bringing a pail of water over the bluff from a neighbor's well, stopped and looked out to sea.

"Guess we're goin' to have a gale," he remarked when he entered the house. Emmy, helping her mother get breakfast, thought to herself that Jim was going out that afternoon. All that morning she watched the sky. There was a strange, wild glow in it, and the wind increased. There were patches of ghastly green light, like rafts on the sea. At noon when Isaac came home to dinner he had the weather gossip from the store where he had been.

"They say down to Capen's," he reported, "that there's goin' to be the biggest blow of the season. Old Cap'n Lawrence says he ain't never see it look much worse in this part of the world. If he was in the West Indies, he says, he'd be certain there'd be a hurricane. They say Jim Parsons's goin' over to Rockland this afternoon anyhow, an' they think he's crazy to do it. He ain't got no sense to start out a day like this, nor his crew neither. They're all young fellers as careless as he is. Three on 'em's over to Rockland anyhow. I guess if the rest had any folks here, there'd be a time about their startin'."

"Well, I don't want nobody to get drownded," said Mrs. Sands, "but I must say I wouldn't care if Jim Parsons got pretty well scared."

"I guess there ain't much scare in him; he's a crazy-headed young feller," responded Isaac, grimly.

Emmy said nothing. She did not eat much dinner. Afterward she watched the sky again. Her mother kept watching her with a severe and impatient air. "Emmy Sands, what ails you this afternoon?" she said once, harshly.

"Nothin'," replied Emmy. Then she sewed faster.

About five o'clock her father came in. "Jim Parsons ain't gone yet, an' if he goes to-night he an' his crew will go to the bottom before they ever get to Rockland," said he. "'T ain't far there, but it's one of the roughest little cruises on the coast. He'd ought to have gone in the daytime if he was goin' at all. He's gone to carry that Marsh girl out to ride, and he ain't got home yet. It'll be dark as a pocket before he gets started. Old Cap'n Lawrence says he's been out in about as rough water as anybody, but he'd be hanged if he'd sail that boat over to Rockland to-night. An' there won't none of them other fellers say nothin'; they're hangin' round waitin', an' they look as uneasy as fish out of water, but they ain't goin' to hang back. Young Blake he's the oldest on 'em, an' he ain't over twenty-five. I guess if they had any folks here they wouldn't start out; but they ain't."

"If Jim Parsons don't know no better than to start out to-night he'd ought to be taken up," said Mrs. Sands. "If he wants to go get drownded himself I dunno as anybody'd care much, but when it comes to drownndin' other folks it's a different thing."

"They're all a crazy set," said Isaac. He was not working that afternoon, he was too nervous with the approaching storm. He went back and forth between the house and the store on ostensible errands, but in reality for the gratification of his restless spirit. Pretty soon he arose again. "Well, I s'pose I've got to go down to Capen's again," said he. "I forgot to ask him if he wanted any of them turnips."

After her father had gone Emmy went too, slipping out the front way; her mother was in the kitchen. She pulled her hat down over her ears to keep it on, and went down the little footpath over the crest of the bluff. She had not put on any shawl or sack; her meager little figure, wavering in the blast, stood out darkly against the wild sky. Everything on the bluff looked gigantic in the wind, which seemed to widen and lengthen everything. The fringe of coarse grass on the edge of the bluff looked like a weedy forest. Emmy passed by the row of summer cottages all shut up and deserted now; and the great festoons of spiders' webs on the piazza, oscillating in the wind, held spiders which looked like tropical ones. Emmy went on. There were some sails in the harbor. There was one in the west which she eyed intently. Anchored opposite it lay a dory; there were some men on the beach near it. Jim was not among them. Emmy, swaying in the wind, stood on the bluff behind them and made sure of that. She turned and ran back along the bluff. She passed her own house and went on to the store. The rough weather had driven the row of lounging men inside. There was scarcely a clear space between the visitors perched upon boxes and barrels and propped against counters and walls. Emmy's father was sitting on a barrel. She pushed up to him. "Is he goin' to-night, father?" she whispered.

He stared at her. "What?"

"Is he goin' to-night?"

"Who goin'—Jim?"

"Yes."

"Course he's goin'. He's just come in, an' gone upstairs to pack his things."

Nobody had overheard Emmy's and her father's whispered conversation, but one of the men took it up. It was the topic of the day, coming uppermost in intervals like waves.

"I wouldn't give that for his chances," he exclaimed. "That boat will go to the bottom with all on board afore they heave in sight of Rockland."

Then a chorus arose like the crying of a flock of ominous birds.

Emmy hurried out of the store without another word. Her father called after her, but she did not hear him. She ran along the bluff again. The sun was low in a red glare of sky and ragged violet and orange clouds. The sky and clouds appeared as close to the sea as the coast; it was as if the sun was passing to some infernal shore. Emmy went nearly to her own house, then she struck across lots to the high- way. She hurried down the road until she came to the house where Flora Marsh lived. It was a fine house for this little coast village. It had green blinds, and a bay window at one side. Emmy knocked at the front door, and Flora opened it.

"Why, hullo, Emmy!" said she. Then she stood staring at her. There was a soft pink glow all over Flora's delicate blonde face that showed she had just been out in the wind. She was prettily dressed.

"Can't you stop his goin'?" Emmy said in a quick, dry voice.

"What?"

"Can't you stop his goin'?"

"I don't know what you mean, Emmy Sands." Flora's manner was at once pert and confused.

"Can't you stop Jim Parsons's goin' out to-night?"

"Stop his going?"

"Yes; can't you? They say it's awful dangerous. There's a terrible gale comin'. He'll be drowned."

"Oh, I guess there won't be much of a gale. He says it's safe enough."

"It ain't. They all say it ain't. He's terrible careless. He'll be drowned. Can't you stop him?"

Flora looked at her; her sweet, full brows contracted. The wind blew so that the girls could hardly stand against it; their very words seemed to be tossed about passing from one to the other. "Come in a minute," said Flora; "we can't talk here."

"There ain't any time to lose."

"It won't take any longer in the house than it will here. Some-body'll hear us if we talk here, we have to holler so."

Emmy followed Flora into the house, into the parlor. Flora shut the door. "I wish you'd tell me now what you mean—what you want me to do?" said she.

"Stop his goin' out to-night."

"How can I stop him, I'd like to know?"

"Go down to the shore where his dory is, and when he comes ask him not to go."

Flora hesitated. She fingered a tidy on the back of a chair. "To tell the truth," said she, "I've told him once I didn't think he ought to go; but it didn't do any good. You can't keep him back an inch if you tell him it ain't safe. He ain't afraid of anything. If I ask him to stay because it's dangerous to go it'll just make him all the fiercer for going."

"I know that. Don't ask him not to go because it's dangerous."

"How shall I ask him then, I'd like to know?"

"Tell him you want him to come up and see you to-night."

Flora looked at Emmy. She drew a long breath. "I don't know what to make of you, Emmy Sands."

"He'll be gone if—you don't go quick," Emmy almost gasped.

"Emmy Sands, how you act! I ain't engaged to him. I can't make him stay any more'n you can."

"Yes, you can; he likes you. Oh, go quick!"

"Why don't you go yourself and ask him not to go?"

"I ain't no reason to."

There came an odd look into Flora's face. "Look here," said she; "do you know what you're doing? I ain't engaged to him. Jim Parsons is an awful flirt. He's going off to be gone quite awhile. Maybe when he comes back he'll come to see you again. I've bid him good-by, and we ain't engaged. It would be a good deal safer for you if you let him go. There, I like him well enough, but I'm going to tell you the truth about it, anyhow. It would be a good deal safer for you if he didn't come to see me again before he goes. You know what I mean."

Emmy threw her head back; her voice rang out sharply. "What do you suppose I care about that?" said she. "Do you suppose I'm comin' here because I want to marry him? Do you suppose, if he wants you and you want him, I'd lift my finger to get him back? Get him back—there ain't any gettin' him back; he ain't never said he thought of marryin' me. Marryin'! What's marryin'? It ain't marryin'; it's life an' death that's to be thought of! What difference do you suppose it makes to me who he marries, if he ain't drowned in that awful sea to-night? Why don't you go if you care anythin' about him? What are you stoppin' for? He'll be gone before you get there."

"You are the strangest girl I ever saw," said Flora.

She went out into the entry and put on her hat and jacket. Emmy opened the outer door and stood waiting. "I don't imagine it'll do any good," Flora said when she came out.

The two girls hurried across to the bluff. Emmy kept looking at Flora. "Tuck up your hair a little under your hat; it's comin' down," she said once as they ran along.

When they reached the bluff Emmy turned towards her own house. "You're going home?" said Flora.

Emmy nodded.

"Well, I'll do the best I can. If I get him, I'll come up the other steps and go by your house. You watch."

Flora sank from sight directly, going down some steps over the face of the bluff, and Emmy went home. It was time to get supper, but she stole upstairs to her own room and sat down at the window that overlooked the sea. The breakers gleamed out in the dusk like white fire. It was not long before two figures, a man and a woman, passed below her window. The woman uplifted her face and looked at the house.

Mrs. Sands called at the foot of the stairs: "Emmy, where be you? Supper's all ready."

"I'm comin'," answered Emmy. She went down into the lamp-lighted room, and her father and mother looked at her, then at each other. She appeared almost pretty. There was quite a red flush on her sallow cheeks, and her eyes shone like blue stars.

After supper Isaac Sands went down to the store again. Emmy and her mother sat by the kitchen fire and sewed. The gale increased; they could hear the breakers on this side of the house with all the windows closed. "I ruther guess Jim Parsons will wish he'd staid on shore," remarked Mrs. Sands. "Well, if folks will be so headstrong and fool-hardly, they've got to take the consequences." There was a grim satisfaction in her tone.

Emmy said nothing.

When Isaac came home he was dripping with rain. "It's an awful night," he burst forth when he opened the door. "Guess it's lucky Jim Parsons didn't go out."

"Didn't he go?" asked Mrs. Sands.

"No. Young Blake was down to Capen's; he said Jim backed out. The Marsh girl come down an' talked to him, an' he guessed she per-

suaded him not to go. Guessed it would have been his last cruise if
he had."

"Served him right if it had been," said Mrs. Sands, severely.

Emmy lighted her lamp and went to bed.

That night the gale was terrific; the rain, driven before it, rattled
upon the windows like bullets. The house rocked like a tree. Nobody
could sleep much. In the morning it rained still, the spray from the
ocean dashed over the footpath on the bluff, the front windows were
obscured by a salt mist. Jim Parsons with all his recklessness could not
put out to sea that day. It was three days before he could go. Then the
sun shone, the sea was calmer, although still laboring with the old
swell of the storm, and he went out in the afternoon, steering down
the coast to Rockland.

The day after he went Emmy met Flora Marsh on the bluff. She was
going by with only a greeting, but Flora stopped her.

"He did stay; you knew, didn't you?" said she.

Emmy nodded. "Yes; I saw you go by with him."

Flora stood before her as if wanting to say something. She blushed
and looked confused. Emmy made a motion to pass her.

"I guess he'd run considerable risk if he had gone that night," Flora
remarked flutteringly.

"He'd been lost if he had," returned Emmy. Then she passed on.
Flora stood aside for her. Suddenly Emmy turned. "You didn't say
anythin' to him about me, did you?" said she.

"No, I didn't."

"You won't, will you?"

"No, I won't."

Then the two girls went their ways. It was not long before the news
of Flora Marsh's engagement to Jim Parsons was all over the village.

Emmy's father and mother heard it, but they said nothing about it
to her; they wondered if she knew. It was said that the couple were to
be married when Jim returned from his cruise.

If Emmy knew it, it did not apparently affect her at all. She kept
faithfully on in her homely little course. She was interested in all that
she had been; there was no indication that any sharp, unsatisfied, new
taste had dulled the old ones. Her mother felt quite easy about her,
although her pride and indignation rallied whenever she thought of

Jim Parsons. When he returned from his cruise, and the wedding was appointed the week after, she was unable not to speak of it to Emmy. The day but one before the wedding she began suddenly in a harsh voice, "I s'pose you've heard the news."

"Yes, I heard it," replied Emmy.

"Well, I hope he'll stick to his wife."

"I don't see why he shouldn't."

"Don't see why he shouldn't after the way he treated you?"

Emmy faced her mother. "Mother, once for all, he didn't treat me bad. I guess I know more about it than you do. There ain't any reason for you to say such things about him."

"Well, if you want to stick up for him, you can. I'm sure it ain't nothin' to me who he marries, if it ain't to you. If you don't feel bad, I'm sure I don't."

"I don't."

"Well, I'm glad of it," said her mother.

It was just after dinner. Emmy went to the door to shake the table-cloth and saw her aunts driving into the yard. They had come to make a visit; they were going to spend the night, and drive home the next morning.

The aunts had not been seated very long before the subject of the wedding was opened. Flora Marsh had been to their town to buy her wedding clothes, the dressmaker there had made her dress, and they had seen it. They knew all about the matter, how it was to be only a family wedding, and how Jim and Flora were going to Boston. Emmy sat and listened quite calmly. Once, when she had gone out of the room for a minute, Mrs. Elkins turned to her sister.

"I forgot he used to go with her once," she whispered. "She don't mind hearin' it, does she?"

"Land, no," replied Mrs. Sands. "She didn't care nothin' about him. Emmy ain't one of the kind to set her heart much on any feller. I'm thankful enough she didn't have him. He ain't got no stability, an' never will have. He wouldn't have made no kind of a husband for her."

The morning of the wedding the Sands family arose early. The aunts wished to start for home in good season. The sun was only a little way above the horizon when Emmy opened her window and looked out. It was a beautiful morning. Over in the east the sun stood; behind him lay what looked like a golden land of glory. The sea was calm, the ripples in the forward path of the sun shone like sapphires and rubies and emeralds.

Emmy's small, plain face looked upon it all from her window. Her cheeks were dull and blue with the chilly air; there was no reflection of the splendid morning in her face. But beneath it, in the heart of this simple, humble young woman of the seaboard, with a monotone of life behind her and one stretching before, was love of the kind, in the world of eternity, that is better than marriage.

Juliza

There was a sewing-circle and sociable in the little Baptist church in Stony Brook. The sewing-circle had begun early in the afternoon, the older women had come with their best white aprons trimmed with knitted lace, and their needle-books and thimbles in their pockets, and had sewed busily, gathered around the great wood stove in the vestry. It was a cold day. They sewed until dusk; then they lighted the lamps, warmed the tea and coffee which had been brought ready made in great cans, and set out the buttered biscuits, the cold meat, and the cake and pies. The young people began to flock in.

Only the young girls with their carefully frizzed tufts of front hair and their shining braids in the back gathered around the stove; the young men stood aloof in stiff, amiable groups near the door. They made way for Juliza Peck when she entered, and she walked through them calmly, looking neither to the right nor left, and greeting none of them. Greeting young men in the aggregate at a sociable was not in the social code of the girls of Stony Brook. Juliza was a heavily-built girl with a back as broad as a matron's. She wore her best blue cashmere dress with rows of velvet ribbon over the bust, her mother's best brooch, which was black, with a beautiful little bunch of pearl grapes on it, and new shoes, which creaked as she advanced.

There was a certain importance about her entrance; the young girls all stared around at her and whispered; and several women in flaring white aprons spoke to her and asked where her mother was. Juliza replied with dignity that her mother had a cold, and had not thought it prudent to come out.

"I s'pose you're all prepared," said one woman whose thin crimped hair was trained carefully over thin flushed cheeks. She held a pile of plates under her arm; the plates rattled, her starched apron crackled, and her black silk hissed as she spoke with nervous haste and pleasantry. "Yes, ma'am," replied Juliza.

"You mustn't make us all cry, the way you did before," said the woman. Juliza laughed. When she approached the group of girls by the stove they all nodded stiffly, and she returned it.

"Goin' to speak to-night?" asked one of the girls, after a little.

"Yes," said Juliza.

"Don't you dread it?" asked another.

"Not a mite."

"I don't see how you do it." The girls all stared at Juliza as she stood in their midst, but she did not seem to realize it. Her dark-brown hair curled naturally, and she had brushed it back crinkling from her fresh-colored face with its rounding profile, and had tied it in a bunch at the back. She warmed her hands, then she sat down; the girls did not talk to her any more. She was not in reality, although near their ages, a companion of theirs. She was an only child. She had lived alone with her parents, had never been to school nor associated with girls of her own age. The result was not shyness when she was brought in contact with them,—she had too steady a nervous system for that,—but a demeanor like that of a woman of fifty. She felt years away from the other girls, and they also felt it.

As she sat waiting, she looked calmly over at the group of young men near the door. Frank Williams had come; she could see his shining blonde head above the others. He was quite tall and his shoulders sloped boyishly in his best coat. She looked steadily at him, and presently he turned his eyes toward her. He did not speak, nor did she; but she could see a wave of red flash over his long throat and his smooth face. Juliza did not blush at all.

When they gathered around the supper-table amid an embarrassed hush, Juliza found herself far away from the other young people, next the minister. When the blessing had been asked by the minister towering over her, she looked around to see where Frank Williams was. He was sitting between two young girls at the lower end of the table. Juliza sat back and ate a hearty supper. After supper, when the table was cleared away, the entertainment began. There was playing on the parlor organ and singing; then Juliza Peck spoke.

"There will now be a recitation by Miss Juliza Peck," announced the minister; and Juliza arose and went unflinchingly in her creaking shoes to the platform, took her position, bowed, and lifted up her voice. Her voice was heavy and low-pitched, and she spoke with a solemn intonation; now and then she gestured deliberately. She spoke a long poem describing an heroic deed and a tragic death; people had their handkerchiefs to their faces. When she finished and stepped down from the platform, there was a murmur of admiration all over the vestry; clapping was not allowed in the church. "Beautiful!" the women whispered to one another, and nodded.

There was more music, then Juliza spoke again,—she spoke three times in all,—and the subdued enthusiasm grew stronger.

Juliza Peck's speaking was held in great repute in Stony Brook. It was quite generally believed that very few of the people who go around the country speaking for money in town-halls could speak as well as she. Women had talked to Juliza's mother about it, but Mrs. Peck had shaken her head. "There ain't any need of Juliza's doing any such thing," said she, with dignity. "I'm willin' she should speak to accommodate as she does here in town, but I ain't willin' to have her go round speakin' in public. It ain't a woman's place. An' Juliza's got enough; she don't need to."

Juliza Peck was considered quite an heiress. There had been two aunts on her father's side who had been left widows with small properties; Juliza had been named for both of them by a judicious combination of Julia and Eliza, and had inherited their money. She had quite a little sum in a savings-bank, and she owned a house in a neighboring village.

The sociable ended about ten o'clock,—there had been a little social time after the entertainment,—then people began to go home.

Juliza pinned her mother's plaid long-shawl firmly and comfortably over her shoulders and tied on her blue hood. The young men stood thickly around the outer door. Now and then when a girl passed out a young man left the group softly and slyly, and followed her. When Juliza Peck appeared, Frank Williams shrank back; several of the young men tried to push him forward, laughing, but he stood his ground. Juliza paused in the doorway, and stood looking back at him calmly, as if waiting. The scuffle among the young men ceased; Frank Williams stepped forward, and he and Juliza went out of the door.

An icy north wind came full in their faces when they turned into the road. The snow was drifted at the sides, so they walked in the middle in the sleigh-ruts. Frank did not offer his arm to Juliza, and she plodded solidly along at his side, with her mittened hands warmly folded under her shawl. "It's an awful cold night, ain't it?" said she, presently. Frank grunted assent; his coat-collar was pulled up over his ears, and his hands were in his pockets. Juliza kept looking at his dusky, forbidding figure. "What's the matter?" said she.

"Nothin's the matter; why?"

"Don't you feel well?"

"Feel well enough."

"What makes you act so, then?"

"Act how? I didn't know I was actin' any way uncommon. I'm cold, and I want to get home."

"Yes, it is dreadful cold," said Juliza, soberly. "Your overcoat's thick, ain't it?"

"Thick? I've been wearin' it all winter."

"Look here, Frank; I've got on this scarf, an' I don't need it with this shawl; I wish you'd put it round your throat."

"No, I don't need it; my coat-collar's warm enough."

"Now, do."

"I don't need it." Frank swung on so rapidly that Juliza panted keeping up with him. It was cloudy, but there was a full moon behind the clouds, so there was a soft, pale light over all the snowy landscape. It was a lonely road, and they had a mile and a half to go. Here and there, back in the fields, twinkled a light in some house-window.

"Frank?" said Juliza.

"What say?"

"What makes you act so?"

"Act how? Well, if you want to know, mother's miserable. She's miserable the whole time. I hadn't ought to have come off an' left her to-night; but she made me. She ain't fit to do a thing about the house, an' she won't have a hired girl. I don't believe mother'll ever be any better; she'll always be feeble; she's just the way her mother was for years. I'm tryin' to do the cookin', but I don't make out much."

Juliza took out a hand from under her shawl and caught hold of Frank's arm. "Don't walk quite so fast," said she. "Look here!"

"What say?"

The young man's tone was softer than before, and he slackened his pace. Juliza looked up in his shadowy face. She had to speak quite loudly to be heard in the strong wind. "There ain't but one thing to do," said she, "I'll come over there whenever you want me."

"You!"

"Yes; there ain't any need of me at home. Of course they'll miss me, but mother's real strong and well. I can come any time next week, if you say so. I haven't much to do to get ready. I've got clothes enough. I never thought I'd want to lay in a great stock when I was married. Anyway, I always thought it was foolish."

"Juliza, you don't mean"—

"I mean I'll get married to you right away, and come over to your house. That'll settle it. I'm a good cook and a good housekeeper: mother says I am." The young man fairly gasped; he trembled violently. "Why, what is the matter?" asked Juliza; "are you so cold as all that?"

"No; it ain't that. Juliza, you're awful good. I know you can cook splendid. I—don't know what to say. Oh, dear! I ain't—thought about gettin' married yet awhile. That't the whole of it, Juliza. I'm just as much obliged to you."

Juliza stopped short. "You don't mean you don't want me to marry you, Frank Williams," she said.

"Why, see here, Juliza"—

"You don't mean it."

"Why, Juliza, you know if—I was goin' to marry anybody. I've always liked you first-rate."

"I hadn't a thought but you wanted me to," said she, and began walking on. "I don't see what you'll do if I don't marry you."

"Oh, we'll worry along somehow. We'd better walk fast, Juliza, or we'll catch cold." He pulled Juliza's firm hand and arm closer against his.

"I ain't cold," said she, "it's you; you've been shiverin' ever since we started. I'm glad we're most home. There's the light in the sittin'-room window."

Juliza's house came first on the brow of a long hill; the Williams house was close to it; and there was no other dwelling in sight either way. Frank and Juliza went to her side-door; the front-yard was blocked in with snow. Frank released Juliza's hand from his arm.

"You musn't think I shall say anything about this to-night," he said in a hesitating voice; "I shan't ever speak of it."

"I don't care if you do," returned Juliza; "I haven't done anything I'm ashamed of; if anybody has, it's you. I supposed you took it for granted I was goin' to marry you, an' I don't think you show much common-sense about it. I don't believe anybody else would think so, either."

"There's something to be considered besides common-sense, some-times," said Frank, feebly. They were a little sheltered in the south yard from the wind. Juliza's cat came mewing loudly around her feet.

"I begin to think there is," said Juliza. "Well, it's for you to say, of course. I ain't goin' in anywhere where I ain't wanted; but I must say I'm surprised. Good-night, Frank."

"Good-night, Juliza." Juliza opened the door and let in the cat, then she stood looking for a moment after Frank's retreating figure, and listening to the sound of his footsteps crunching the snow.

"Juliza! that you?" called a voice from the sitting-room; and she went in hastily and closed the door. When she entered the sitting-room she found her mother there alone, in the warm, light atmo-sphere full of the odor of green flowering-plants; the windows were all set with tiers of them. There was a curious majesty about Mrs. Peck's large figure and long face; she wore her black hair in punctilious water-waves around her temples; she sat in her rocking-chair as if it were a throne; and her black cashmere skirt fell over her knees in stately folds. "You are pretty late, ain't you?" said she; and her voice was deep, with solemn inflections like Juliza's.

"I don't know. The entertainment was pretty long."

"Did they act as if they liked your pieces?"

"Yes, I thought they did."

"Did anybody ask after me?"

"Yes, a lot did."

"What did you tell 'em?"

"I told 'em you had a cold, an' didn't think it was quite prudent to go out." Juliza's voice took on exactly the tone with which she had replied to the inquiring women. She had taken off her shawl and hood, and was standing over the stove. Her face was all a deep pink glow from the cold wind. "Mother," said she, suddenly, "what do you suppose the reason is that Frank don't want me to marry him?"

"Juliza Peck, what do you mean?"

"What I say. What do you suppose the reason is he don't want me to marry him?"

"How do you know he don't?—what are you talking about?"

"He said he didn't, just now."

"How came he to?"

"He was tellin' me how miserable his mother was, an' what a hard time he had gettin' along, an' I said I was willin' to marry him, an' go over there, whenever he said. I knew you could get along without me."

"Juliza Peck, you didn't ask Frank Williams to marry you?"

"No, I didn't ask him; I told him I would."

"Do you know what you've done?"

"What?"

"What? You've made yourself a laughin' stock all over Stony Brook."

"I don't see why I have, I'm sure."

"Don't you know girls don't tell young men they'll marry 'em unless they're asked."

"I don't see why they don't."

"You needn't tell me you didn't know better than that." Juliza turned about, and fronted her mother calmly.

"No I didn't, an' I don't," said she. "I don't see why it's any worse for a girl to speak than 'tis for a man. I always supposed he wanted me to marry him, I've never wanted to marry anybody else, an' I knew his mother was so miserable, and I'd have so much work to do if I went there, that he'd think it was kind of mean to speak of it himself. I don't see a single thing to be ashamed of."

"He'll tell of it all over town."

"No, he won't, he said he wouldn't; an' I told him he could if he wanted to. I don't see what I've done to be laughed at. I don't think he's shown common-sense."

Mrs. Peck looked at Juliza with angry eyes, black and full under her water-waves. Juliza looked at her and never flinched.

"I should have thought your own modesty would have taught you."

"Modesty," returned Juliza in bewildered contempt as if she didn't know what the word meant. "I think it's you that's immodest, mother. I'm too modest to see how I wasn't."

"Well, you've done it, that's all I've got to say," said her mother rising, "now you'd better go to bed. I've been sittin' up here waitin' for you this hour; your father went to bed at nine o'clock. I feel like givin' up, myself; a girl with all your advantages, with money at interest, an' speakin' the way you can, havin' a young man tell you right to your face he didn't want to marry you. I should like to know what he thinks he is—the Williamses warn't never much; they've picked up a little late years, but I remember the time when they was jest as poor an' low down as they could be. Your father an' me look a good deal higher than he for you; I can tell him that."

"He's high enough for me," said Juliza, lighting her lamp.

"I'm ashamed of you," said her mother, fiercely.

"I ain't goin' to run him down because he don't want to marry me." Then Juliza went up stairs to her own room, slowly and ponderously.

The next morning she awoke with a firm resolution in her mind. "I'm goin' to know about this thing," she muttered to herself, and bore down heavily with her wet brush upon her crinkly front hair, then tied her bunch of curls with a jerk.

Her mother treated her with cold stiffness when she appeared down stairs; her father, who was an old man and very silent, ate his breakfast and then went away with a load of wood.

"Be sure you get back in good season," his wife called after him, standing in the door, "I want you to take me down to the village after dinner." The old man made no reply, but it was certain that he heard and would be home in good season. He never dreamed of disobeying his imperious wife, but covered his docility with taciturnity, which gave him a show of masculine dignity.

After the house-work was done, Mrs. Peck called Juliza into the sitting-room and drilled her in a new selection. She stood majestic in her morning calico which swept about her like the robe of a tragedy queen, repeating the poem line by line, and Juliza followed her, imitating the modulations of her voice. Her gestures she could not well imitate; there was something fairly impressive about the backward fling of her mother's head and the sweep of her great arms; her black eyes were full of energetic fire. "You plank your arm up an' down like a pump-handle"; said she, "your arm ain't put in with a hinge, it's put in with your feelin's, when you're speakin'." Juliza worked her arm with patient vigor, but she could not equal her mother. "I s'pose it's because you're built so solid," said Mrs. Peck. "Well, you speak it pretty well. I thought it would be a good piece for the next sociable, if you don't get married."

Juliza answered not a word, she did not flush or look confused. She sat down and sewed silently on a dress she was making. She had a certain dignity of taciturnity like her father at times.

After dinner, her father put the horse in the sleigh, and her mother bundled herself in cloaks and shawls, until she looked like a massive pillar standing in the door-way. "Look out for the fire, Juliza," said she, "an' you'd better study that last piece over some."

"Yes'm," said Juliza.

After her mother had gone, she sat by the sitting-room window and watched the snowy road stretching away in cold blue furrows where the sleighs had passed. Her hands lay idle in her lap. She sat there an hour, then she arose and got her shawl and hood. When she was tying on her hood at the sitting-room glass, she saw Frank Williams going by. She rushed to the window, and pounded on it and beckoned.

He looked up, smiled and nodded confusedly, and was passing on. Juliza had to reach between the flower-pots, and he could scarcely see her face behind them. She hurried to the front-door, unlocked it, and pulled it open with a desperate jerk, for the snow had frozen on the sill. "Frank," she called out, "Frank Williams, come in here a minute, I want to see you." The young man hesitated.

"Is it anything particular?" he called back.

"Yes, 'tis. I've got to see you a minute."

"I've left mother all alone, an' I've got to go down to the store."

"I won't keep you but just a minute." Frank turned up the path leading to the side-door; Juliza kicked off the ridge of snow on the sill, pushed to the door, and went around to let him in.

"I can't stay but a minute," he said, and he looked sulky.

"I won't keep you but just a minute." Juliza led the way into the warm sitting-room; she did not ask him to sit down, they stood confronting each other. "Father and mother have gone to the village," said she. "I've called you in because I wanted to ask you something, and it was a good chance."

Frank was blushing; he looked down at his snowy boots, saw the snow melting on the carpet, and thought fiercely to himself that he did not care if it was spoiled. He tried to smile. "Well," he muttered.

"Now, Frank, I want to ask you something, an' I want you to tell me the truth. I think you owe it to me. We've known each other ever since we were children; you're all the one I've ever known outside this house. You know mother never let me go to school, nor play with other girls. You lived next door, you know, an' she couldn't help it."

"What is it you want to know, Juliza?" said Frank in a constrained voice.

"I want to know why you don't want to marry me?"

Frank threw up his chin with a jerk. "See here, Juliza Peck," he cried, "you may not know it, but you're doin' a dreadful thing. How do you suppose I can answer you a question like that if I'm a man. You know I like you well enough; I always have, but—oh dear, I don't know what to say."

"Is there anybody else you like better?" Juliza asked calmly.

Frank gave a sudden start and looked at her. "I don't know as there is."

"Who is it?"

"I tell you, I don't know as there's anybody."

"Now, Frank Williams, you've got to tell me. You owe it to me. Is it any girl here in Stony Brook?"

"No, it isn't."

Juliza looked at him reflectively. "I know who 'tis," said she.

"No, you don't."

"Yes, I do, an' I'll tell you, too. It's that Lily Emmons that came here once with your cousin Jenny." Frank blushed deeper; he cast a glance at Juliza that was almost piteous.

"I knew 'twas," said she, "you can't cheat me. She came here last summer; I remember her. She was real pretty; I never saw such pink cheeks as she had, an' she had a pink dress with cambric edging on it."

"It's no use talkin' about it," said Frank.

"Yes, there is, too. See here, Frank, have you asked her?"

"Asked her? I haven't seen her since she was here."

"Haven't you written to her?"

"No. Jenny's written to me about her, that's all."

"An' you've sent a word to her sometimes, haven't you?"

"Well, I don't know, I may have, once or twice."

"Frank, you sit down here a minute,—you've got to tell me about this." Juliza pulled forward a rocking-chair and Frank settled into it.

Juliza sat opposite. "Now," said she, "you tell me the whole story. Do you think she likes you?" Frank looked at her like a bashful child, blushing, and half-smiling. "Tell me all about it," said she.

"I've never told a livin' soul, Juliza."

"That's all the more reason why you should. Did anything happen while she was here?"

"You know she wasn't here but two weeks with Jenny," began Frank, hesitatingly, "I suppose you wouldn't think anything could happen in that length of time, but Jenny was with mother, an' she an' I were thrown together a good deal, an' we got acquainted fast. It seemed to me I never got acquainted with anybody so fast; an'—well, it was the day before she went away, we walked down in the orchard, an' I don't know how it happened, but we were standin' there under the trees, an' she was looking up at me, an'—well, any way, I kissed her; an' just then Jenny came runnin' down through the field."

"Did she act mad?"

"No, I don't think she did. I was afraid she was, afterward, but she didn't act so."

"Of course she liked you, then."

"See here, Juliza—should you, if you'd been in her place, that is, if any one had acted so by you? You're another girl, an' you ought to know."

"Yes, I should."

"May be she did like me a little, then. I don't see how she could. Oh Juliza, wasn't she pretty?"

"She's prettier than any girl in Stony Brook."

"I guess she is." Frank's face was full of a tender radiance, his blue eyes looked up into Juliza's face with the love that belonged to the other girl. Juliza was now standing over him. "See here," said she, "why don't you write to her, or go to see her, or something?"

"Jenny asked me to come over to Hillbrook, an' visit. She hinted somebody else would be glad to see me, she guessed; but I can't go."

"Why not?"

"I can't leave mother."

"You could write to that girl," said Juliza, after a reflective pause.

"No, it's no use: I can't. I tell you what 'tis, Juliza, I have written fifty letters, an' torn 'em up. I don't even know how to begin 'em."

"I should say, 'Dear Friend,'" said Juliza.

"Should you? Well, I didn't know. You see I wasn't sure she was in earnest that time in the apple-orchard. I was afraid of writin' as if she was, and afraid of writin' as if she wasn't. Then I tried to write news, but there wasn't any. I had to give it up."

"I could help you write a letter, I suppose," said Juliza, "but I think you had better see her. I'll tell you what I'll do. You get ready an' go to Hillbrook, an'—I'll stay with your mother while you're gone."

"Oh Juliza, you don't mean it!"

"Yes, I do, too."

"Oh! I tell you what 'tis, Juliza, I never saw a girl as good as you are. I don't believe *she* is; at least, I don't believe she's any better."

"I just as lives as not," said Juliza, "it ain't anything, you get ready an' go, an' I'll come over any day. When do you want to go?"

Frank hesitated. "It's Thursday, now," said he, "when do you think I'd better go?"

"Why don't you go to-morrow, an' stay a week?"

"Had you just as soon come to-morrow?"

"I can come to-morrow just as well as any day."

"Well, then," said Frank, getting up, "I'll go home an' tell mother. I guess she'll be willin'. She's always thought everything of you, Juliza."

"How is she to-day?"

"She's miserable."

"Don't she take any medicine?"

"Yes, she takes the doctor's medicine, an' then she has her own little doses. I've just been makin' her some anise-seed tea."

When Frank went, Juliza resumed her sewing and waited for her father and mother to return. It was dusk, and she had lighted the lamp before they drove into the yard. Juliza opened the door, and her mother came in, panting, in a swirl of cold air. She had her arms full of bundles, and she put them down on the lounge with emphasis.

"It's a terrible raw wind," said she, "I'm lucky if I don't get more cold." Suddenly she stood still, and sniffed; her thick green veil moulded itself to her large features.

"What's that I smell?" said she, "anise?" Juliza made no reply.

"Yes, 'tis anise," repeated her mother, "You can't cheat me. Frank Williams has been in here. Mis' Williams is always havin' anise tea, an' their clothes are always scented with it." Suddenly Mrs. Peck made a step forward, slipped up her veil, and peered down at the carpet. "What's that great spot?" she cried out. "He's tracked in snow, an' you know water spots this carpet. I should think you were crazy, Juliza Peck. Why didn't you put a mat under his feet?"

"I didn't think."

"I should think you'd better think. There's that great spot on the carpet. What did he come in here for, anyway?"

Juliza stood looking at the spot. "He wants to go away a few days, but he can't leave his mother. I—told him I'd go over there an' stay with her, so he could go."

"You did!" Juliza looked at the spot. "I guess you won't go a step, not if I know it."

Juliza had always been frank and artless even to bluntness and stupidity. Now she suddenly displayed art which would have done credit to a diplomat. "He's goin' to his cousin Jenny's," said she, "but he's really goin' to see that Emmons girl who was here last summer. If—I go over there to stay while he's gone, he won't think, an' nobody else will think, I want him."

Her mother looked at her sharply. She had taken off her veil and bonnet, the stiff water-waves were unruffled, her cheeks were a purplish-red with the cold wind. "If I ever hear anybody hint you wanted him, they'll get a piece of my mind," said she.

The next morning Juliza went over to the Williams house; her mother had made no further opposition; she even helped her off, grudgingly. "Don't you try to work ter hard now," said she, "you make Frank draw you some water, an' get in a stock of wood before he goes. I'll run over this afternoon, an' see how you're gettin' along."

When Juliza entered the sitting-room of the other house, she found Mrs. Williams sitting at the window in her rocking-chair. She was a little woman, doubled up limply in pillows, like a baby. Her small, gently querulous face was tear-stained, and she looked up pitifully at Juliza. "He's out in the kitchen, shavin'," said she. "He's goin' on the ten o'clock train."

"You an' I will get along first-rate," said Juliza.

Mrs. Williams turned her face toward the window, and wept feebly.

"Now, you mustn't feel so," said Juliza, "you'll make it dreadful hard for him. He won't take any comfort at all, if you do so."

"I don't know—anything about that—girl," sobbed Mrs. Williams. "She's a real pretty girl, an' Jenny knows her."

"I don't want him bringin' home a strange girl, here, and me not able to lift a finger. I don't see why he couldn't have married you, if he'd wanted to married anybody."

"Now, Mis' Williams," said Juliza, "you mustn't do so; it ain't right. You want him to be happy, don't you?"

"Course I do. I want him to be happy more'n anything in the world; he knows I do."

"Then you mustn't take on so. Have you had any breakfast, Mis' Williams?"

"Yes, all I want."

Juliza had laid her shawl and hood away in a closet. She began to straighten the furniture in the sitting-room and to set things to rights. Presently Frank came in, all ready, his black valise in his hand. He looked sharply at his mother, then he set the valise down, heavily.

"Look here, mother," said he, "I ain't goin' a step if you feel this way. I think more of you than I do of anybody else, an' I ain't goin' to have you plagued."

Mrs. Williams began weeping again. Juliza caught up the valise, took hold of Frank's arm, and pulled him out into the kitchen. "Now, you go right along," said she, "an' don't stop to argue. She's all right. She's only nervous. I'll look out for her."

"Oh, Juliza, do you really think I'd ought to go?"

"Of course, I do. Don't you make any more words about it. Go in there, and kiss her, an' say good bye, and don't make any fuss. Here, give me your hat while you go. It needs brushin'."

When Frank was fairly started Juliza stood at the kitchen-window, and watched him down the road with steady eyes; then she went back to Mrs. Williams in the sitting-room. She had no easy task during the next week. The invalid's feeble nerves were all at loose ends and quivering over her son's absence. Then, too, there was much to be done to put the house in order. Frank's housekeeping was eccentric; it seemed to Juliza that everything was where it did not belong. Mrs. Peck came over and helped her several times, but she had a cold, and there was much stormy weather. Juliza had little leisure to grieve, if she had wished to, even at night. She slept in a room out of Mrs.

Williams's, kept a lamp burning, and was ready to spring up at her slightest call.

On the day Frank returned there was a heavy snow-storm; it was dark at half-past four, and Mrs. Williams had gone to bed. Juliza was out in the kitchen; she had been baking biscuits, and had just lifted the pan out of the oven, when Frank opened the door. The minute she looked at him she knew. His face was all wet and rosy like a child's, from the snow and the wind. He was trying not to smile, or rather laugh out with joy, but his whole face shone.

"Well; so you've got home?" said Juliza.

"Yes. How's mother?"

"She's pretty comfortable. She's just gone to bed."

Frank went up to the stove and stood over it. "You don't ask me how I got along, Juliza?" said he.

"How did you?"

"Well, I guess it'll be all right." Suddenly Frank flung up one arm on the shelf, and rested his head on it. "Oh!" he cried out, almost sobbing like a child, "I'm so happy! She's liked me all along, ever since she was here. I don't know what I've done to deserve it. I can't believe it. Oh, I'm so happy it seems as if I couldn't live."

"I'm real glad for you," said Juliza. She was quite pale, but her voice was steady. She went into the pantry and brought out some cookies in a plate. The table was all set for Frank's supper. "You'd better go in an' just speak to your mother," she said; "she must have heard you come in, an' she'd be nervous waiting."

"Well, I'll go in," said Frank, raising his head and showing his radiant, quivering face. "Oh, Juliza! you've been the best friend to me I ever had in my life, comin' over here. I'll never forget it."

Juliza smiled. "I'd just as lives as not," said she. "Go in kind of quiet." The minute the sitting-room door had closed after Frank, Juliza caught her shawl and hood from a peg, put them on, opened the door softly, and sped out. Then she tramped sturdily down the snowy road toward the lights of her own home.

Frank was married some six weeks afterward at his bride's home in Hillbrook. The newly-wedded couple, with quite a large company of relations, came over to Stony Brook for a wedding party at the bridegroom's house. Juliza had a new black silk to wear, and her mother had made her take some of her money and buy a garnet breastpin. "You might just as well have things," she said, with a defiant air. She thought to herself that Juliza looked better than the bride, but the bride was beautiful. She stood smiling and blushing beside Frank, in her pink gown and her veil. Juliza had pinned on the veil; the bride had brought it over from Hillbrook in a box.

The evening was nearly over when Mrs. Peck came up to Juliza and took hold of her arm forcibly—"They want you to speak a piece," she whispered.

"Oh, mother! I don't believe I can to-night."

"Yes, you can, too; that last one. They all want you to. Mis' Williams does, an' Frank, an' *she* does, too. There! the minister's goin' to tell 'em."

There was a sudden hush. Then the minister spoke: "We will now listen to a recitation by Miss Juliza Peck," said he. "She has kindly consented to grace still further this happy occasion."

There was a soft clapping of hands. Juliza stood forward and bowed. She was exactly in front of the wedded pair. She began to speak, and she spoke as she had never done before. Her gestures were full of fire; every line of her form and face seemed to conform to the exigencies of the situation; her voice rang out with a truth that was deeper than her own personality. Everybody listened. The bridal couple were forgotten. When Juliza finished, everybody crowded around her; her mother stood aloof proudly smiling. The beautiful bride told her she had never heard anybody speak so well. Frank stood close to her, and as soon as the others drew off a little he leaned over her and whispered.

"I want to tell you, Juliza," he said, "how much we thank you for every thing you've done. I've told Lily about it, an' we both feel as if it's all due to you."

"I haven't done much."

"Yes, you have, an' there's another thing. Juliza, I want you to forgive me for—that night. I haven't told a soul, not even Lily, an' I never shall. I know you just meant to be kind, that was all."

Juliza smiled. She had the same proud lift to her head, that she had had when reciting. "It's all right," said she, "don't you worry."

A Tragedy from the Trivial

The great double doors of H. F. Crosby's Dry Goods Emporium faced south, and the wind was that way. The ribbon counter, where Charlotte May stood, was directly in front of the door, and all the gay ribbons hanging overhead from a wire and those suspended from their rolls on the edge of the case swung and waved, and wove together in the gusts of the wind. Those overhead were mostly in shades of orange, those on the case in blues. Between those dancing streamers of colour Charlotte's face—triangularly shaped, almost like a cat's, with a mild fulness about the temples and innocently speculative blue eyes—appeared. Her hair was very fair, almost white, and she wore it in a quaint extreme of fashion which often caused people to turn and look after her. Her blue gingham short waist fitted her nicely, and her blue ribbon tie was wound tightly around her throat, and fastened with a cheap brooch with a stone of turquoise blue china. Charlotte's friend, Maud Lockwood, who stood beside her at the ribbon counter, had told her many a time that no one could tell it from the real thing, and Maud Lockwood was regarded as an authority and was much admired.

It is quite true that there are spheres which would make us all stars could we but find them for our revolutions, and Maud Lockwood had found hers. She was a handsome girl, with such a subtle consciousness of her fine trimly girded figure that she seemed to fairly thrust it upon one's attention. It was also well known that she was not obliged to work in a store, being led to such a step only by the desire of certain extras in the way of dress somewhat beyond the reach of her father's purse. It is only choice, not necessity, which dignifies labour in the estimation of many who have always laboured from necessity, and their fathers before them. A girl like Charlotte May, who had to work or starve, looked with envious respect at a girl like Maud Lockwood, who had to work or give up her frills. Maud wore a real turquoise brooch, and the girl beside her often looked at it with a sentiment of complacency and no envy. She could not see that it was any prettier than her own, and she was not one to be disturbed by any pretence, if it were clever.

The third girl, or rather woman, at the ribbon counter looked with gravity and ill-concealed contempt upon both of them—the wearer of the real turquoise and the wearer of the sham. She would have worn neither. Neither the real nor the false ornamental superfluities of life had any place in her conception of its structure. She would have dispensed with all perianths and gargoyles in her architecture, and left but the pillars and brackets of support. In her opinion only use redeemed the existence of ornament. If she wore a brooch it was to fasten something, otherwise she left it in its little box in her bureau drawer. She had a plain gold one which had belonged to her mother.

This woman, Eliza Green, had been employed in Crosby's for years, and was trusted. She went now and then to New York to purchase ribbons, and her judgment as to quality and value was good, although her own taste was scarcely showy enough to suit the folk of this cheap, provincial, manufacturing city. She bought ribbons, as she looked upon the jewellery of her mates at the counter, with keen recognition of the taste of others, and contempt for it. She would under no circumstances have worn any of the ribbons which she purchased.

Eliza Green was supposed to be quite well to do, having doubtless saved from her salary, which had been increased from time to time, and having her own house free from encumbrance. Eliza had inherited a comfortable square house, half of which she rented out and lived herself in the other half. The house was some three miles from the city, in a farming district. Next door lived John Woodsum, who presently came into Crosby's, after hitching his horse before the store.

It was hot that afternoon. The concrete sidewalks yielded and sprang underfoot like sponge. The drug-store clerks wore white linen coats, and the waiting lines at the soda fountains were long.

John Woodsum had no work that day. The factory in which he was employed was running low, the midsummer heat seeming to affect the current of trade like that of a brook. He was going to marry Charlotte May, though few knew it. He had himself requested Charlotte not to speak of it.

"Not that I'm doing anything I'm ashamed of, nor you either," he said, "but I don't want folks talking about my affairs more than I can help. There's three times a man has to be talked about, whether or no—when he's born, when he's married, and when he dies. I mean to get rid of all the others that I am able."

So John Woodsum had taken the girl to drive, and escorted her home from meeting, and, as she had many other admirers, nobody was sure. Indeed, the general opinion was that she would not marry John Woodsum. Eliza Green dismissed the matter with a single reflection when Maud Lockwood told her that John Woodsum had taken Charlotte to drive the Saturday before.

"She has not enough sense," she thought.

Then she matched some ribbon for a customer, and thought no more about it. But when the young man stood in the store door that afternoon she felt a little surprise. She glanced quickly at Charlotte and saw that her delicate face was a deep pink. John himself advanced upon the counter with no embarrassment or change of colour, presenting that singular anomaly of utter rusticity with neither confusion nor shame-facedness. He wore his best clothes, but rose superior to even their clumsy stiffness. His face, large and somewhat heavy, had a certain dignity of expression which made up for the want of alertness. People were wont to say that John Woodsum wasn't so quick as some, but it would take a mighty smart man to get round him. Even his new hat, much too large for him, which he did not remove when he approached the counter, did not detract from his air of self-establishment.

Eliza Green, who was rolling up some yards of blue ribbon, said, "How do you do, John?" and went on with her work. Maud Lockwood said, "Good afternoon, Mr. Woodsum," in her sweet, artificially modulated voice, with a nod and smile which she saw as plainly as in a looking-glass.

Charlotte said nothing. She turned red, then pale, and half shrank away as John approached.

"Are you ready?" John inquired, in a deep voice, with no hesitation whatever; and Charlotte gazed at him hesitatingly for a second, her lips trembling, and her cheeks quite pale between her loops of flaxen hair.

"Are you ready?" the young man asked again, this time with a note of surprise. Then Charlotte replied, "Yes," hurriedly, and took her hat—a white, broad-brimmed one with perky bows of pale blue, turned up at the back with a profusion of cheap pink flowers—from under the counter, put it on with trembling hands, and slipped past her mates.

"What's Mr. Crosby going to say, dear, if you run away half an hour before it's time to close?" inquired Maud Lockwood. "I saw him just now looking over here; and he didn't look any too sweet: I can tell you that."

"Mr. Crosby knows, and he'll say nothing," John Woodsum returned shortly. Then he and Charlotte went out, she walking rather weakly and carrying her head bent, with never a backward glance, and he assisted her into his open buggy before the store.

Maud Lockwood turned to Eliza Green, with a brilliant flash of eyes and teeth.

"Know what that means?" said she.

Eliza Green shook her head.

"They're going to be married."

Eliza Green did not change colour, but there was a swift contraction of the muscles around her mouth, and her eyes narrowed as before too much light.

"What makes you think so?" she asked, in her quiet, sustained voice. She rolled up some orange ribbon as she spoke, and not getting it quite straight unwound it, and re-rolled it carefully.

"Didn't you see she had on her new white dress and her best hat?"

Eliza nodded. She had noticed the flying white frills, and the pink flowers, as Charlotte went out of the store.

"Well, John Woodsum had on his Sunday clothes, and they had arranged it with Crosby, and two and two make four. They've gone to get married. It's just the way a stick like John Woodsum would set about getting married—no wedding and no anything. Charlotte has never had an engagement ring. I shouldn't wonder if he didn't give her a wedding one. Settling down with a man like that, to cook and to mend—a pretty girl like her!"

"Maybe she hasn't."

"Oh, yes, she has. Didn't you see her face when he came in? A girl don't look like that unless she's going to get married, or buried, or do something out of the common. Here's Crosby. Ask him."

Mr. H. F. Crosby, who just then came sauntering up, passing some customers with a suave hitch of his shoulders and an impatient wrinkle of his forehead, was unmarried, and people credited him with an admiration for Maud Lockwood. She put her hand to her hair and pulled her shirt waist straight as he drew near.

"Mr. Crosby," she called, with confidential softness. Eliza Green went on rolling ribbons.

"Well?" returned Crosby, and the frown deepened. His hair was of a deep shade of red, and his eyes were like blue sparks. He was considered handsome, except for his hair.

"You needn't look so cross," said Maud Lockwood, with a pout, carefully lowering her voice, that its familiarity should not be noticed. "What has Charlotte May gone off half an hour before shutting up for? If you are getting partial I want to give notice."

Maud laughed and her employer seemed to quail before her. There was a steady impetus about this girl which intimidated his nervous, irascible temperament, whose irascibility had no firm roots. Sometimes H. F. Crosby felt that Maud Lockwood could marry him if she chose, and he felt afraid of her. He tried to laugh, but with poor success, and his lips were pale.

"They've gone to call on the minister, I guess," said he.

Maud laughed triumphantly.

"There, you can't cheat me," she cried to Eliza, who was interweaving the ribbons hanging from the line overhead as imperturbably as a fate. "How long have you known it?" she asked Crosby.

"Last night," he replied shortly, and turned away as some one spoke to him. "First aisle to the left, madam," he said to the inquiring woman, and was gone.

Maud laughed again with shrewd malice. "He's hit. I suspected it," she said.

Eliza looked at her with the faintest shade of inquiring interest.

"Oh, you never see things. He's hung around this counter to see Charlotte, day in and out. Folks thought it was me, but it wasn't.

However, I didn't want it to be me. I wouldn't marry a man like Crosby and put up with his tantrums. He'd have to get over 'em grand lively. But, on the whole, I'd just as soon take somebody that didn't need to be made over. Made-over things never fit so well," said she, with an approving laugh at her own wit.

Not another customer approached the ribbon counter that afternoon. When it was time to close Eliza Green went home with her little lunch bag. She always carried her lunch, for motives of economy. She walked, although the electric cars ran near her house, for the same reason.

When she came within sight of John Woodsum's house, which was just before her own, she saw a white flutter at the door, and knew that the bridal couple had got home. Eliza heard Charlotte's little soft giggle, as she turned in at her own gate. She had no sooner entered her own room than the woman who lived in the other side entered hastily, the scent of tea and baking biscuit following her, and a child calling her back shrilly.

"Do you know what has happened?" she whispered, as slyly as if John and his bride were within earshot.

"Yes," replied Eliza, taking off her hat carefully and folding her veil.

"Got married, without no weddin' nor a word to nobody! Drove over to the minister's in his own team, and brought her trunk under the seat. Land! I never had much to do with, but I got married in better shape than that. Had she said anything about it to you?"

"No, not a word," replied Eliza.

The woman looked at her sharply.

"I didn't know but she had, as long as she worked at the same counter."

"She didn't," Eliza said. "If you can let me have a little hot water I guess I won't make up a fire to-night, it's so warm."

"You can have it jest as well as not. I see she's got a handsome white dress on, and a hat with pink flowers. Had she worn 'em before?"

"Yes, I guess she had."

"I wonder if she's got a new silk dress."

"I don't know," replied Eliza, getting a pitcher out of her pantry.

"I don't believe she had," said the woman. "It would be just like

John Woodsum not to want her to, even if she bought it with her own money. He's awful tight-fisted."

"She didn't have much to spend on silk dresses," said Eliza; "not much beside her board and washing."

There was a scream from the woman's child on the other side, and she ran, Eliza following with her pitcher.

Every night when Eliza came home from the store the woman gave her a bulletin of the happenings next door. She had seen the bride at work in an old calico which had belonged to John's mother, much too large for her, folded over, and pinned up. She knew John would not let her wear her store dresses at work. The bride had done the washing, and there were disgusted pointings at the drabbled garments hanging on the line. Eliza thought with incapable reachings of imagination of Charlotte at the wash-tub, rubbing away at her husband's heavy under-garments with those slender little hands of hers. Charlotte's hands were the tiniest things: long-fingered and blue-veined.

"John Woodsum ought to hire a washerwoman," said the other, and Eliza acquiesced, though calmly. She did not call on the bride, but when she caught a glimpse of her in the yard she saw that she was greatly changed. Once, too, she came into the store to buy some needles and thread and gingham, and Maud Lockwood remarked upon it.

"Such a pretty girl as she was," she said after she was gone. "It seems to me sometimes as if matrimony was nothing but a tomb for good looks. Sometimes I think I'll never get married."

However, Charlotte had not lost her prettiness; it was simply veiled and hidden beneath unwontedness and awkward plainness of attire. Her face was too delicately sharp and her forehead too high for her to wear her hair strained tightly back into a hard knot, yet that was the way she had arranged it since her marriage.

"I don't like your hair falling over your ears in that way," John had said; "put it straight back and show your forehead." And she had obeyed.

Charlotte also, when she was bidden, discarded all her little tricks of style and fashion, which, regarded from her husband's practical point of view, were void of sense. There were no more wide collars of crumpled ribbons; no jaunty puffings of blouses, no garniture of cheap flowers, and, above all, no cheap jewellery—no jewellery of any kind except her wedding ring. John had given her a wedding ring, though it was not the ostentatiously heavy article which her crude fancy had pictured. Charlotte had her girlhood fripperies packed away in her bureau drawers, and sometimes she looked at them, not so much with regret as with anxious bewilderment. She was not unhappy, being as fond of her husband as a spaniel, but was more or less anxious and bewildered, having developed within herself since marriage a painful willingness of obedience without entire capacity. Charlotte, having lost her parents when young, had never been under the active necessity of obedience to anything, except Providence, and it is very easy to confuse Providence with one's own wishes, especially in trivialities. It was easy enough for her to strain her hair back from her blue-veined temples; she could leave off her ribbons and brooches, but in housewifely matters lack of training made her wilful against her will.

It was a woefully kept house unless John Woodsum rose at dawn, and toiled until midnight after his daily work was done. And the waste, to one of his frugal turn, amounted to actual crime. Charlotte seemed absolutely incapable of learning the lesson of household thrift. She was devoid of domestic instincts. There was no guile in her and a great tenacity of affection; but she was simply organised, and her feet went swiftly only in the ways in which they had been set. Her duties had been, as it were, single-threaded. The measuring and selling of ribbon, and furbishing up of her own pretty person, had no relation to the financial diplomacy required in the simplest housekeeping to advantage. Her pleasures had been firemen's balls, and park entertainments, and electric car excursions, with vacations at a cheap shore resort. All these she had forfeited by her marriage. There were for her no more dances, nor summer vacations, nor, as a rule, electric rides. John regarded those as a waste of money. He still kept the horse which his father had used on the farm. Charlotte was never impatient, but sometimes, jogging to town behind the heavy, slow-plodding animal, meekly sitting at her husband's broad left shoulder, she looked with wistful eyes at the crowds whizzing past on the electrics. Her mind was forced back upon itself, and thought was to her hard exercise, and she liked crowds and rapid motion to take its place. She was like a butterfly deprived of its wings, yet with all its instincts of tremulous motion left, as she sat beside her husband, behind the solemnly advancing horse, but she looked often at him with perfect belief and devotion. By some idiosyncrasy John's old horse now and then shied violently at the electric cars, though at nothing else—even steam rollers had failed to move him. Charlotte's eyes would flash with sudden life when the old horse jumped. She was afraid, but she liked to be afraid, since the fear gave her a sensation of life and individuality. Though Charlotte did not enjoy driving in such wise, it was to her a respite from her household tasks, which daily filled her with more consternation and despair. John never lost his temper, never scolded her, but his steady disapproval was as the face of a rock before her eyes. He was fond of the toothsome, though perchance unwholesome, village fare which his mother had set before him from boyhood. He wanted light biscuits, and cake, and pie, though all must be concocted with a careful calculation as to the best possible results from the fewest and cheapest ingredients.

When Charlotte made a cake or a pie it was not only poor in quality, but she wasted her husband's substance unmercifully. When he pointed out to her the flour left on the board, the sugar in the bowl, her very soul was bowed in pitiful humiliation, and the depressing certainty that it would be no better next time.

When Charlotte had been married three years she had become that sad anomaly—a creature at cross purposes with itself. She was completely under the sway of her husband's will as regarded her own, yet she was unable to accomplish perfect obedience to its mandate.

Charlotte acquired a piteous little wrinkle between her eyes. She lost all her soft, childlike confidence of manner. She looked at her husband before she spoke, and yet never spoke wholly to please him, as she never did anything wholly to please him. She knew that John was not saving as much as he had expected to. He had wished to purchase a piece of land adjoining his own, but another purchaser had anticipated him while he was hoarding his money. John had a fierce ambition to acquire a competency, and Charlotte knew she was constantly balking it, although he never accused her of it and never reproached her. The waste in the little household was considerable, though they lived poorly, by reason of her bad cookery. Charlotte seldom dared essay a cake or a pie, since her efforts had been so disastrous in that direction that John had prohibited them. He had even placed her upon an allowance of flour, butter, sugar, and such things.

"You must use no more than this for a month," he told Charlotte with that intense soberness of his which amounted in its effect to sternness. "If you do we must go without the rest of the time."

Ever since Charlotte had studied the resources of the supply bags in her pantry as anxiously as a shipwrecked mariner. However when the first of a month came, with its replenishment of supplies, she sometimes felt a little more confidence, and used them a little more recklessly. She was still so childish that she had visions as of eternity and inexhaustibility at the beginning of things.

When John's birthday fell upon the same day that the flour and sugar bags were renewed a reckless spirit took possession of her. She would make him a birthday cake. She waited until John had gone to the factory for the day, carrying his poor luncheon; then she got out her mixing bowl and set to work. She studied laboriously a recipe in the cook book which John had bought for her, and strove to follow it as if it had been a commandment, but somehow she failed. When she took the cake from the oven it was a soggy, heavy mass.

Charlotte sat down and wept. And then the woman who lived in Eliza Green's house came in, with a child tugging at her skirt.

"Why, what's the matter?" said she sympathetically. She was a curious woman, but not kindly.

"I—I made a cake for John's birthday, and—and it's fell," sobbed Charlotte.

"Why, make another; what do you sit down and cry for?" said the woman easily. She had a fair, pretty face, and her stout figure was draped in a baggy, pink calico wrapper. "I've got a rule I never knew to fail," said she. "I'll send it over by Stevy."

"Oh, I can't, I can't!" cried Charlotte in horror. "I can't do that, and waste all this! I don't know what my husband would say."

"Well, why don't you make it over, then?"

"Make it over?" repeated Charlotte, vaguely.

"It's as easy as can be. You just put in an egg and a little molasses, and a little milk, and a little baking powder, and a little more flour, and stir it together, and bake it over again. I've done it dozens of times."

"What's your rule?"

"Oh, I haven't got any rule. Just put in a little more of everything. You can't fail. I never did. Use your judgment. Will you lend me your glass pitcher? My cousin and her husband are coming on the noon train, and mine got broken the other day, and the common one doesn't look hardly fit to set on the table for company. You can't fail on that cake. I wouldn't cry any more. It ain't worth it."

Then the woman hurried away with the glass pitcher, while the child was tugging backward at her pink skirts, and Charlotte, with hope springing anew in her young heart, set to work to make over the cake.

She added a little of everything, as the woman had directed, but there was a result of which she had not been advised. The mixture filled two cake-tins instead of one, and the two went into the oven, and the two fell lamentably and utterly, as the first had done.

When Charlotte took them out and surveyed them she did not cry any more. A curious change had come over her. All her individuality, which had been overawed, but not obliterated, by those years of wedlock with a stronger nature, erected itself in full vigour, freed from all restraint by the courage of utter despair.

Charlotte's mouth was set hard; her eyes were like blue stars; there were red spots on her cheeks. She was utterly desperate and reckless. She made over the two cakes, and they were four, and she put them in the oven and they fell.

Then she went on and on, and always the cakes increased by that terrific rule of progression which has the awe of infinity in it, and the cakes always fell. She used all her baking tins. She put the mixture in china bowls which she feared would crack in the heat, but she was too desperate to heed that. At the last she even used her best china teacups.

The oven would not accommodate them all, and the pans stood about on the table, chairs, and floor, awaiting their turn. She mixed and baked until she had used all her month's supplies, and the cupboard was as bare as Mother Hubbard's. She exhausted the pile of wood which John had split that morning, and split more herself with her weak, girlish arms, and at last, in the middle of the afternoon, the pantry shelves, the kitchen floor, the table, the chairs, were laden with that nightmare of utterly fallen and uneatable cake.

Charlotte took out the last loaves and looked at them. She burned her fingers, but did not seem to feel it. Her eyes were still dry. Then without a moment's hesitation she went into her bedroom, took her muslin dress, in which she had been married, out of her closet, put it on, and her old hat, with the cheap pink flowers. Then she packed a change of linen and some little things in a bag. She took nothing which her husband had bought for her. Charlotte pinned the neck of her muslin gown with the sham turquoise brooch which she had not worn since her marriage, because John disliked it, and tied on a dotted veil, which he had also prohibited, over her face.

Then she went out of the house, locked the front door, put the key under the blind, and took the next car to town. She had not a cent with her, not enough to pay her fare. She knew the conductor, and asked him, with a revival of her old childishly familiar manner, to trust her till the next time, which he was glad enough to do, paying her fare out of his own pocket.

"You're a great stranger," he said, with a smile, as he slipped back along the foot rail. He was quite a young man.

"Yes, I am," assented Charlotte; "but I guess I sha'n't be so now."

The conductor gave her a half admiring, half curious look. Her eyes showed that she had been weeping, but there was an expression of gaiety that was almost abandon on her face. Her cheeks reddened in the fresh wind, her flaxen hair tossed about her temples. People turned to look at her.

Charlotte stopped the car at Crosby's store.

That night, when John Woodsum came home and found his house redolent with sweets and spices, and the shelves laden with poor Charlotte's multiplicity of cakes, and she gone, he was overwhelmed by misery, and the more so by the very absurdity and grotesqueness of the guise in which it came. He looked at the cakes, and laughed while he groaned. It was like a strong man being drowned in sugar and water. He had not a doubt of it at all. These miserable, soggy attempts at cake, filling all his dishes, had their unequivocal significance in his eyes. Under a quiet and taciturn exterior he was abnormally sensitive and suspicious. He judged this to be a manifesto of all renunciation of wifely obedience, and a mockery. Still he made up his mind that she would return, and he would be very mild with her.

"After all she is childish, and I ought to have seen it when I married her," he argued, without so much regret at a false step for himself as pity for her. "She might have done better with a rich man like Crosby, who could have kept a hired girl," he thought.

He did not disturb the cakes, but kindled the kitchen fire anew, and sat down to wait for his wife; but she did not come. The fire went out. At nine o'clock he began to believe that she had rebelled utterly—made a mock at him and his frugality, and set in open defiance of him this enormous waste upon his very heart.

Then he went out to the barn, put the old horse in the buggy, and drove to town. It was a very hot night. As he passed an ice-cream saloon he looked in the windows, glittering with electricity and astir with electric fans. At a table full in sight sat Crosby, Maud Lockwood, and his wife. Charlotte had both round elbows on the table, and as he passed she looked up with that sweet, soft giggle of hers—more like an ebullition of general enjoyment than actual mirth—and it seemed as if she saw him, but she did not.

John tied his horse and entered. He stood beside the table before they saw him. Then Charlotte looked up, and her jaw dropped and her blue eyes stared. But Maud Lockwood sprang to her feet, glowing with anger.

"You have come to look for your wife, have you, Mr. Woodsum?" said she. "Well, she is making me a visit, and she is going to stay some time; and I am going to see that she has enough to eat, so she will look a little more as she used to before you married her. She is having some ice-cream now. I doubt if she has had any since she was married. You can go home and let her alone; she is staying with me."

John gave one glance at Charlotte, and opened his mouth to speak; but she looked at him as a bird might have, with a round-eyed fascination of terror. That stung him into a coldness and stiffness of pride which seemed like death. John went out, saying not a word, turned his old horse about, and went home.

Then he recommenced his solitary life. He packed away all Charlotte's little foolish flipperies and trinkets which he had held in such contempt, because they did not harmonise with his conception of her. Could he have put his feeling about them into words he would have inquired the need of hanging ribbons and laces upon a flower for its further adornment. But poor Charlotte was no flower—only a girl with many follies of nature upon which the follies of life could catch and cling.

John Woodsum's nature was so essentially masculine that these little girlish possessions touched him only to that selfsame contempt as he thrust them into the trunk. Yet he loved his wife, and his heart was well-nigh breaking for the loss of her, though she had, as he believed, deserted him and mocked him with such an extravagance of absurdity that it seemed to fairly rob his grief of its own dignity. John was not jealous; no doubt as to his wife's faithfulness ever dawned upon him. That was no more in his conception of her than her help-less shallowness of nature had been.

John sent the trunk to his wife, who had left Maud Lockwood and was boarding in her old quarters and working at the ribbon counter at Crosby's. He was painfully conscious and angry at himself for it when he gave the address to the express-man who took the trunk away. He knew that he knew—that all the neighbours knew. One morning the woman who lived in Eliza Green's house sent him some muffins for breakfast, and he sent them back.

"Thank your mother, and tell her I've had my breakfast," he said to the little round-faced boy who bore them aloft in both hands.

That night the woman told Eliza Green; and Eliza for some reason felt indignant almost to repulsion with John's wife when she stood next her at the ribbon counter the following day.

Charlotte was prettier than when she had stood there before, for the little shade of unhappiness and anxiety on her face accentuated it and gave it an interest beyond that of mere sweetness of colour and outline. She had resumed some of her coquettish tricks of dress, and the sham turquoise again gleamed in her neck ribbon; but she still wore her hair as John had directed.

"Why don't you do your hair the old way? You'd look a heap pret-tier," asked Maud Lockwood; and Charlotte giggled and said she didn't know; but she never looped her flaxen locks over her ears as she had been used to do.

Charlotte did not talk as much as before her marriage. Her blue eyes had often a retrospective look. For the first time in her life she had a clearly defined object—a definite goal for progress. She was intent upon saving enough money to replace all the ingredients she had wasted in her luckless cake-making. Her weekly stipend was small;

she had almost nothing left after her board was paid, but she saved every penny. She even did her washing in her own room, and dried her clothes overnight in her window. She paid not a cent for car fares, always walking unless some one invited her to ride. She bought no new trinkets; she went without new flannels when winter came, and wore her old thin ones. Still she could save only penny by penny. She reckoned the cost of the supplies which she had wasted as about fifteen dollars. Then she took cold from wearing damp clothing, only partly dried in her room, and thin flannels, and she was out of the store some weeks, with the doctor and medicine to pay for. Mr. Crosby paid her salary while she was out, and sent her fruit and flowers; and she began to realise that she had only to speak for still more.

"He's gone mad over you," said Maud Lockwood. "Why don't you get divorced and marry him?"

Charlotte coloured all over her thin, sweet face and her neck. She had grown very thin during her illness, and strange fancies were always in her brain. She did not feel like her old self at all. Sometimes she experienced a momentary surprise at seeing her familiar face in the glass. Possibly she was not the same. Nobody can tell what changes the indulgence of a foreign trait may work in a character; and it was with Charlotte as if a butterfly had developed a deadly intensity.

It seemed to her as if she could never scrape together that fifteen dollars; but none the less she persevered. She did not definitely plan what would happen should she succeed—whether she would return to her husband or not—but the fifteen dollars she must have, for some reason. Whether it was love or revenge, or the instinct of blind obedience to a stronger nature, she did not know. She was not equal to self-analysis, but she began to think and grow cunning with that cunning which springs most readily from the greed of acquisition. The next time Mr. Crosby sent her flowers she did what she had never done before—sent him a pretty note of thanks.

Then he wrote to her, sending more flowers and fruit, and begging her not to return to the store until she was entirely restored to health.

Charlotte returned to the store the next week, though she was not able. She was very thin, and she coughed hard. She was indescribably pathetic and pretty, with her hollow blue eyes and her appealing smile, when her employer came to greet her.

She thanked him, and let her hand remain in his. He chided her gently for returning to the store, and invited her to drive with him that afternoon—the air would do her good—and she consented.

Eliza Green had heard the conversation, and when Mr. Crosby had gone she turned severely to the other girl.

"Do you realise what you are doing?" she asked, with more excitement than she had ever shown. "As long as you bear a man's name you have no right to lay it in the dust."

But Charlotte stared at her with utterly childish wonder.

"What do you mean, Eliza?" said she. Then she coughed.

"She means that you mustn't flirt with one man till you're quit of another," said Maud Lockwood clearly, and laughed.

"I am not going to," Charlotte replied simply between her coughs; but she blushed guiltily, for she had an under-motive which no one suspected.

Charlotte did not get over her cold as she should, perhaps from her continuing to do her washing in her room and wearing poorly aired linen, and perhaps because she did not buy the medicine ordered by her doctor.

After a while she could not be in the store at all. Mr. Crosby used to send delicacies and sometimes call on her. On pleasant days he took her to drive in an easy carriage. People did not know whether to talk pityingly or reproachfully. Maud Lockwood defended her stoutly. But neither she nor any one dreamed for a moment of her real aim and motive, which was ridiculous to grotesqueness—she wanted to get that fifteen dollars. She alone knew by what childish wiles and cunning, planned in her sleepless nights while she lay coughing, drenched with the sweat of exhaustion, she brought it about; but Crosby one day brought her something which he had been made to know would please her—a real turquoise brooch set with pearls. The girl's eyes flashed when she saw it. She fairly laughed.

"What a tonic a bit of jewellery is to a woman!" Crosby said, laughing in return.

"Thank, oh, thank you!" cried Charlotte. "Is it mine to do just what I want to with? Do you mean that?"

"Of course I do," replied Crosby wonderingly.

That evening after dusk Charlotte stole out of the house, though she had been forbidden the night air. When she returned, stifling her cough on the stairs, lest her landlady should hear her, Crosby's turquoise brooch had been sold, and the fifteen dollars' worth of provisions ordered sent to John Woodsum's.

The next day when John Woodsum returned from work he found the parcels heaped on his porch.

He was looking at them in a bewildered way when he heard a cough, and saw Charlotte shrinking back in the corner. John had heard some of the talk about Crosby, and his heart was bitter. He was about to turn away when he caught sight of her face.

"Are you sick?" he asked, almost roughly.

"I guess so," she returned, shrinkingly.

Then she made a weak little run to him, and he put an arm around her.

"That is every bit as much as I used, every bit as much," she said, pointing to the parcels.

"What do you mean?"

Charlotte told him incoherently, and he listened.

"Oh, my God!" cried he. "Come into the house, poor child."

The next day Crosby's turquoise brooch was returned to him. John carried it to his boarding-place, and the two men had a talk, at first with angry voices. At last they shook hands. The next day Crosby sent some white roses, and John himself put them in a vase beside Charlotte's bed.

"He's been real good," said she, "and if it hadn't been for him I don't know as I ever could have come home."

Charlotte lived only two months after her return. There was consumption in her mother's family. Then, too, her willingness to yield to forces was a fatal element in this case.

It was only the day before she died when Eliza Green came in to see her, bringing some jelly. Eliza looked unusually well; her face was clear and good; her voice was calm and pleasant. Charlotte's nurse was not very tidy.

Eliza moved softly about the room, setting things to rights. She covered up a dish, lest the flies should get into it; she put a cork in a bottle. Charlotte watched her with a wise regard in her hollow blue eyes.

That night she said to John:

"John, do you like Eliza?"

"Well enough; why?"

"Nothing," replied Charlotte. "Only—she is a good girl, and she is very neat and orderly, and I don't believe she would ever waste anything. John—"

"Oh, hush, darling!" cried John, in an agony.

But Charlotte smiled. At the last she had learned her little lesson of obedience and thrift against all her instincts, and all her waste of life was over.

The Prism

There had been much rain that season, and the vegetation was almost tropical. The wayside growths were jungles to birds and insects, and very near them to humans. All through the long afternoon of the hot August day, Diantha Fielding lay flat on her back under the lee of the stone wall which bordered her stepfather's, Zenas May's, south mowing-lot. It was pretty warm there, although she lay in a little strip of shade of the tangle of blackberry-vines, poison-ivy, and the gray pile of stones; but the girl loved the heat. She experienced the gentle languor which is its best effect, instead of the fierce unrest and irritation which is its worst. She left that to rattlesnakes and nervous women. As for her, in times of extreme heat, she hung over life with tremulous flutters, like a butterfly over a rose, moving only enough to preserve her poise in the scheme of things, and realizing to the full the sweetness of all about her.

She heard, as she lay there, the voice of a pine-tree not far away—a solitary pine which was full of gusty sweetness; she smelled the wild grapes, which were reluctantly ripening across the field over the wall that edged the lane; she smelled the blackberry-vines; she looked with indolent fascination at the virile sprays of poison-ivy. It was like innocence surveying sin, and wondering what it was like. Once her stepmother, Mrs. Zenas May, had been poisoned with ivy, and both eyes had been closed thereby. Diantha did not believe that the ivy would so serve her. She dared herself to touch it, then she looked away again.

She heard a far-carrying voice from the farm-house at the left calling her name. "Diantha! Diantha!" She lay so still that she scarcely breathed. The voice came again. She smiled triumphantly. She knew perfectly well what was wanted: that she should assist in preparing supper. Her stepmother's married daughter and her two children were visiting at the house. She preferred remaining where she was. Her sole fear of disturbance was from the children. They were like little ferrets. Diantha did not like them. She did not like children very well under any circumstances. To her they seemed always out of tune; the jar of heredity was in them, and she felt it, although she did not know enough to realize what she felt. She was only twelve years old, a child still, though tall for her age.

The voice came again. Diantha shifted her position a little; she stretched her slender length luxuriously; she felt for something which hung suspended around her neck under her gingham waist, but she did not then remove it. "Diantha! Diantha!" came the insistent voice.

Diantha lay as irresponsive as the blackberry-vine which trailed beside her like a snake. Then she heard the house door close with a bang; her ears were acute. She felt again of that which was suspended from her neck. A curious expression of daring, of exultation, of fear, was in her face. Presently she heard the shrill voices of children; then she lay so still that she seemed fairly to obliterate herself by silence and motionlessness.

Two little girls in pink frocks came racing past; their flying heels almost touched her, but they never saw her.

When they were well past, she drew a cautious breath, and felt again of the treasure around her neck.

After a while she heard the soft padding of many hoofs in the heavy dust of the road, a dog's shrill bark, the tinkle of a bell, the absent-minded shout of a weary man. The hired man was driving the cows home. The fragrance of milk-dripping udders, of breaths sweetened with clover and meadow-grass, came to her. Suddenly a cold nose rubbed against her face; the dog had found her out. But she was a friend of his. She patted him, then pushed him away gently, and he understood that she wished to remain concealed. He went barking back to the man. The cows broke into a clumsy gallop; the man shouted. Diantha smelled the dust of the road which flew over the field like smoke. She heard the children returning down the road behind the cows. When the cows galloped, they screamed with half-fearful delight. Then it all passed by, and she heard the loud clang of a bell from the farm-house.

Then Diantha pulled out the treasure which was suspended from her neck by an old blue ribbon, and she held it up to the low western sun, and wonderful lights of red and blue and violet and green and orange danced over the shaven stubble of the field before her delighted eyes. It was a prism which she had stolen from the best-parlor lamp— from the lamp which had been her own mother's, bought by her with her school-teaching money before her marriage, and brought by her to grace her new home.

Diantha Fielding, as far as relatives went, was in a curious position. First her mother died when she was very young, only a few months old; then her father had married again, giving her a stepmother; then her father had died two years later, and her stepmother had married again, giving her a stepfather. Since then the stepmother had died, and the stepfather had married a widow with a married daughter, whose two children had raced down the road behind the cows. Diantha often felt in a sore bewilderment of relationships. She had not even a cousin of her own; the dearest relative she had was the daughter of a widow whom a cousin of her mother's had married for a second wife. The cousin was long since dead. The wife was living, and Diantha's little step second cousin, as she reckoned it, lived in the old homestead which had belonged to Diantha's grandfather, across the way from the May farm-house. It was a gambrel-roof, half-ruinous structure, well banked in front with a monstrous growth of lilacs, and overhung by a great butternut-tree.

Diantha knew well that she was heaping up vials of cold wrath upon her head by not obeying the supper-bell, but she lay still. Then Libby came—Libby, the little cousin, stepping very cautiously and daintily; for she wore slippers of her mother's, which hung from her small heels, and she had lost them twice already.

She stopped before Diantha. Her slender arms, terminating in hands too large for them, hung straight at her sides in the folds of her faded blue-flowered muslin. Her pretty little heat-flushed face had in it no more speculation than a flower, and no more changing. She was like a flower, which would blossom the same next year, and the next year after that, and the same until it died. There was no speculation in her face as she looked at Diantha dangling the prism in the sunlight, merely unimaginative wonder and admiration.

"It's a drop off your best-parlor lamp," said she, in her thin, sweet voice.

"Look over the field, Libby!" cried Diantha, excitedly.

Libby looked.

"Tell me what you see, quick!"

"What I see? Why, grass and things."

"No, I don't mean them; what you see from this."

Diantha shook the prism violently.

"I see a lot of different colors dancing," replied Libby, "same as you always see. Addie Green had an ear-drop that was broken off their best-parlor lamp. Her mother gave it to her."

"Don't you see anything but different lights?"

"Of course I don't. That's all there is to see."

Diantha sighed.

"That drop ain't broken," said the other little girl. "How did she happen to let you have it?" By "she" Libby meant Diantha's stepmother.

"I took it," replied Diantha. She was fastening the prism around her neck again.

Libby gasped and stared at her. "Didn't you ask her?"

"If I'd asked her, she'd said no, and it was my own mother's lamp. I had a right to it."

"What'll she do to you?"

"I don't know, if she finds out. I sha'n't tell her, if I can help it without lying."

Diantha fastened her gingham frock securely over the prism. Then she rose, and the two little girls went home across the dry stubble of the field.

"I didn't go when she called me, and I didn't go when the supper-bell rang," said Diantha.

Libby stared at her wonderingly. She had never felt an impulse to disobedience in her life; she could not understand this other child, who was a law unto herself. She walked very carefully in her large slippers.

"What'll she do to you?" she inquired.

Diantha tossed her head like a colt.

"She won't do anything, I guess, except make me go without my supper. If she does, I ain't afraid; but I guess she won't, and I'd a heap rather go without my supper than go to it when I don't want to."

Libby looked at her with admiring wonder. Diantha was neatly and rigorously, rather than tastefully, dressed. Her dark blue-and-white gingham frock was starched stiffly; it hung exactly at the proper height from her slender ankles; she wore a clean white collar; and her yellow hair was braided very tightly and smoothly, and tied with a punctilious blue bow. In strange contrast with the almost martial preciseness of her attire was the expression of her little face, flushed, eager to enthusiasm, almost wild, with a light in her blue eyes which did not belong there, according to the traditions concerning little New England maidens, with a feverish rose on her cheeks, which should have been cool and pale. However, that had all come since she had dangled the prism in the rays of the setting sun.

"What did you think you saw when you shook that ear-drop off the lamp?" asked Libby; but she asked without much curiosity.

"Red and green and yellow colors, of course," replied Diantha, shortly.

When they reached Diantha's door, Libby bade her good night, and sped across the road to her own house. She stood a little in fear of Diantha's stepmother, if Diantha did not. She knew just the sort of look which would be directed toward the other little girl, and she knew from experience that it might include her. From her Puritan ancestry she had a certain stubbornness when brought to bay, but no courage of aggression; so she ran.

Diantha marched in. She was utterly devoid of fear.

Her stepmother, Mrs. Zenas May, was washing the supper dishes at the kitchen sink. All through the house sounded a high sweet voice which was constantly off the key, singing a lullaby to the two little girls, who had to go to bed directly after they had finished their evening meal.

Mrs. Zenas May turned around and surveyed Diantha as she entered. There was nothing in the least unkind in her look; it was simply the gaze of one on a firm standpoint of existence upon another swaying on a precarious balance—the sort of look a woman seated in a car gives to one standing. It was irresponsible, while cognizant of the dis-comfort of the other person.

"Where were you when the supper-bell rang?" asked Mrs. Zenas May. She was rather a pretty woman, with an exquisitely cut profile. Her voice was very even, almost as devoid of inflections as a deaf-and-dumb person's. Her gingham gown was also rigorously starched. Her fair hair showed high lights of gloss from careful brushing; it was strained back from her blue-veined temples.

"Out in the field," replied Diantha.

"Then you heard it?"

"Yes, ma'am."

"The supper-table is cleared away," said Mrs. May. That was all she said. She went on polishing the tumblers, which she was rinsing in ammonia water.

Diantha glanced through the open door and saw the dining-room table with its chenille after-supper cloth on. She made no reply, but went up-stairs to her own chamber. That was very comfortable—the large south one back of her step-parents'. Not a speck of dust was to be seen in it; the feather-bed was an even mound of snow. Diantha sat down by the window, and gazed out at the deepening dusk. She felt at the prism around her neck, but she did not draw it out, for it was of no use in that low light. She could not invoke the colors which it held. Her chamber door was open. Presently she heard the best-parlor door open, and heard quite distinctly her stepmother's voice. She was speaking to her stepfather.

"There's a drop broken off the parlor lamp," said she.

There was an unintelligible masculine grunt of response.

"I wish you'd look while I hold the lamp, and see if you can find it on the floor anywhere," said her stepmother. Her voice was still even. The loss of a prism from the best-parlor lamp was not enough to ruffle her outward composure.

"Don't you see it?" she asked, after a little.

Again came the unintelligible masculine grunt.

"It is very strange," said Mrs. May. "Don't look any more."

She never inquired of Diantha concerning the prism. In truth, she believed one of her grandchildren, whom she adored, to be responsible for the loss of the glittering ornament, and was mindful of the fact that Diantha's mother had originally owned that lamp. So she said nothing, but as soon as might be purchased another, and Diantha kept her treasure quite unsuspected.

She did not, however, tremble in the least while the search was going on down-stairs. She had her defense quite ready. To her sense of justice it was unquestionable. She would simply say that the lamp had belonged to her own mother, consequently to her; that she had a right to do as she chose with it. She had not the slightest fear of any reproaches which Mrs. May would bring to bear upon her. She knew she would not use bodily punishment, as she never had; but she would have stood in no fear of that.

Diantha did not go to bed for a long time. There was a full moon, and she sat by the window, leaning her two elbows on the sill, making a cup of her hands, in which she rested her peaked chin, and peered out.

It was nearly nine o'clock when some one entered the room with heavy, soft movements, like a great tame dog. It was her stepfather, and he had in his hand a large wedge of apple-pie.

"Diantha," he said, in a loud whisper, "you gone to bed?"

"No, sir," replied Diantha. She liked her stepfather. She was always aware of a clumsy, covert partizanship from him.

"Well," said he, "here's a piece of pie. You hadn't ought to go to bed without any supper. You'd ought to come in when the bell rings another time, Diantha."

"Thank you, father," said Diantha, reaching out her hand for the pie.

Zenas May, who was large and shaggily blond, with a face like a great blank of good nature, placed a heavy hand on her little, tightly braided head, and patted it.

"Better eat your pie and go to bed," he said. Then he shambled down-stairs very softly, lest his wife hear him.

Diantha ate her pie obediently, and went to bed, and with the first morning sunlight she removed her prism from her neck, and flashed it across the room, and saw what she saw, or what she thought she saw.

Diantha kept the prism, and nobody except Libby knew it, and she was quite safe with a secret. While she did not in the least comprehend, she was stanch. Even when she grew older and had a lover, she did not tell him; she did not even tell him when she was married to him that Diantha Fielding always carried a drop off the best-parlor lamp, which belonged to her own mother, and when she flashed it in the sunlight she thought she saw things. She kept it all to herself. Libby married before Diantha, before Diantha had a lover even. Young men, for some reason, were rather shy of Diantha, although she had a little property in her own right, inherited from her own father and mother, and was, moreover, extremely pretty. However, her prettiness was not of a type to attract the village men as quickly as Libby's more material charms. Diantha was very thin and small, and her color was as clear as porcelain, and she gave a curious impression of mystery, although there was apparently nothing whatever mysterious about her.

But her turn came. A graduate of a country college, a farmer's son, who had worked his own way through college, had now obtained the high school. He saw Diantha, and fell in love with her, although he struggled against it. He said to himself that she was too delicate, that he was a poor man, that he ought to have a more robust wife, who would stand a better chance of discharging her domestic and maternal duties without a breakdown. Reason and judgment were strongly developed in him. His passion for Diantha was entirely opposed to both, but it got the better of him. One afternoon in August when Diantha was almost twenty, he, passing by her house, saw her sitting on her front doorstep, stopped, and proposed a little stroll in the woods, and asked her to marry him.

"I never thought much about getting married," said Diantha. Then she leaned toward him as if impelled by some newly developed instinct. She spoke so low that he could not hear her, and he asked her over.

"I never thought much about getting married," repeated Diantha, and she leaned nearer him.

He laughed a great triumphant laugh, and caught her in his arms.

"Then it is high time you did, you darling," he said.

Diantha was very happy.

They lingered in the woods a long time, and when they went home, the young man, whose name was Robert Black, went in with her, and told her stepmother what had happened.

"I have asked your daughter to marry me, Mrs. May," he said, "and she has consented, and I hope you are willing."

Mrs. May replied that she had no objections, stiffly, without a smile. She never smiled. Instead of smiling, she always looked questioningly even at their beloved grandchildren. They had lived with her since their mother's death, two pretty, boisterous girls, pupils of Robert Black, who had had their own inevitable little dreams regarding him, as they had had regarding every man who came in their way.

When their grandmother told them that Diantha was to marry the hero who had dwelt in their own innocently bold air-castles of girlish dreams, they started at first as from a shock of falling imaginations; then they began to think of their attire as bridesmaids.

Mrs. Zenas May was firmly resolved that Diantha should have as grand a wedding as if she had been her own daughter.

"Folks sha'n't say that she didn't have as good an outfit and wedding as if her own mother had been alive to see to it," she said.

As for Diantha, she thought very little about her outfit or the wedding, but about Robert. All at once she was possessed by a strong angel of primal conditions of whose existence she had never dreamed. She poured out her very soul; she made revelations of the inmost innocences of her nature to this ambitious, faithful, unimaginative young man. She had been some two weeks betrothed, and they were walking together one afternoon, when she showed him her prism.

She no longer wore it about her neck as formerly. A dawning unbelief in it had seized her, and yet there were times when to doubt seemed to doubt the evidence of her own senses.

That afternoon, as they were walking together in the lonely country road, she stopped him in a sunny interval between the bordering woods, where the road stretched for some distance between fields foaming with wild carrot and mustard, and swarmed over with butterflies, and she took her prism out of her pocket and flashed it full before her wondering lover's eyes.

He looked astonished, even annoyed; then he laughed aloud with a sort of tender scorn.

"What a child you are, dear!" he said. "What are you doing with that thing?"

"What do you see, Robert?" the girl cried eagerly, and there was in her eyes a light not of her day and generation, maybe inherited from some far-off Celtic ancestor—a strain of imagination which had survived the glaring light of latter days of commonness.

He eyed her with amazement; then he looked at the gorgeous blots and banners of color over the fields.

"See? Why, I see the prismatic colors, of course. What else should I see?" he asked.

"Nothing else?"

"No. Why, what else should I see? I see the prismatic colors from the refraction of the sunlight."

Diantha looked at the dancing tints, then at her lover, and spoke with a solemn candor, as if she were making confession of an alien faith. "Ever since I was a child, I have seen, or thought so—" she began.

"What, for heaven's sake?" he cried impatiently.

"You have read about—fairies and—such things?"

"Of course. What do you mean, Diantha?"

"I have seen, or thought so, beautiful little people moving and dancing in the broken lights across the fields."

"For heaven's sake, put up that thing, and don't talk such nonsense, Diantha!" cried Robert, almost brutally. He had paled a little.

"I have, Robert."

"Don't talk such nonsense. I thought you were a sensible girl," said the young man.

Diantha put the prism back in her pocket.

All the rest of the way Robert was silent and gloomy. His old doubts had revived. His judgment for the time being got the upper hand of his passion. He began to wonder if he ought to marry a girl with such preposterous fancies as those. He began to wonder if she were just right in her mind.

He parted from her coolly, and came the next evening, but remained only a short time. Then he stayed away several days. He called on Sunday, then did not come again for four days. On Friday Diantha grew desperate. She went by herself out in the sunny field, walking ankle-deep in flowers and weeds, until she reached the margin of a little pond on which the children skated in winter. Then she took her prism from her pocket and flashed it in the sunlight, and for the first time she failed to see what she had either seen, or imagined, for so many years.

She saw only the beautiful prismatic colors flashing across the field in bars and blots and streamers of rose and violet, of orange and green. That was all. She stooped, and dug in the oozy soil beside the pond with her bare white hands, and made, as it were, a little grave, and buried the prism out of sight. Then she washed her hands in the pond, and waved them about until they were dry. Afterward she went swiftly across the field to the road which her lover must pass on his way from school, and, when she saw him coming, met him, blushing and trembling.

"I have put it away, Robert," she said. "I saw nothing; it was only my imagination."

It was a lonely road. He looked at her doubtfully, then he laughed, and put an arm around her.

"It's all right, little girl," he replied; "but don't let such fancies dwell in your brain. This is a plain, common world, and it won't do."

"I saw nothing; it must have been my imagination," she repeated. Then she leaned her head against her lover's shoulder. Whether or not she had sold her birthright, she had got her full measure of the pottage of love which filled to an ecstasy of satisfaction her woman's heart.

She and Robert were married, and lived in a pretty new house, from the western windows of which she could see the pond on whose borders she had buried the prism. She was very happy. For the time being, at least, all the mysticism in her face had given place to an utter revelation of earthly bliss. People said how much Diantha had improved since her marriage, what a fine housekeeper she was, how much common sense she had, how she was such a fitting mate for her husband, whom she adored.

Sometimes Diantha, looking from a western window, used to see the pond across the field, reflecting the light of the setting sun, and looking like an eye of revelation of the earth; and she would remember that key of a lost radiance and a lost belief of her own life, which was buried beside it. Then she would go happily and prepare her husband's supper.

The Hall Bedroom

My name is Mrs. Elizabeth Jennings. I am a highly respectable woman. I may style myself a gentlewoman, for in my youth I enjoyed advantages. I was well brought up, and I graduated at a young ladies' seminary. I also married well. My husband was that most genteel of all merchants, an apothecary. His shop was on the corner of the main street in Rockton, the town where I was born, and where I lived until the death of my husband. My parents had died when I had been married a short time, so I was left quite alone in the world. I was not competent to carry on the apothecary business by myself, for I had no knowledge of drugs, and had a mortal terror of giving poisons instead of medicines. Therefore I was obliged to sell at a considerable sacrifice, and the proceeds, some five thousand dollars, were all I had in the world. The income was not enough to support me in any kind of comfort, and I saw that I must in some way earn money. I thought at first of teaching, but I was no longer young, and methods had changed since my school days. What I was able to teach, nobody wished to know. I could think of only one thing to do: take boarders. But the same objection to that business as to teaching held good in Rockton. Nobody wished to board. My husband had rented a house with a number of bedrooms, and I advertised, but nobody applied. Finally my cash was running very low, and I became desperate. I packed up my furniture, rented a large house in this town and moved here. It was a venture attended with many risks. In the first place the rent was exorbitant, in the next I was entirely unknown. However, I am a person of considerable ingenuity, and have inventive power, and much enterprise when the occasion presses. I advertised in a very original manner, although that actually took my last penny, that is, the last penny

66

of my ready money, and I was forced to draw on my principal to purchase my first supplies, a thing which I had resolved never on any
account to do. But the great risk met with a reward, for I had several
applicants within two days after my advertisement appeared in the
paper. Within two weeks my boarding-house was well established, I
became very successful, and my success would have been uninter-
rupted had it not been for the mysterious and bewildering occurrences
which I am about to relate. I am now forced to leave the house and
rent another. Some of my old boarders accompany me, some, with the
most unreasonable nervousness, refuse to be longer associated in any
way, however indirectly, with the terrible and uncanny happenings
which I have to relate. It remains to be seen whether my ill luck in
this house will follow me into another, and whether my whole prosperity in life will be forever shadowed by the Mystery of the Hall
Bedroom. Instead of telling the strange story myself in my own words,
I shall present the Journal of Mr. George H. Wheatcroft. I shall show
you the portions beginning on January 18 of the present year, the date
when he took up his residence with me. Here it is:

"January 18, 1883. Here I am established in my new boarding-
house. I have, as befits my humble means, the hall bedroom, even the
hall bedroom on the third floor. I have heard all my life of hall bedrooms, I have seen hall bedrooms, I have been in them, but never
until now, when I am actually established in one, did I comprehend
what, at once, an ignominious and sternly uncompromising thing a
hall bedroom is. It proves the ignominy of the dweller therein. No
man at thirty-six (my age) would be domiciled in a hall bedroom,
unless he were himself ignominious, at least comparatively speaking.
I am proved by this means incontrovertibly to have been left far behind in the race. I see no reason why I should not live in this hall
bedroom for the rest of my life, that is, if I have money enough to pay
the landlady, and that seems probable, since my small funds are invested as safely as if I were an orphan-ward in charge of a pillar of a
sanctuary. After the valuables have been stolen, I have most carefully
locked the stable door. I have experienced the revulsion which comes
sooner or later to the adventurous soul who experiences nothing but
defeat and so-called ill luck. I have swung to the opposite extreme. I
have lost in everything—I have lost in love, I have lost in money, I

have lost in the struggle for preferment, I have lost in health and strength. I am now settled down in a hall bedroom to live upon my small income, and regain my health by mild potations of the mineral waters here, if possible; if not, to live here without my health—for mine is not a necessarily fatal malady—until Providence shall take me out of my hall bedroom. There is no one place more than another where I care to live. There is not sufficient motive to take me away, even if the mineral waters do not benefit me. So I am here and to stay in the hall bedroom. The landlady is civil, and even kind, as kind as a woman who has to keep her poor womanly eye upon the main chance can be. The struggle for money always injures the fine grain of a woman; she is too fine a thing to do it; she does not by nature belong with the gold grubbers, and it therefore lowers her; she steps from heights to claw and scrape and dig. But she can not help it oftentimes, poor thing, and her deterioration thereby is to be condoned. The landlady is all she can be, taking her strain of adverse circumstances into consideration, and the table is good, even conscientiously so. It looks to me as if she were foolish enough to strive to give the boarders their money's worth, with the due regard for the main chance which is inevitable. However, that is of minor importance to me, since my diet is restricted.

"It is curious what an annoyance a restriction in diet can be even to a man who has considered himself somewhat indifferent to gastronomic delights. There was to-day a pudding for dinner, which I could not taste without penalty, but which I longed for. It was only because it looked unlike any other pudding that I had ever seen, and assumed a mental and spiritual significance. It seemed to me, whimsically no doubt, as if tasting it might give me a new sensation, and consequently a new outlook. Trivial things may lead to large results: why should I not get a new outlook by means of a pudding? Life here stretches before me most monotonously, and I feel like clutching at alleviations, though paradoxically, since I have settled down with the utmost acquiescence. Still one can not immediately overcome and change radically all one's nature. Now I look at myself critically and search for the keynote to my whole self, and my actions, I have always been conscious of a reaching out, an overweening desire for the new, the untried, for the broadness of further horizons, the seas beyond seas, the thought beyond thought. This characteristic has been the primary cause of all my misfortunes. I have the soul of an explorer, and in nine out of ten cases this leads to destruction. If I had possessed capital and sufficient push, I should have been one of the searchers after the North Pole. I have been an eager student of astronomy. I have studied botany with avidity, and have dreamed of new flora in unexplored parts of the world, and the same with animal life and geology. I longed for riches in order to discover the power and sense of possession of the rich. I longed for love in order to discover the possibilities of the emotions. I longed for all that the mind of man could conceive as desirable for man, not so much for purely selfish ends, as from an insatiable thirst for knowledge of a universal trend. But I have limitations, I do not quite understand of what nature—for what mortal ever did quite understand his own limitations, since a knowledge of them would preclude their existence?—but they have prevented my progress to any extent. Therefore behold me in my hall bedroom, settled at last into a groove of fate so deep that I have lost the sight of even my horizons. Just at present, as I write here, my horizon on the left, that is my physical horizon, is a wall covered with cheap paper. The paper is an indeterminate pattern in white and gilt. There are a few photographs of my own hung about, and on the large wall space beside the bed there is a large oil painting which belongs to my landlady. It has a massive tarnished gold frame, and, curiously enough, the painting itself is rather good. I have no idea who the artist could have been. It is of the conventional landscape type in vogue some fifty years since, the type so fondly reproduced in chromos—the winding river with the little boat occupied by a pair of lovers, the cottage nestled among trees on the right shore, the gentle slope of the hills and the church spire in the background—but still it is well done. It gives me the impression of an artist without the slightest originality of design, but much of technique. But for some inexplicable reason the picture frets me. I find myself gazing at it when I do not wish to do so. It seems to compel my attention like some intent face in the room. I shall ask Mrs. Jennings to have it removed. I will hang in its place some photographs which I have in a trunk.

"January 26. I do not write regularly in my journal. I never did. I see no reason why I should. I see no reason why any one should have the slightest sense of duty in such a matter. Some days I have nothing which interests me sufficiently to write out, some days I feel either too ill or too indolent. For four days I have not written, from a mixture of all three reasons. Now, to-day I both feel like it and I have something to write. Also I am distinctly better than I have been. Perhaps the waters are benefiting me, or the change of air. Or possibly it is something else more subtle. Possibly my mind has seized upon something new, a discovery which causes it to react upon my failing body and serves as a stimulant. All I know is, I feel distinctly better, and am conscious of an acute interest in doing so, which is of late strange to me. I have been rather indifferent, and sometimes have wondered if that were not the cause rather than the result of my state of health. I have been so continually balked that I have settled into a state of inertia. I lean rather comfortably against my obstacles. After all, the worst of the pain always lies in the struggle. Give up and it is rather pleasant than otherwise. If one did not kick, the pricks would not in the least matter. However, for some reason, for the last few days, I seem to have awakened from my state of quiescence. It means future trouble for me, no doubt, but in the meantime I am not sorry. It began with the picture—the large oil painting. I went to Mrs. Jennings about it yesterday, and she, to my surprise—for I thought it a matter that could be easily arranged—objected to having it removed. Her reasons were two; both simple, both sufficient, especially since I, after all, had no very strong desire either way. It seems that the picture does not belong to her. It hung here when she rented the house. She says if it is removed, a very large and unsightly discoloration of the wall-paper will be exposed, and she does not like to ask for new paper. The owner, an old man, is traveling abroad, the agent is curt, and she has only been in the house a very short time. Then it would mean a sad upheaval of my room, which would disturb me. She also says that there is no place in the house where she can store the picture, and there is not a vacant space in another room for one so large. So I let the picture remain. It really, when I came to think of it, was very immaterial after all. But I got my photographs out of my trunk, and I hung them around the large picture. The wall is almost completely covered. I hung them yesterday afternoon, and last night I repeated a strange experience which I have had in some degree every night since

I have been here, but was not sure whether it deserved the name of experience, but was not rather one of those dreams in which one dreams one is awake. But last night it came again, and now I know. There is something very singular about this room. I am very much interested. I will write down for future reference the events of last night. Concerning those of the preceding nights since I have slept in this room, I will simply say that they have been of a similar nature, but, as it were, only the preliminary stages, the prologue to what happened last night.

"I am not depending upon the mineral waters here as the one remedy for my malady, which is sometimes of an acute nature, and indeed constantly threatens me with considerable suffering unless by medicine I can keep it in check. I will say that the medicine which I employ is not of the class commonly known as drugs. It is impossible that it can be held responsible for what I am about to transcribe. My mind last night and every night since I have slept in this room was in an absolutely normal state. I take this medicine, prescribed by the specialist in whose charge I was before coming here, regularly every four hours while awake. As I am never a good sleeper, it follows that I am enabled with no inconvenience to take any medicine during the night with the same regularity as during the day. It is my habit, therefore, to place my bottle and spoon where I can put my hand upon them easily without lighting the gas. Since I have been in this room, I have placed the bottle of medicine upon my dresser at the side of the room opposite the bed. I have done this rather than place it nearer, as once I jostled the bottle and spilled most of the contents, and it is not easy for me to replace it, as it is expensive. Therefore I placed it in security on the dresser, and, indeed, that is but three or four steps from my bed, the room being so small. Last night I wakened as usual, and I knew, since I had fallen asleep about eleven, that it must be in the neighborhood of three. I wake with almost clock-like regularity and it is never necessary for me to consult my watch.

"I had slept unusually well and without dreams, and I awoke fully at once, with a feeling of refreshment to which I am not accustomed. I immediately got out of bed and began stepping across the room in the direction of my dresser, on which I had set my medicine-bottle and spoon.

"To my utter amazement, the steps which had hitherto sufficed to take me across my room did not suffice to do so. I advanced several paces, and my outstretched hands touched nothing. I stopped and went on again. I was sure that I was moving in a straight direction, and even if I had not been I knew it was impossible to advance in any direction in my tiny apartment without coming into collision either with a wall or a piece of furniture. I continued to walk falteringly, as I have seen people on the stage: a step, then a long falter, then a sliding step. I kept my hands extended; they touched nothing. I stopped again. I had not the least sentiment of fear or consternation. It was rather the very stupefaction of surprise. 'How is this?' seemed thundering in my ears. 'What is this?'

"The room was perfectly dark. There was nowhere any glimmer, as is usually the case, even in a so-called dark room, from the walls, picture-frames, looking-glass or white objects. It was absolute gloom. The house stood in a quiet part of the town. There were many trees about; the electric street lights were extinguished at midnight; there was no moon and the sky was cloudy. I could not distinguish my one window, which I thought strange, even on such a dark night. Finally I changed my plan of motion and turned, as nearly as I could estimate, at right angles. Now, I thought, I must reach soon, if I kept on, my writing-table underneath the window; or, if I am going in the opposite direction, the hall door. I reached neither. I am telling the unvarnished truth when I say that I began to count my steps and carefully measure my paces after that, and I traversed a space clear of furniture at least twenty feet by thirty—a very large apartment. And as I walked I was conscious that my naked feet were pressing something which gave rise to sensations the like of which I had never experienced before. As nearly as I can express it, it was as if my feet pressed something as elastic as air or water, which was in this case unyielding to my weight. It gave me a curious sensation of buoyancy and stimulation. At the same time this surface, if surface be the right name, which I trod, felt cool to my feet with the coolness of vapor or fluidity, seeming to overlap the soles. Finally I stood still; my surprise was at last merging into a measure of consternation. 'Where am I?' I thought. 'What am I going to do?' Stories that I had heard of travelers being taken from their beds and conveyed into strange and dangerous places,

Middle Age stories of the Inquisition flashed through my brain. I knew all the time that for a man who had gone to bed in a commonplace hall bedroom in a very commonplace little town such surmises were highly ridiculous, but it is hard for the human mind to grasp anything but a human explanation of phenomena. Almost anything seemed then, and seems now, more rational than an explanation bordering upon the supernatural, as we understand the supernatural. At last I called, though rather softly, 'What does this mean?' I said quite aloud, 'Where am I? Who is here? Who is doing this? I tell you I will have no such nonsense. Speak, if there is anybody here.' But all was dead silence. Then suddenly a light flashed through the open transom of my door. Somebody had heard me—a man who rooms next door, a decent kind of man, also here for his health. He turned on the gas in the hall and called to me. 'What's the matter?' he asked, in an agitated, trembling voice. He is a nervous fellow.

"Directly, when the light flashed through my transom, I saw that I was in my familiar hall bedroom. I could see everything quite distinctly—my tumbled bed, my writing-table, my dresser, my chair, my little wash-stand, my clothes hanging on a row of pegs, the old picture on the wall. The picture gleamed out with singular distinctness in the light from the transom. The river seemed actually to run and ripple, and the boat to be gliding with the current. I gazed fascinated at it, as I replied to the anxious voice:

"'Nothing is the matter with me,' said I. 'Why?'

"'I thought I heard you speak,' said the man outside. 'I thought maybe you were sick.'

"'No,' I called back. 'I am all right. I am trying to find my medicine in the dark, that's all. I can see now you have lighted the gas.'

"'Nothing is the matter?'

"'No; sorry I disturbed you. Good-night.'

"'Good-night.' Then I heard the man's door shut after a minute's pause. He was evidently not quite satisfied. I took a pull at my medicine-bottle, and got into bed. He had left the hall-gas burning. I did not go to sleep again for some time. Just before I did so, some one, probably Mrs. Jennings, came out in the hall and extinguished the gas. This morning when I awoke everything was as usual in my room. I wonder if I shall have any such experience to-night.

"January 27. I shall write in my journal every day until this draws to some definite issue. Last night my strange experience deepened, as something tells me it will continue to do. I retired quite early, at half-past ten. I took the precaution, on retiring, to place beside my bed, on a chair, a box of safety matches, that I might not be in the dilemma of the night before. I took my medicine on retiring; that made me due to wake at half-past two. I had not fallen asleep directly, but had had certainly three hours of sound, dreamless slumber when I awoke. I lay a few minutes hesitating whether or not to strike a safety match and light my way to the dresser, whereon stood my medicine-bottle. I hesitated, not because I had the least sensation of fear, but because of the same shrinking from a nerve shock that leads one at times to dread the plunge into an icy bath. It seemed much easier to me to strike that match and cross my hall bedroom to my dresser, take my dose, then return quietly to my bed, than to risk the chance of floundering about in some unknown limbo either of fancy or reality.

"At last, however, the spirit of adventure, which has always been such a ruling one for me, conquered. I rose. I took the box of safety matches in my hand, and started on, as I conceived, the straight course for my dresser, about five feet across from my bed. As before, I traveled and traveled and did not reach it. I advanced with groping hands extended, setting one foot cautiously before the other, but I touched nothing except the indefinite, unnameable surface which my feet pressed. All of a sudden, though, I became aware of something. One of my senses was saluted, nay, more than that, hailed, with imperiousness, and that was, strangely enough, my sense of smell, but in a hitherto unknown fashion. It seemed as if the odor reached my mentality first. I reversed the usual process, which is, as I understand it, like this: the odor when encountered strikes first the olfactory nerve, which transmits the intelligence to the brain. It is as if, to put it rudely, my nose met a rose, and then the nerve belonging to the sense said to my brain, 'Here is a rose.' This time my brain said, 'Here is a rose,' and my sense then recognized it. I say rose, but it was not a rose, that is, not the fragrance of any rose which I had ever known. It was undoubtedly a flower-odor, and rose came perhaps the nearest to it. My mind realized it first with what seemed a leap of rapture. 'What is this delight?' I asked myself. And then the ravishing fragrance smote my sense. I breathed it in and it seemed to feed my thoughts, satisfying some hitherto unknown hunger. Then I took a step further and another fragrance appeared, which I liken to lilies for lack of something better, and then came violets, then mignonette. I can not describe the experience, but it was a sheer delight, a rapture of sublimated sense. I groped further and further, and always into new waves of fragrance. I seemed to be wading breast-high through flower-beds of Paradise, but all the time I touched nothing with my groping hands. At last a sudden giddiness as of surfeit overcame me. I realized that I might be in some unknown peril. I was distinctly afraid. I struck one of my safety matches, and I was in my hall bedroom, midway between my bed and my dresser. I took my dose of medicine and went to bed, and after a while fell asleep and did not wake till morning.

"January 28. Last night I did not take my usual dose of medicine. In these days of new remedies and mysterious results upon certain organizations, it occurred to me to wonder if possibly the drug might have, after all, something to do with my strange experience.

"I did not take my medicine. I put the bottle as usual on my dresser, since I feared if I interrupted further the customary sequence of affairs I might fail to wake. I placed my box of matches on the chair beside the bed. I fell asleep about quarter past eleven o'clock, and I waked when the clock was striking two—a little earlier than my wont. I did not hesitate this time. I rose at once, took my box of matches and proceeded as formerly. I walked what seemed a great space without coming into collision with anything. I kept sniffing for the wonderful fragrances of the night before, but they did not recur. Instead, I was suddenly aware that I was tasting something, some morsel of sweetness hitherto unknown, and, as in the case of the odor, the usual order seemed reversed, and it was as if I tasted it first in my mental consciousness. Then the sweetness rolled under my tongue. I thought involuntarily of 'Sweeter than honey or the honeycomb' of the Scripture. I thought of the Old Testament manna. An ineffable content as of satisfied hunger seized me. I stepped further, and a new savor was upon my palate. And so on. It was never cloying, though of such sharp sweetness that it fairly stung. It was the merging of a material sense into a spiritual one. I said to myself, 'I have lived my life and always have I gone hungry until now.' I could feel my brain act swiftly under the influence of this heavenly food as under a stimulant. Then suddenly I repeated the experience of the night before. I grew dizzy, and an indefinite fear and shrinking were upon me. I struck my safety match and was back in my hall bedroom. I returned to bed, and soon fell asleep. I did not take my medicine. I am resolved not to do so longer. I am feeling much better.

"January 29. Last night to bed as usual, matches in place; fell asleep about eleven and waked at half-past one. I heard the half-hour strike; I am waking earlier and earlier every night. I had not taken my medicine, though it was on the dresser as usual. I again took my matchbox in hand and started to cross the room, and, as always, traversed strange spaces, but this night, as seems fated to be the case every night, my experience was different. Last night I neither smelled nor tasted, but I heard—my Lord, I heard! The first sound of which I was conscious was one like the constantly gathering and receding murmur of a river, and it seemed to come from the wall behind my bed where the old picture hangs. Nothing in nature except a river gives that impression of at once advance and retreat. I could not mistake it. On, ever on, came the swelling murmur of the waves, past and ever past they died in the distance. Then I heard above the murmur of the river a song in an unknown tongue which I recognized as being unknown, yet which I understood; but the understanding was in my brain, with no words of interpretation. The song had to do with me, but with me in unknown futures for which I had no images of comparison in the past; yet a sort of ecstasy as of a prophecy of bliss filled my whole consciousness. The song never ceased, but as I moved on I came into new sound-waves. There was the pealing of bells which might have been made of crystal, and might have summoned to the gates of heaven. There was music of strange instruments, great harmonies pierced now and then by small whispers as of love, and it all filled me with a certainty of a future of bliss.

"At last I seemed the centre of a mighty orchestra which constantly deepened and increased until I seemed to feel myself being lifted gently but mightily upon the waves of sound as upon the waves of a sea. Then again the terror and the impulse to flee to my own familiar scenes was upon me. I struck my match and was back in my hall bedroom. I do not see how I sleep at all after such wonders, but sleep I do. I slept dreamlessly until daylight this morning.

"January 30. I heard yesterday something with regard to my hall bedroom which affected me strangely. I can not for the life of me say whether it intimidated me, filled me with the horror of the abnormal, or rather roused to a greater degree my spirit of adventure and discovery. I was down at the Cure, and was sitting on the veranda sipping idly my mineral water, when somebody spoke my name. 'Mr. Wheatcroft?' said the voice politely, interrogatively, somewhat apologetically, as if to provide for a possible mistake in my identity. I turned and saw a gentleman whom I recognized at once. I seldom forget names or faces. He was a Mr. Addison whom I had seen considerable of three years ago at a little summer hotel in the mountains. It was one of those passing acquaintances which signify little one way or the other. If never renewed, you have no regret; if renewed, you accept the renewal with no hesitation. It is in every way negative. But just now, in my feeble, friendless state, the sight of a face which beams with pleased remembrance is rather grateful. I felt distinctly glad to see the man. He sat down beside me. He also had a glass of the water. His health, while not as bad as mine, leaves much to be desired.

"Addison had often been in this town before. He had in fact lived here at one time. He had remained at the Cure three years, taking the waters daily. He therefore knows about all there is to be known about the town, which is not very large. He asked me where I was staying, and when I told him the street, rather excitedly inquired the number. When I told him the number, which is 240, he gave a manifest start, and after one sharp glance at me sipped his water in silence for a moment. He had so evidently betrayed some ulterior knowledge with regard to my residence that I questioned him.

"'What do you know about 240 Pleasant Street?' said I.

"'Oh, nothing,' he replied, evasively, sipping his water.

"After a little while, however, he inquired, in what he evidently tried to render a casual tone, what room I occupied. 'I once lived a few weeks at 240 Pleasant Street myself,' he said. 'That house always was a boarding-house, I guess.'

"'It had stood vacant for a term of years before the present occupant rented it, I believe,' I remarked. Then I answered his question. 'I have the hall bedroom on the third floor,' said I. 'The quarters are pretty straitened, but comfortable enough as hall bedrooms go.'

"But Mr. Addison had showed such unmistakable consternation at my reply that then I persisted in my questioning as to the cause, and at last he yielded and told me what he knew. He had hesitated both because he shrank from displaying what I might consider an unmanly superstition, and because he did not wish to influence me beyond what the facts of the case warranted. 'Well, I will tell you, Wheatcroft,' he said. 'Briefly all I know is this: When last I heard of 240 Pleasant Street it was not rented because of foul play which was supposed to have taken place there, though nothing was ever proved. There were two disappearances, and—in each case—of an occupant of the hall bedroom which you now have. The first disappearance was of a very beautiful girl who had come here for her health and was said to be the victim of a profound melancholy, induced by a love disappointment. She obtained board at 240 and occupied the hall bedroom about two weeks; then one morning she was gone, having seemingly vanished into thin air. Her relatives were communicated with; she had not many, nor friends either, poor girl, and a thorough search was made, but the last I knew she had never come to light. There were two or three arrests, but nothing ever came of them. Well, that was before my day here, but the second disappearance took place when I was in the house—a fine young fellow who had overworked in college. He had to pay his own way. He had taken cold, had the grip, and that and the overwork about finished him, and he came on here for a month's rest and recuperation. He had been in that room about two weeks, a little less, when one morning he wasn't there. Then there was a great hullabaloo. It seems that he had let fall some hints to the effect that there was something queer about the room, but, of course, the police did not think much of that. They made arrests right and left, but they never found him, and the arrested were discharged, though some of them are probably under a cloud of suspicion to this day. Then the boarding-house was shut up. Six years ago nobody would have boarded there, much less occupied that hall bedroom, but now I suppose new people have come in and the story has died out. I dare say your landlady will not thank me for reviving it.'

"I assured him that it would make no possible difference to me. He looked at me sharply, and asked bluntly if I had seen anything wrong or unusual about the room. I replied, guarding myself from falsehood with a quibble, that I had seen nothing in the least unusual about the

room, as indeed I had not, and have not now, but that may come. I
feel that that will come in due time. Last night I neither saw, nor
heard, nor smelled, nor tasted, but I—felt. Last night, having started
again on my exploration of, God knows what, I had not advanced a
step before I touched something. My first sensation was one of disappointment. 'It is the dresser, and I am at the end of it now,' I thought.
But I soon discovered that it was not the old painted dresser which I
touched, but something carved, as nearly as I could discover with my
unskilled finger-tips, with winged things. There were certainly long
keen curves of wings which seemed to overlay an arabesque of fine leaf
and flower work. I do not know what the object was that I touched.
It may have been a chest. I may seem to be exaggerating when I say
that it somehow failed or exceeded in some mysterious respect of being
the shape of anything I had ever touched. I do not know what the
material was. It was as smooth as ivory, but it did not feel like ivory;
there was a singular warmth about it, as if it had stood long in hot
sunlight. I continued, and I encountered other objects I am inclined
to think were pieces of furniture of fashions and possibly of uses unknown to me, and about them all was the strange mystery as to shape.
At last I came to what was evidently an open window of large area.
I distinctly felt a soft, warm wind, yet with a crystal freshness, blow
on my face. It was not the window of my hall bedroom, that I know.
Looking out, I could see nothing. I only felt the wind blowing on
my face.

"Then suddenly, without any warning, my groping hands to the
right and left touched living beings, beings in the likeness of men and
women, palpable creatures in palpable attire. I could feel the soft
silken texture of their garments which swept around me, seeming to
half infold me in clinging meshes like cobwebs. I was in a crowd of
these people, whatever they were, and whoever they were, but, curiously enough, without seeing one of them I had a strong sense of
recognition as I passed among them. Now and then a hand that I
knew closed softly over mine; once an arm passed around me. Then
I began to feel myself gently swept on and impelled by this softly moving throng; their floating garments seemed to fairly wind me about,
and again a swift terror overcame me. I struck my match, and was
back in my hall bedroom. I wonder if I had not better keep my gas

burning to-night? I wonder if it be possible that this is going too far? I wonder what became of those other people, the man and the woman who occupied this room? I wonder if I had better not stop where I am?

"January 31. Last night I saw—I saw more than I can describe, more than is lawful to describe. Something which nature has rightly hidden has been revealed to me, but it is not for me to disclose too much of her secret. This much I will say, that doors and windows open into an out-of-doors to which the outdoors which we know is but a vestibule. And there is a river; there is something strange with respect to that picture. There is a river upon which one could sail away. It was flowing silently, for to-night I could only see. I saw that I was right in thinking I recognized some of the people whom I encountered the night before, though some were strange to me. It is true that the girl who disappeared from the hall bedroom was very beautiful. Everything which I saw last night was very beautiful to my one sense that could grasp it. I wonder what it would all be if all my senses together were to grasp it? I wonder if I had better not keep my gas burning to-night? I wonder—"

This finishes the journal which Mr. Wheatcroft left in his hall bedroom. The morning after the last entry he was gone. His friend, Mr. Addison, came here, and a search was made. They even tore down the wall behind the picture, and they did find something rather queer for a house that had been used for boarders, where you would think no room would have been let run to waste. They found another room, a long narrow one, the length of the hall bedroom, but narrower, hardly more than a closet. There was no window, nor door, and all there was in it was a sheet of paper covered with figures, as if somebody had been doing sums. They made a lot of talk about those figures, and they tried to make out that the fifth dimension, whatever that is, was proved, but they said afterward they didn't prove anything. They tried to make out then that somebody had murdered poor Mr. Wheatcroft and hid the body, and they arrested poor Mr. Addison, but they couldn't make out anything against him. They proved he was in the Cure all that night and couldn't have done it. They don't know what became of Mr. Wheatcroft, and now they say two more disappeared from that same room before I rented the house.

The agent came and promised to put the new room they discovered into the hall bedroom and have everything new—papered and painted. He took away the picture; folks hinted there was something queer about that, I don't know what. It looked innocent enough, and I guess he burned it up. He said if I would stay he would arrange it with the owner, who everybody says is a very queer man, so I should not have to pay much if any rent. But I told him I couldn't stay if he was to give me the rent. That I wasn't afraid of anything myself, though I must say I wouldn't want to put anybody in that hall bedroom without telling him all about it; but my boarders would leave, and I knew I couldn't get any more. I told him I would rather have had a regular ghost than what seemed to be a way of going out of the house to nowhere and never coming back again. I moved, and, as I said before, it remains to be seen whether my ill luck follows me to this house or not. Anyway, it has no hall bedroom.

Humble Pie

There are some people who never during their whole lives awake to a consciousness of themselves, as they are recognized by others; there are some who awake too early, to their undoing, and the flimsiness of their characters; there are some who awake late with a shock, which does not dethrone them from their individuality, but causes them agony, and is possibly for their benefit. Maria Gorham was one of the last, and for the first time in her life she saw herself reflected mercilessly in the eyes of her kind one summer in a great mountain hotel. She had never been aware that she was more conceited than others, that she had had on the whole a better opinion of her external advantages at least, than she deserved, but she discovered that her self-conceit had been something which looked to her monstrous and insufferable. She saw that she was not on the surface what she had always thought herself to be, and she saw that the surface has always its influence on the depths.

Maria Gorham was an old young woman in her early thirties. She had taught school in her native village in one of the New England States since she was seventeen. She had been left quite alone in the world, five years before, when her mother died. She lived entirely alone in the house in which she had been born. It was one of the cottages prevalent in certain localities. She was entirely fearless. So quietly poised was she in her own self esteem that it had never occurred to her that anybody could possibly have any ill will, or even any uncomplimentary feeling, toward her. She had always heard herself called good-looking, and it had not occurred to her to doubt the opinion of others. She had also heard herself called industrious, capable and more than ordinarily clever, and she acquiesced with that opinion also. She had also heard her taste in dress extolled, and she had packed her little trunk with entire confidence. Dexter Ray's sister Emma had run across the street, and was watching her. "I thought I'd like to see you put all them pretty things in, I suspected you was packin'," said Emma, with a gentle admiration, and not a suspicion of jealousy. Maria noted Emma's faulty English with a superiority which gave her a certain pleasure. "Poor Emma," she thought, and replied all the more sweetly. "Yes," said she, "I am going on the eight o'clock train to-morrow morning, and I must have my trunk all ready to-night."

Emma watched Maria fold her blue foulard gown daintily. "Well," she said, "I guess there won't be many to that hotel where you are goin' that has any prettier things than you."

Maria laughed. "Nonsense," she replied, but in her heart she quite agreed with Emma. She had entire faith in her wardrobe, which she and the village dressmaker had prepared.

"I suppose you'll wear that handsome pink wrapper mornin's," said Emma.

"Yes, I have planned to," replied Maria. Just as she spoke there was a ring at the front door bell, and Emma started and blushed, altho she had herself nothing for which to blush. "I rather guess that must be Dexter," said she.

Maria frowned.

"Dexter said he guessed mebbe he'd jest run in an' say good-by," said Emma, timidly, and with even more embarrassment.

Maria herself blushed, but, as it seemed, with anger rather than embarrassment. However, she tried to speak politely. Dexter Ray was the only man who had ever wanted to marry her, and while she thought herself too good for him, she considered that he was to be rewarded at least with politeness for his pretensions.

"I really don't see how I can stop my packing," she said, "I wonder if you wouldn't just run down stairs and tell your brother that I am real sorry, but I am packing."

Emma stood up with dignity. She had at times a little sense of injury on her brother's account. "All right," said she.

"I have been working very hard all day finishing up some sewing and getting the house ready to leave, and, if I stop now, I don't know when I would get to bed," Maria added, with more conciliation in her tone.

"All right," said Emma, and went out. Maria heard her tell Dexter. "She's says she's real sorry, but she's awful tired, she's been workin' so hard all day, and she's got to get her trunk packed to-night." There was more sorrow in Emma's voice than there had been in Maria's. Maria stole a glance out of the window, and saw Dexter going meekly down the path between the flowering shrubs after his rebuff. He was quite a tall man, a little older than she, and there was an odd faithful bend in his shoulders. Maria sighed, she could not have told why. Sometimes she wished that Dexter had been a more fitting match for her.

Sometimes she had actually felt angry with Dexter Ray that he did not try to make more of himself, but he spoke no better English than his sister. He also, in her opinion, had no ambition. He kept the village drug store, and several times he had had an opportunity to be selectman, and once town clerk, but he seemed to have no interest except in measuring out drugs and dispensing soda water. It would have puzzled Maria had she been required to mention by what right in view of her own antecedents she regarded herself as on a higher social scale than Dexter Ray. Her father had been a small farmer, and his father before him. On her father's death she had sold all the farming land, and that made her little nest egg in the savings bank. She had never saved much from the money which she earned teaching. She had a weakness for pretty things, both for her own person and for her house. She had had a bay window and a piazza put on the house since her father's death. She had also a very splendid carpet in the parlor and a set of plush furniture. She had never traveled. There was in the depths of her soul a feminine timidity about setting forth alone on strange paths, in spite of her steady egotism. It was almost as if she feared lest her faith in herself would desert her, if she were deprived of the accustomed support of admiring friends and subjected to the cold scrutiny of strangers. However, nothing could have made her admit the slightest hesitation, and the next day she was to set out alone to spend a whole month at a great mountain hotel. "I declare," Emma Ray said, when she returned. "I should think you'd sort of dread startin' out all alone to-morrer, Maria."

"I don't know why," replied Maria, calmly.

"I should think you'd sort of dread goin' into the dinin'-room all alone."

"I don't know why."

"Of course, I know you'll look as fine as anybody," said Emma in a conciliatory tone.

"I don't know why I should dread it, however I looked. This is a free country."

"I suppose there's a lot of rich folks at that hotel."

"Well, riches don't make any difference in a country like this, do they?"

"I don't know," replied Emma.

"They ought not to, anyway," said Maria, firmly, substituting the principle for the fact with a fairly great loyalty.

"Mebbe they don't," said Emma.

Presently Emma added. "Of course, it ain't as tho you wasn't educated. Of course, you have been school-teachin' all your life, and I s'pose lots of them rich folks couldn't teach school any more than they could fly."

"They haven't been obliged to," replied Maria.

"They couldn't, anyway."

Maria made no dissent to that. In her heart she agreed with Emma. She folded carefully a white lawn sacque trimmed with frills of embroidery, and laid it in one of the top trays of her trunk.

"That will be real pretty to wear with your black silk skirt," said Emma.

"Yes, I thought it would," said Maria.

"It looks as if you might have a dreadful hot day to-morrow," said Emma, glancing out of the window which faced the west. The sun was setting like an awful ball of fire for the ultimate consumption of the world.

"Yes, it seems as if it might be hot," assented Maria.

"What are you going to wear travelin'? You'll have quite a long journey, most nine hours, Dexter said. He studied it out on the time table."

"I'm going to wear my gray mohair I had last summer."

"Well, that sheds the dust fine."

"Yes, and I'm going to put my black silk skirt in the top of the trunk where I can get at it easy, and put it on with this cambric sacque to go to supper in, if it's a warm night," said Maria.

"That will be a real good idea," said Emma, approvingly. "It won't be so much work as getting into a dress, and you'll feel tired."

"That's what I thought. I'll wear this cambric sacque to supper, and then I suppose I shall sit in the parlor and listen to the music. They say there's music and dancing every night."

"Well, there ought to be something when they ask such prices."

"Yes, that is so," replied Maria. She was herself secretly dazed at the wild extravagance into which she was about to launch, but a spirit of defiance had suddenly seized her. It was a hot electric summer, prone to burst forth in fierce storms, and Maria, in spite of her great self poise, had an irritable, high-strung nervous temperament. All at once it had seemed to her that she could no longer remain where she was and go her daily rounds. She hated the very sight of all the old articles of furniture, which had heretofore been to her almost like members of her family. She had acquired the habit of sitting in the front parlor, a room which had never been used unless there was company in the house. She also slept in the front chamber instead of her own for weeks. From these rooms she could look across the street and see Dexter Ray coming and going, and sometimes she was conscious of a distinct anger against fate which had not provided her with a better lover. She had an unacknowledged humiliation because of her single estate. She was afraid that people would think nobody had ever wanted to marry her. She took a pleasure of which she was ashamed in having Emma Ray run in often and in her apparently unappreciated hints concerning her brother. Emma had been almost aghast when Maria told her of her resolution to go to the mountains and spend a month.

"Why don't you wait and go on one of them fifteen-dollar excursions?" said she. "There will be time enough before your school begins."

"I am not going with a rabble. I would rather stay at home," replied Maria, firmly.

"But it must cost an awful sight at that hotel."

"I don't care. I'm going to take the money out of the bank, and I am going. I need a change. I have been getting nervous lately, and, if I go at all, I am going the way I want to go. I don't care if it does cost. I have made up my mind."

Dexter was almost as much aghast as his sister when she told him of the proposed flitting, but after a minute, he said: "Well, I guess she's right. She'd better go the way that's a-goin' to do her good, if she goes at all. I'm glad she's goin' to have a little vacation. She has worked hard all her life." The expression of Dexter Ray's face as he said that was gentle, almost noble. The tears sprang into his sister's eyes. "I don't know as she has worked any harder than lots of other folks," said she, and she spoke almost crossly to cover her pity for her brother. "Go right up an' down the street here," she added. "How many women or men have ever had a real vacation?"

"That don't alter it any," replied Dexter, still with the same gentle, noble expression. "I'm real glad *she's* goin' to have one, anyway." The emphasis which he put upon the she was like a benediction. It almost transfigured the face of the man, which was homely with a commonplace homeliness. He was a good druggist, and the village people held him, after all, in esteem, altho he had always been, in a measure, a butt, because of his awkwardness and shyness. He stumbled on all the thresholds of social intercourse with his kind, but he never made an error in putting up a prescription. The night they were talking about Maria's going away he proposed timidly to his sister that perhaps Maria would like to have him carry her to the railroad station in his buggy. "There'd be plenty of room in front for her trunk tipped up on end, and it would save her fifty cents," he said.

"Land, she'd turn up her nose at the bare idea," replied Emma.

"Well, maybe she would ruther have the stage come for her," returned Dexter, meekly. "I was only thinkin' of savin' her some money."

"It would make no end of talk," Emma said, with more leniency toward Maria.

"Well, I s'pose you are right," responded Dexter, with a sigh.

However, Emma was so sorry for him that the night before Maria left, when the trunk was packed, and she was about to go home across the street, she said, timidly, "I s'pose you've got the stage ordered to take you to the station in the mornin'."

"Of course," replied Maria. "It isn't very likely I would leave that until after nine o'clock at night, when the train left in the morning." She spoke with some asperity. She seemed to have a glimpse of Emma's meaning in putting the question, "Why?" she demanded further.

"Nothin'," replied Emma, meekly. She felt cowed, and as if she had done her brother's cause great harm. "Only—"

"Only what?"

"Oh, it wasn't nothin', only Dexter, he said he'd jest as lief take you and your trunk down to the train, and save you the expense."

Maria's face flushed. "Well, I rather think I wouldn't go down to the station with Dexter Ray right in the face an' eyes of all the people, with my trunk tilted up in front," said she. "I should think your brother would have known better than to propose such a thing."

Emma Ray was almost in tears. She was capable of evanescent spurts of assertion, especially on her brother's account, but she was easily intimidated, especially by Maria, to whom she looked up with the greatest admiration and love. However, she also loved her brother, and she made a feeble feint in his defense. "He didn't mean nothin' but kindness," she said, and Maria's heart smote her.

"Oh, I know it!" she replied, "and I'm much obliged to him, but you know, Emma, yourself, it wouldn't do."

"Maybe it wouldn't," said Emma, "but Dexter he didn't think of that. Men ain't apt to. He jest meant to be kind, and save you expense." There was something almost piteous in her tone.

"Well," said Maria, "when I started out planning this trip I made up my mind to spend some money, and not worry about the expense, but I'm just as much obliged to your brother." Maria always said, "your brother" instead of Dexter.

That night after she had gone to bed she thought about it all, and she felt almost angry again with fate, or with Dexter himself, she could scarcely have told which, that the one man who had fallen in love with her had been Dexter Ray and not some one whom she could consider as her equal, and who spoke better English. The position, socially speaking, she did not think of at all. A druggist was as good as anybody in her little village; in fact, it was considered a decidedly genteel calling. It was only Dexter's own personal drawbacks which she considered.

The next morning she started on her trip, and a queer little qualm of something like self-pity smote her when she saw one of the village women being driven to the station by her husband in his buggy, with a small trunk tilted up in front. She herself clambered out of the village stage coach, which was a relic preserved with pride, and she tripped a little and a bit of the braid ripped off the hem of her gray mohair. She was obliged to pin it up when she got on the train. The thought came to her that a woman was better off with a husband to take her to the station, and assist her out, and check her baggage. Then she straightened herself, and realized with pride that she was going to the mountains to stay a month in a great hotel at an enormous price, and the other woman was only going to pay a visit to her sister in Maine, and going on an excursion at that. It was almost dark when Maria arrived at her destination, then she had a drive of a mile through the woods, which rose and sank and beetled on mountain sides. The air was cooler, and she was conscious of a strange vigor in it. She rode in a mountain wagon which was filled with passengers, altho Maria could not remember seeing one of them on the train. They had all been on Pullman coaches. It had never occurred to Maria to take a Pullman coach. On the seat with Maria was a corpulent woman in a long black silk traveling cloak, and a hat draped with a chiffon veil. She cast one glance at Maria, then looked away, and it was as if she had not seen her at all. With this woman were her two young daughters in tailor-made suits and a young son carrying golf sticks. The two daughters were nearly of an age, and very pretty with pert tilts to their chins, and they carried themselves like princesses. They talked but little, but what they said was as the language of an unknown world to Maria. Both of the girls glanced at Maria very much as their mother had done, only they gave each other an almost imperceptible glance of amusement afterward. Maria wondered why. She caught the glance, as any self-centered person would have done. She shortly afterward raised her hands and straightened her bonnet. She wore a bonnet with strings tied under the chin, altho she was not nearly so old as the girls' mother. She also wore a nice little brown and white checked shawl over her shoulders. The shawl had belonged to her mother, and Maria always used it for an extra wrap on a journey, without a thought that its day as regarded fashion had passed. When she had seated herself in the mountain wagon she put the shawl over her shoulders and sat up straight with her school teacher air, which was almost majestic. She did not dream that the combination of majesty, and little checked shawl, and bonnet, and face, which was almost too young for such head gear, could possibly afford any amusement to the girls beside her. When she heard a soft subdued chuckle she did not dream that she was the cause of it. "Two silly girls," she said to herself, and eyed the mountains, and realized her own superiority, inasmuch as she was intent upon those majestic slopes, while the girls were chattering over their own petty little affairs. She made up her mind that she would write Emma Ray while she was away, it would please her so much, and she thought of a fine sentiment to put in the letter. She would say that she had never realized her own littleness so much as when she had her first glimpse of the mountains, and she did not know that in reality she realized her own superiority instead of her littleness. They reached the hotel, and she was shown to her room. She felt a slight inward tremor, because she had never been in a hotel before, but she fairly strutted across the office, holding her bonneted head high, with her little checked shawl still over her shoulders. And she carried out her intention of slipping on her black silk skirt and her white cambric sacque, in which to appear at supper. But for the first time in her life Maria Gorham had an awed sensation as she saw the other women sweep into the dining-room in evening gowns. She looked around furtively, and she saw not another woman in a sacque. But she was not easily daunted, not even when some other ladies in low neck gowns seated themselves at her table, and she saw them looking askance at her sacque.

She ordered her supper with dignity, and ate it, and when she had finished she marched stiffly the whole length of the dining-room. They had placed her at a table at the extreme end. She heard furtive chuckles, but she did not admit that they were laughing at her, Maria Gorham, and that she did not still believe in her sacque and its entire appropriateness to the occasion, and she would not weaken. She went into the music-room, and seated herself composedly and listened to the orchestra and watched the young people dance. When at last she went up to her room, and divested herself of the sacque, she did not own that she would not wear it again to supper while she was in the hotel. Instead she hung it up carefully with a little defiant air, under the cretonne curtain which served in lieu of a closet on one side of the room. "I don't care what other folks wear, I rather think I have a right to wear anything I choose which is tidy and comfortable," she told herself. The next morning she attired herself in the pink wrapper and went down to breakfast, and she was soon aware that not another woman in the dining-room wore a wrapper. She became aware that furtive fun was made of her. The people in the hotel were, on the whole, a well bred and good-natured lot, and were incapable of down-right ridicule. But now Maria Gorham's spirit was up. Out on the verandah she went and walked up and down holding up her wrapper daintily. Then she sat down in one of the verandah chairs, and watched people pass her with furtive stares at her wrapper, and she felt fairly warlike. She said to herself that she would not persist in wearing the white cambric sacque to supper, since she had not planned that, altho if there came a warm night when she did not feel like putting on a tight dress she would wear it, but as for the wrapper she would not give in one whit. It was a pretty wrapper, and nicely made, trimly belted with a pink ribbon. She had intended to wear it mornings during her stay at the hotel, and she would wear it. And she did, but as the time went on she suffered tortures. Ridicule was the hardest thing in the world for one of her kind to endure. Open warfare would have been more to her liking, but ridicule it was that she had to prepare herself for every morning, and ridicule the worse because it was covert and could not be met with open resentment. Several times in the evening when she was wearing one of her best dresses, which somehow seemed not so fine as she had thought them, she heard herself alluded to as the woman who wore the wrapper mornings. She knew that was the name she went by, but the more she suffered the more obstinate she grew. She walked the verandah in her wrapper. She even climbed a mountain, a small one, marching to the summit as grimly and unflinchingly as the youth in "Excelsior," holding up the wrapper carefully above her starched petticoat. She wore on that ex-pedition her little bonnet with a small black lace veil, and the black flies crawled under the veil and bit her cruelly. The next day her face was so swollen that she was obliged to call in the hotel physician, and it was on that day that Mrs. Evans came in the afternoon. There was a gentle knock at Maria's door, and Maria said, "Come in," and a woman as gentle as the knock entered, and asked if she could not do something for her. She had heard that she was ill. Maria answered her gratefully at first, then she caught a swift glance of the other woman's eye at the pink wrapper, a fold of which obtruded from behind the calico curtain, and she understood that this woman, sweet and gentle and kind-hearted as she was, had looked upon her in the wrapper as the others had. Then she spoke grimly, altho grimness only lent renewed absurdity to her distorted face. "There is nothing you can do, thank you," she said. "I have had medical advice." The "medical advice" alone would have proclaimed her the school teacher. The other woman was rather persistent in her kindness, she offered to read to her, but Maria refused more and more brusquely. The woman went away, but soon she sent by a bell boy a plate of grapes, having selected the choicest from some which had been sent to her from New York. "Now, she'll be coming again," Maria said to herself, and she was right. Next day Maria was better, still her face was too badly swollen for her to leave her room, and the woman came again. Even after she had quite recovered Maria was liable to a call from her, altho she never encouraged it. In fact, the woman, who had an obtrusively benevolent heart, had set herself the task of quietly leading up to the wrapper. She had talked it over with some other ladies, and they had agreed that it was a shame that a woman as good as Maria seemed to be should make herself so ridiculous. But the other ladies had not the spirit of this one. "I am going to tell her," said she, and she did about a week after she had first spoken to her. The woman was calling upon Maria one morning and Maria was wearing the wrapper, and the woman spoke out with exceeding sweetness, which still had a sting in it. "What a lovely wrapper that is you are wearing," said the woman.

Maria's face changed. She looked at her suspiciously, altho she answered with dignity. "Thank you!" she said.

"What a pity it is that wrappers, no matter how pretty they are, are not worn in large hotels," said the woman. Then her face colored piteously before the indignation in Maria's. "It does not make the slightest difference to me what is worn in hotels, or is not worn in hotels," said Maria, sternly. "I wear whatever I please as long as it is tidy and respectable."

Tears actually sprang into the other woman's eyes. "Oh, dear, I am so sorry you take it so!" said she. "I meant well. It was only because I hated to have—" She paused.

"Hated to have what?" asked Maria, pitilessly.

"Hated to have you made fun of," almost sobbed the other woman.

"If I am not made fun of for anything worse than wearing a wrapper in the morning, it does not worry me at all, not at all," said Maria, with her head up in the air.

The other woman rose. "Well, I meant it kindly, and I am going away in the morning," said she.

"Oh, I am not at all offended!" said Maria, in a somewhat softer voice, "and I thank you for your interest, but I do not allow even my dearest friends to interfere in matters so purely personal as my attire."

The next morning Maria in her wrapper shook hands with the other woman, as she went out of the hotel on her way to the train. "I do hope you don't lay up anything against me," said the other woman.

"Not at all," said Maria, briskly and kindly. Then the woman went her way. She was the only one of the guests who had spoken to Maria, and she had been in the hotel two weeks. Nobody at all spoke to her during the remaining two weeks of her stay. Maria was, on the whole, more lonely than she had ever been in her life, and she did more thinking. She thought a good deal about Dexter Ray. She thought how if she had a husband with her like many of the other women she would not have felt so defenseless and isolated in her wrapper, which she had begun to regard as a matter of principle. She felt sure that Dexter would admire the wrapper. She could see just the kindly, worshipful expression that would come into his brown eyes at the sight of her in it. She recalled how Emma had believed in the wrapper. She began to reflect as she had never done on the pettiness and worthlessness of externals. She wished she could see Emma, and hear her talk in her bad English. She began to understand that the bad English might be very much like the wrapper, something beneath a loving soul to notice, if the heart of the speaker were right. She remembered how very plain Dexter Ray was, and how clumsy, and how he talked just as Emma did, and it all seemed to her like the wrapper and the cambric sacque, something for people who had not love and appreciation in their hearts to make fun of, but nothing of any consequence to those who could see what was underneath; the honesty, and the affection, and the faithfulness. Two days before Maria went home she wrote to Emma Ray, and told her when she was coming, and asked her and her brother to come in and spend the next evening with her. Maria was pale when she posted the letter in the little hotel office. She had never asked Dexter to spend the evening with her before, and she knew what it would mean. Emma Ray, when she got the letter the day before Maria's return, read it aloud to Dexter. When Emma read that Maria would like to have them both come in and spend the evening the brother and sister looked at each other. Dexter's homely, faithful face flushed, then turned very pale. Emma gazed at him with the sympathy of a mother, rather than of a sister. Nobody knew how she had pitied him, and how hard she had tried to help him. She smiled with the loveliest unselfishness, then she looked again at the letter in her hand. "Guess Maria has been eatin' humble pie," she thought to herself, then she reflected how much she thought of Maria, and her brother, and how glad she was. "Well, I guess Maria thinks that the old friends that have always set store by her are the best after all," she said, and a moral perfume, as of the sweetness of humility itself, seemed to come in her face from the letter.

The Slip of the Leash

Whether it was in his blood or not, as they say it is in the blood of some wild animals which invariably, sooner or later, revert to utter savagery, or whether he was unduly restrained by the conditions of his life, which made a reaction inevitable, Adam Andersen, at a time of life when most men have settled into the calm of acquiescence with fate which is to endure until death, broke his bonds. In other words, he went wild, he freed himself from all which had hitherto held him, and was for himself alone,—or perhaps for that which was in reality greater than himself or anything which had held him. Perhaps in returning to nature he also returned, in a sense, to God, although he broke, to the execration of all who knew of it, like the woman of the Scriptures, his jar of precious ointment.

Adam Andersen was over forty when he left a wife and four children, and a comfortable home, and went, not to the bad—that was not the word for it—but to that which is outside the good or the bad, to freedom from all cords and weights of civilized life. He lived, anyway, on the outskirts of civilization, where he could hear and see, and smell with his sharpened nostrils, that which was outside. He lived in one of the far Western States, on a fine farm which he himself had wrested from the wild. He had a house which was in those parts considered sumptuous, and furniture in those parts considered luxurious. There was a piano, and his daughters took music lessons. In the yard was a croquet set, and he used to watch his children playing the game with a sort of whimsical and admiring contempt. When he had been the age of his eldest boy—eight—he had played with a shovel and a hoe in grim earnest for his bread and butter. The eldest boy was eight, the next was five, then there were two girls, one ten, the other nine.

Andersen's wife was still good to see—large, and blonde, with a seeming decision of character which, some said, had driven her husband afield. However, people, for the most part, were on her side.

The day after Andersen disappeared, leaving no trace,—for he had planned his escape well,—and his wife appealed to the people in the scattered settlement to aid her, there had been no lack of volunteers, and there had been fierce blame for the man, although he had left his family in easy circumstances, and his wife was considered to have the brain of a man and to be as competent to run the farm as Adam.

Adam Andersen had simply attired himself in some stout clothes and put a few necessaries in the rude old knapsack which he had borne over his shoulders when he first came to those parts, and one night when his wife and family were at a Christmas gathering in the schoolhouse, three miles away, he had stepped—or rather leaped, so glad was the new sense of freedom in him—over the indefinite barrier which kept the settlement from the wild, the civilized man from the savage, and in a trice he was what he had been before he had known himself. He loped like a young wolf along the road farther west. He was a small and wiry man, and his muscles had still the strength and suppleness of youth. He had chosen a strange time for his exit, a night of intense cold, when the stars overhead swarmed in myriads seemingly laced together in a net of frost; but he was warmly clad, and besides he did not mind the cold. He loved it with a fierce animal yearning, for his forefathers had come of a cold climate, and it was the spur of their old impulses which now urged him on. He forged ahead as a Viking might have done at a battle-call, although before him were only wastes of land, instead of sea. He did not seem to feel the cold at all. He thought, it is true, of his wife and his children, and, paradoxical as it may seem, with intense love, yet still with exultation that he had broken away from that love and its terrible monotony of demand. The going to bed every night to sleep in his carved bedstead underneath the patchwork quilts which his wife had made, to realize beside him that other personality which had become a part of him, and which he had realized as extraneous, even while he loved it; the invariable rising in the morning and going about his tasks; the three meals a day; the sound of his daughters' pounding on the piano which he had purchased for them, and in which he himself took the greatest pride; the sight of his wife about her household tasks; the smell of the bread baking and the sweet cake; the wrangling and playing of the younger children in which he delighted,—he was free from now, and instead was an infinite preciousness of renewed individuality.

"I was being tore to pieces betwixt them all," he said to himself as he leaped along, "and soon there would have been nothing at all left of me." He looked up at the stars, and a sense of his own soul which he had lost for a long time was over him, and along with it, as a matter of sequence, was the sense of God. In his belt were pistols and a hunting-knife; over his shoulder, a rifle. He meant to hunt and trap the valuable game farther off, but when he reached the hunting-fields the desire left him. He was not a man of sentiment. It simply did not appeal to him to hunt, for the sake of profit, his fierce brothers of the out-of-doors. Once he had a good chance to shoot at a deer, and leveled his rifle, but did not fire. Instead of shooting the deer, he made his way to the nearest settlement and purchased some venison which another man had shot. He wore a money-belt. Once, even, he might have killed a bear and had a valuable skin, but let the great shaggy free thing lumber away. That was in the spring, when he had been on the tramp for six months.

At last he fell in with some men on their way to the mines, and he fared along with them. They were not the kind usually seen on such roads, but a meek set rather intimidated by their own adventure, and they had come from the East. They all rather feared Andersen, who kept himself to himself even while with them, and they had a theory that he was some escaped criminal. Andersen understood, and it filled him with the grim humor that a wild animal might have had. He knew himself that he would not hurt these men, that in reality he had never hurt anything, and the suspicion as to his evil doings seemed to him a fine joke. He listened to the innocent prattle of his companions concerning the gold they would dig out of the earth, and what they would do with it, and he had a sort of wonder concerning his own motives for joining them.

He was too simple to understand that the thirst for gold is in itself as primeval a thing as the thirst for freedom, inasmuch as gold is often the price of it. Then, too, the desire of discovery is as old as the world, and Andersen in setting himself free had become at once as old and as young as the world. It was therefore that he went on with the men to the mines. But he was the one of them all who made a rich find, although it was not for a year's time, and in the mean time there had been hardships which he had borne lightly, since he had not borne them with his soul. Frost-bites which do not affect the soul have little sting in them, and neither has hunger under burning suns. Several of the party succumbed, and Andersen surprised them all by his roughly tender care of them, although they still feared him. They called him the wild man. Indeed, he had let his hair and beard grow, and was as shaggy as a bear, and almost as speechless. He never talked with his companions, and none of them knew anything of his antecedents.

When he made his great find it was in the early spring, and he struck out toward home. He did not know why he did so, but it seemed a part of his freedom, the natural impulse of a living thing which has discovered, toward a hole of hiding. It was a long and arduous journey, but he went on doggedly, his pistols in his belt, his rifle over shoulder. Except for the general wildness of his aspect, largely owing to the great growth of his hair and beard, he looked no more worn nor old than when he started. In reality, hardships had not injured him in the least. They had rather served as a tonic to a peculiar nervous nature which civilization had been rasping beyond endurance.

When he reached the outskirts of the settlement in which he had lived before his exit, he slunk cautiously, as if he had been a beast of prey with designs upon the folds. However, he was really in no danger of discovery. Before his departure he had gone clean shaven, and now so hirsute was he that his own wife and children could not have recognized him. There was about the settlement a great growth of forest, and in this he concealed himself. The weather was quite warm, and he had no trouble about living in the open; all his trouble was the lack of food. He had been obliged by necessity to overcome his dislike to slaughter for the sake of food, but even now he had a repugnance to it. At last he hit upon a plan. Under cover of night he stole into the village and robbed a baker's shop, leaving on the counter gold sufficient to twice pay for what he had taken. He also in the same fashion appropriated the contents of hen-coops.

As the summer advanced he built himself a rude shack under the shag of a hill, and laid in a stock of fire-wood. It began to be known in the settlement that there was a wild man living in the woods, but as he always paid for his raids upon the provisions of the place, no rancor was aroused against him, and wild things awakened no particular surprise or curiosity in that vicinity, so frequent they were, not even that wildest of all wild things—a wild man. It is true that some mothers lately from the East forbade their children to stray far into the woods in the locality where the wild man had been seen, but the children themselves, more fearless, made little raids in large companies for mutual protection, and boasted that they had seen the wild man and the wild man's house, and astonishing tales, tinctured with their childish fancy, they told of both. The man, in particular, was described as being in appearance something like a prehistoric giant. Nobody in the settlement dreamed of the true state of the case, and yet Adam Andersen had been away only a little over a year. Once it happened that his own two young children came with the exploring party, and both gazed at him round-eyed, from a flowering thicket, and neither dreamed that he had ever seen him before.

That night Andersen had a bad hour. The hunger of natural affections was upon him again, and crowded out that hunger of the soul which kept him in the wild. Those two utterly common little faces, those young of his flesh and blood, but not of his true self which he had let loose, had filled him with a torture of yearning. He wanted his wife and his children and his home. Once he started up to try to put himself in fitting trim to go home, and then it was over. The smell of the damp spring earth, and the multitude of young growing things which were the music of the first man, were loud in his senses, and his own spirit awakened to the life which satisfied him. Again, while he loved and longed for his wife, he resented his bonds, for in bonds she had held him, and the children, which were all like her rather than like him. He had cut the knot of his conditions of life, and he realized that not yet could the break be made entirely whole, and yet he never for one moment lost sight of his family, or lost his sense of care over them. He slunk on the borders of the fields, to make sure that his wife kept the men to their work; many a night the house dog barked and howled and strained at his leash because he was under the windows, and they did not know who was there, although the youngest boy suggested fearfully that it might be the wild man, and Andersen heard the grate of the bolt in the door.

It was doubtful, when Andersen went away that night, moving with a curious free padding lope, like a wild animal, which he had acquired since he had left home, if he had ever in his life loved as he did then his wife and children and home. But they had become to him as the angel with whom Jacob wrestled for the sake of a mystery which was more than earth and life and all the natural affections thereof. As Andersen retraced his steps to his shack deep in the heart of the wood, he even wept a little, like a child. It was a damp night, and the wind came from the south full of moisture. Presently it began to rain. Andersen lay out in the warm rain and let it soak through him, and felt the winds, and soon the old sense of attaining his full stature—the sense of freedom from trammels which held him to an encumbering happiness—was over him. Still, as he lay there he felt his heart dislocated as Jacob felt his hip after the angelic encounter. He remembered with solicitude that his wife's face had looked thinner and older, that much of the look of decision and feminine imperiousness which had in reality fed upon him had vanished. The woman, bereft of her gentle, subservient husband, settled back into what she really was—a rather incompetent, timid female of her species. Adam had overrated her capability; her manner had misled him. The next year he, covertly observant, saw with concern that the fields had begun to suffer for want of his overlooking. Still his wife and his children retained their prosperous air.

Adam saw that his wife wore a rich silk dress, and bonnet loaded with flowers, and that she held her head high, while her mouth had a pleased, self-conscious expression. He understood her thoroughly. He knew that her beautiful clothes soothed as with a soothing emollient any ache in her heart because of his desertion of her. She was a type of the perfectly common feminine. She was a good woman, she kept the Commandments, but the material frivolity of her had overrun the spiritual, as weeds will overrun the flowers of a garden. And it was the same with the children, who resembled their mother, and it had been becoming the same with Adam. He had been losing the feeling of his own soul, and that from which the soul emanates, by reason of these harmless and pleasant, but utterly earthly and petty, interests. His children were as smartly attired as his wife; none of them looked downcast. He realized that for the time at least, in this atmosphere of religious festivity, and enveloped in their fine feathers, they were not troubled because of him, and his own misgivings were laid at rest. He had placed half of his gold which he had discovered in trust, and the interest was to be sent quarterly to his wife. He told himself that even if she did let the farm go to waste, she would have enough. And there was the remainder of his wealth, which he had buried as a dog might have buried a bone in a secret place in the woods. He used very little of it. His needs, the needs of a primitive and wild man which he had become, were few, and mostly supplied without coin of the realm. In summer there were always succulent greens, mushrooms, and berries. In winter there was the game which he had now forced himself to kill and eat, for savagery had returned in a degree with his freedom. He really needed little except cartridges, and now and then a rough garment.

All this time, although conscious of a never-ceasing ache of hunger in the earthly heart of him, he had the exaltation of a martyr, the sublime happiness of one who forfeits the good for the sake of the better, and the consciousness of that beyond his earthly life, which had been slipping away from him, was never lost. Always the wonderful perfume of a broken box of ointment was in his nostrils, and his sense of Him for whom it had been broken never left him. A religion so deep and vast that it seemed to furnish his soul with wings toward immensity possessed him. God and his relation to Him became more than his relation toward his kind. He became in the fullest sense himself. His growth, which had been checked, again reasserted itself.

Yet always he kept that watch upon that which he had left. Year after year the fields which had yielded so bountifully under his care suffered. The time came when it was hard for him not to enter the house and ask his wife what it meant, why she did not see to things, but he never did. He knew that she had enough, even if the broad fields, as finally happened, were converted into gardens of flaming weeds instead of grain. But soon after that—it was now three years since his exit—he began to notice that his wife no longer went dressed as richly as formerly, and that his children were even shabby. Then he saw them walking when properly they should have been riding; and one night, stealing into the barn, he found that the horses were all gone. He began to ask himself if anything could have gone wrong with that trust money. He tramped to the nearest town and possessed himself of papers, and soon enough found what he wanted. The man in whom he had trusted had defaulted. The money was gone. He then began to dole out the money which he had remaining. He was at his wits' end to do so without discovery, but by tramping miles first in one direction, then another, he contrived to send it in quarterly instalments, and he saw with delight that his wife had a new dress and the flowers on her bonnet bloomed anew. But the worry was upon him that the money, since he was using the principal, would soon be gone. He felt that he should invest the remainder. He tramped fifty miles one spring with the money concealed about him, and his pistols in his belt, and he invested it, and it was not long before the investment proved an utter loss. Then he knew that his wife had mortgaged the farm. Still, although the thought of it all was always with him, he seemed to live in his solitude with God, and realize himself that which he should be.

But finally the time came when by spying and listening he found out that his family could not live much longer unless something was done for them. One afternoon, slouching along in the shadows of the woods, he saw his wife and his slender daughters and eldest boy trying to plough the fields with an old horse which they had hired. That was too much for him. There was a man in the settlement who had owed him money for years. Andersen had returned to the simplest notions of right and wrong. That night he went to the great barn of the man who owed him, and got out two stout horses, and he worked all night ploughing his fields. In the morning, when the deserted wife saw what had been done, she thought it was the work of a benevolent neighbor, a widower, who had for some time been making advances to her. There had been a well-grounded report that Andersen was dead. However, Andersen's wife would not listen to the man, and although she saw with delight the work done on her fields, still she made up her mind that she would not admit any knowledge of the man who had done it. Adam worked night after night, and it was the seventh night that his second daughter discovered him. He was working quite near the house, and guiding the horses in silence, yet it was bright moon-light, and the girl, who was nervous and wakeful, looked out and saw him. He heard her shriek, and hurried with the horses out of the field.

The girl ran down to her mother, who slept on the ground-floor, and she was fairly gasping in hysterics. "Oh, mother! oh, mother!" she cried, catching her breath.

Her mother, white and gasping also, rose up in bed and looked at her.

"It is the wild man who is ploughing our fields," said the girl, choking.

"I don't believe it."

"Yes; I saw him. His beard blew out like a flag as he walked behind the horses."

"I don't believe it. You were dreaming. It was Silas Edgett."

"No, it was the wild man. I saw him."

The next night Adam did not come. He felt that it was of no use. He knew they would all be on the watch. He waited. He thought, if he waited, they might cease to watch. On the third night he stole up to the barn of the neighbor whose horses he had borrowed, and caught the gleam of a lantern from the wide-open doors. They, too, were on the watch. They had discovered that their horses had been used. He waited still three days longer, and made a third attempt. Passing his wife's house, skirting like a shadow the edge of the woods which bordered the road, he distinctly saw white gleams in the windows; he kept on to the barn, and there was still the lantern gleam. A man was actually pacing like a sentinel before the open door. He retreated. The next day he left his shack, taking with him his scanty possessions, for he had a presentiment. He was quite right. The sheriff had been sent for, and that very night his shack was visited, but the wild man had gone. After all, there was nothing very serious in the charge against him. He had merely borrowed without leave a man's horses and ploughed the fields of a poor deserted woman. The widower who was her covert admirer advised the withdrawal of the search party, without further efforts to find the man.

The next day but one, Adam returned to his shack, but he was in despair. That had come which he had foreseen. All day he sat on a ledge of stone near his shack, reflecting. It was a beautiful day in spring, and a sudden warm spell had brought out the leaves on the trees. His feet were sunken in a bed of wild flowers. He heard running water and pipes of birds, and it seemed to him that he also heard something else—the trumpet of freedom of life and earth which calls a man to the battle-field of God. But he knew that the time was come when he must return to the trammels of love and happiness and anxiety, which his day and generation had made incumbent upon him, and which, although his soul after a manner delighted in them, were yet not the best for a man of his kind who had in him the memory of the old which is the new.

It was late afternoon when Adam rose up and entered his shack and got out a razor and a bit of looking-glass which he had kept all this time, and he shaved himself and cut his hair. Then he put on a decent suit of clothes which he had also kept, and when it was all done he looked a thin and meek man, and not one to ever kick over his traces of life. Then he left his shack, and went along the road toward his old home. He stopped at the house of a man who owned a mule, a half-mile from his own home, and found the man's wife at home, and bargained with her, with a little money he had left, for the hire of the mule for a few days. These people were newcomers in the settlement and did not know him, but the woman looked at him wonderingly when he told her what fields he wished to plough.

"But," she said, "I thought that man was dead. I thought he ran away and died."

"No," said Adam, "he is alive."

"But they told me he died," persisted the woman.

"No, he is alive."

"Are you him?" asked the woman.

"Yes, I am," replied Adam, and left the woman gaping after him as he went away with the mule. She half feared that she had seen a ghost; then she looked at the solid silver in her hand.

Adam went on, leading the mule with his ragged sides. He was a strong mule, although he showed those ragged patches. Adam went, when he had reached his old home, into the barn and got the plough, and the dog strained at his leash to get at him, barking with joy.

Adam's wife and children in the house heard the dog bark and ran out, and there was Adam ploughing the field,—a small, meek-faced man with an expression of sublime patience and love. Adam's wife screamed.

"It is your father come back!" she cried out. Then she and the slender young girls and the little boys all ran out in the field and up to Adam, and he turned from his ploughing and clasped his wife and then his children in his arms, and his face was beaming, and his heart aching with excess of joy, and his leash was upon him again.

But he still had the sense of blessing which had come to him from his wrestling with that which was the holiest and best of earth and humanity, but which had come between himself and the best of himself.

For the Love of One's Self

Against the south wall of the shoe-factory stood a tall spruce-tree. One branch of it crossed like an arm Amanda Dearborn's window, in front of which she stood at work on her machine. At first, when she was learning her monotonous task, she scarcely noticed the branch of the tree; now that she had worked a year, she sometimes glanced up at no risk, and her glance of bitter patience fell upon the everlasting greenness of it. She got, in spite of herself and her attitude of spiritual revulsion against comfort, a slight amelioration in the hot midsummer days in the suggestion which the tree gave her of coolness and darkness and winter. In the winter itself the arm draped with changeless green did not suggest so much; still, she sometimes noticed it, and it was a relief to her weary eyes.

Nobody knew how the girl hated her work in the great factory, or how she hated life, yet endured it with a sort of contemptuous grimness. She had a highly strung nervous organization; everything in her surroundings jarred upon her,—the noise, the odors, the companionship. She was herself superior to those about her—that is, to the most of them, although she never realized it. All that she did realize was that she stood day after day at work, at a task which stretched her nerves and muscles to breaking-point, to maintain a life in a world which honestly appeared entirely unattractive to her. She was neither hysterical nor sentimental, but she was naturally pessimistic, and she naturally reasoned from analogy. She was, besides, clear-visioned, and her outlook on the future was not apt to be dazzled by hope. She saw herself exactly as she was, as she had been, and in all probability as she would be. She had not yet reached middle age, but she was no longer exactly young; in fact, she had never been exactly young as

some of the girls around her were. She listened to their chatter as she might have listened to a language of youth which she herself had never spoken. She did not understand, and she had a sort of unconscious contempt for it, as she had for most of the girls themselves. She saw their innocent attempts to be beautiful—to be like those who had not to toil like themselves, to the quick wasting of youth and beauty,—and she in a way despised them for it.

Nothing would have induced her to arrange her abundant brown hair in a fluffy crest, as the girl who stood next her arranged hers. She wore her own hair brushed straight back, exposing her temples, which showed faint lines of care and weariness, but which had nevertheless something noble about them. Nothing would have induced her to muffle her throat in stocks; she had a plain turn-over collar, of the same material as her waist. She indulged in no eccentricities of belts and buttons. She was saving all that she was able from her hard earnings against an old age of inability to work, and want. And yet she might have been distinctly pretty had she cared to make herself so. As she was, she was homely with a hard, stern homeliness. She was stiff and straight and flat-chested; her long arms were becoming every day more and more bony from the strain upon them, but her rigid back of burden was never yielding.

Perhaps she came the nearest to happiness when she went to the savings-bank to make a tiny deposit. The ignoble greed of the miser had an attraction to a nature like hers, non-acquiescent with its conditions, yet with a contemptuous sense of its own helplessness, rather than with any leaning to rebellion. When a strike was talked about she held a position aloof, although her sympathies were entirely with the party who wished to strike. It was only that she realized the futility of fighting with weapons of straw. Had they been weapons of steel, she might have been the most dangerous of them all; but she saw too clearly the ultimate outcome of it all, just as she saw her own face in the looking-glass of her little room in the boarding-house. However, in that she did not see quite as clearly, since she saw only facts, and not possibilities. She saw only a dark, harsh, sternly set face, not one which was susceptible of other things, as in fact it was.

She had never thought much about her personal appearance, except with regard to its subservience to cleanliness and order and good-

ness. Her training was partly responsible for that. Her mother had been a very plain-visaged woman, and quite destitute of sentiment or romance. Marriage itself had been in her case a queer coincidence. She had married a widower older than herself, who had died when Amanda was a child; she could scarcely remember him. In his younger days he had held a petty rank in the civil war, and her mother, as long as she lived, had a small pension. It was that pension which had enabled Amanda and her mother to have a home. The house was heavily encumbered; Amanda's father, who had worked like herself in the factory for a living, had been obliged to lay off much on account of an old wound. He had not been able to leave even the house clear to his family. The pension money had paid the interest on the mortgage, the taxes, the repairs; and Amanda's mother took boarders—shopgirls— to eke out the remainder of their living.

After Amanda was old enough, and had graduated from the high school, in a cheap white dress, coming forward in her turn and reading gravely—for she had even as a young girl much self-poise—her stupid little essay, heavy with platitudes, she assisted her mother with the housework. It was necessary, for her mother was growing old; she was not very young when she married. However, she remained still of so much assistance that when she died Amanda realized the impossibility of going on with her work of keeping a boarding-house. They had barely made both ends meet as it had been. When the pension stopped, and the interest, taxes, and repairs were to be paid for out of the small sums received from the boarders, and she would also be obliged to hire help, she saw nothing ahead except bankruptcy. Therefore she sold at auction, with a resolute stifling of her heartache, most of the old household goods with which she had been familiar since her infancy, keeping only enough to furnish one room, and her mother's bed and table-linen and wedding-china, which she had obtained permission to store in the garret of the house after it had ceased to belong to her. After the mortgage was paid there was a small sum remaining, which she placed in the savings-bank. She took a certain comfort in thinking of that as a last resource in case of illness and inability to work. Her mother had been in the habit of saying often, "Everybody ought to have a little laid by in case they are took sick." Amanda had the same pessimistic habit of thought, though not of speech—for she had no intimate friend.

She boarded in a house where there were several other girls and one married couple who worked in the factory, but she had nothing to do with them. They resented it, and said that Amanda Dearborn was "stuck up," while she had no good reason for being so.

"What if her mother did take boarders, and kept her out of the shop as long as she lived?" said they; "she's there now, and she ain't no call to turn up her nose at them as is as good as she is."

However, they were wrong; Amanda did not feel above them; she simply realized nothing in common with them; and when she came home from work she preferred remaining alone in her own room, sewing or reading. She was fond of books of a certain kind,—simple tales which did not involve much psychological analysis. Overwork in a shoe-factory does not fit the mind for strenuous efforts, except in its own behalf. Amanda used all her reasoning powers upon her own situation in the world and life. Sometimes while she sat sewing of an evening her thoughts were anarchistic, almost blasphemous; then, as always, came the contemptuous realization of their futility. Sometimes, as she sat there, she realized with a subtle defiance and rebellion that she was not in a spiritual sense a good woman. She realized that she was a woman without patience, destined to a hard monotony of life, and non-acquiescent with it. And yet in reality her demands from life, could she have made them, were small enough. She did not ask so very much, only a house no better than she had been accustomed to have, away from the buzz of the machines and the pressure upon her sensitive soul of the most heterogeneous elements of humanity. She was entirely willing to work beyond her strength, but she wanted herself to herself, and she wanted her home.

Often she took a pencil and paper and calculated at what age, if she had in the mean time no illness or disaster to infringe upon her small resources, she might possibly be able to buy a little house and set up her home again. At such times the impulse of saving grew fairly fierce within her. She went without everything that she possibly could; she patched and darned, although she always looked neat. She had learned that of her mother as she might have learned a tenet of faith. There was never a spot on the black gown she wore in the shop. It smelled of leather, but it was tidy. She was a good worker. One day not long before Christmas the foreman came to her and told her that her wages were to be raised at the beginning of the year. She had

been, in fact, considered hitherto as only learning the art of stitching shoes, and her wages had been only nominal. Amanda looked at the foreman as he gave her the information, and there was a curious expression in her serious eyes. In fact, she was not only considering the raise in her wages, but she was considering him, as a brown sparrow, a dusty plebeian among birds, might consider a bird of paradise. She looked upon him as a male of her species, of course, but with a certain wonder, and even intimidation, because of his superior brilliance.

Frank Ayres, the foreman, was in fact an unusually handsome young man. He came of a good family. He was distantly related to the senior member of the firm, and might even in time belong to it. In the mean time he had his own personal advantages, which were enormous. He was only a year younger than Amanda, but he looked almost young enough to be her son. Hair as soft and golden and curly as a child's tossed above his white forehead, which had a childlike roundness. His cheeks were rosy, his lips always smiling, and with it all he was not effeminate. There was rather about him the triumph of youth and joyousness, which seemed never-ending. He, although only a foreman in a shoe-factory, carried himself like a young prince. The girls all adored him, some covertly, some boldly. He appealed to them all in a double sense, as a lover and as a child,—and the man who appeals to women after that fashion is irresistible. However, he did not take advantage of his power. He smiled at all the girls, but particularized none.

Amanda had watched with furtive disdain the other girls pushing up the fluffs of their pompadours as he drew near, and seeing to it that their shirt-waists were fastened securely in the back, straightening themselves with that indescribable movement of the female of the day, which involves at once a throwing back of the shoulders, a lengthening of the waist, a hollowing of the chest, and a slight bend of the back. She had always continued at her dogged work, and paid no attention to him. However, to-day, when he approached her (it was the hour of closing, and the girls in the vicinity had quitted their machines), she was conscious of a different sentiment. Almost the same expression entered her grave brown eyes that might have entered those of the other girls as she looked up in the joyous, triumphant face of the man. All at once a feeling of tenderness seemed to contract her

heart, but it was the feeling that she had sometimes experienced at seeing a beautiful child. It was compounded of admiration and an almost painful protectiveness. In reality the maternal instinct came first in her, and the young man consequently reached it first. She gazed at him with eyes in which was no coquetry, but a gentle tenderness which transformed her whole face. The young man himself started and gazed at her as if he had seen her for the first time. She appealed to a need in his nature, and that is the strongest appeal in the world. That night he remarked to his younger brother, who was a foreman in the packing-room, that the prettiest girl in the factory was Amanda Dearborn. The brother stared. The two were smoking in Frank's room in their boarding-house.

"What! that Dearborn girl?" he said. "You are crazy."

"She is the best-looking girl in the factory, and I am not sure that she is not the best-looking girl in town," repeated Frank, stanchly.

"Why, good Lord!" cried his brother, staring at him, "she is the homeliest of the lot. Hair strained tight back from her forehead, and she dresses like her own grandmother."

"I like it a good deal better than so many frills," replied Frank, "and I am dead tired of those topknots the girls wear nowadays, and I am dead tired of the way they look at a fellow."

"Nothing conceited about you," remarked his brother, dryly. Although younger than Frank, he looked older, and was of a heavy build. He had not much attention from the other sex—that is, not much gratuitous attention.

"It is just because I am not conceited that I am tired of it," said Frank. "I would rather a girl would look at me as if she would nurse me through a fever than as if I was a handsome man, and that is the way that Dearborn girl looked at me to-night when I told her her wages were raised. It is high time they were, too. She has been working under rate too long as it is."

As the two young men talked, the snow, or rather sleet, drove on the windows. It was a bitter night—so bitter that neither thought of going out. Amanda Dearborn also remained at home. There was a sociable in the church vestry, and she had thought a little of going, although it was not her usual custom. But when it began to storm she decided to remain where she was. Her room was cold. It was a northeast room, and when the wind was that way little heat came from the register. She sat in the dark beside her window, wrapped in an old shawl which had belonged to her mother, and which always seemed to her to partake of the old atmosphere of home, and she gazed out at the white slant of the frozen storm. The sleet seemed to drive past the windows like arrows. There was an electric light a little farther down the street, and that seemed a nucleus for the swarming crystals. Amanda sat there huddled in her shawl and thought.

All thoughts are produced primarily by suggestion, and so were hers. A little package which had been found on her bureau on her return from the shop produced hers. She knew what was in it before she opened it. It required little acuteness to know, because a week before Christmas she and her mother for years had received a similar package from a distant cousin in Maine, and it contained invariably the same thing. Amanda opened the package, and found, as always, an ironing-holder. This year it was made of pink calico bound with green, and the year before, if she remembered rightly, it had been made of green calico bound with pink. Back of that she could not remember. An enormous package of these holders was stored away up in the garret of her old home. Amanda, although she was pessimistic, had a sense of humor. When she regarded this last holder she laughed, albeit a little bitterly.

"What on earth does Cousin Jane Dearborn think I want of an ironing-holder now?" she said, quite aloud. Then she considered that soon, by the last mail that night or the first in the morning, would come another package, from Cousin Maria Edgerly, and that that package would contain as usual a knitted washcloth. She then reflected upon the speedy arrival of another package from still another cousin in the second degree, containing a hemstitched duster of cheesecloth. She and her mother in the old days had often smiled over these yearly tokens, and said to each other that if they ironed every week-day, and bathed every hour, and dusted betweenwhiles, they would have enough of these things to last for a lifetime. But her mother's smile had always ended with an expression of sympathetic understanding.

"Poor Maria," or "Poor Jane," or "Poor Liza," as the case might have been, the mother always remarked, "she wants to do something,

and she ain't got any means and no faculty, and it's all she can do."
Amanda's mother had had a curious tenderness for these twice and
third removed cousins of hers, whom she had not seen for years, and
Amanda took comfort in the reflection that she had never expressed
the conviction uppermost in her mind on the receipt of these faithful
tokens a week before Christmas. It had been a dozen times on her
tongue's end to say, "She is just sending this so as to make sure she
gets something from us," but she had never said it. Instead she had
aided her mother in preparing the best return presents they could
afford—presents which meant self-denial for themselves. She recalled
how the very Christmas before her mother died they had sent Cousin
Jane a pair of black kid gloves, although her mother's were shabby.
"Poor mother, she did not need gloves very long after that, anyway,"
Amanda reflected; then she also reflected that, knowing what she was
now earning, they kept up this absurd deluge of holders and wash-
cloths and dusters, in the hope of a reward. They were to her understanding nothing more than so many silent requests for benefits. Suddenly she became filled with an ignoble anger because of it all.

"Why should I drudge all my life and go without, in order to send
Christmas presents to these cousins of mother's whom I have not seen
more than two or three times in my life, and who send me things
which I don't want, like so many machines?" she asked. Suddenly she
resolved that this year she would not. They should get nothing. She
had planned to spend fifteen dollars—an enormous sum for her—
upon these cousins. She had made up her mind, since she did not
know what they needed, to send the money this year, five dollars to
each cousin. Suddenly she resolved that she would not. She considered how much she herself needed a new gown—a really nice black
gown,—how if she had gone to the sociable that night she had not
one gown which was suitable. She reflected, not fairly realizing that
she did so, that Frank Ayres might have been at the sociable, and,
also without fairly knowing, she saw herself as she might have looked
in her poor best dress, in those dancing blue eyes of his. She imagined
also herself as she would look, in those same eyes in a dainty costume
of black crêpe, similar to one which a girl had who worked in the
same room with her. She imagined the fluffy sweep of the long skirt,
the lace trimming.

"That fifteen dollars would just about buy the material for the dress," she said to herself. Fifteen dollars when she had paid her board, due the first of the month, was nearly all the ready money she had. She did not dream of drawing upon her little bank-account. Her increase in wages would not begin until the following Monday. She remembered that there was to be a New-year's festival at the church the week following Christmas, and how she might have the dress made and wear it to that.

Suddenly she thought further; her feminine imagination became sharpened. She thought of a rosette of black lace in her hair. "Why should I give all that money to those far-away cousins?" she asked of herself. "While mother was alive we gave to please her, but now— Why should I in return for all these holders and wash-cloths and dusters, which are absolutely valueless to me, go without things I really need?" She thought furthermore in the depths of her heart, even veiling her thought from her own consciousness, how her youth was fast passing, and she thought again how she would look, in Frank Ayres's eyes. She had an under-realization of what that new black dress might mean to her. After all, in spite of her steadfastness and even severity of character, she was only a woman, and a woman untaught except by her own nature and that of her mother. She thought of this girl and that girl whom she had known, who had had her love affair, and had married and become possessed of a happy home, and she wondered if, after all, she was so without the pale as she had always thought. She began to have dreams as she sat there staring out into the storm, of chance meetings with Frank Ayres, of what he might say and do, of what she might say and do. A warmth stole all over her from her fast-throbbing heart in spite of the cold. She trembled, she smiled involuntarily, and all seemed to hinge upon the new black dress and the lace rosette for her hair.

Suddenly she gave her head a resolute shake. "What a fool I am!" she whispered. She was distinctly angry with herself. She got up, lit her lamp, and looked in the glass. There had been a flush on her cheeks, but that and the smile had gone. Her face looked back at her from the glass, above her flat chest, and her uncompromising collar hostile to that which was the legitimate desire and need of her kind. She glowered at herself in the looking-glass. "What a fool I am!" she said again.

She took a little stationery-box from the shelf under her table, and got her pen and ink from the shelf. Then she proceeded to cut little slips of paper, and write on them, "For Cousin Jane, with a merry Christmas from Amanda," and so on. She did not own any visiting-cards. She proposed to put a slip with a five-dollar note in each envelope, and send to the three cousins by registered mail. But now the cold of her room struck her again. Her hands felt stiff with it.

"There isn't any hurry," she said to herself. "Mother never sent anything until the day before Christmas. She thought they liked to get their presents on Christmas day." Then, too, she began to wonder if, after all, it was best to send the money,—if the value of money in gifts would not please them better. She thought that she might buy a pair of blankets for Cousin Jane, who was the poorest of the lot, and a silk waist for Cousin Liza, who had not quite given up, in her remote corner of Maine, the vanities of life, and about whom there had been rumors of a matrimonial alliance with an elderly widower. She also thought that a chenille table-cloth might please Cousin Maria. She decided, on the whole, that she had better wait until the next day before she got the five-dollar notes ready to send, although she was not conscious of a faltering in her determination to send the presents. Therefore she put away her paper carefully—she was very orderly—and went to bed, and lay for a long time awake watching the storm drift and swirl past the window in the electric light.

Amanda probably caught cold that night, for cold air instead of heat came from her register, and the covers on her bed were not so very thick, being well-worn quilts which had belonged to her mother. She had taken a sort of comfort in using them instead of the coverings which the mistress of the boarding-house would have furnished. Sometimes at night she felt, as she nestled under the well-worn quilts, which were heavy rather than warm, as if she were still under the wing of home. Every bit of calico in these quilts had been connected in some way with her family. However, she caught cold that night, and the next day was so ill that she was obliged to stay away from the shop. She did not even feel equal to getting the presents ready for the cousins. She was, moreover, still undecided whether to buy some gifts or send the money, but she felt too ill even to put the money in the envelopes and make arrangements about registering. The next day she was no better, and it was the fourth day before she could drag herself out of bed and go to the factory. Frank Ayres came and spoke to her, after she had been at work an hour, and inquired if she had been sick, and she felt the blood rise to her steady forehead. A chuckle from the girl at her right after he had gone made her angry, not only with the girl, but with herself and the foreman. The imagination of anything particular in his attention had come to her, but not the belief in it. She simply felt that he was making her an object of ridicule by a notice which must in her case mean nothing.

When she got home that night she was so worn out that she was obliged to go directly to bed. She resolved that the next evening, since the stores were open in the evening during the holiday season, she would go out and look for gifts for her cousins. But the next eve-ning—she had caught a little more cold during the day—she was even more unable to go out. Then she resolved that she would send the money, as she had planned to do in the first place. It was the day but one before Christmas at last, when she dragged herself home, and took out the three new five-dollar notes to put in the envelopes. She had not taken off her wraps, for she wanted to go to the post-office, which was only a block away, to post them and have them registered. Then all at once a revulsion seized her. She again thought of the new black dress which she needed. She thought of the pile of miserable holders and dusters and wash-cloths. She looked at the money.

"What a fool I am!" she said to herself,—"what a fool! Here I shall not have one Christmas present for myself,—not one *real* present, for these are not presents; these are only reminders to me to send the cousins something. Here I am, with no Christmas presents coming to me, going to give away money which I actually need!" Again she seemed to see the foreman's happy, handsome face before her. She remembered the display which the girls around her had made of their gifts that very day. Suddenly she made up her mind that this year she would give her Christmas present to herself. "There is nobody else in this whole world to give me a Christmas present," she thought, "but myself. I will give myself the present."

When she had made this resolve a singular sense of guilt, as if she had blasphemed, was over her, but with it came a certain defiance in which she took pleasure. She began planning how she would have the new black dress made. There was, moreover, all the time the oddest conviction, for which she could not account, of something unfamiliar about the room. It was as if some strange presence was there. Every now and then she looked about. She had her lamp lighted and was seated beside her table doing some mending, but she saw nothing for a long while. She told herself that the quinine which she had taken for her cold affected her nerves. Then all at once she gave a great start. She saw, what it seemed inconceivable that she had not seen before, a package on a little ancient stand, which had belonged to her maternal grandmother, and had always stood by the side of her mother's bed in her lifetime, and now stood beside her own.

She gazed a moment at the package, which was done up in glossy white paper and tied with a gold cord; then she rose, and went across the room, and took it up. She saw what it was—a two-pound box of candy. It was directed to Miss Amanda Dearborn. She carefully took off the glossy white wrapping-paper, and a beautiful box of gold paper decorated with bunches of holly and tied with green ribbon appeared. She opened it, and on the lace-paper covering the candy was a card—"Frank Ayres." Amanda turned pale; she actually felt her limbs tremble under her; but all the while she was assuring herself that there was a mistake, that the candy did not belong to her. She reflected that there was another girl in the factory, working in another room, of the same surname, although her Christian name was different—Maud. This other girl was very pretty—a beauty some considered her. "This was meant for her," she said to herself, and at the same moment a deep, although ungrudging, jealousy of the other girl seized her. Amanda had good reasoning powers. She admitted that it was quite right and proper that Frank Ayres should send a Christmas token to this other girl in preference to her. She admitted that it was entirely right that the girl should have it instead of her. She was a good girl, besides being pretty and having all the graces which Amanda lacked. She had not one doubt but the box was intended for this other girl, and the more so because she herself knew quite well a young woman who was employed in the store from whence the candy came. She told herself, and with much show of reason, that this young woman, in preparing the package to be sent, had, from knowing her so well, absently confused the two names.

She carefully laid back the folds of lace-paper and looked at the dainty bonbons and fruits glacés. Then she replaced the paper, and neatly folded up the box in the outer wrappings and tied it with the gilt cord, after which she laid it on another table where it would not come to harm, and stood for a moment regarding it. It was only a box of candy, a gift which a man could send to any young woman without in the least compromising himself; it was so slight a matter that taking it seriously would in any case have been absurd, but she thought how she would have felt had it been really intended for her, and if Frank Ayres had sent it. There was something about the very uselessness of the thing which gave it a charm to her. She was not even very fond of sweets, but she had never had a Christmas present except those which savored of the absolutely essential, and which somehow missed something in being so essential. Of course there had been the holders and wash-cloths and dusters, and when her mother was alive they had been accustomed to give each other things which they really needed. That had been all. Amanda, reflecting, could not remember that she had ever had in her life, not even when she was a child, such an expensive and utterly needless gift as that box of candy. "Such a large box!" she considered, looking at it, "and such a lovely box in itself, and such a waste of ribbon, and if Frank Ayres had sent it, too!"

She began to imagine so intensely what her state of mind would have been in that case that her whole face changed; the downward curves at the corners of her mouth disappeared, she actually laughed. For a second she was as happy as if the box had actually been hers. Then her face sobered, but a change of resolution had come to her with that instant's taste of happiness on her own account. The sweet had been in her heart and relieved it of selfishness because of the joy of possession. One need not covet if one has, and the imagination of having had served her as well as the actuality, accustomed as she was to having little. She wondered how she could for a second have thought of depriving those poor cousins, those women who had had so little of the joys of life, of the Christmas gifts which she and her mother had always bestowed upon them. Her mother's dear reproach-ful face seemed to look upon her. She imagined the three women going to the post-office—the single one had a mile to go—and finding nothing, and her own heart ached with the ache of theirs. She seemed to put herself completely in their places, to change personalities with them. She looked at her clock and found that she had time enough, and hurried on her coat and hat, took the box of candy, and set out. The candy-store, with its windows radiant with the most charming boxes of bonbons, with evergreens and holly, was first on her way. She entered, and waited patiently for a chance to speak to the young woman whom she knew and who had been an old schoolmate of hers. She had to wait a few minutes, for the shop was packed with customers. Finally she found her chance, and approached the counter with the box.

"Alice," she said, in a low voice, almost a whisper, "here is something which has been sent to me from here by mistake." She spoke in a low tone both because she was embarrassed and because she was afraid that she might make trouble for her friend.

But the young woman, who was fair and plump, with a slightly imperious air, although she had greeted her pleasantly, stared at her, then at the box. "Why, I did not sell this, Amanda," she said. "I don't know anything about it." Then she called to another girl. "Nellie," she said, "did you sell this box of candy?"

There was a moment's lull in the rush of customers. The other young woman leaned her elbows on the counter and stared with distinct superciliousness at Amanda in her plain garb. She had an amazing bow at her throat, and her blond locks nearly reached Amanda's face with their fluffy scoop. She examined the box with an odd haughtiness which nothing could exceed. She might have been a princess of the blood examining a crown jewel. This girl who worked in a shoe-factory seemed to her immeasurably below her. She felt a contempt for the girl at her side because she treated her so pleasantly.

"Yes, I sold that box to Mr. Ayres," said she. "Why?" She raised her eyes in interrogation rather than pronounced the why.

"It does not belong to me," said Amanda. "It belongs to Miss Maud Dearborn instead of me."

"I am certain Mr. Ayres said Amanda," replied the girl, icily.

But Amanda had also a spirit of her own. She straightened herself. She pushed the box firmly toward the girl. "The box does *not* belong to me," she said, sternly. "Will you be kind enough to erase the Amanda and write Maud instead and have it sent to its proper address?—Good night, Alice." Then she walked out of the candy-store like a queen. She distinctly heard the haughty young woman say that she guessed there must have been a mistake, although she was almost sure he had said Amanda, for she could not imagine what any man in his senses would want to send a box of candy to a cross, homely old thing like that for.

But Amanda did not mind; she was quite accustomed to her own estimate of herself, which was so far from complimentary that its confirmation did not sting her as it might have otherwise done. She went on to the other stores, and bought a beautiful pair of blankets with a blue border—which she had sent by express—for Cousin Jane, a table-cloth for Cousin Maria, and a silk waist for Cousin Liza. Then she returned home and enclosed her slips of paper with her name and Christmas greetings with the waist and the table-cloth, and got them ready for the mail. She also wrote a letter to Cousin Jane, which she sent the next morning, that it might reach her at the same time the blankets arrived. Then she went to bed and thought of the delight which the other girl would feel when she received the box of candy from Mr. Frank Ayres. She seemed to enter so intensely into her state of mind that the same happiness came to her. The suggestion precipitated a dream. She dreamed, when at last she fell asleep, that she was the other Dearborn girl—the one with the pretty face—and that the candy had come to her, and she wondered how she could ever have thought she was anybody else. Then she awoke and remembered herself, and it was time to get up, although not yet light; still the unreasoning happiness had not yet gone.

She went to the shop, and saw Maud Dearborn, looking unusually pretty, standing near the office door. She was evidently waiting for Frank Ayres to come out, and, in fact, he did at that moment. "Thank you so much for the lovely box of candy," Amanda heard Maud say, in her pretty voice; then she passed on to her own room and took her place at her machine. She wondered a little when after a while Mr. Ayres came up to her and said good morning and asked her if she was quite recovered. She answered him quietly and resumed work, and heard the girls near her chuckle as he went away; and again the feeling of anger and injury that they should make a mock of one like her came over her. She reflected how she had gone her own way, and never knowingly hurt any one, and the feeling of revolt against a hard providence was over her. She thought of Maud Dearborn, and how prettily she had thanked Mr. Ayres, and again she seemed to almost change places with her. A great gladness for the other girl who was more favored than she irradiated her very soul. Then she fell to thinking of the joy of the cousins when they would receive their gifts. Her face relaxed, the expression of severity disappeared. She fairly smiled as she bent over her arduous, purely mechanical task. For the first time she seemed to realize the soul in that, as in all work, or rather the power in all work, for spiritual results. "If I did not have this work," she thought, "I could not have given those presents. I could not have made those poor souls happy."

That night when she went home she reflected with delight that the next day was a holiday, and she would be free of the humming toil of her hive of work for one day at least. She went directly up-stairs to her own room to wash her face and hands and remove her wraps before supper. The minute she entered the room she had, as she had the night before, that sense of something strange, almost the sense of a presence. She looked involuntarily at the little stand beside her bed, and there was another package of candy, directed plainly to her. She opened it with trembling fingers, and there was Frank Ayres's card. Even then she did not dare to understand. The thought, foolish as it was, flashed through her mind that Mr. Ayres might be making presents to all the girls, that she was simply one of many. Even as she stood divided between joy and uncertainty she heard a quick step on the stairs, and there was a knock on the door. The maid employed by the boarding-house mistress gave her a note from the young woman whom she knew in the candy-store. It was this:

"DEAR AMANDA,—Do, for goodness' sake, keep this box of candy. Mr. Ayres just bought it of me, and when I said Miss Maud Dearborn, he fairly snapped me up. I guess the other was for you fast enough. Guess you've made a mash.

ALICE."

Even the rude slang of the note did not disturb the joy of conviction that came to the girl. She knew that the present, the sweet, useless, very likely meaningless present, was hers. She realized the absurdity of her suspicion that Mr. Ayres was presenting two-pound boxes of candy to all the girls in the factory. She laughed aloud. She opened the box, and folded back the lace-paper, and gazed admiringly at the sweets. She no more thought of eating them than if they had been pearls and diamonds. She gazed at them, and she again seemed to see the foreman's handsome, laughing face.

Suddenly she made a resolution. There was a Christmas tree in the church that evening and she would go. She had not taken off her wraps. She hurried down-stairs and into the busy, crowded street. She went to a store where a young woman whom she knew worked at the lace-counter.

"See here, Laura," she said, "I want to buy a lace collar. I want to go to the tree to-night, and my dress is too shabby to wear without something to smarten it up a bit. But I can't pay you till Saturday night."

"Lord! that's all right," replied the young woman. She gave a curious glance at Amanda's face, and began taking laces out of a box. She looked again. "How well you do look!" she said; "and I heard you were laid up with a cold, too."

"My cold is all gone," replied Amanda. She selected a lace collar which would cost a third of her week's wages.

"Well, you *are* going in steep," said the young woman.

"I would rather not have any lace than cheap lace," Amanda replied.

"Well, I guess you are right. It don't pay in the long run. That will look lovely over your black dress. I wish I could go to the tree, but I can't get out; my steady will be there, too. You are lucky to work in a shop, after all."

"Maybe I am," laughed Amanda, as she went away with her lace collar.

When she got home there was a loud hum of voices from the dining-room, and an odor of frying beefsteak and tea and hot biscuits. She tucked her lace collar in her coat pocket and went in and drank a cup of tea and ate a biscuit. Then she hurried up to her room and got out her best black dress and laid it on the bed. Then she smoothed her hair, and gazed at herself a moment in her glass. She loosened the soft brown locks around her face, and saw that she was transformed. There was a pink glow on her cheeks; the smiling curves of her lips were entrancing. She put on her dress and fastened the lace collar, which hung in graceful folds over the shoulders, with a little jet pin which had been her mother's. Then she looked again at herself. She looked a beauty, and she wondered if she saw aright. She looked away from the glass, then looked again, and the same beautiful face smiled triumphantly back at her. She was meeting herself for the first time, and not only admiration and joy but tenderness was in her heart. The woman who sees herself beloved for the first time sees something greater and fairer in herself than she has ever seen. Amanda glanced at the beautiful box on the stand—she had not replaced the wrapping-paper,—and the gold of the box, decorated with holly, gleamed dully. She had become quite sure that Mr. Ayres would not have sent it to her unless he had singled her out from the others; she had become sure that the first box had been meant for her. She laughed aloud when she thought of the other Dearborn girl; then she felt sorry—so careful had she always been of money—that he had been obliged to buy another box,—of the most expensive candy, too. Then she put the box in her bureau drawer and locked it. The thought had come to her that the maid might enter the room and take a piece, and that would seem like sacrilege.

Amanda put on her coat and hat and went to the Christmas tree. She was rather late, and the gifts were nearly distributed. She took a seat at the back of the vestry, which was fragrant with evergreen. She listened to the names which were called out, and saw those called go forward for their presents. Her name was not called, and she did not expect it to be. She had from a side glance a glimpse of Frank Ayres near her. After the presents were distributed, and people began moving about, she felt rather than saw him coming toward her. She was quite alone on the settee.

"Good evening, Miss Dearborn," he said, and she turned quite sedately—she had much self-control.

"Good evening," she replied. Then she thanked him for his present. He laughed gayly, and yet with a certain tenderness of meaning.

"I meant the box that Miss Maud Dearborn got for you," he said, "but somehow there was a mistake in sending it."

"It was sent to me," replied Amanda, in a low voice, "but I thought that you could not have meant it for me."

"Why not?" asked Frank Ayres, gazing at her with an admiration which she had never seen in his eyes before. He was in reality thinking to himself that, much as he had liked her, he had never known she was so pretty.

Amanda stole a glance at him. "Oh, because," she said.

"Because what?"

"Why, I thought she was a girl you or any man would be more likely to send a box of candy to," she said, simply, and a soft blush made her face as pink as a baby's.

"Nonsense!" said Frank Ayres. "You underrate yourself." Then he added, "But a man rather likes a girl to underrate herself."

When Amanda went home that night, Frank Ayres went with her. When they reached the door of her boarding-house they stopped, and there was a pause.

"You must miss your home dreadfully since your mother died," he said.

"Yes, I do," replied Amanda.

"I have missed mine a good deal, too," Frank Ayres said. There was another pause. "I have been thinking pretty hard about setting up another one before long," he said, in a low, almost timid voice.

Amanda said nothing.

"I saw last week that the house you used to own was for sale," said Frank Ayres.

"Yes, it is, I believe," replied Amanda, faintly.

"It is a good house, just the kind I like."

"Yes, it is a good house."

There was another pause. Frank Ayres's face had lost its gay, laughing expression; he looked sober, afraid, yet determined. "May I come and see you sometime?" he asked.

"I shall be very glad to have you," replied Amanda, in a whisper.

They shook hands then, and Amanda went into the house. When she was in her own room she took the pretty box out of the drawer and sat with it in her lap, thinking about Frank Ayres and her mother, and kept Christmas holy.

The Witch's Daughter

It was well for old Elma Franklin that Cotton Mather had passed to either the heaven or hell in which he believed; it was well that the Salem witchcraft days were over, although not so long ago, or it would have fared ill with her. As it was, she was shunned, and at the same time cringed to. People feared to fear her. Witches were no longer accused in court, and put to torture and death, but human superstitions die hard. The heads thereof may be cut off, but their noxious bodies of fear and suspicions writhe long. People in that little New England village, which was as stiff and unyielding as its own poplar-trees which sentinelled so many of its houses, knew nothing of that making of horns which averts the evil eye. They shuddered upon their orthodox heights at the idea of the sign of the cross, but many would have fain taken refuge therein for the easing of their unquiet imaginations when they dwelt upon old Elma Franklin. Many a woman whispered to another under promise of strict secrecy that she was sure that Elma bore upon her lean, withered body the witch-sign; many a man, when he told his neighbor of the death of his cow or horse, nodded furtively toward old Elma's dwelling. In truth, old Elma's appearance alone, had it been only a few years ago, would have condemned her. Lean was she, and withered in a hard brown fashion like old leather. Her eyes were of a blue so bright that people said they felt like swooning before their glance; and what right had a woman, so old and wrinkled, with a head of golden hair like a young girl's? Her own hair, too, and she would wear no wig like other decent women of less than her age. And what right had she with that flower-like daughter Daphne?

Young creatures like Daphne are not born of women like Elma

125

Franklin, who must have been old sixteen years agone. Daphne was sixteen. Daphne had a Greek name and Greek beauty. She was very small, but very perfect, and finished like an ivory statue whose sculptor had toiled for his own immortality. Daphne had golden hair like her mother's, but it waved in a fashion past finding out over her little ears, whose tips showed below like the pointed petals of pink roses, and her chin and cheeks curved as clearly as a rose, and her nose made a rapture of her profile, and her neck was long and slowly turning, and her eyes were not blue like her mother's, but sweet and dark, and gently regardant, and her hands were as white and smooth as lilies, whereas hands had never been seen so knotted and wickedly veined as if with unholy clawing as her mother's.

Daphne led however, as lonely a life as her mother. People were afraid. Dark stories, vile stories, were whispered among that pitiless, bigoted people. Old Elma and Daphne lived alone in their poor little cottage, although in the midst of fertile fields, and they fed on the milk of their two cows, and the eggs of their chickens, and the vegetables of their garden, and the honey of their bees. Old Elma hived them when they swarmed with never any protection for that strange face and those hands of hers, and people said the bees were of an evil breed, and familiars of old Elma's, and durst not sting her. Young men sometimes cast eyes askance at Daphne, but turned away, and old Elma knew the reason why, and she hated them; for hatred prospered in her heart, coming as she did of a strong and fierce race. Elma combed her daughter's wonderful golden locks, and dressed her in fine stuff made of a store which she had in a great carved chest in the garret, and would have had the girl go to meeting where she could be seen and admired; but Daphne went once, and was ever after afraid to venture, because of the black looks cast upon her, which seemed to sear her gentle heart, for the girl was so gentle that she seemed to have no voice of insistence for her own rights. When her mother chid her, saying, with the disappointment of a great love, that she had with her own hands fashioned her wonderful gown of red shot with golden threads and embroidered with silver flowers, and had wrought with fine needlework her lace kerchief and her mitts and her scarf, and that it was a shame that she must needs, with all this goodly apparel, slink beside her own hearth and be seen of no one, the girl only kissed her mother on her leathery brown cheek, and smiled like an angel. Daphne was a maiden of few words, and that would have enticed lovers had it not been for her mother. However, at last came Harry Edgelake, and he was bolder than the rest, and the moment he set eyes upon the girl clad in green with a rose in her hair and a rose at her breast, spinning in a cool shadow at her mother's door, his heart melted, and he swore that he would wed her, came she of a whole witch-tribe. But Harry had more than he recked at first to deal with in the way of opposition. He came of a long line of eminent ministers of the Word, and his grandfather and father still survived, and were of the Cotton Mather strain. Although they talked none, they would, if the good old days had endured, have had old Elma up before the judges; for all the cattle in the precinct, and all the poor crops, and every thunder tempest and lightning stroke, and all strange noises they laid at her door, nodding at each other and whispering.

Therefore when it came to their ears that Harry, who had just come home from Harvard, and was to be, had he a call, a minister of the Word, like themselves, had been seen standing and chatting by the hour beside the witch's daughter as she spun in the shade with her golden head shining out in it like a star, he was sternly reasoned with. And when he heeded not the counsel of his elders, but was seen strolling down lovers' lane with the maid, great stress was laid to bear upon him, and he was sent away to Boston town, and Daphne watched and he came not, and old Elma watched the girl watch in vain, and her evil passions grew; for evil surely dwelt in her heart, as in most human hearts, and she had been sorely dealt with and badgered, and the girl was her one delight of life, and the girl's sorrow was her own magnified into the most cruel torture that a heart can bear and live.

And whether she were a witch or not, much brooding upon the suspicion with which people regarded her had made her uncertain of herself, and she owned a strange book of magic, over which she loved to pore when the cry of the hounds of her kind was in her ears, and she resolved one night, when a month had passed and she knew her daughter to be pining for her lover, that if she were indeed witch as they said, she would use witchcraft.

The moon was at the full, and the wide field behind her cottage, which had been shorn for hay for the cows, glittered like a silver shield, and upon the silver shield were little wheels also like silver woven by spiders for their prey, and strange lights of dew blazed out here and there like stars. And old Elma led her daughter out into the field, and Elma wore a sad-colored gown which made her passing like the passing of a shadow, and Daphne was all in white, which made her passing like that of a moonbeam; and the mother took her daughter by the arm, and she so loved her that she hurt her.

"Mother, you hurt me, you hurt me!" moaned Daphne, and directly the mother's grasp of the little fair arm was as if she touched a newborn babe.

"What aileth thee, sweetheart?" she whispered, but the girl only sobbed gently.

"It is for thy lover, and not a maid in the precinct so fair and good," said the mother, in her fierce old voice.

And Daphne sobbed again, and the mother gathered her in her arms.

"Sweetheart, thy mother will compel love for thee," she whispered, and the girl shrank away in fear, for there was something strange in her mother's voice.

"I want no witchery," she whispered.

"Nay, but this is good witchery, to call true love to true love."

"If love cannot be called else, I want not love at all."

"But, sweetheart, this is not black but white witchery."

"I want none, and besides—"

"Besides?"

The girl said no more, but the mother knew that it was because of her that the lover had fled, and not because of lack of love.

"See, sweetheart," said old Elma, "I know a charm."

"I will have no charm, mother; I tell thee I will have no charm."

"Sweetheart, watch thy mother cross the field from east to west and from north to south, and criss-cross like the spiders' webs, and see if thou thinkest it harmful witchcraft."

"I will not, mother," said the girl, but she watched.

And old Elma crossed the field from east to west and from north to south, and crisscrossed like the spiders' webs, and ever after her trailed lines of brighter silver than the dew which lay up the field, until the whole was like a wonderful web, and in the midst shone a great silver light as if the moon had fallen there, although still in the sky.

Then came old Elma to her daughter, and her face in the strange light was fair and young. "Daughter, daughter," said the mother, "but follow the lines of light thy mother's feet have made and come to the central light, and thy lover shall be there."

But the daughter stood in her place, like a white lily whose roots none could stir save to her death. "I follow not, mother," she said. "It would be to his soul's undoing, and better I love his soul and its fair salvation than his body and his heart in this world."

And the mother was silent, for she truly knew not as to the spell whether it concerned the soul's salvation.

But she had still another spell, which she had learned from her strange book. "Then stay, daughter," said old Elma, and straightway she crossed the paths of light which she made, and they vanished, and the meadow became as before, but in the midst old Elma stood, and said strange words under her breath, and waved her arms, while her daughter watched her fearfully. And as she watched, Daphne saw spring up, in the meadow in the space over which her mother's long arms waved, a patch of white lilies, which gave out lights like no lilies of earth, and their wonderful scent came in her face. And her mother hurried back, and in her hurrying was like a black shadow passing over the meadow.

"And go to the patch of lilies, sweetheart," she said, "and in the time which it takes thee to reach them thy lover will have gone over the forests and the waters, and he will meet thee in the lilies."

But Daphne stood firm in her place. "I go not, mother," she said. "It would be to his dear soul's undoing, and better I love his soul and his soul's heaven than I love him and myself."

Then down lay old Elma upon the silver shield of the meadow like a black shadow at her daughter's feet.

"Then is there but one way left, sweetheart," came her voice from among the meadow grasses like the love-song of a stricken mother-bird. "There is but one way, sweet daughter of mine. Step thou over thy mother's body, darling, and cross to the patch of lilies, and I swear to thee, by the Christ and the Cross and all that the meeting-folk hold sacred, that thou shalt have thy lover, and his soul shall not miss heaven, neither his soul nor thine."

"And thine?"

"I am thy mother."

And Daphne stood firm. "Better I love thee, mother," she said, "than heaven on earth with my lover; better I love thee than his weal or mine in this world, better than all save his dear soul."

"I tell thee, sweet, cross my body, and his soul and thy soul shall be safe."

"But thy life on earth, and thy soul?"

"I am thy mother."

"I will not go."

Then came a wail of despair from old Elma at her daughter's feet upon the silver shield of the meadow, and then she was raised up by young Harry Edgelake, and she stood with her leathern old face like an angel's for pure joy and forgetfulness of self. For her daughter stood in her lover's arms and his voice sounded like a song.

"Nothing on earth and nothing in heaven shall part me from thee, who hold my soul dearer than myself, and thy mother dearer than thyself, for, witch or no witch, thy mother has shown me thy angel in the meadow to-night," he said.

Old Elma stood watching them with her face of pure joy, and all the fierceness and the bitter grief of injury received from those whom she had not injured faded from her heart. She forgot the strange book which she had studied, she forgot her power of strange deeds, she forgot herself, and remembered nothing, nothing save her daughter and her love, and such bliss possessed her that she could stand no longer upon the silver shield of the meadow. She sank down slowly as a flower sinks when its time has come before the sun and the wind which have given it life, and she lay still at the feet of her daughter and the youth, and they stooped over her and they knew that she had been no witch, but a great lover.

The Horn of Plenty

"It would," said Mrs. J. M. Armstrong, "be enough sight worse to have your horn of plenty overflow than to have it half full. It is natural to be swamped in misery, but sort of monstrous to be swamped in the good things of life."

Mrs. Armstrong's sister, Lucilla Childs, who had also a strain of philosophy, spoke. "A horn of plenty," said she oracularly, "could not in the nature of things be lacking in anything. If it were, it would not be a horn of plenty."

"That is true," said Mrs. J. M. Armstrong, "I did not make myself clear. I ought to have said folks should get the exact size of their horns of plenty, then there would never be any complaining. We would always know when we had enough."

"Some people," stated Lucilla, "may not own horns of plenty."

"Nobody was ever born without one in the soul," answered Mrs. Armstrong.

"I see you are hitting me," said Lucilla.

"Yes," assented Mrs. Armstrong calmly; "hope I hit hard enough."

"You don't hit hard enough to upset my horn of plenty," returned Lucilla. She laughed, but her blue eyes remained strained and sad. Lucilla was Mrs. Armstrong's half-sister, and young enough to be her daughter. Her mother had been the second wife, a mere girl, who had died soon after Lucilla's birth. Lucilla was a beautiful girl, or young woman. She was a little past thirty. She was very fair, and her skin was wonderful. She wore a blue dress of soft wool, and the blue of her costume was like that of her eyes, only one was opaque, and the others were translucent with light like jewels. Lucilla stared at nothing as if it were something of tremendous interest, after a peculiar fashion of her own, and her eyes were very round and large, like a baby's when it first glimpses something which awakens its mind. Lucilla looked very young, so young as to be pathetic; she was a little anemic, and there was a frown of dissent, although of gentle dissent, between her eyes. She even stooped a bit as though under an invisible burden of grief, sitting with her slenderness hunched upon itself.

Her sister Abby was paring apples. Her hands were never idle, Lucilla's always were. Lucilla at that time of her life seemed pure emotion and mentality, her sister was more complex. "I am going to speak very plainly," said Mrs. Armstrong. "You have been home six weeks now. You seemed to me not to have enjoyed your visit with Ada Green in New York."

"I never said I did not."

"If you would say things right out, it would be better for yourself, and everybody else," returned Mrs. Armstrong.

"Well, I did not have such a very enjoyable visit," said Lucilla with a passive agreement.

"Why?"

"Well, I don't know exactly."

"Didn't Ada and her husband do everything they could to make you have a good time?"

"Oh, yes, everything, sister Abby."

"Well, I suppose then that you thought your horn of plenty wasn't as full as theirs."

Lucilla colored sweetly. "I would not have married Winslow Green if he had been the last man in the world," said she, "and as for Ada's baby, it is a very large, squashy baby, and has always to wear an unpleasant bib, and cries all the time. Ada has a lovely home, though, and she does seem happier than almost anybody I know."

"It is the whole of it, then, that you think of?"

Lucilla colored more vividly, but the blue light of her eyes was defiant and virginal. "Why not?" she demanded.

"I don't suppose there is any why not. I suppose it is only natural. But I do suppose that perhaps your horn of plenty can only hold just what you have without slopping over; do you suppose, for instance, that it would hold Armstrong?"

Lucilla paled a little and stared at her sister, for Armstrong, who had deserted his wife for another younger woman, and decamped for parts unknown, years before, had been a tabooed topic.

"I suppose," said Abby Armstrong, "that you think my horn of plenty does not hold Armstrong—well, it does, and it is a pretty good load. You see, I was happy with Armstrong before—well, before that other woman came along, and I can tell you one thing, Lucilla—a happiness that is passed takes up a terrible amount of room in a horn of plenty; sometimes it crowds out happiness which hasn't passed. Well, you know Armstrong, when he went away, was six feet tall and weighed about two hundred, and then there were the two little girls who died. Do you think your horn of plenty would hold all that?"

Lucilla did not smile, and the miserable parallels of woe remained on her forehead between the lovely loose puffs of fair hair. Still, her pretty mouth dropped; still, her blue eyes gazed straight ahead as if at a landscape of terrible futures.

Abby Armstrong looked at her shrewdly. "I think," said she, "that you need somebody with horse sense to translate your own situation in life into language that you can read. You are not the first girl whose life has been written, as far as she was concerned, in one of the unknown tongues. Now here you are a young, handsome woman."

"I am over thirty," said Lucilla.

Her sister sniffed. "Thirty! You are a baby. Lord! you speak as if the world had come to an end because you are thirty. I can tell you that you are a mighty young thing in a mighty old world. And you don't look a day over twenty, even when you scowl and pucker and do your best to make lines on a face that's like a rose and a lily, and that the Lord intended to last nice and smooth till you are a good deal older than you are now. Now you are going to hear some pretty plain language for the first time in your life. I know it's the first time. Your mother died when you were a baby, and our father died when you were pretty young, and anyway he sort of spoke in precepts, and didn't fire the truth at folks straight. He hit all creation, but not anybody in particular. I used to think it was a great pity that father hadn't lived in Bible times. He might have written a chapter in Ecclesiastes, or a psalm, though possibly I am wicked to think of such a thing. I know father wasn't inspired, although he was a very good man, with a good mind, and enough sight better than King David, or King Solomon in all his glory, as to his acts. They may have meant better than father, but they came short sometimes, if they did sing songs about it and lay down the laws. Now I am going to speak plain. You are a young woman and as pretty as a picture, and you have all your wits and plenty to live on, if you are careful. You can do about as you are a mind to—travel or stay at home—and if it is too quiet here for you, you can start up any time you want to and have a change to where it's livelier. There's nobody to say you shall or you shan't. You ought to be as happy as the day is long, and here you are eating nothing and looking glum, just because you think you haven't quite all that ought to come to you, when you don't exactly know what that is for the life of you. The first thing you know you will turn out exactly the way Rebecca Reddy did."

"I don't know what you mean, sister."

"Well, you just sit still and wait, and I'll tell you what I mean. You have so much to be thankful for that it is not safe to rebel because you haven't got more. Now I've got these apples pared, and I'm going to roll out my pie crust, and I'm going to tell you about Rebecca Reddy, and you can see what you think then. Another thing you've got to be thankful for is this nice kitchen to sit in, when it's snowing the way it is outside. There isn't such a kitchen in this village, if I do say so. It is the biggest for one thing, and I knew what I was about when I had the floor painted yellow. If the sun isn't shining it don't show."

Abby Armstrong rose, and made preparations for her pastry, and her sister looked about with a listless and silent assent. The kitchen was lovely. Abby Armstrong, in spite of her provincialism, had kept up in many respects with her day and generation. Her kitchen was one evidence of it. It was large, with floor painted a clear pumpkin yellow. The walls were papered with yellow and covered with glass. The glass walls had almost caused a scandal in the village, and the man who had done the work had been in his inmost soul afraid of the woman who had instigated it. But the result was beautiful and sanitary. Tables covered with glass and holding pots of flowers stood in the two south windows. Abby's kitchen table was painted yellow and glass-covered. There were two rocking-chairs upholstered with yellow and white chintz, and the other chairs were yellow. She had a corner cupboard with glass doors, containing yellow and white ware, and cleats on the walls were hung with shining cooking utensils. There was even a yellow cat in a round coil of slumber in one of the rocking-chairs.

Abby wore an indigo blue dress and apron, and her hair, still yellow, shone compactly like a little gold ball at the top of her head. She had been pretty, and now was charming like a dried yellow flower which had kept its shape, and lost nothing except the summer juices at the advent of frost. When she had her pastry under way she continued talking to her sister, telling her story in a whimsical, tender fashion. "Rebecca, she was old Squire Reddy's daughter, and she lived in the big white house on the hill where Doctor Lane and his son Sammy live now. I don't know that Squire Reddy would be called rolling in riches nowadays, but he was a rich man when Rebecca was a girl. She was a grown-up young lady when I was a little girl going to school past her house every day, dressed in my long-sleeved apron and sunbonnet. Old Squire Reddy was looked up to as the richest man in the town, and coming from the best of families, all college-educated men. And his house was built in the fear of the Lord, with nails that were driven in to hold, and plaster put on to stay. In those days, too, it didn't cost all creation to live, and live well. Rebecca certainly did live well in her father's time. I used to see her sitting on her front porch in her beautiful organdie muslins, with her long curls falling over her shoulders, and she was as smooth and handsome as a cat that has always been stroked the right way. She was a beauty, and the young men knew it. I used to see them sitting on the porch looking at her as if she were an angel with a harp and crown. There was one young man always there. His name was Thomas Dean. He was as good as gold, though he was very small, and he had a handsome face. He was well-to-do, too. He was a lawyer. He didn't have much practice, but he didn't need it. His father had left him plenty to be comfortable. Thomas set his eyes by Rebecca. He never made any secret of it, and folks used to sort of laugh. Sometimes I have wondered if that was the reason why Rebecca didn't seem to care more for him. He was so within her reach always, and she knew it, and she knew that everybody else knew it, that he didn't look worth so much to her. Anyway, he used to sit on her porch whether the young men were there or not, and he was always ready to fetch and carry for her, if nobody else was handy; but time went on, and Rebecca didn't get married to him or anybody else. There was some talk about her falling in love with a grand young gentleman once when she visited in Boston, and his not fancying her, handsome as she was, but nobody ever really knew. It was all surmise. I always thought that it was just because she set such store by her own self, and thought more of her own self than anybody else, until her father died, and she got old. I say old. She wasn't exactly old, but it was as if she had stood still and let youth run past her. She began to have an old-fashioned look, and she seemed older than the women of her own age who had married, even though they were all dragged down by hard work and children. I suppose people make so much allowance for hard work and children in a girl's looks that they do a queer kind of example in subtraction, and think of her as being just as young and pretty as she ever was without them. Finally she didn't have any beaux left. Thomas Dean always kept up visiting her, but folks stopped thinking of him as being her beau. He just worshiped the ground she trod on, and seemed something like it, I guess, to her—that is, for a long while. The time comes once in a while when folks who have been trampling the ground all their lives look down and see flowers worth more than the stars in the sky to them. I guess it was that way with Rebecca, but I am getting ahead of my story.

"Rebecca was a good deal older than I was. You can't remember her at all I know. I wish you could. It seems like you're missing a beautiful picture that I have hanging right before my eyes. I wish you could remember her the way she used to look, coming up the church aisle on Sabbath days, dressed in the sweetest organdies and the prettiest bonnets with wreaths of roses in the summers, and winters in beautiful rich silks and mantillas edged with fur. Rebecca had very handsome clothes as long as her father lived. Then they found out that he had bought a lot of land that wasn't worth anything and sold good securities to pay for it. I suppose as he grew older he was childish, and played with his dollars as if they had been blocks—built up things just to see them tumble down. When everything was settled, there wasn't much left for poor Rebecca, although there was enough.

"She had the house and a little money at interest, enough to pay taxes and just keep her going. There wasn't anything over for new clothes, so it was lucky she had such a store of them. It would have been luckier, though, if she had had sense enough to wear them the way they were, or had any knack at fixing them over. She didn't have a mite. Every time the fashion changed, Rebecca would try to make her clothes over, and they were always sights. It was all anybody could do not to laugh right out in meeting when Rebecca walked up the aisle after she had been fixing over her dresses. If she had only let them alone. Such beautiful things as she had—India shawls and lace shawls, and everything—but she made over one India shawl into a coat, and it was enough to make a cat laugh. But Rebecca Reddy wasn't satisfied with what a higher Providence had lotted out to her, and she reached up beyond her height for more, and pulled things all to pieces, and lost her own balance.

"There she had a beautiful old house to live in, and enough money at interest to pay the taxes and keep it in repair, and she had to pity herself, and complain, and get herself and everybody else stirred up. People used to drop in to see her a good deal, and she used to neighbor a lot as she grew older, and all she talked about was her deprivations and her hardships. I suppose she was honest enough about it. She had been such a beauty and a darling that she felt puzzled and injured because she didn't have what she knew she wanted and didn't know she wanted. Anyway, she got the whole town up in arms over her hard lot. Everybody was pitying her and thinking she had an awful time. She never lost a pretty little way she had, and she coaxed everybody round to her way of thinking until we were all about as mad as she was herself that she couldn't go dressed in the top notch of style and take trips round the world and live on roast swans. It was about a week before Thanksgiving, a good many years ago, that Aurelia Ames came to see me about Rebecca, and she shed tears. Aurelia was one of the sweetest women that ever lived, and most of her tears were for the troubles of other folks. When one came to think of it fair and square, Aurelia hadn't had any too fine a time in this world herself. Her husband had got the old-fashioned consumption before her two little girls were grown up, and she had had to dressmake. Then just when her husband had finally died, and she could draw a long breath, because, though she had thought a lot of him, he had been an awful care, and cross as a bear all the time, one of her girls got married to a worthless sort of chap, and had a baby and died, and her husband skipped, and Aurelia had to take the child. Then the other girl, who was a real help to her mother, got consumption, the quick kind, and died, and Aurelia wasn't very strong herself, and working hard to support the baby, and the baby wasn't a pretty child, and sick a good deal, and when it was well chock full of mischief, but Aurelia never seemed to think she was an object of pity, not even for herself. So in she comes and shed tears over Rebecca Reddy. 'Poor soul,' says she. 'There she was born Squire Reddy's daughter, and used to have everything, and she can't even have a turkey for her Thanksgiving dinner.' All Aurelia was going to have was a roast of pork, but she didn't seem to think of that, and all I was going to have was a chicken, but I must say I didn't think of that myself. I remember that I felt about as much wrought up as Aurelia did over Rebecca. I don't think I shed any tears. I never was easy to cry, but I was wrought up. 'It is dreadful,' says I. You see, I called to mind that beautiful girl sitting all dressed up with her beaux around her on her front porch when I was going by to school, and I remembered how grand the great dining room in the squire's house was, with its Turkey carpet, and mahogany furniture, and great sideboard, and solid silver service, and willow ware, and pictures with wide gold frames, and the dinners Rebecca must have been used to, and it did seem rather dreadful to think of her sitting down on Thanksgiving Day to eat a hen that she had raised herself, or most likely it would have been a rooster. She would have kept the hens, of course. But Aurelia, she put it hen. It did sound more pitiful. She just sat and wept in a soft, quiet way that made me feel about as sorry for her as for Rebecca. 'To think of that poor soul, brought up as she was, not having even a turkey—nothing but a he·n,' says Aurelia, in that lovely trembling voice of hers. Then I sat up straight. 'If you don't think she will be offended she shall have the very best turkey that I can buy at Peters's,' says I.

"'She needn't know it—that is, she needn't know who sent it,' says Aurelia. 'I thought I would send her a couple of my mince pies, with just a line saying they came from a constant old friend and admirer, not because she needed them, but just because she lived alone, and might not be making mince pies just for herself. I haven't got it worded just right yet.'

"I said I thought it was a good plan, and I would send the turkey, and would write something after Aurelia's plan to go with it. Aurelia went home a little comforted, but I could see her wipe her eyes now and then as she went down the street. If everybody were as tender-hearted as Aurelia Ames was, one-half of creation would drown out the other half with tears of pity for its troubles. As I look back I think Aurelia was almost too tender-hearted. I wasn't so much so, but I think sometimes such things are sort of catching. There really was no more hardship for Rebecca to have a chicken for her Thanksgiving dinner than for me, but it looked so then, and I couldn't seem to see it any other way.

"So I went to Peters's market. We always called it Peters, but Sam Rumson kept it. Peters had moved out West long before. I didn't get to the market till two days before Thanksgiving. I had a bad cold, and when I did go I was a little afraid I might be careless. But I kept thinking of poor Rebecca Reddy with nothing for her Thanksgiving dinner but a hen, and I bundled up and I went, though it was a raw day. When I got to the market, Rumson had just two turkeys left, one was big enough for a hotel, weighed somewhere around eighteen pounds, and the other wasn't worth looking at, not much bigger than a good-sized chicken, with a long, thin neck, and all bristling with pin feathers, as miserable-looking a turkey as any I ever set eyes on. 'Seems to me you have pretty well sold out your turkeys,' says I to Sam Rumson, and he grinned. 'Well, it's near time to,' says he.

"'Haven't you got any except these two?' says I, looking at the big one and the little skinny one.

"'These are all I have left,' says Rumson. Then he looks at the big one. 'That's the finest bird I've had brought in this year,' says he. 'That is a prize bird for a State fair, that is.'

"'But I don't want a prize bird for a State fair,' says I. 'I only want a turkey for one woman, and I should think she could never live long enough to dispose of that, even if he kept.'

"'Keep all right,' says Rumson. He was a sharp one. 'It's cold enough now to keep anything.'

"'That's so,' says I, 'but I never heard of buying a turkey that size for one woman.'

"'I've seen women that eat as hearty as men,' says Rumson, 'and this bird will make mighty good eating.'

"Well, the outcome of it was I was goose enough to buy that turkey.

He was big enough to send to the President, weighed over eighteen pounds, and I sent with it, written real nice on gilt-edged paper, a note. I can remember every word of it. I made it up when I was housed with my cold. This was what I wrote: 'Miss Rebecca Reddy, Dear Madam—Please accept from an old friend this slight token of a life-long admiration and respect, and may it conduce to a happier Thanks-giving than you would otherwise have had.' I wasn't quite satisfied with what I wrote. I did wish I had your father to word it for me, and I must say I felt kind of tickled when I thought of calling that mon-strous turkey a 'slight' token. It struck me, whatever else he was, he wasn't slight. When I told Rumson to have the turkey sent to Miss Rebecca Reddy, I noticed his face change a little. He looked as if he'd started to laugh, then choked it back, and acted as solemn as a dea-con. I paid him for that turkey, and went home as fast as I could, because it was getting late, and I was afraid of catching more cold. I stopped in the drug store and got some horehound drops and went right home. I had my little Thanksgiving work about done, a few pies made, and the chicken was all ready to stuff next day. After I had had my supper, I sat down and read the night paper, then I got to thinking hard about that big turkey, and Rebecca Reddy, and then I felt sort of dizzy with it all. I began to wonder what I had to be thankful for myself. I had enough to live on and a little over, but not much, and I was all alone, and I had influenza. I began to feel sort of complaining myself. Then all of a sudden I gave it all up. Says I to myself: 'It's just right and as it should be that you have what you have. It's your slice of the good things of life. Take it and hold your tongue, or you'll get something worse.'

"After I had finished the paper, I read a while in a real interesting storybook I had from the village library, and sucked my horehound drops, and toasted my feet. Then I went to bed and had a good night's rest, and when I waked up next morning my cold was about gone, and I went to work stuffing my chicken and making a little pudding, and was as happy as could be, though every now and then the queer, puzzled feeling about Rebecca Reddy and that whopping turkey I had sent her would come over me. I remembered how Aurelia had shed tears, and how the whole village was harrowed up over Rebecca, and I could not just understand it all.

"Well, Thanksgiving morning came. It was a beautiful day. I thought I would go to meeting. I knew I could leave the stove so the chicken wouldn't burn, and I had just got it in the oven, and was going upstairs to get dressed, when in comes Aurelia as pale as a sheet and all of a-tremble. 'Oh,' says she, 'do come over to that poor soul's just as quick as you can! Get the camphor bottle and come. I've got a bottle of my blackberry wine. I don't know as it will do a mite of good.'

"'What are you talking about?' says I.

"'Oh,' says she, and sort of sobs: 'Poor Rebecca!'

"'What about her?' says I.

"'She's got a bad spell,' says Aurelia. 'Do come quick as you can! I didn't fetch my camphor bottle. Maria Liscom just run in and told me. Her little girl had been over to carry some celery, and she found that poor soul in a spell, and she run all the way home to tell her ma. Maria has gone right over there.'

"'How about the doctor?' says I, getting my shawl and knit hood out of the sitting-room closet.

"'Maria sent her Lilly for the doctor,' says Aurelia. 'Have you got the camphor bottle?'

"I had a good-sized camphor bottle, and I hugged it up under my shawl and we started on a run for the Reddy house. On the way the doctor passed with his old horse at a gallop. 'Oh, dear; oh, dear!' says Aurelia. 'There goes Doctor Simson, but I know it's too late. Poor Rebecca!'

"'She isn't dead yet,' says I, all out of breath.

"'You don't know. Oh, you don't know,' says Aurelia.

"I certainly didn't know, but I remember feeling thankful that she couldn't have had time to even cook that big turkey, let alone eat him, so if she was dead, I hadn't killed her. Then we went on till we come in sight of Squire Reddy's, and there was a whole crowd of folks standing around the front door and going in, and horses and buggies were hitched outside the fence beside the doctor's.

"When Aurelia and I got to the door we heard what everybody standing there was listening to. It was a queer noise. It wasn't crying and it wasn't laughing, and it wasn't groaning, and it wasn't talking—at least not then, but it was something betwixt them all.

"'She must be dreadful sick,' says Clara Todd. Clara was a pretty young girl, and she had run without her hat, and her yellow hair was ruffling all over her head, and her cheeks were pale and her blue eyes big.

"'It is a dreadful spell,' gasps Aurelia. 'She never will get over it.'

"Then Aurelia and I went through the crowd into the house. As soon as I went in I smelled celery and cake and spice. The whole house smelled rich and sweet. Folks were standing peeking into the dining room, and Aurelia and I headed for there. There lay Rebecca on the floor, with the doctor down on his knees feeling her pulse, and she was keeping right on making those awful noises, but in spite of my feeling so scared about her, I couldn't help fairly jumping at the sight that room was, and the sight the sitting room was—the door stood open—and the sight the hall was. It did look for all the world like a county fair, or a great grocery establishment. Chickens and turkeys and roasts of pork and hams were lying all around. The air seemed fairly bristling with those stiff fowls' legs. And there were bunches of celery everywhere and stacks of pies and cakes and puddings, and nice little glass dishes of jelly, and bowls full of nuts and raisins, and vegetables. There were bushels of onions and turnips and potatoes and beets. There were hubbard squashes and pumpkins. There were baskets of apples and oranges and eggs, and paper bags full of goodness knew what. I never had seen anything like it. I felt as if I might have a spell myself. 'What in creation does it all mean?' says I to Aurelia. Then she gives me a nudge and sort of pointed with her chin, and I looked, and there was poor Thomas Dean. He had an enormous paper bag under his arm, and the paper had broken and some nuts and candy were tumbling out. There Thomas Dean stood looking at that woman he had worshiped ever since he knew what worship meant having a spell, and the tears were rolling right down over his cheeks. Thomas Dean had kept his looks better than Rebecca had done. He was a real handsome little man, and he was so good and so worried over his precious Rebecca.

"Aurelia looked at him, then at me, and the tears ran down her own cheeks. 'She must have had all this sent in,' says Aurelia, sort of choking, 'and it must have been too much for her.'

"That was exactly what had happened. Rebecca had had her piece of pie, that Providence thought suited to her, lotted out to her, and she had rebelled, and this was the outcome. Doctor Simson looks round finally and sees me, and I guess he knew I was to be depended on, for he calls out real rough—he was a pretty rough-spoken old man—'Mrs. Armstrong, for God's sake, come here and shut the doors and keep all the rest of the fools out.'

"When I came to think of it afterward, it didn't sound so very complimentary to me—sounded as if he classed me in with the rest, but I did just as he told me to. I faced round on the others, and I says: 'You all hear what the doctor says,' and with that the folks seemed to scurry out like a parcel of hens, and I locked the doors. When I turned round, though, there was Thomas Dean left. He had sort of huddled into a corner, and there he stood, staring with his pitiful brown eyes, holding his paper bag, with the things all dropping out of it. Doctor Simson saw him, and he sort of laughed. 'You are the biggest fool of all, Thomas,' says he, 'but you can stay. Now, Abby Armstrong, get me a tumbler half full of water.'

"I had to slip out into the kitchen for that, and the folks were all out in the entry staring, and the kitchen was heaped up with things worse than the other rooms. There was a turkey half stuffed on the table, and my big turkey was on the floor, and Rebecca's cat was smelling it, and I drove her away. I got the water, and went back, and locked the door after me, and the doctor dropped some medicine into the tumbler. Then he lifted poor Rebecca's head, and it actually waggled, and he fairly yelled at her: 'Here, you, stop this confounded noise and drink this,' and Thomas Dean gave a sort of leap forward, and Doctor Simson shouted at him: 'Keep away, man. It is the only way to treat her.' Then the doctor yelled at Rebecca again: 'Here, you, drink this or—' and poor Rebecca, she stopped and swallowed the medicine as meek as a lamb. But in a second, after she had got her wind, she talked connectedly. 'Oh,' says she, in that high, screeching, cackling voice, that sounded like a parrot's. 'Oh, oh! Twenty-seven turkeys, fourteen chickens, seven roasts of pork, sixteen hams, eighteen cakes, fifty-three pies. Oh, twenty-two!' Then the doctor shook her, though Thomas Dean made as if he would knock him down for it. 'You let me alone, Thomas,' says Doctor Simson. 'I know what I am about.' Then he shook her again, and she stared at him like a helpless baby. 'You just stop,' says he, and she did stop.

"'Now,' says he to me, 'you do seem to have a few wits left. Thomas and I will help her upstairs, and you can undress this woman and get her to bed.'

"It was lucky that there was a staircase running out of that room beside the one in the front entry. Doctor Simson and Thomas Dean—Thomas had set his paper bag down on the floor, and it was slowly collapsing, while nuts and raisins and oranges and all sorts of things gathered round it—helped Rebecca upstairs, and I got her undressed and put her to bed. I don't know what Doctor Simson had given her—he had the name of giving real strong medicine—but her head hadn't more than touched the pillow before she was quiet, and she sunk right off to sleep, like a baby. I heard afterward that the doctor said he had never seen a worse case of hysterics, and she had a weak heart and it might have been dangerous.

"When I got back downstairs, Doctor Simson was talking to the folks. 'Now,' says he, 'all of you take what you have brought, or sent here, and get it home. I have been as big a fool as anybody else, and pretty near killed a woman I've known since she was knee-high and always thought a good deal of. I knew Rebecca had enough to get along with, and that she was only amusing herself nursing her grievances instead of a baby, and didn't want to part with them, and I sent her a turkey, when she would enough sight rather have had one of her own chickens, and thought while she ate it that she was a blessed martyr. My turkey is the one she was fixing to cook. I'll leave that, but the rest of you sort out what you have sent her and get it out of this house, or I won't answer for the consequences.'

"Well, they just hustled around, and it was like a moving grocery establishment. Thomas Dean left his paper bag and went home, walking sort of slow, with his head bent, but everybody else took away their contributions. Aurelia and I stayed and finished dressing the turkey and getting the rest of the dinner started. Then Aurelia took hold of the neck of my big turkey, and I took hold of the feet, and we carried him out in the woodshed. 'I will get Sammy Joyce to come with his express wagon and get him by and by,' says I; 'then you and your grandchild come over Sunday and help eat him. He'll keep.'

"We finished getting Rebecca's dinner, and by that time Susan Jones, the nurse, had come. Doctor Simson had sent her. She said as soon as Rebecca waked up, she would see that she ate her dinner, and she had seen a great many cases of hysterics and she knew just what to do. Then Aurelia and I went home."

Lucilla had been listening interestedly. "Is that all?" said she.

"No," said her sister. "Rebecca Reddy, she got married to Thomas Dean the next June, and came out bride the first Sunday in a beautiful old organdie that she hadn't made over. It had a sort of running pattern of roses over it, and the skirt was full and just showed the little pointed tips of her feet when she stepped up the church aisle with Thomas, and she wore a narrow green ribbon round her waist, and a big hat trimmed with lilacs, and a fall of white lace over the brim, and she looked beautiful, like a rose that had been freshened up in some queer kind of water of the spirit. As for Thomas Dean, he looked as if he had reached the goal that he had been looking forward to all his life. Then they lived together in the old Squire Reddy house, and were as happy as could be, and they both died within a week of each other, and are buried in the Reddy lot with myrtle all over their graves, and I for one don't doubt that they are happy together in heaven. Rebecca must have liked Thomas all the time, only she was looking too high, and missed the flower at her feet for the sake of straining after the star in the sky that maybe wasn't worth while if she had got it."

Lucilla looked at her sister, and smiled with a charming little shamed blush. "Maybe I am like Rebecca Reddy," said she.

Her sister looked puzzled. "I don't know what you mean, I guess, Lucilla."

"Maybe I have been staring at stars, which I wouldn't have any use for if I got them, and not taking the flower at my feet that I really need to round out my horn of plenty," said Lucilla, "for my horn of plenty has not been quite complete after all, sister."

"I don't know what you mean now."

Lucilla's blush deepened. "I mean Sammy Lane," said she.

Abby laughed. "You mean Sammy Lane is the flower?"

Lucilla laughed, too, a little nervously. "I suspect he always has been," said she, "but you see, Abby, I got accustomed to thinking he was just Sammy, and he has always been at my feet, and when I went to New York I saw men who were not just Sammy, and had not always been at my feet, and though I didn't really want them, I got more unsettled, but now I think I may as well make up my mind that a flower which will always be at its best for me is about all I need, though Sammy is a funny kind of flower." Lucilla laughed again, and Abby also.

"Sammy is rather a good-sized flower," said she. "You might as well call him a tree."

"But that does away with your lovely horn-of-plenty idea," said Lucilla. "No, Sammy is a flower, and I'll look no higher than Sammy for the rest of my life."

"You will have a good home and a good husband," said Abby with a little sigh, "and you will never have to fill your horn of plenty with lost happiness, as some do, unless you lose to find, and that is not really losing."

"I saw Sammy last night at Lizzie's," said Lucilla, "and he asked me again coming home, and I told him I would give him his answer to-day."

"That is why you put on your blue dress?"

"Yes."

"When do you expect him?"

"Any time now. He had to make some calls over in Amity this afternoon, and he said he would stop on his way home."

"I hope he won't get the medicines mixed wrong, because he doesn't know exactly what you will say."

"Sammy will never get the medicines mixed wrong, no matter what I say," returned Lucilla rather proudly. "I think possibly that is what makes Sammy a flower." Lucilla had all the time been stealthily peering out of the window through the drifting veil of the northeast snowstorm to the obliterated road. Now she saw a shadowy movement through the gray blue of the storm. "I think he is coming now," said she.

"Take him into the parlor," said Abby Armstrong, "and ask him to dinner to-morrow."

Lucilla ran out with a flutter of blue skirts, and Abby Armstrong continued her homely tasks, which are as the accompaniment to the melody of love in life. "To think she was just fretting because she didn't know what she really wanted was hers all the time," she thought.

Abby Armstrong listened to the hum of tender voices from the parlor, and commenced beating eggs in a yellow bowl.

She had a restrained but poetical soul. She seemed to see her young sister holding in her two fair hands a gilded metaphorical horn of plenty, crowned with young Sammy Lane's handsome face set about with flower petals.

And she saw in the rapturous grasp of her own heart her happy past days and others happy beyond belief waiting for her.

"Everybody has all they really need for the good of their own souls if they count up the past and future as well as the present," Abby Armstrong said quite aloud, and in her voice was a true chord of thanksgiving.

A Guest in Sodom

Yes that was Benjamin Rice. He has been that way ever since the affair of the automobile. His mind was run over and killed by that machine, if minds can be run over and killed, and sometimes I think they can. I have known Benjamin Rice ever since we were boys together, and he was smart enough, but he never quite got through his head the wickedness of the world he had been born into. He thought everybody else was as good and honest as he was, and when he found out he was mistaken, it was too much for him. His wife feels just as I do about it.

"That automobile was too much for pa," she often says. "Poor pa didn't make a god of his money, but he knew the worth of it, through he and his father before him workin' so hard to get a little laid by, and losin' so much was an awful shock to him; but that wasn't the worst of it. Findin' out what an awful wicked place this world he was livin' in was, and what kind of folks there was in it, just broke his heart."

Benjamin's daughter Lizzie says the same thing.

"Yes, that car just broke poor pa's heart," says she. Lizzie calls it car instead of automobile. Sometimes she calls it motor-car. Lizzie has had advantages. Her father didn't spare money where she was concerned. She went to the Means Academy in Rockland, and then her father bought a type-writer for her, and she took lessons. She hasn't worked for money yet, and I don't suppose she needs to, but she may, if she don't get married young; for she favors her father's folks, and they don't like to spend and get nothin' back.

I don't know whether it was mostly on Lizzie's account that Benjamin got that car (guess I will call it car, like her; it's easier) or on his own. For quite a while Benjamin had been sayin' to me sort of mys-

148

terious: "One of these days, Billy, I'm goin' to spend a little money for something extra. I've never had anything that I could do without, and I would like *one* thing, and I'm goin' to have it." When he said that, Benjamin would look real decided for him. Take him in the long run, he was a real meek, mild-spoken kind of man. He was good-lookin' too, with handsome blue eyes, and a high forehead, and a real fair complexion. I always thought Benjamin wasn't an appropriate name for him. He ought to have been christened Joseph. He was just the sort to let his brothers chuck him into a pit and take away his coat of many colors, if he owned one.

That makes me think: after Benjamin bought the car, he got a fur coat. I don't know what kind of critter it come from, but Benjamin he looked real funny in it. My wife said she'd heard of wolves in sheep's clothin', but Benjamin Rice was a sheep in wolves' clothin'. Benjamin's wife didn't have any fur coat,—she wrapped herself up in all the old shawls in the house,—but Lizzie had a real pretty blue coat lined with gray fur.

It is some years ago that Benjamin sold the nine-acre lot and bought the car. He used that money. He sold the land to a real-estate man from the city, and that was where some of the trouble came in. That night Benjamin came to my house and showed me the check he'd got for the land. He looked real excited. There were red spots on his cheeks, and his blue eyes were shinin'.

"Guess you never saw a check as big as that, Billy," says he, and he was right. Big checks have never come in my way, though I've made a fair livin'. I looked at the check, and then Benjamin put it back in his old wallet real careful.

"Guess what I'm goin' to spend that for?" says he.

"Guess you'll put it in Blendon school bonds," says I, laughin', for I couldn't imagine Benjamin spendin' that much money except for more money.

Then he just fired the news right at me.

"I'm goin' to buy an automobile," says he, and then he gives his head a toss, and looked at me as if he thought I might have something to say against it.

"A what?" says I.

"An automobile," says he.

"What for?" says I.

"What folks generally buy 'em for," says he: "to go ridin' round and get a little pleasure out of livin'. Look at here, Billy," says he, "I'm gettin' on in years, and I ain't never had much except my board and lodgin' for my hard work. Now I'm goin' to take this money, and I'm goin' to buy an automobile, and I'm goin' to have a little fun, and my wife is goin' to, and Lizzie is goin' to before *she* gets old."

"What kind of an automobile are you goin' to buy?" says I, sort of feeble.

"I am goin' to buy an automobile off the Verity Automobile Advance Company of Landsville, Kentucky," says he.

"Why don't you buy nearer home?" says I.

"Sammy Emerson is agent for them automobiles, and he says they are the best to be had for the money, and he knows all about them, and he's goin' to show me how to run it, and maybe Lizzie can learn, and he's goin' to keep it in order," says he.

"Have you got a guaranty?" says I.

"Lord! yes," says he; "I'm dealin' with real square and above-board people. If the first car don't work to suit me, they'll send me another, and they'll supply all the parts that get broken for nothin'; but Sammy says nothin' is goin' to get broken. He says that machine is built to last fifty years."

"Well, Sammy Emerson ought to know," says I.

Sammy Emerson we all think is a genius. We shouldn't be surprised if he did anything. He is a real mechanical genius. We found it out when he stole the works of the Baptist church organ when he was only a boy. That organ began to act queer, and it acted queerer and queerer, and one Sunday Lemuel Jones, the organist, couldn't get a solitary squeak out of it, though little Tommy Adkins was blowin' till he almost dropped. Then they found out what the trouble was. The works were gone, and Sammy Emerson had another organ most rigged up in his ma's barn.

There was an awful fuss about it. That organ had to be made over, and all the works carted back from the Emerson barn. Sammy had stolen them piece by piece. He had made a key that would unlock the church door. Mrs. Emerson had to pay a lot of money; for of course it cost, and they wouldn't let Sammy help set up the organ again, though he offered. But after that we all felt that he was a genius, though we were rather scared. My wife said she didn't know but Sammy would try to steal her sewin'-machine and make a flyin'-machine out of it; but Sammy didn't do much harm after that. He just tinkered away, and almost did pretty wonderful things. His ma had money, and she let him have the barn to tinker in, and she let him buy lots of old junk that he thought he could make something of. Sammy had almost made an automobile himself. Everybody thought it would go if he could once get it started; but he never quite fetched the startin'. Then he took the Verity agency. I dare say his ma begun to think he was spendin' too much, and had better try to earn a little to exercise his genius on.

"Well," says I to Benjamin, "I suppose Sammy Emerson knows about it. He ought to."

"Of course he does," says Benjamin. "He says it's the best car on the market, and there's millions back of it."

"Who is back of it?" says I.

"The Variable Tea-Kettle Corporation of Vermont," says Benjamin.

"Seems to me rather queer that a tea-kettle concern should take to making automobiles," says I.

Benjamin never got very mad, but he did look a little riled.

"Don't see anything queer about it," says he. "Anybody knows what the observation of boilin' tea-kettles led to, and everybody that has seen one dancin' on the stove at full boil can figure out for himself that if it had wheels and tires it might get somewhere. Accordin' to my way of thinkin'," says he, "a tea-kettle jest naturally leads up to an automobile."

"Does it run by steam?" says I, a little surprised.

"Do you think me and ma and Lizzie is goin' to take any chances of bein' bu'st up by a steam-engine?" says Benjamin. "Of course it runs by gasolene."

"Where be you goin' to get your gasolene?"

"I'm goin' to buy it in Rockland," says Benjamin.

"You'll have to cart it."

"Can't I run the automobile over there,—it's only ten miles,—and have it put in?" says Benjamin. "And I've cleared out the barn where I kept my haywagon and tip-up cart for the automobile."

"What be you goin' to do with those?" I asked.

"Oh, I've made room in the big barn. I had the carryall and the buggy taken over to Rockland, too, to be sold. No use keepin' them if I have an automobile."

Well, Benjamin went home pretty soon, and I am afraid he was a little disappointed. I tried to act real elated with his scheme and pleased because he said me and my wife and daughter should go to ride in his car, but I was really pretty well taken aback.

Well, it seemed that Benjamin had had his car ordered three months before he told me about it, and it didn't come until the first of September. However, the fall was late that year, and it looked as if he might get a good deal out of it before cold weather set in. Everybody was anxious to see it, and when it came up from the freight-station, Sammy Emerson drivin',—Lord knows how he found out the way; some folks claimed he never took any lessons,—and Benjamin sittin' beside him in his fur coat, although it was an awful' hot day, pretty near all Blendon was out to see. Well, that car came on a Friday,—I remember the day because my wife said it was unlucky,—and they kept it goin' next day, Saturday, and it stayed in the barn Sunday, and Benjamin and his wife and Lizzie walked to church. They had always driven to church, but now they had sold their carryall, and Benjamin thought from the first that it was wicked to go out in the car Sundays.

But Monday mornin' they had it out again, and Benjamin was tryin' to learn to drive, leanin' 'way over, and starin' ahead through his far-sighted glasses. In the afternoon they went out, and Sammy drove real nice and slow, and Benjamin sat 'side of him in his fur coat, and Mrs. Rice and Lizzie were on the back seat. There was room for three, and they stopped to see if my wife or daughter wouldn't like to go, but both of them was afraid. My wife said she wouldn't ride on a tea-kettle with Sammy Emerson drivin', and she was sure she wouldn't ride in an automobile drove by Sammy and backed by a tea-kettle company.

That evening Benjamin came over to see me. He looked real excited and pleased, but sort of scared, too.

"It's great, Billy," says he; "but I never can crank her." He showed me his hand all bruised. "It's a knack," says he. "You have to let go of her jest so, or she fetches you an awful blow; and, besides, I never was quite right in my side since that pleurisy two year' ago. My side is lame to-night," says he. "Guess I can't ever crank her, Billy."

"How be you goin' to manage?" says I.

"Sammy is goin' to crank her for me, and he says Abel has sense enough for that, he thinks," says he. Abel was Benjamin's hired man, and none too bright.

"I shouldn't think Abel could do anything that needed a knack," says I.

"Sammy says he can," says Benjamin again, but he did seem kind of sad because he couldn't crank it himself. He was just like a baby with a rattle over that car. Well, Abel did learn to crank it, but I don't think he ever could have except he happened to use both hands alike: he was left-handed and right-handed. When one hand was too used up, he could crank with the other; for he never did learn the knack of it, and the car always hit him a crack before he could get clear from her. Then, too, he wasn't bright enough to know how lame he was, and say he wouldn't crank; and, too, the car wasn't in shape to run, let alone crank, much of the time.

The trouble began the Tuesday after it came. That evenin' poor Benjamin came down to my house, limpin' and lookin' dreadful cast-down.

"What is the matter?" says I.

"She broke down in Rockland," says he, "and ma and Lizzie had to come home by train, and I walked. It is going to cost so much to keep that car that I must begin to save somewhere. I walked all the way, and my corns are bad, and the bunion on my right foot, and I hadn't ought to have come down here to-night, but ma and Lizzie keep askin' me if I think I have got a good car, and I wanted to get away from it. Women mean well, but they don't know when not to talk. Oh, Billy," says poor Benjamin, "I am dreadful' afraid I haven't got a good car, and I have sunk all that money into it! The man over in the automobile place in Rockland says the drivin'-shaft is bent, and he says it is made of tin, when it ought to be steel. Oh, Billy, should you think they would have sold me tin instead of steel?"

Of course I knew better than that. "Couldn't have been tin," says I.

"Mighty poor steel, then," says Benjamin, dreadful' mournful. "I'm afraid I've thrown my money away, and, worse than that, I'm afraid there is more wickedness in the world than I've ever dreamed of. I paid them for good steel, Billy. It don't make much difference whether it is tin or poor steel, anyway; it's bent, and something else they call the traditional is twisted so it won't work. I'm afraid it's a pretty bad business, Billy, and they are goin' to put up twenty little, cheap houses on the nine-acre lot, and ma and Lizzie say only cheap people will live in them, and it will spoil our place. Should you have thought that a man could do such a thing as that, Billy?"

I pitied Benjamin that night, but I agreed with him that he had made a pretty bad bargain, and we were both right.

Once in a while, after Sammy Emerson had done an extra lot of tinkerin', the car would run real nice a day and a half or two days, but she never run over two. I went out in her once, and I was so sorry for Benjamin that I chipped in and helped him pay a man with a team to drag her to Rockland, then we walked home. That settled me. I was glad to have poor Benjamin come and tell me his troubles, but I didn't want to walk home.

Well, things went on from bad to worse. Finally Lizzie Rice wrote a real nice, ladylike letter to the Variable Tea-Kettle Company, and asked for the money back; but they didn't take a mite of notice of it. Then Benjamin got a lawyer to look at the contract, and the lawyer said it was so open that an elephant could walk between every word without jostlin' them. Then Benjamin gave up gettin' righted by the tea-kettle concern, but he was real charitable. He said that he was sure that they made splendid tea-kettles, and all the trouble was in tryin' to apply their tea-kettle rules to automobiles. He said he didn't doubt they meant well.

It was a beautiful fall that year, not a mite of snow and splendid weather up to Christmas. Benjamin and Sammy tinkered and tinkered, and the car would run a little while between tinkerin's, then it would have to be all done over again. And poor Benjamin had to keep sendin' to factories for the parts that got broken or dropped out. Once Benjamin came to my house with a paper bag full of little broken steel things. "I picked them up in the barn, Billy," says he; "I don't know what they be."

One evenin' he came to my house and almost cried like a baby.

"Now she has busted her transgression, Billy," says he, "and a new one will cost a lot, and we have to wait an awful time for it, too."

I always suspected that Benjamin must have got some of the names of the parts wrong, but I didn't know. What I did know was that Benjamin, who had never cheated his fellow-men out of a penny, had not been treated likewise. I never knew what was really the matter with the car, and I don't believe anybody else did. Our doctor said it was an instance of congenital malformation, which had a terrible sound, and seemed to me to fit the case exactly.

They tinkered in Sammy Emerson's barn, but they tinkered mostly in Benjamin's, for Sammy had so much junk around there wasn't much room. Then two men come from the city, and Benjamin's wife fed them real high, and kept them a week; but though they said they got the car in splendid order, they swore so that Benjamin paid them and sent them off. He said he wouldn't have such language used over any property of his, even if it was an automobile. But after that he hired a driver from the city. They said he had worked in automobile factories and been to an automobile school, but he only ran the car a week before she gave out entirely. Then he left, and Lizzie she wrote to the Kentucky company, and they wrote right back a real nice letter, and Benjamin was tickled 'most to pieces. He showed the letter to me, and it did read real fair.

"That's what comes from dealin' with an honest company," says he, for they wrote to ship the car back to Kentucky, and they would send a brand-new one right from the factory.

Well, the car was shipped back to Kentucky, and Benjamin had an awful bill to pay for freight, and after about six weeks the new car came, and he had freight to pay on that, but he was so tickled he didn't complain. That new car run just twice to Rockland and back before she broke down, and the tinkerin' begun again. They took her over to Rockland and had her tinkered there by a man who said he had been born and brought up in an automobile school, but after he was through they were six hours and a half runnin' her home. Then Benjamin and Sammy tinkered again, and finally the cap-climax came. Benjamin Rice had never lost his patience within the memory of man. Folks had always said he was too good to live; but he was tried too far. He and Sammy were out in the car, and they had only got half a mile in an hour, when something went off like a pistol, and the car wouldn't budge. It was right in front of the store, too, and a lot of folks came runnin'. I was there. Benjamin he just stood up in that car and he damned for the first time in his life.

"I don't care whether it's the traditional, or the tin drivin'-shaft, or the transgression that's bu'st," says he—"damn, damn, damn!"

Sammy Emerson he was so scared that he slid out of the car and stood gapin' up at him, and Abel, who had his right hand tied up,—they had taken him along to crank,—sat in the back seat and shook all over. Benjamin went on, and it was something sort of solemn and awful and made you think of the Psalms.

"I am an old man," says he; "never in my whole life have I taken the name of the Lord in vain, but now I am pushed on beyond my strength by the devil and his work. These things"—and he pointed down at the car, which was smoking up in his face—"are the work of the evil one himself. I have lived a decent, honest life, I have never wronged my fellow-man, and now it has come to me in my old age to see evil and have it worked upon me. I have spent for this worthless thing, the work of dishonest hands and dishonest hearts, money which was earned by honest labor in the fear of the Lord."

Then he goes on to tell us something which *did* make us stare. It seemed that Lizzie Rice had lost in the first car a little gold breastpin, and she had found it that very mornin' slipped into a little hole in the linin' of one of the pockets; and Benjamin knew by that that the company had not sent him a new car, but his old one painted up, and I suppose they changed the numbers and things. Folks said they must have, but maybe poor Benjamin never thought about the numbers, anyway, and as for Sammy Emerson, he was brighter about mechanics than about some other things, and maybe he never thought either.

Anyway, the point was that Benjamin had his same old car back again, and he knew it. So he keeps on, after tellin' us that. "I will have nothin' more to do with this, so help me God!" says he. "Any man who dares face the father of all lies and tamper with his works can take this automobile and welcome. As for me, I am done with it. I would not sell it for a penny: I should wrong the buyer. I would not give it away: I should wrong the receiver. But I leave it here to be disposed of as any man among you may wish. It is the work of iniquity, which I would have died rather than seen with my old eyes. Oh, if I could have died before I lost my faith in my fellow-men, and seen the wickedness of the world!"

With that Benjamin gets down sort of stiff and majestic, and walks away, and leaves the car starin' at us with its two glassy eyes. But poor Benjamin had not gone far before he began to stagger, and then down he went as if he had been hit on the head. He had a stroke, and they (I was one of them) got him into the storekeeper's wagon, and carried him home, and got the doctor. It was all dreadful. It meant a good deal more than an automobile, as the doctor said. He put it just the way it was. Says he, "that good, simple man has encountered the deadly juggernaut of progress of the times, and has gone down before it."

But Benjamin didn't die, of course, because you just saw him. That automobile stood right there in the road several days while he was so dreadful sick. The horses shied at it, and the women dragged their children past for fear it might start up of its own accord. Then one mornin' comes the doctor, and says that Benjamin had come to himself as much as he ever would, and could speak, though not very plain. "And he wants this confounded rattletrap of a machine," says the doctor, glarin' at the car. The doctor never had any use for automobiles, but drove good horses till he quit doctorin'.

So that car was towed back to Benjamin's, and it has set there in his yard ever since. Benjamin's wife and Lizzie made a waterproof cover for the thing in wet weather, and it's just as good as it ever was, which ain't sayin' much. Lizzie and her mother see to it that it's kept dusted off and real clean, and they have had it painted once. When the house was painted, there was some paint left over, and they had it put on the car to save it. That's the reason why it's white with green stripes. The green was left from the house-blinds. The car was dark blue when it was new.

Well, Benjamin sits in that car every day, dressed up in his fur coat, with his shakin' hand on the wheel, and now and then when he sees anything out on the road he toots the horn. And, though of course it's a dreadful thing, because he ain't what he used to be, you can't seem to sense it, because, if ever there was a man happy in this world, it's Benjamin Rice. He just seems to smile on livin', and you saw yourself how fat and rosy he is. There he sits in that car, that won't stir a peg till the day of judgment, and—*he thinks he's goin' forty miles an hour!*

The Doll Lady

Minnie, sitting in the arbor, walled in and roofed over by closely set grape-leaves through which only a dim green light of day filtered, taking dainty stitches on the hem of a muslin gown for herself, a charming muslin pattern with delicate little flowers scattered as on a summer field, heard every word. She could not help it. She could not make her presence known without causing a most unpleasant shock of embarrassment both to herself and others. She had not had time to escape, because the remark came like an explosive, and she did not even get a whiff of the cigar smoke until afterward.

"Marry Minnie!" proclaimed the masculine voice. "Marry Minnie, Wilbur! Why don't you propose that I marry a doll and be done with it?"

In reply came a voice which Minnie loathed. It was the voice of a man, but it had an almost feminine softness of tone. "My dear fellow," said that voice, "Minnie is not such a doll as you think."

"Looks like one, acts like one," returned the other voice, which was manly, although full of unproven authority. That was the voice of the Rev. Edward Yale, the young minister who boarded with Minnie's widowed mother and her widowed sister, Mrs. Emma Prior; not in any sense with Minnie. Minnie never had any voice in household arrangements. She was much younger than her sister Emma, and she had been the child of her mother's more than middle age. She had been a petted darling of her old father, who had died the year before, and for whom she was just leaving off mourning. She was always the petted darling of her mother and sister, but being a petted darling sometimes involves a slight underestimation, even unconscious contempt. Petting implies superiority; being petted may imply inferiority, although a beloved and graceful inferiority.

Minnie continued to listen. She stopped sewing. "She is not at all," said the unpleasant voice, which belonged to Wilbur Bates. She and Wilbur had been schoolmates, and he had always, she supposed, been in love with her, and she had certainly never been in love with him, had been more and more repelled as they grew older. Now his defense of her was hateful as his expressions of distaste could never have been. She knew just the expression of Wilbur's face as he spoke—his long, blond face, with its thin, much-curved mouth and his narrowing blue eyes. "Minnie has a great deal of character," said Wilbur. "I have known her all my life, and I am sure of it."

"It is well concealed, then," said Edward Yale. He certainly spoke as no gentleman should have spoken regarding a woman who, whatever her faults of character, had always treated him well.

"All strong character is apt to be well concealed," replied Wilbur Bates. The two had stopped just beside Minnie's arbor, and were seated, smoking, on the stone wall which separated the garden from the adjoining estate.

"I rather take issue with you regarding that," said Edward Yale.

"I say, I am sure."

Edward made no reply. A stronger whiff of cigar smoke penetrated the arbor.

"I have never," continued Edward Yale in a crescendo of authority, "known a really strong character which was not indicated in some way by the face."

"You can never be quite sure what soft pink curves and dimples conceal," replied Wilbur.

Now Edward Yale laughed a pleasant, arrogant, boyish laugh. "In dolls they usually conceal sawdust," said he.

Minnie turned pale. That was too much. It was even unchristian for a minister of the gospel to assume that any human being was stuffed with sawdust. She sat still, almost rigid. The young minister spoke of something else, but Wilbur persistently brought the conversation back to herself. Then she knew that Wilbur knew she was within hearing and compelled to listen to his praises and the other man's disdain.

Minnie did not take another stitch. Her heart beat like a trapped thing, but her wrath served as a stimulus. Her soft, curved cheeks bloomed again. Minnie had a temper which sustained her and which, although unholy, was a resource.

She sat perfectly still. She reasoned that the two men could not talk forever, sitting there on the stone wall. She knew that Mr. Yale could not have finished his sermon, although it was Saturday afternoon. He had procrastinating habits. As for Wilbur, who was a man of leisure and wealth, he could remain if he chose, but she was sure that he would leave when Mr. Yale did. He would not choose that Minnie should know that he had been conducting this discussion for her benefit.

At last Edward Yale said, rising, "This will not finish my to-morrow's sermon," and Wilbur, also rising, returned: "Well, Yale, you had better think over what I have said. There is nothing like a wife and a settled home for a man of your profession. Then you can make sure that all the unmarried females of your flock are intent upon spiritual benefits when they listen to your discourses."

"The whole idea is a shame," said the other, hotly, and Minnie, in spite of her anger, liked him for the rejoinder.

She waited until there had been ample time for the minister to gain his study and until she had heard the trot, trot of Wilbur's horse recede entirely; Wilbur never drove, but rode a fine, high-headed animal of price and blood. Then she folded her work with a final air and put her sewing utensils in her little silk bag and returned to the house by a path which was invisible from the study.

Minnie's father had been a minister, and young Yale used the old study. When Minnie entered the house, her sister, Emma Prior, was writing a letter on an old-fashioned writing-desk, and her mother was peacefully reading a book from the village library. It was, Minnie considered, a stupid book, full of sweet platitudes, but her mother, who was somewhat of a sweet platitude herself, enjoyed such. Mrs. Abbot was always spoken of as a dear old lady, and she looked worthy of her reputation as she smiled serenely at Minnie. "It is a fine day, isn't it?" said she.

"Very fine, mother," replied Minnie.

Emma, who had a long, nervous, but rather pretty face, glanced up from her letter. It was a duty letter written twice every year to a cousin out in Ohio whom she had never seen. Emma had many small duties with which she filled in the chinks of the larger ones. She was a very busy woman, and she was writing a most conscientious letter, with lines beneath the paper, that she might avoid optimistic upward slants and pessimistic downward ones. There was a nice pen-wiper on the desk, a blotting-pad, and a small dictionary. "Will you please look at the kitchen clock and tell me the time, Minnie?" said she. "I think this clock is not quite right."

Minnie disappeared. Emma's pen moved smoothly again, filling in the slight chink.

"It is ten minutes of five, sister," replied Minnie, returning. Her mother smiled happily at something in her book.

"What is Maria doing?"

"She is sitting beside the window."

"It is time to put the biscuits in the oven, and they must be ready, but she will not do it unless I tell her to," said Emma, rising.

"I will tell her, dear," said Minnie.

"You!" repeated Emma in a tone of loving contempt, as if she were addressing a pet animal. "You know Maria would not put the biscuits in for you, dear."

"I could put them in myself," replied Minnie, with a slight note of rebellion in her voice which caused both her mother and sister to stare at her. "You!" said Emma again. Mrs. Abbot laughed pleasantly and turned her eyes again upon her book. Emma wiped her pen carefully upon the inside of the pen-wiper and left the room. Minnie also left by another door and ran up-stairs.

She went into her own room and closed the door. Then she sat down in a little rocking-chair which had survived her childhood, leaned her elbows on the open window-sill, and stared out into the green, overlapping spread of a cherry-tree. This was a favorite occupation of hers, or, rather, a favorite lack of occupation, for she was not only idle as to her body, but not consciously mentally active. She sat brooding over nothing as far as she knew, but always afterward came action. As she sat there the girl belied the young minister's description of her. She did not look in the least like a doll, in spite of the rounded figure in the little rocking-chair and the dimpled face resting in a cup of dimpled hands. Her eyes, staring into the glossy bosses of the cherry-tree, looked black instead of blue, and were set in reflective and reminiscent hollows. Her curved mouth was a straight line. She saw and did not see the cherry branches stirred now and then by a seeking robin, although the cherries were long since gone. She heard and did not hear her sister Emma and Maria moving about below preparing the evening meal to the accompaniment of tinkling china and silver.

Presently she rose and went to the glass which surmounted her old-fashioned mahogany bureau and looked at herself. Her look was severe. She told herself, angrily, that there was no semblance of a doll in that face. Then she tipped the glass and surveyed her figure, and she felt cold. Minnie's lack of height had always been a sore affliction to her. She was much below the average height, and her little body was absolutely void of angularity. If she bent her elbows even, one got the curve of a crescent moon instead of a triangle between waist and hips. Her whole form was undoubtedly on the plan of a doll's, and no corset could remedy that—Minnie had secretly tried it. Now she bent her whole energy to the work of discovering other means. She wore a white, embroidered blouse, with her black skirt belted with black ribbon with a dull jet buckle. Minnie recognized that her costume decreased her height. Then came action. There was a scant half-hour before supper. She was thankful that biscuits were to be baked, and the fire must have got low, for she could smell smoke from the kitchen chimney.

Minnie owned one dress which with a slight alteration would meet her new taste, but that was her very best. She could not wear that. She got an old black silk blouse out of her little dimity-covered shirt-waist box, snipped the sleeves to the elbow, cut out the collar, sewed with long stitches patches made from the snipped sleeves over worn places. Then she got out of her top bureau drawer a long, black veil, cut it in two, sewed the two lengths together, leaving holes for the arms, hollowed the neck, basted a bit of flat, black trimming around that, slipped it over her head, and began pinning skilfully with small black mourning-pins. The girl displayed, suddenly awakened, the first of all feminine talents, the talent of dress impelled to life by sheer vanity of sex. She pinned in marvelous fashion those soft folds of veiling. She draped her arms, she draped her waist, and girded herself with a black silk cord. The result was rather surprising. She had, apparently, gained in height. What were, in fact, her own curves seemed the flutter and fluff of the veil. She also looked much older. She pulled her crisply curling yellow hair straight back from the forehead in the center and fastened it securely. The result was a sweetly curved triangle of strength and womanliness.

Then she heard her sister call, and went down-stairs to the supper-table. Edward Yale stood there politely waiting until all the ladies were seated before he took his own chair. Minnie sat down. Her sister regarded her in a puzzled fashion. She resolved that she would ask her after supper what she was wearing. Meantime she poured the tea from the ancient silver pot and dispensed cream and sugar from its associates. Mrs. Abbot sat serenely opposite the minister, ate genteelly, and now and then made one of her obvious remarks. She said of the clear primrose-yellow sunset visible from the dining-room windows, "It is indeed a beautiful sunset." She said of a breath of roses which came in from the open, "The roses are very sweet." She said of a gust of warm air, "It is warmer." She said, hearing the whining snarl of a mosquito in the room, "There is a mosquito."

Everybody nodded assent or spoke assentingly to these remarks. Mrs. Abbot had never in her whole life received even a covert snub. She did not know the meaning of one, and yet she had gently wearied everybody with whom she had had to do. Mrs. Abbot did not notice Minnie's altered appearance. When she had once seen a person, she had seen her forever. Minnie could never make any new impression upon the placid imperturbability of Mrs. Abbot's mind. As for the minister, Minnie, watching furtively, suspected that he did not see her at all. Then her wrath grew, the righteous wrath of a really strong nature belittled and driven into petty ways to assert itself.

Because the minister did not look at her, Minnie stayed away from the preparatory lecture in the church vestry that evening. The next Sunday was that of the administering of the communion, and there was always a preparatory lecture. Directly after supper Edward Yale hurried to his study. Minnie knew that he was horribly pressed for time with regard to his sermon. "He had better have been writing that than talking about me to Wilbur Bates," she thought, indignantly, sitting in her room in the little rocking-chair as she had sat before.

As she sat there the soft, summer twilight fell like a veil. The fragrance of the garden intensified by the dew drifted against her face. She heard the katydids and a whippoorwill singing to the accompaniment of a little river whose silvery rush she could just hear. Then came the rather discordant peal of the church-bell, and out of the yard passed three figures in black—her mother, her sister, and the minister. Then, scurrying to be in time, came another figure around the house corner, that of Maria, the servant-girl, also a church member in good and regular standing and intent upon being prepared for the solemn rite of the morrow.

Minnie realized that she was alone in the house, and felt a little thrill of dismay. She did not like being alone in the house, nor alone anywhere. After a while she could not endure the vacant house longer, and went down-stairs and out in the front yard. She stood in the gravel walk between the rows of shrubs, and started at a long light flung across them. The minister had left the study lamp burning.

Minnie went into the house to extinguish the lamp. When she entered the small, square room, lined with books, she shivered before a bitter-sweet memory. She had spent many hours with her old father in this room, and she resented its being occupied by another. Her father had never underrated her. He had a knowledge that she had an imbibing intelligence. In this very room he had taught her Latin and a smattering of Hebrew. Minnie pulled down the curtains; then she saw the minister's sermon on the table, one sheet in the shiny black typewriter. Edward Yale composed sermons on the typewriter, and some people considered it sacrilegious.

Minnie eyed the typewriter. It was a very innocent curiosity which impelled her, in spite of her wrath against the minister; an innocent curiosity and also an unconfessed anxiety lest the sermon should not be finished in time.

Minnie examined the sermon. That is, she looked at the number of the page on the typewriter. She saw at once that it was not more than half written. Minnie puckered her mouth, but she did not whistle. She could not. She could only manage that premonitory pucker. "Goodness! he will have to sit up half the night to finish it," she thought.

She regarded the sermon, her chin dipped, intensifying her dimples;

a peculiar tiny gleam like a bird's came into her eyes. The sermon was very neatly arranged. Edward Yale was an orderly man. The sheets of paper lay exactly placed, their edges meeting. Minnie could use the typewriter. She looked at the sheet thereon. It contained very little.

Minnie read: "We have now to remember carefully what has been before said, in order that the succeeding passages may be clearly understood. Sequence is a fundamental law of all human undertakings, as it may be of divine methods. It is 'first the seed, then the ear, then the full corn in the ear.' The law of creation may well set the pace for our poor, little, futile efforts at performing our petty tasks. Therefore, I beg you, before I proceed, to consider well what has gone before."

Minnie shook her head. That paragraph was not good. It was a mere hiatus. It was a begging for time. The church-bell had begun to ring, and the minister had played that off upon the machine simply with a view to so much space covered. He, however, would allow it to remain. Edward Yale had a trick of writing these hiatus paragraphs. It was due, no doubt, to his habit of procrastination and working under pressure. While his idea momentarily failed him he wrote like that, instead of stopping to consider, as many would have done. "What," thought Minnie, "has come before?"

She took up the topmost sheet of neatly typewritten manuscript. She glanced over it, and the queer, bird-like gleam was more pronounced in her blue eyes. Here also haste was evident, although not in the neatness of the page nor the accuracy of the work. But the minister had left space enough for a very long paragraph before laying the sheet aside and inserting another in the typewriter. Minnie stood, her head on one side. Then she laughed—a rather uncanny laugh, taking into consideration the laughter. Minnie did not look capable of that sort of laugh. She glanced around quickly, then she removed the sheet of paper from the typewriter, took up the sheet preceding, with its blank space at the foot, inserted it carefully, and sat down and wrote. She did not hesitate. The machine ticked as rapidly as with the minister. The text of the sermon was, "Judge not, that ye be not judged." The last words of the paragraph which the minister had written upon that page were a repetition of the text.

Minnie was very clever. She also repeated the text, adding emphasis to emphasis and doing away with any immediate and violent transition which might have caused quick suspicion and alarm in the mind of the minister. Then she also repeated in a slightly different fashion an allusion which the minister had made earlier in the sermon to the double-faced shield and the dispute over the color, and the proving that each of the disputants was right.

"Let us not forget that double-faced shield," typed Minnie, "the shield which has been one of the valuable object-lessons of humanity. Let us remember and understand that it is always possible for our wrong to be another's right, and be merciful and charitable, and humble our minds to a readiness of conviction as to our own mistakes. Who can even say, and be certain that he speaks the fundamental truth, that those gods of the heathen which were overthrown by the law and the prophets had not for their worshipers some meaning of good which we have never grasped? Are we fit judges even of Baal? Judge not, that ye be not judged." Minnie, with her head on one side, considered. There was space for a line more, but she felt that, on the whole, she had written enough. She read it over. She did not see how the minister, once fairly launched upon her work by means of the deceptive mind slide of the text repetition, could avoid reading the whole. She did not know, but she could imagine the result. There were some very orthodox members in Edward Yale's church, even for this day and generation.

Minnie removed the sheet from the machine and inserted the other with its hiatus paragraph at the top. Then she stood trembling a little. She thought about undoing her work, copying over what Yale had written on the preceding page and omitting her emendation. She began to be frightened and conscience-stricken. Consequences began to multiply in her imagination.

Then she heard the scrape of a foot on the gravel walk outside, and she was possessed by a mad impulse of concealment. Aside from the matter of the sermon, she must not be caught in the minister's study. There had been plenty of talk already; she was such a beautiful girl and so much admired, and the minister was so young. It was fortunate that Minnie's brain worked rapidly. In one dart she was across the room and in the closet.

In the closet hung the minister's overcoats and hats, stood his umbrella. His two suit-cases were stacked neatly one on the other. Minnie was on the suit-cases and enveloped in the folds of the minister's winter overcoat before the front door opened. The bell had rung sharply twice first, and she had had plenty of time. She was beautifully concealed. She was thankful then for the minister's procrastinating habits, otherwise that coat would have been stored away in camphor and moth-balls by her careful sister. Yale had been intending to send it to a tailor for repairs, and had neglected to do so. Only that very morning Minnie had heard Emma remark to her mother, "That over-coat of Mr. Yale's will be eaten up by moths if he doesn't get it off before long, but I don't like to say anything." "Moths were never in that closet in your father's time," Mrs. Abbot had returned, giving Minnie the impression that the odor of sanctity might drive away moths.

Now Minnie got the odor of stale tobacco, which she loved, al-though the love puzzled her. It was rather well known that the min-ister smoked an occasional cigar out-of-doors, and many thought it unbefitting his profession. It was Wilbur Bates who, when he called on Yale, made a business of stripping the telltale bands of costliness from the minister's cigars and saying much about the cheapness of the brands which did not bear them. Yale was commonly credited with smoking two three-cent cigars per day, and, inasmuch as they would not buy two postage-stamps for the use of foreign missionaries, he was condoned. Minnie heard the talk among the women, and she knew that three-cent cigars had not the odor of the minister's, but she said nothing. As for the minister, he did not know of his reputation for cheap cigars, or an explanation from the pulpit might have ensued. Yale was nothing if not a hero of frankness. He only smoked out-of-doors, because he knew that the study of the former minister might be considered as desecrated if he smoked there. It involved much self-denial, and he often wondered if his sermons might not have been improved had he smoked while writing. He had been an inveterate smoker in college. Strangely enough, to-night for the very first time he had absently lit a cigar upon returning to his study after supper. He had almost immediately extinguished it, but Minnie had noticed the faint, fresh odor of tobacco in the room. That, however, was now lost in the stale odor with which the coat was permeated of the cigars which the young man had smoked.

When Minnie heard the front door being opened, a sudden pang of fear, aside from the mere fear of being found in the study, seized her. For the first time she thought of the possibility of a burglar. He might be in quest of this very coat, and, if so, what of her sheltered in its folds? Then she heard a snatch of song in a very good tenor, and knew it was Wilbur Bates. He was in the habit of first ringing the bell, and then, if nobody answered, walking in and entering the study. He and Yale were very intimate. Minnie was always puzzled by this intimacy, but it was largely an intellectual affair. Bates was a thoroughly educated, much-traveled man, and a rather subtle thinker. There was not another his equal in those respects in the town. Yale, therefore, had found him congenial, although neither man pretended to have any deep regard for the other. Bates's covert good-nature with regard to the belted cigars showed in reality some affection that the minister did not suspect. "Why, in the name of common sense, if I may ask, can you find any amusement in pulling those adornments off my cigars?" he had asked once.

"Hate them," had been Bates's laconic reply. "Always pull them off on principle. Savor of snobbery—want to be looked upon as brother to the bootblack and all that sort of thing."

"It strikes me I have seen a bootblack before now smoking a belted cigar," Yale had returned, with a puzzled look.

"Then that particular bootblack should have been tempted to pick up a bomb," replied Bates. "The hauteur of the poor is more abominable than that of the rich, for it is not even the real thing. It is veneered, gilded." Then he had continued stripping the cigars and replacing them carefully in their box.

Now as Minnie stood concealed in the coat, in a measure relieved, because it was hardly rational that Bates would investigate the minister's closet, he entered the study still singing. The words of the song from some opera were in Italian and Minnie could not understand them. What she did understand was, she would be a prisoner in the coat while the man remained, and he might easily wait until the meeting was over, and he might easily stay for a long while afterward. It would not make the slightest difference to him that he was delaying a sermon. Bates was absolutely without consideration for his friends' pursuits. He was selfish to the core, although he had, when it did not interfere with his own pleasure, a good-natured readiness to serve them.

Minnie in the closet heard Wilbur aimlessly strolling about the room in a way he had before sitting down. He was a restless man, although he spoke slowly and gave an impression of calmness. Minnie knew him to be idly scrutinizing the books on the walls. She knew with a guilty conviction that, much as she disliked him, she was entirely safe, as far as he was concerned, from the discovery of her tampering with the sermon. She knew Wilbur Bates would no more even glance at a written line of his friend's study table than he would murder him. She was not sure that, under strong provocation, he would not prefer the murder to the subtler offense. After a while Wilbur sat down and smoked. Now and then he removed his cigar and went on with his Italian song.

Minnie was having a rather dreadful experience. For one thing, it was very warm in the closet in the folds of that heavy winter coat. It was almost smothering. Minnie thought of Ginevra and her smothered demise in the chest, although the cases were not at all parallel, except that she also might be found smothered. Then, irrelevantly, Minnie thought, as she had done many times before, with what irony she had been named Minnie. If she had been named Ginevra, even her dimples might have assumed importance, and the minister might not have spoken so cruelly as he had done that afternoon. Minnie in itself was a doll-name. That in combination with her appearance was fatal. If she had been named Margaret, for instance, she felt that she might have in time tiptoed up to the level of her name, but Minnie dragged her down. However, now it made little difference. She was having a horrible time, and her conscience began to torment her. She would have given—what would she not have given?—to undo what she had done! If only Wilbur Bates had not come, she knew very well that by now that page of the sermon would have been copied on the type-machine, her interpolated words omitted, and the former page destroyed. She was horribly sorry. She knew what would probably happen. The poor minister, led on so artfully by deluding words, could no more help reading what she had written than he could have helped stumbling into a pit. She had dug a pit for him, and she loved his very old coat, his coat reeking with stale tobacco.

She had some grievance. The minister had fallen from a high place in her faith when he had said those things about her. She did not mind the marrying part. Minnie colored with a red of shame besides the red of heat. He had never spoken to her about marrying, and Minnie was one of the maids who deem it a sacrilege done themselves to ponder upon such a matter with regard to any particular man before he has offered himself. It was not that. But he had spoken disparagingly of her; he had called her a doll with a doll character, and that he had no right to do. For the minister had, after all, not been insensible to Minnie's wonderfully perfect beauty and her charm, and he had looked with eyes which betrayed him, and he had said things which were naught in themselves, but his tones had been much, and he had pretended to be a good friend of hers, and this was traitorous to friendship. Besides, he had done her an indignity. He had refused in marriage to another man her whom he had not asked. He had assumed that she would be his for the asking. Even now resentment raged in her heart, but above it arose her sorrow and regret that she had done what she had done. Nothing could ever excuse that. And there sat Wilbur Bates. She made up her mind to remain just where she was until the minister returned, until Wilbur left, until the minister finished his sermon and retired for the night. Then she would steal out, and with soft taps at the machine she would undo the evil she had done.

However, the girl's fright made her illogical. She did not reckon the obvious results of such a course. She stood there, sweltering with heat, not daring to move, but feeling safe from discovery, when she heard Wilbur rise and approach the closet. Her mind, always a very quick one, leaped to his purpose. The minister kept his cigars in the closet. Wilbur was coming for them in order to strip them of their labels.

Wilbur opened the closet door. Minnie held her breath. He fumbled. His fumbling hands actually touched her feet, but, strangely enough, he did not apparently realize it. He was intent upon cigar-boxes and not looking for a girl's feet, and Wilbur Bates's mind moved in straight lines when he had any definite end in view. He had thought the cigar boxes might be where the suit-cases were. When he touched Minnie's feet he simply remarked, "Damn!" Then he lit a match and explored the closet shelf at its farthest end, where the boxes were neatly piled. Wilbur took them down and went out, leaving the lighted match on the floor. Minnie peered out of the coat and watched that match. She was obliged to. It was close to an inflammable duck suit of the minister's, and it was not her policy to be burned alive.

Wilbur had left the closet door open. Minnie reflected that men always left doors open, always threw lighted matches on floors. She reflected that women were superior, then that she loved the minister, though not in the way to induce her to marry him, partly because he had led her to love him in ancient ways and partly because he had injured her and she had injured him. The match went out. Minnie softly drew her eyes under the dark, tobacco-scented smother of the coat. Her hearing seemed preternatural. She could hear Wilbur stripping the gay little bands from the cigars and replacing them in the boxes. She wondered if he would finish before the minister returned and himself replace the boxes in the closet, or if it would fall to the minister's lot. She hoped Wilbur would replace them. He had failed to discover her once and might fail again, but Mr. Yale might be keener.

The time went on. Minnie heard the clock on the study shelf tick. It struck the half-hour, then, after what seemed ages, the hour. Then Minnie waited for the return of the minister, her mother, her sister, and also Maria. The church was near. They would come soon. Wilbur had not finished his work. The agony of waiting for one thing would soon be over, at all events. She would hear the front door flung open, the voices, the footsteps, then Edward Yale would enter the study and—she thought unreasoningly in a sudden panic—might rush at once to the closet and discover her. She did not stop to consider how very unlikely it was that he should be seized with a desire to inspect his winter coat upon this soft June night. Everything seemed horribly possible.

The front door opened; she heard the steps, the voices. Then Edward Yale entered the study.

"Hullo, Yale!" remarked Wilbur Bates.

"Good-evening, Bates," returned the minister, in a voice whose dismay he endeavored vainly to conceal. The other man laughed easily with a queer mixture of malice and good-nature. Wilbur Bates was a tormentor from the cradle. Teasing was to him the condiment, the essential one, of all life.

"I call that a pretty welcome," said he, "a mighty cordial welcome for a man who comes in and spends his precious time doing what might be called fancy work for a friend."

"Oh, gammon!" replied the minister. "I am always glad to see you, but you know what the trouble is."

"Your confounded sermon," said Bates, coolly.

"Yes, just that. Saturday night and not half done."

"Read an old one."

"That I will not do."

"You flatter yourself that a man or a woman in all your congregation would remember, O thou puffed up one!"

"I flatter myself with nothing. I dare say you are right and nobody would recall a word of a sermon I preached six months ago. I'm not sure that I could myself, but I am here to write new sermons, not palm off old ones."

"Lord, what an inconvenience it must be!" said Bates, going on with his work.

"What is an inconvenience?"

"A conscience. Why don't you dump it, as Christian did his in the *Pilgrim's Progress?*"

"It was not his conscience, but his sins, which made his heavy burden," said the minister, a trifle didactically.

"Rot! The sins would not have weighed a feather if it had not been for the conscience. When he dumped the sins, he dumped the conscience and walked off, like the cock of the walk, drums beating and plumes flying. Did you never learn that, man? That was the conscience that Christian was bent double under, not the sins."

"I can't argue, Bates. I must finish my sermon."

"Come on, then." Bates got up and took another chair, leaving the one before the type-machine vacant. "Sit thyself and play off the law and the gospel."

Then Minnie heard the tick of the machine, and she could picture to herself the poor minister, with a worried face, striving to write a sermon under such difficulties. Wilbur Bates had the decency to refrain from his humming song while Yale continued with his work. Neither of the men spoke. Minnie was suffering tortures from standing so long in one position. She began to fear lest overwrought muscles and nerves should give way and she go down with a crash. After a while Bates finished his work and moved upon the closet with his cigar-boxes. Minnie held her breath while he stacked the boxes on the shelf and retired.

"Whew!" he exclaimed, with a sniff.

"What is the matter?" asked the minister, absently.

"What a dandy you are, Yale!"

"Don't know what you mean."

"You hang little dinky bags of violet sachet in your closet, I'll swear you do."

"Rot!"

"You do. I am going to close the door."

When the door was closed Minnie sank down in a little heap of weak collapse upon the suit-cases.

"Mice in your closet, too," she heard Wilbur state.

"Very likely. Don't care if there are. My best clothes are up-stairs," returned the minister, rather irascibly. Bates eyed him with malicious enjoyment, and yet his glance was kindly. Minnie, huddled upon the suit-cases, knowing that if the door were opened suddenly she would certainly be discovered, waited.

Then that which ordinary logic should have taught her happened. There was an outcry, a dismayed outcry in the house, and the study door was flung open after a sharp knock. Of course, Minnie had been missed, by her mother and sister and Maria, and it was after ten o'clock at night. Minnie heard the sharp, staccato notes of alarm. She heard the minister and Wilbur Bates respond. She heard questions, answers, wild surmises. This surpassed all which she had imagined. There was no way out of the difficulty. She had not thought of her mother and sister and Maria, and the inevitability of their missing her.

She heard Emma's sharp explanatory words: "Came very near not knowing that she was gone. I happened to hear distant thunder—and Minnie is so apt to have all her windows wide open—and she has new curtains—and I thought they would be ruined, so I hurried into her room and—"

"The bed had not been slept in," stated Maria.

"There was no one at all there," came in her mother's mild tones of wonder, as if she had been surprised at not finding a large crowd.

Minnie's head swam. For one second she thought desperately of giving up this miserable ship, of disclosing herself. Then the thought of the utter impossibility of such a course kept her huddled stiff and still.

"We will go and search the house and grounds and rouse the village if necessary," rang out suddenly in the minister's voice, and Minnie heard a note of anxiety in it. Then there was a rush of feet and silence except for vague, distant calls. Minnie could think of nothing better than to slip out of the closet and fly up-stairs. When they should find her at last she did not know whether she would be obliged to lie or not. She never had lied, but the possibility of the necessity of such a course occurred to her.

She waited until she could not hear a sound, then she slid stiffly down from the suit-cases, opened the closet door softly, and emerged, and there stood Wilbur Bates. He had just re-entered the room and had closed the door behind him. He turned as white as she when he saw her. "So I was not mistaken," he said, in a hoarse whisper. Minnie regarded him in a sort of fascinated way. Her little, beautiful face was woefully scared and piteous, so scared and piteous that it was almost terrible to behold. The panic-stricken soul completely dominated all the soft flush of rose and gold and blue, the sweet curves and dimples. The girl stood naked as to her inner self before the man who loved her in his own way. He moved toward her and patted her shrinking shoulder. "Don't be frightened," he whispered, "I'll find a way out."

Then the quick compassion faded from his face, which became menacing and stern. "What," he demanded, in such a loud voice that Minnie glanced apprehensively at the windows—"what were you do-ing in that closet, hiding in Edward Yale's closet?—*you!*" There was infamous suspicion and horror in his look and voice. Minnie told. She kept nothing back. She repeated what she had interpolated in the sermon, and Wilbur took up the page and read it with a grin. "You know I overheard this afternoon," said Minnie.

"What a girl you are!" said Wilbur. He bent with silent laughter. "Lord," said he, "that poor fellow will be certain to read it; he will think it witchcraft, and the congregation will think it heresy."

"No, he will not read it," said Minnie.

"What do you mean?"

"I shall tell him."

Wilbur took her by the shoulders. "Do you realize what he will think of you?"

Minnie nodded. Her blue eyes looked black, her face was so pale.

"You know, of course, that he is head over ears in love with you." Minnie gasped. "Didn't you know it? Well, I will tell you, because what you have done proves conclusively that you have no love for him."

"But he said—"

Wilbur laughed. "That was nothing. I led him on. I was profaning his holy of holies, and he threw all his old boots in front of it to stop me. You can think yourself lucky that he said nothing worse. You women don't understand a man like Yale. Neither do I, entirely, for that matter. But I wanted him to say things which you would hear and which would not be flattering, and I had my way. I am, I presume," stated Wilbur, with a queer, critical air, as if he stood before some spiritual looking-glass, "not altogether what poets term the soul of honor. I will grant that I do think Yale has been in some doubt about the expediency of marrying you; whether you are not too much of a beauty and a petted darling to make what is popularly called 'a suitable minister's wife.' Yale has an enormous appreciation of the demands of his profession. However, he is in love with you and—" Wilbur started. "You, too!" he cried.

"I am in love with nobody," stated Minnie. But she was too late to conceal the flash of heavenly joy at the revelation of love.

Wilbur was silent for a moment. His curved lips were white. When he spoke it was very slowly, as if he had to make an effort not to stammer. "You know perfectly well," said he, "that, whatever his sentiments have been, they would undergo a change the minute he knew of this. You know that—when he knows—"

Minnie nodded.

"Well, it is like this, then: if he knows, he will put you out of his mind and heart. If he does not know and marries you, such a secret would be like a deadly poison between husband and wife, especially when the husband was Yale and the wife you."

Minnie nodded. She tried to moisten her lips.

"In any light, everything is over, then," said Wilbur. "Here is my proposition: You do not tell Yale, and I will not. Nobody will ever know. If he does read what you wrote" (Wilbur grinned)—"I know what people are—it will go in one ear and out of the other. He may puzzle over it awhile, but it will amount to nothing. You keep quiet, and I will. I have a plan to shield you. There is not much time. And—you must promise not to definitely refuse me for two years. I know you don't love me, but the years are alchemists. Promise, Minnie, quick! I hear them coming."

Minnie heard, too. A horrible panic seized her. To be found here with Wilbur Bates! To have him tell the truth! And how many might come? There might be more than her mother and sister, Maria and the minister. She looked helplessly at Wilbur. He caught her arm, forced her out of the room into the hall to the stairs. "Run for your life," he whispered. "Go into your room and lie down. Leave the door open and you can hear what I tell them. Then you can close it. Nobody will disturb you."

Minnie obeyed. She fled up the stairs and into her room and flung herself on her bed, where she lay panting. She heard Wilbur's voice as through running water.

Wilbur had invention. It was a clever tale which he told. It would require, later on, certain precautions to establish it upon a lasting basis, but it was clever. "She is in her own room," said Wilbur, finally. "She seemed quiet. I would advise nobody, not even her mother, to disturb her to-night. I have never seen any human being in such a panic of terror." Wilbur had been telling a tale of Minnie coming home from the house of one of her girl friends down a lonesome side street, of a following man, of a détour, a mad scamper to the shelter of some thick undergrowth until she encountered Wilbur. "She seemed quiet at last," Wilbur went on. "When we passed my house I made her stop, and my housekeeper gave her a glass of port and a quieting powder which she herself takes for insomnia. She will sleep if not disturbed."

Minnie rose and closed her door softly. Then the house became very still. After a few minutes, however, her door was opened by degrees and a head thrust in. "She is there," proclaimed Maria quite audibly, evidently to Minnie's mother and sister. There were warning hushes, and the door was closed again.

Minnie lay waiting. She had no doubt whatever of what she was to do. She had not the shadow of a doubt. She was not going to remain silent with regard to what she had done. She was going to destroy not only love, but the merest respect for herself in Edward Yale's heart. She thought with hot scorn of Wilbur Bates guarding her secret and waiting for her possible yielding to his suit. She was going to tell the truth. There was absolutely no struggle whatever in her mind, which was fixed in its purpose. She only waited until she was sure that her mother, sister, and Maria were in their rooms. She knew that the poor minister would have to remain in his study writing his sadly interrupted sermon.

Finally she rose and stole down-stairs. She dared not knock at the study door, and was relieved to find it slightly ajar, with a long glimmer of light marking its length. She pushed the door gently open. The minister did not hear her. He sat with his side face to her, and he looked very young, very tired and disheartened. The minister was young, and he had a boyish air which caused him to seem younger than he was. Minnie entered and closed the door softly behind her. Then he saw her.

He started up, looking fairly frightened, and tried to speak, but Minnie interrupted him. She told in a low, mechanical voice, as if she were repeating a lesson, her whole pitiful, absurd little story, but she did omit her eavesdropping in the arbor. That involved too much. She simply said, "You had vexed me about something, and I took that awful way to get even."

To her astonishment, the young man looked relieved. "Goodness!" he exclaimed, like the veriest boy. "You do take a load off my mind. I have been reading that sentence over, and I had an uncle who was crazy, and I wondered if anything were going wrong with me."

Minnie stared. The tears welled up in her blue eyes. She felt as if she had brought her feet down with a horrible jolt upon nothing at all. "I am sorry," she almost sobbed.

Edward Yale looked at her: little, dimpled, feminine thing, weak and strong, harmonies and discords, altogether darling and the beloved of his soul. Then he took her in his arms. "I nearly went mad when I thought you were lost, that something dreadful had happened to you," he said.

"Why?"

"Because I love you. Haven't you known it all along?"

"Then why did you say what you did to Wilbur this afternoon?"

"He did not tell!"

"No, I heard. I was in the arbor. I could not help hearing."

Edward Yale hesitated. He colored. Then he spoke out like a man and called himself names. "I was a coward and a cad to speak so to Bates," he said. "But—well, I will not excuse myself. I was a coward and a cad, but I loved you; only— You shall have the whole truth. You deserve it. I loved you—who could help it?—but I did have doubts, even if you would so honor me, as to whether you would prove just the best wife for me in view of my—sacred calling. You are so very beautiful and you have always been so petted and—"

"Made such a doll of," said Minnie, piteously, looking up at him. "I know that very well, Mr. Yale."

"Will you marry me?" asked the minister.

"I am afraid I am not best for you. What I did shows that you were right. I am just a doll."

"What you did shows you are not a doll—coming down here and telling me the truth. Will you be my wife?"

"If you are sure—"

"No doll ever tells the truth," said the minister. "She cannot, because she is just a pretty little lie herself. Will you?"

"If you are sure.—Poor Wilbur!"

"Oh, he told me. He is going around the world. He said he would get over it, and he will. He hates being unhappy."

"When did he tell you?"

"Ran in here before he went home. Told me he was off to-morrow, and said good-by and told me how you had refused him. He gave a queer reason, though, for going."

"What?"

"He said he was going not because you had refused him, but because he had found out that my doll was a woman. Said he was hit harder than Pygmalion. Now, sweetheart, run up-stairs to bed."

"You will not get your sermon done!" said Minnie after a little. She looked ruefully at the manuscript on the table.

"Of course not, dear. It is Sunday now, and I can't write sermons on Sunday."

"What will you do?"

"Preach an old sermon to a new tune," said the minister.

The Blue Butterfly

She undoubtedly led a double life, but the life of which nobody knew was wonderful, innocent, and tragic. She, who was known as Miss Keyes, who "did dressmaking," as the people expressed it, on a very small scale, with only one regular assistant and another at call for emergencies which seldom arose, who lived a life as austere as a nun's, eating meat seldom, and inhabiting a forlorn little house of which the parlor was the fitting-room (all her poor little decorations having been pushed aside to make room for a platform and a looking-glass purchased on the instalment plan), lived unto herself a life which would, if known, have made her a stranger beyond ken to those who thought they knew her best.

Even Marcia Keyes's own mother did not know her in that strange solitary life of hers. To her Marcia was a good daughter who worked hard and honestly, and who ought to have more patronage. She was also called not at all pretty, and had never had a chance to marry, and, moreover, had not thought of marriage to an extent which had made her unhappy. Sometimes old Mrs. Keyes, Marcia's mother, felt a bit mortified because of her daughter's single estate, and calmly and shamelessly lied to any who cared to listen.

"Marcia has had heaps of chances, perfect heaps," old Mrs. Keyes would say, who was herself a beauty even in old age, and who had in her time numbered lovers by the score. "There was one man threatened to shoot himself, but Marcia wouldn't look at him. I was sort of scared myself. His heart was set on her, and no mistake."

"Did he shoot himself?" inquired the neighbor to whom she told the tale. She was also an old woman, of an investigative turn of mind, and covertly incensed because of Mrs. Keyes's fragile old loveliness, while she was as if made of leather.

Then would the face of old Mrs. Keyes assume an expression of subtlety, although she was not in the least subtle. Upon the contrary, she was so transparent as to be incredible. "I never knowed, for certain," said she. "He went right away out West. He didn't have any near relations round these parts. I never knowed, but he certainly acted as if he might be driv to most anything."

"Was your daughter prettier when she was younger?" inquired the leathery neighbor with open impertinence.

"She always favored her pa's folks," replied old Mrs. Keyes. "But, as for that, if folks had eyes in their heads and looked sharp, they'd see she's enough sight better-looking than most folks now."

The neighbor sniffed offensively, but curiously enough old Mrs. Keyes was right. Her daughter Marcia still had a prettiness so regular and delicate and unobtrusive that it remained unrecognized as such. There was no beauty of color. Marcia had no rose-bloom. Her hair was of a negative blond shade. Her features were very small, and no one of them obtruded itself; still her face was in a way faultless. Marcia knew it, but she cherished absolutely no resentment because others did not know it. Her whole heart was in her work. She cared very little for herself, but she was as devoted to her work as any artist might have been. Marcia would have been an artist under different environments. Canvas and paints had not been at hand, needles and thread and fabrics had, hence her form of expression.

It was a trial to Marcia that she hitherto had not been allowed to express herself as fully by these humble means as she wished. Her patrons were for the greater part poor women, or at least women of moderate means, who could afford to pay very small sums for work. And she had never numbered one young beauty among all her patrons, one who could really display her costume to the enhancement of her own charms and the credit of the dressmaker. Sometimes Marcia had fits of despondency because of it. She confided in Emma White, the elderly woman who worked with her. "Miss Daisy Wheelright is the only really young woman we work for," said she, "and look at her shape!"

"Her shape," agreed Emma White, who was of a sad disposition and poor digestion, which influenced her temper, "is bad."

"Bad! Why won't she put her corset on right? That last dress we made for her was pretty, although it didn't cost much, but she spoiled it by putting on her corset wrong. She looked lopsided and round-shouldered. And that was a pretty dress."

"It was a beauty," said Emma White with sour enthusiasm. Emma had been married and her husband had deserted her, and she was supporting an anemic little girl with white hair and rather wonderful blue eyes. Marcia employed the child to pick out basting-threads, and she was usually in evidence in the box of a workroom with her mother and Marcia. She had been taken out of school, she was so delicate.

Little Mildred was there the day when Miss Alice Streeter and her mother arrived with the proposition that Marcia make Alice her coming-out dress. Mrs. Streeter had never employed Marcia. Mrs. Julius Streeter had gone to exclusive and fashionable *modistes* for her own and her daughter's costumes, but she had seen Daisy Wheelright's last dress, and in spite of the ill-fitting corset had appreciated it; and, since there were just then financial straits in the Streeter family, she had made inquiries, and as a result had descended upon Marcia. Alice had wept at the decision. "I would almost rather not come out at all—give up the dance—than not have Madame Soule make my gown," said she. "I know this new dressmaker will make me look like a perfect fright."

"My dear," said her mother, who had firmness, "if you do have Madame Soule you will most assuredly not come out this year, and the dance will be given up, and I for one have not the face to confront Madame Soule with that last long bill unpaid. Your father has lost lately."

Alice looked alarmedly at her mother. "Not seriously?"

"I don't know about that, but we have to retrench, and I for one thought Daisy Wheelwright's gown a creation."

"I thought she looked a perfect dowdy."

"That," said Mrs. Streeter, "was Daisy."

It ended in the descent of the Streeters in their gleaming limousine upon the little establishment of Marcia Keyes. Old Mrs. Keyes was trembling from head to foot when she made the announcement to her daughter, at work with Emma White on a cheap one-piece suit for a lank elderly girl who worked in a store. "Those Streeters are here in their auto," quavered Mrs. Keyes. "Oh, Marcia!"

Marcia, although she had always been balked by untoward circumstances, had the poise of a conqueror. She rose calmly and untied her apron. "Are there any threads on the back of my dress, Emma?" said she.

Emma scrutinized her narrowly, thin cheeks flushed, thin mouth pursed. She picked off two white threads. Her little daughter Mildred made a weak spring and seized a long black silk filament dangling from Marcia's shoulder. Mildred's wonderful blue eyes gleamed under her drab crest of hair tied with a perky blue bow. She also was impressed.

When Marcia had gone down-stairs, old Mrs. Keyes and Emma looked at each other. "How Marcia can be so calm, I don't see," said old Mrs. Keyes.

"I couldn't," said Emma.

"If the Streeters are coming it will be the making of Marcia," said Mrs. Keyes.

"They are awful stylish folks. Minnie Snyder says they be," remarked the little girl in her thin sweet treble.

"I wonder you let her go with that Snyder girl," said old Mrs. Keyes. "The Snyders ain't much."

"She sat next her in school when she went," said Emma in an apologetic voice. The Streeters were inducing her to feel her *own* need for exclusiveness.

The Streeters came of one of the best old families of the little seaport city. They lived in a really beautiful old mansion-house on The Bluff, and The Bluff was the aristocratic quarter. There had been college, and European travel, even far Eastern travel; and there were friends with famous names from New York who came often. Port Avon had reason to plume itself on the Streeters. In fact, it wore, as it were, the Streeters like a plume upon its urban brow.

But Marcia Keyes, fair hair arranged in tight little crinkles, regular-featured face calm, slender figure erect in well-fitting blue serge, stood before the Streeters, mother and daughter, as more than an equal. The wonderful pride of the artist was upon her. She, in the presence of these who could make her art a possibility, ceased to be Marcia

Keyes. It seemed strange that she owned to her own personality when Mrs. Streeter, large and opulent, seated in a wide dark spread of richness as to skirts and fur-lined wrap, questioned her. Alice, young and exquisite, looked at her with sidewise sulkiness.

"Miss Keyes?" said Mrs. Streeter.

"Yes, I am Miss Keyes," replied Marcia calmly.

She stood looking down upon the Streeters. Mrs. Streeter occupied her little sofa, Miss Alice sat gracefully cross-legged in her best red plush chair. Marcia saw Alice' costume and reflected that a very good tailor must have made it, and not her rival Madame Soule. Madame Soule refused to make tailor gowns. She, however, was sure that Madame had made the exquisite fluffy blouse disclosed by the girl's thrown-open coat.

Alice Streeter was more than a pretty girl. She was a beauty, even a great beauty. She was flawless, face and figure. Marcia, regarding her, realized that to make even one costume for this superb young thing would be bliss. Marcia absolutely required means to the end of her talent, and she had certainly lacked those means. She had made gowns for scrawny women and fat women, for sloppy women and girls. She had never really made one gown for a woman with a perfectly good figure who was well corseted. She was like an artist with poor paints and canvas. She was like a musician with an untuned instrument. Her talent might be a humble one, but of necessity it had only shown dimly under a bushel of untoward circumstance. Now here, for the first time, might be her chance to allow it to show forth its little glory to the full. She waited outwardly calm, to a great extent inwardly calm, but she realized fully what the happenings of the next few minutes might signify to her.

Mrs. Streeter began after a pause of dignity which accentuated all her conversation. "I have heard of you Miss Keyes," she said, "through Miss Wheelright, or rather through Mrs. E. K. Wheelright. I saw a gown which Miss Wheelright wore at Mrs. Stuyvesant's tea last week, and thought it really quite charming. Mrs. E. K. Wheelright informed me that you made it. It was a blue cloth with touches of silver embroidery."

She ended her statement with a slightly interrogative accent, and Miss Keyes replied simply, "Yes, I made that dress for Miss Wheelright."

"My daughter," said Mrs. Streeter after another pause of dignity, indicating Alice by a slight movement of her feather-crowned head. Alice did not look up, her expression intensified in sulkiness. Alice was in a temper, which, however, she knew how to restrain. She was aware that strenuous outbursts of temper were not desirable; moreover, she was not a bad sort.

"My daughter," continued Mrs. Streeter, quite unmoved by Alice' sulkiness,—she knew her daughter would give in gracefully when the time arrived,—"is to have a dance, her first dance, in fact, on New Year's eve, and she will require a new gown, something simple and girlish, but of course *chic.*" Mrs. Streeter made a perceptible hesitation before the last word. She wondered if Miss Keyes knew what *chic* meant.

"Yes," said Miss Keyes.

"I liked Miss Wheelright's gown so much that it occurred to me that possibly you might succeed in making one for my daughter. Do you think you could attempt to make a gown of that description?"

"I can try," said Marcia, and her voice shook slightly. The suspense was becoming intense even for her. Marcia was after all emotional to a high degree. Her self-poise was acquired—well sustained, but in the beginning acquired. Marcia was a very proud woman, and did not wish to endure the contempt for herself which a display of undue excitement and elation would have forced upon her.

When the climax was reached, the decision made, and she knew that she, Marcia Keyes, was to make Miss Alice Streeter's débutante costume, that costume which would be seen by guests from the mighty city as well as by the best of her little native town, that would be described in the papers—when she knew all this, even when she was taking Miss Streeter's lovely measurements, she was perfectly self-possessed, so much so that the Streeters, mother and daughter, commented upon it when they were in their limousine. "She didn't act as if she were at all keen about making that gown for me," said Alice. She was still pouting, but a pleasant look had crept into her eyes. She had taken a fancy to Marcia, whose evident admiration of herself, although unexpressed, had conveyed the subtlest and most delicate flattery. She had caught a look in those blue eyes of the dressmaker which would have befitted a lover.

"Well, she has reason to be," said Mrs. Streeter. "Even if we do not pay her Madame's price, the mere fact of your débutante costume being made by her is a great benefit to an unknown dressmaker."

"Of course," acquiesced Alice easily, nestling the rose tip of her chin in her furs; "still, she was not in the least obsequious, not as much so as Madame, and I liked her for it. I simply detest obsequious people. Of course one knows one's position, that one is not a dressmaker, but I never want anybody to make a door-mat of herself on my account. I feel vicious, like really using her for one."

"I don't like those expressions, Alice," said Mrs. Streeter.

"What is there besides door-mat, Mama?" asked Alice.

Marcia, after the great luxurious car had glided away, sat down alone in her miserable little crowded parlor. She did not quite realize what had come to her. She above all wished to be alone for a few minutes. She had never before known what it was to be perfectly happy—happy with a sense of riotous freedom. Marcia's life had contained few emotional experiences; she was now passing through one, and she felt as if her sense of spiritual modesty would be outraged were anybody to spy upon her. It was only a few minutes, however, before her mother came tiptoeing in with a curious expression as of peaked solemnity upon her pretty old face. Behind came Emma White, with the face of a scenting hound; behind Emma came her little girl, pulling out basting-threads.

"Be you goin' to?" asked old Mrs. Keyes.

"Yes," answered Marcia.

Old Mrs. Keyes laughed with a sort of triumphant cackle. "Sakes, I wonder what Madame Soule will say!" said she.

Emma laughed too, triumphantly but gratingly.

Marcia rose abruptly and left the room. Emma's little girl ran after her, clutching a fold of her dress.

"She acts as if it was nothing at all," said old Mrs. Keyes fretfully.

"She ain't given to saying much, is she?" said Emma White.

"She takes after her father's folks," replied old Mrs. Keyes. "My husband could talk, but he had two brothers that acted as dumb as posts; and as for Grandfather Keyes, he would set and set by the hour together and never open his mouth. For my part, I like folks to speak out when something is on their minds. Of course Marcia is tickled most to death, and she knows what the Streeters coming to her is going to mean. The Wheelrights never meant so much. I guess they've got more money than the Streeters, but they ain't quite so much in it; and, besides, old man Wheelright is as close as the bark to a tree; and that Daisy don't show off her clothes no matter how much pains Marcia takes with them. She's awful slouchy. Marcia is tickled enough, but what I want to know is, why can't she tell her own mother how she feels?" Old Mrs. Keyes, although she spoke fretfully, did not scowl. Her delicately aged face remained smirkingly serene, always intent upon its own prettiness. It was even more smirkingly serene that afternoon when Marcia had gone to New York to purchase material for Alice Streeter's gown, and the neighbor came in.

"So Marcia has went to New York," observed the neighbor with a little tense, spiteful smile. She spoke bad English with an elegantly defiant air. Mrs. Keyes had once corrected her, and she had maintained that her use of verbs was entirely right, and had taken much pleasure since in not departing from her accustomed ways.

"Yes," said old Mrs. Keyes, "Marcia has gone to New York."

"I thought she had went when I see the depot carriage had came for her," said the neighbor.

"Marcia was obliged to go in a hurry," said Mrs. Keyes. "The Streeters came this morning and want her to make a dress for Alice Streeter to wear to her party New Year's eve."

"For Alice Streeter?" gasped the neighbor.

"Yes," replied Mrs. Keyes calmly. "Marcia has gone to buy the material."

"I thought the Streeters had Madame Soule dressmake for them," said the neighbor feebly.

"I rather think they have had, but now they have come to Marcia. Seems they saw that last dress she made for the Wheelright girl."

"Was they so took with that, they had to came to Marcia?"

"I think," said old Mrs. Keyes precisely, "that they did admire Miss Wheelright's dress so much that they felt as if they must come to Marcia."

The neighbor did not stay long after that. She went home with a subdued air. She belonged to the large class whom the triumph of others subdues.

As for Marcia, she came home late. She was tired, but her face was radiant. She had planned a gown for Alice Streeter, and it was to her as if she had written a great poem or composed a sonata. Mrs. Streeter had said that she was to use her own taste in the planning of the gown—she had only fixed the price. Marcia knew that she would far exceed the price, that she would lose money on the gown, but what was money to this, her first real jar of precious ointment? Mrs. Streeter had stipulated that the gown was to be of white; that is, of white primarily; otherwise Marcia had her way, and she reveled. Alice Streeter, although a beauty, was in reality a beauty of a somewhat difficult type to dress when it came to a question of white. She was a blonde, with fair hair showing no gold lights, but rather shadows in its folds. Still she was not an ash-blonde. Her complexion was radiant, her eyes of the intensest living blue. "Just pure white would kill her hair," Marcia reflected, "and nobody would notice how blue her eyes are."

When Alice went home from her second trying-on—the first had been a mere matter of linings—she was enthusiastic. "Mother, that gown will be a dream, I do believe," she said. "Of course it is not finished, but I do think it will be a dream."

When the costume arrived the day before the dance, and was lifted tenderly from its box, and its tissue wrappings removed, Mrs. Streeter looked triumphantly at her daughter. "What did I tell you?" she inquired.

Alice was rapt over the lovely thing. It was in fact rather marvelous. Marcia had gone without some furs and shoes to purchase more expensive materials and trimmings than the price agreed upon would admit. It was a poem, a symphony, of white lace, white chiffon, silver, gold, and touches of blue. With it was a great blue butterfly with silver and gold spangles on his quivering gauze wings, fastened to a silver band for the hair. Marcia had, with the revelation of an artist, seen that a brilliant bit of color was essential in that wonderful shadowy fair head to complete the effect of the whole. "Mother," said Alice before the looking-glass, "look at me with this lovely band on my hair!"

Alice looked at her mother, and the blue butterfly danced in her lovely hair, and her blue eyes shone. "It is charming," assented Mrs. Streeter, "but it will have to be included in the price."

"Oh, Mother, do you think it is fair?"

"Fair or not, it will have to be. I simply will not ask your father to give me another dollar for the occasion."

"Then," said Alice, "Miss Keyes is coming to the dance."

"Alice, are you crazy?"

"No, I am not. Of course I don't mean really coming. How could she? But she is coming to look on. There is the little bay window out of the south chamber that looks on the conservatory on one side and the drawing-room on the other. Nobody will see her there if she sits back. She can see everything and hear the music, and supper can be sent up to her; and you know we are not to use the south chamber except for Aunt Ellen Streeter, and she is so good-natured she will never mind. Anyway, Miss Keyes asked if she might come to help Belle dress me. She said she was anxious to see if everything was right about the gown, and of course I said yes."

"That is a good plan," said Mrs. Streeter. "Something might be wrong with the dress at the last minute, especially with a new dressmaker. If she were Madame Soule it would be different."

"Mother," said the girl, gazing at the lovely shimmer of colors on her bed, "this is prettier than anything Madame ever made for me. Why, you know it is! Look at the detail on the neck, that is all hand-work; and that panel is one mass of hand-embroidery, and that is real lace."

Mrs. Streeter gazed rather suspiciously at the gown. "I do hope she hasn't taken advantage and added to the bill," said she.

"Mother, I know she has not. But, Mother, she will not make one penny on this. What is more, you know she will lose."

"You forget, my dear, how much our patronage means to her," said Mrs. Streeter with her serene smile of confident power.

Alice flushed. She was an honest young creature. "Well, it must mean something, and it shall," said she, "if I have to wear her tag like a brooch on the front of this beautiful gown. Everybody shall know she made it."

"I hope you will not be foolish enough to tell the price; if you do she will go up immediately."

"I would tell the price if I thought it would benefit her," declared Alice hotly, "but I can't see how it would. I will say she charges much less than Madame Soule, anyhow."

"Alice!"

"Yes, Mother, I will."

"Then you are very foolish." Mrs. Streeter went out of the room, filling the doorway with a flounce of silken drapery.

Soon she saw Alice' own little electric car glide out of the drive. "She has gone to invite Miss Keyes," she told herself, and she felt a curious mixture of anger and respect. She knew her own daughter to be of a nobler strain than herself, but was herself noble enough to adore her for it. Besides, the mental vision of the girl in that costume filled her heart with the sweetest anticipation and pride. "Alice will be a dream in her coming-out dress," she told her husband that night.

He smiled; matters had gone a little better with him that day. There had been a change for the better in the market. "If you need more money, Margaret," he said, "I can spare it."

"No, the costume is perfect, and costs just about half what it would have if Madame Soule had made it. It is really rather wonderful, and Alice in it. Well, you will be proud of our daughter, John."

"She will be so pretty that some other man will relieve me of her, I suppose," said the husband a little wistfully. His wife did not understand. She was one of the women to whom marriage is the ultimatum for a girl. She had married off Alice in her cradle, and without a qualm. With the man it was different. "Of course you want Alice to be married to the right sort of man, don't you?" asked the wife wonderingly.

"Yes, I suppose so," said the man with a sigh. He lit a cigar and resumed his reading of the evening paper. Mrs. Streeter took up a magazine. "Miss Keyes furnished a blue butterfly to be worn in the hair, which is the finishing-touch," said she.

"A blue butterfly?" said Alice' father with absent interrogation.

"Yes, a blue butterfly."

Up-stairs Alice at that minute was displaying her new gown to two of her intimate friends, who were exclaiming over it. "You don't mean to say that an unknown dressmaker made that?" cried one, a pretty, nervous, thin girl with eyes like black diamonds, and with a mist of curly black hair over childishly rounded temples.

"Miss Keyes made it," replied Alice. "She made that lovely blue for Daisy Wheelright."

"I thought that was imported," said the other girl, who looked much older than she was, by reason of a stately, mature figure, and the serious gaze of womanhood under smooth folds of hair.

"Fancy E. K. Wheelright having anything imported!" said the dark girl.

"It was imported from 124 Front Street, Port Avon," said Alice. "Miss Keyes made it, and she does not charge anything like Madame; but her prices will go up of course. They ought. I know perfectly well she is losing money on this gown."

"Why?" asked the first girl. "To get custom?"

"No," said Alice, "because of her pride in her work. She is an artist."

"She certainly is," said the second girl thoughtfully. "I don't like my own dress that I'm to wear to your dance—not at all. That is a French thing mother brought over in September, and Madame has been altering it, but I simply don't like it. If there were time I would go to Miss Keyes and have another dress made."

"There isn't, or I would too," said the dark girl. "I don't like my own dress very well. I will get Miss Keyes to make one for your February tea, if you don't mind, Alice."

"Why should I mind?" said Alice. "I want her to get customers. She is the sweetest thing."

Going home, one girl said to the other that certainly Alice Streeter was a dear. "So many would not have told who made that ravishing thing," she said.

"Or wanted others to go to her and have ravishing things made cheaply at first and then send up the price," said the dark girl. "Do you know what will happen, Genevieve, when my brother Tom sees Alice in that gown?"

"No—what?"

"He will wake up," replied the dark girl with a laugh.

"You mean—?"

"I mean that Alice likes him, though she has been a modest violet, and all that sort of thing; and Tom likes her, only he has kept right on seeing a long-legged little schoolgirl intimate with his little sister. But you wait till he sees her in that blue and white and gold and silver."

"You would like it?"

"Like it, my dear Genevieve! Whom would I like for a sister except Alice, unless I could have you, and you are engaged."

"I certainly am," said the womanly girl with a happy laugh. "That is one reason why I want the new dress. I have a green one which Dick doesn't like, and he adores me in blue; and if I can have one for a moderate price for that tea I shall be glad."

Next day the two went to see Miss Keyes. Marcia was pleased, but not enrapt as she had been in the case of Alice. Here was certainly prosperity coming toward her with leaps; these girls also would do her credit. She could lavish upon them with good result, her artist skill, but never again could anything move her as that first gown. She had overdrawn her little bank balance for the materials, but she did not give that a thought. All she lived for was the triumph of New Year's eve, when she would see her lovely work displayed and appreciated. Alice had been charming when she had invited her. She had even been loving, but Marcia had been cold to that. In her was the almost pitiless strain of the great artist. The girl was a darling. She was like an angel for kindness without condescension, but the one thing for Marcia was the fact that she had made her art a possibility. She was sublimely selfish. She was not moved even by her mother's delight over her new customers and the beauty of the coming-out costume. She was not moved even by her own delight, but by something very much beyond all whom she loved and her own self. She lived only for New Year's eve, when she for the first time would see her own art.

The Streeters' limousine was sent for her quite early. Mrs. Streeter had still some doubt. There was a little note suggesting that Marcia bring her sewing implements, in case of possible alterations at the last moment. Marcia put the things in a bag, smiling. As if that work could need alteration! It was perfect, and she knew it.

Marcia Keyes had lived a hard, monotonous life, but after she had fastened the gown on Alice and stood regarding the effect, her life seemed to blossom. She felt for the first time a riotous joy in the fact that she was in the world. She saw for the first time wonderful vistas beyond the world. It was absurd, perhaps, of a dressmaker living in a shabby, hideous little house on a shabby street, a dressmaker under-educated, who had always trodden the narrowest of paths; but she knew the pure joy of a creator as she looked at the girl. Alice was in fact wonderful. Even her own mother gasped when she saw her. Her father passed his hand across his eyes. The maid stared with open mouth; the elderly aunt Ellen exclaimed, then was silent and looked. As for Alice herself, she was not unconscious in one way, but in another. She stood before the long glass, and she recognized herself as being very beautiful, but she was scarcely conscious of the beauty as being her own undisputed possession. It pleased her—she was radiant, she was triumphant, but it was the radiance and triumph of a looker-on. She gazed at herself in the glass as she might have gazed at a portrait of another girl, with the frankest admiration, but quite innocently. She was in reality thinking more of the gown than of herself in the gown. She turned to Marcia.

"You dear thing," she said. "Why, you have made me look like a real beauty!"

Marcia smiled, and her smile was so satisfied, so rapt, that it was almost fatuous. This woman without the usual life of a woman, who had never been wedded, nor borne children, knew in one instant all the joy and sorrow which she had missed. The girl with the blue butterfly atilt in her fair hair, with the beautiful face and figure accentuated by her own beautiful work, was to her more than any daughter could ever have been. She more than loved her; she gained through her the self which she had hitherto missed, the heights of clear joy prophetic of joy to come which she had only dimly sensed upon her little horizon.

"The dress is perfect, Miss Keyes," said Mrs. Streeter finally. She gazed at Marcia with a slightly awed expression. She herself was magnificent in a gown of Madame Soule's, which caused her to glitter and shine with externals, but did not make of herself and itself a true harmony. Alice in her gown was a musical chord ringing perfectly true.

Alice' father went out of the room. When he was in his study he lit a cigar and stood before the open fire. He thought over all Alice' life from babyhood, and a great love, and sadness, and premonition of loss and loneliness, was over him. The child was dancing away from him into the world in her white and blue and silver and gold; she was flying gaily away like a blue butterfly, and he could do nothing. He felt vaguely angry at his wife. She ought to have kept the girl at home for her own parents a while longer. What ailed women, he wondered, that they were so eager to get rid of their daughters?

When his wife came to the door, seeking him, he turned sulkily like

a boy. "Come," said she, "it is time. Doesn't Alice look a dream?"
And the wondering man went with the triumphant woman to the
great drawing-room, decorated and beautiful, where his dearest daughter in her wonderful attire stood, her little gold-slippered foot upon
the threshold of the world.

The Streeters' house, very plain as to its exterior, was rather magnificent otherwise. Much money had been spent upon it, and considerable architectural and decorative talent. It had many unusual features: one was the interior bay window opening from the inner wall of
the yellow room on the second floor. It was an octagonal window,
with leaded panes of almost orange glass. When the window was
closed the effect was as of a great glowing lantern of gold; when open,
nearly the same, for the yellow room was a blaze of golden color,
electric-lighted. Two thirds of this window gave upon the drawing-
room, the remaining third upon the conservatory, which was really a
part of the drawing-room, screened from it by great palms and tapes-
tries instead of doors. That night the window was open, and the
golden light of the room shone out, and Marcia, sitting far to one
side, could see, but could not be seen except vaguely as a dark, slender
shadow.

When the music began she leaned forward and watched. She never
saw anything except the girl, the beautiful girl, in her beautiful dress.
She watched every movement of the lovely young thing. She began
to frown several times when she feared lest Alice might not swirl her
train gracefully; once when a lace flounce caught on a chair her heart
stood still. Then she smiled, and the smile of that hidden watcher of
the festivity of others was full of infinite delight and pathos. Marcia
had never had any real youth of her own. She had never in all her life
participated in a scene like this. The festivity, the merrymaking of the
world had never been for her; but now she entered into it more truly
than any young girl stepping in time to the music. Every dance of the
girl whom she had adorned she danced, every smile of joy she smiled,
and later on came something more. Marcia, watching, saw a young
man dancing with the girl, and she knew what the look in his eyes
meant. She recognized him. He was the brother of the girl who had
come to her for a dress: he was Tom Liston, older than Alice. Marcia
thought him handsome as a prince. A queer vicarious love for him

leapt into her own heart as she saw the face over which the blue butterfly fluttered, upturned to his in the dance. "She loves him, and he loves her. He has just found it out, and it is because she is beautiful in my dress. They are in love, and they will be married, and it is because of my dress," thought Marcia. A maid brought a supper tray to her, and she thanked her, but she did not eat. She waited until Alice and the young man returned from the dining-room. They strolled into the little side room, or conservatory, and sat down near the palms and tapestry. Marcia listened as one who had the right.

"Alice, you are a revelation," she heard Tom Liston say.

And then she heard the girl, her voice raised purposely.

"It is the dress, Tom."

"It is you revealed by the dress perhaps."

"No, the dress."

"Have it the dress then. Alice, I was going right on, never knowing what you were, how I loved you. Why, I might have lost you!"

"If," said Alice very tenderly, and so low then that Marcia could hardly hear, "you would never have known if I had not worn this lovely thing Miss Keyes made, if that is all the reason! If you would never have known otherwise—"

"Heavens," cried Tom Liston, "I knew well enough, only I did not know that I knew, and you in that wonderful harmony of blue and silver and gold and white opened my eyes. Oh, Alice dear, how blue your eyes are!"

"They have always been as blue," said Alice. "It is only the blue butterfly."

"Bless the blue butterfly. Then, Alice, you do, and you will?"

"Perhaps, Tom dear, by and by. Let's not talk more about it to-night. Why, this is my coming-out dance, Tom! By and by."

"You dear!" said Tom, and Marcia heard him, and blushed as if he had spoken to her; but when the blond head and the dark head under the window came close together, Marcia shuddered lest the blue butterfly be crushed. She drew a long breath of relief when the girl and the man came out from under the palms and ferns and swung into a waltz, and the butterfly fluttered intact, and the girl's graceful skirts swept about the flying golden feet, quite unrumpled.

Marcia was sent home in the limousine just after midnight, but before the maid came for her, Alice came hurrying into the room and bent over her, whispering. "Dear Miss Keyes," she whispered, "it is a great secret, although you have heard something while you sat in this window. It is a great secret, not to be known for ever so long, because it will break poor father's heart to lose me anyway, I am afraid, but some time I am going to marry Mr. Liston, and he only found out he wanted me to-night, when I wore for the first time your beautiful dress. And you must promise to make all my dresses after this." Then the girl's soft lips had been on Marcia's cheeks, and she had gone; and for the first time a throb of love for the girl herself warmed the woman's heart, and she realized something really more precious than art.

Marcia realized that as well as art as she lay awake all that night until the sun of the New Year shone in her east window. All night she had lain awake and dreamed of the girl's future joys. Marcia was like a violinist with his first great violin; like a harpist with a harp of heaven; like an artist who sees for the first time upon the canvas the realization of his ideal; like a singer who flings out for the world a voice so sweet she knows it not for her own. Marcia, while the girl slept, composed symphonies of her future joys, and costumes befitting them. She planned wedding garments; she even went farther, and lay with the tiniest delicacies of apparel floating before her vision like shreds of harmonies. The girl slept while the woman whose inspiration she was painted, and sang, and composed, all wonderful combinations of beauty which her future might hold; and so great an artist was she, although but a humble wielder of needle and thread, she knew it all a part of herself, even when the sun of the New Year shone in her east window.

Friend of My Heart

Friend of my heart, tho' many years
We journey thro' this vale of tears;
Tho' eyes grow dim, and white thy hair,
Forever to me young and fair:
To thee this little book I give,
And if you love me, pray receive,
And let the giver be to thee
What thou hast always been to me:
Friend of my heart, for weal or woe,
For time and for eternity.

With a fine pen and in her very best hand, Catherine Dexter had copied the verse of faulty rhythm and rhyme from a yellow old manuscript, which had belonged to her Aunt Catherine, long since dead, considered by her intimates a poetess. Then Catherine, her face still grave and her kind eyes still intent, had sent the verse in an album to Elvira Meredith for a Christmas present, for she considered that Elvira was indeed the friend of her heart. And Elvira had sent in return a sweet little note of thanks, written on gilt-edged paper, and a beautifully embroidered black silk apron.

That afternoon the two ladies had thanked each other in person, and now Elvira was at Catherine's house, and they were making little lace candy-bags for the Sunday-school Christmas-tree the next day. It was the time before the Civil War, when Sunday-school Christmas-trees were at their prime. Both Elvira and Catherine had Sunday-school classes.

"We might just as well admit that we are not girls any longer," Elvira declared, as she reached for another piece of lace.

"Women cannot remain girls forever," replied Catherine, who had a goodly supply of philosophy, and a disposition to accept the inevitable gracefully.

But Elvira was different. She had been a great beauty. She had smiled at and scorned many lovers. She had played the harp and sung. She had possessed all the accomplishments of her day. Now they seemed to pale. She was in a way still a beauty, but a beauty whose charms had been in the world so long that they had become as an unconsidered rose. Elvira herself no longer took pleasure in regarding her face in her looking-glass. She was dainty about her dress from force of habit; but in her heart of hearts it did not seem to her to matter. Nothing of that sort had mattered very much since Lucius Converse had gone away after her last rejection of his suit.

Elvira had not intended the rejection to be final. In those days of her youth, she had been unable to consider any adverse decision with regard to love of herself final. Then it had seemed to her that, once love, it must be always love. Then she had believed in the enduring power of that face in the looking-glass. How many times her thoughts had run in this groove! Until they had worn it so deep they could no longer climb over the sides of it, she now realized. And they would soon give up trying to climb over, she told herself, as she sewed bag after bag. It was because she was growing old. She shook her head hopelessly. There were young girls out in the kitchen, making molasses candy and stringing popcorn for the Christmas-tree, and their happy laughter and chatter made Elvira sadder still.

"I, for one, shall be glad when Christmas is over," she said to Catherine. "I feel too old for Christmas. I feel left out. Hear those young things in the kitchen, talking and laughing! Addie Emerson is telling Faith Wheeler how Tommy Keene took her sleigh-riding. You and I never go sleigh-riding nowadays, Catherine."

"Jonas can take us, any time you wish," said Catherine.

"Thank you," replied Elvira. "Going sleigh-riding behind your hired man, driving your fat old black horse, is not the kind of sleigh-riding I mean. I mean flying over the hard, white snow on a moonlight night, with the horse shying at the shadows and the bells ringing like mad and—a young man driving—with one hand." Elvira laughed a little in spite of herself.

Catherine colored. Then she also laughed. "Elvira Meredith, I am ashamed of you!"

"Well, I am not quite old enough or sour enough not to laugh and be ashamed of myself when I say a foolish thing," said Elvira, "but I do feel sad this Christmas. I realize that I have lost, and by my own fault, so many of the great gifts of life. I wonder whether by another Christmas my hair will not be gray, and I obliged to wear a cap and front-piece?"

Catherine laughed again. "Elvira," said she, "I cannot see a single gray hair."

"There are a few, and I shall look a fright in a cap. I tried on mother's the other day. However, that will not matter." Elvira meant that Lucius Converse would not see her in a cap, and that was a comfort.

"I don't think things of that sort really do matter," said Catherine in her philosophical way, "and I do not think you need to worry about the cap for a good many years, anyway."

"Of course that is unworthy," admitted Elvira, "but you must know, Catherine, that my life is—well—not exactly what I expected, not quite calculated to make me very happy."

Catherine glanced about, and in her face was a covert sense of satisfaction, and of self-accusation before the satisfaction. Catherine had the best house in the village. The room in which she was seated was handsomely furnished. There was a Brussels carpet, there were a haircloth sofa and chairs, and the south windows were filled with blooming oleander-trees. Beyond was a glimpse on one side of a fairly glorious "best" parlor, with red silk-damask sweeps of curtains; on the other, of a dining-room with a Chippendale sideboard, laden with glass and old silver. The house was warm from a hot-air furnace, the only one in the village. "I realize that I have more to make me satisfied with my lot than you have, dear," said Catherine, and her eyes were apologetic.

"Oh, I am glad you have such nice things," said Elvira. "I don't mind that. Of course it is hard, having so very little—we have to manage so carefully. But poor mother is so trying nowadays that I can hardly bear it, although I do try. Henrietta does not seem to mind. She has a better disposition than I have, I suppose." Henrietta was Elvira's older sister.

"Henrietta has never expected so much of life, therefore she is naturally not so disappointed at not having it," remarked Catherine.

"I fear that does not excuse me," said Elvira, "but I will own that this is the saddest Christmas I ever knew—and these foolish little lace candy-bags are driving me crazy!"

Catherine laughed. They were sewing the bags with colored wool, and Elvira's had knotted under her nervous taper fingers. "Here, don't break that wool," cried Catherine. "Give it to me; I will get the knot out!"

Elvira thanked her when she took it back. "What have you for your Sunday-school class?" said she.

Catherine hesitated. "Little coral pins."

"Oh," exclaimed Elvira, "the girls will be delighted. I have nothing for mine except some little books—not very interesting, I fear."

"Girls always like books."

"I don't know. When I was a girl, I would have much preferred a coral pin. I do hope my Sunday-school class and my friends will not give me any more worsted things this year. I had so many last year that I can never use them up if I live to be a hundred; and they are dreadful things for moths. I am not able to give much, but I have tried to give what people would not be miserable over. Oh, the girls are coming! It is time to go home. The days are short now. Well, the candy-bags are done: this is the last."

The young girls flocked in and took formal leave of Elvira and Catherine, whom they considered very old. Elvira, watching them scurry down the path between the box-borders, sighed. She was pinning her shawl. Catherine was also pinning hers. It was after sunset, and Catherine always walked home with Elvira if she remained late. Elvira was a timid soul, and Catherine had never known what fear was.

Elvira lived in the next house, but the road was lonely, skirting a wide field. Elvira's house, the old Meredith homestead, showed in the moonlight a curious vagueness of outline, like a sketch done with a soft pencil. It was out of repair. Its shingles flapped like the very rags of a home. Its sills were rotten; the doors and windows sagged. The interior showed a stately shabbiness.

When Elvira entered, she realized the contrast between her home and her friend's. It was chilly. There was also a not altogether disagreeable, but musty odor, like the breath of the old house. That night when Elvira went up-stairs to her own room the cold was so intense that a rigid chill held her like the arms of a skeleton. There was no heat in the room. Elvira seldom afforded a fire on the hearth. She hurried to bed, and lay there long awake and shivering, with the moonlight lying in a broad blue shaft across the floor.

She could see from the bed a light in Catherine's dining-room; and she wondered why she was up so late, for it was after ten, which was considered very late in Abbotsville.

Catherine, when she had returned, had been accosted by her old servant-woman. "I found some jars of that peach preserve beginning to spoil," said she, "and I didn't dare to leave it, for all it's so cold. So I have been scalding it up. I didn't find it out till I went to the store-room to get the jelly for supper; then I noticed the peach looked sort of queer." Maria wished Catherine to taste of the preserve to make sure that it was right; and Catherine, who was fond of sweets, sat down at the dining-table with a saucer of peaches before her, and began to eat. "It is very nice," said she.

Maria, who was privileged, sat in a chair in the corner, beaming. "I'm glad," she replied proudly. "I know you set store by peach. I'm glad I happened to notice it." Maria was a tall woman, with a thin skin roughened by frequent scrubbing with soap and water, with gray-blonde hair, and a sharp nose terminating unexpectedly in a knob, upward turned. "Mr. Lucius Converse is in town," she added.

Catherine started and paled slightly. "Who told you, Maria?"

"Nobody told me. I saw him go by when I was in the butcher's shop," she replied, with pleased importance.

Catherine took another spoonful of peach preserve. Her hand was quite steady, but she could hear her heart beat.

"He hasn't changed one mite, except he's raised a beard, and mebbe he's a little bit heftier," said Maria.

"Hasn't he?"

"He was dressed real handsome, too. He wore a greatcoat and a silk hat, and he carried a cane."

Catherine took another spoonful of peach preserve.

"The butcher said he was stopping at the tavern," continued Maria; "said he'd spoke to him—just as pleasant as he used to be. Mr. Lucius Converse always was real pleasant spoken."

"Yes, he was," assented Catherine. She took another spoonful of peach preserve, and the sweet, smiling face of a young man of long ago seemed just before her. How Lucius had smiled, had smiled at everybody, at her, Catherine, as well as at Elvira! Perhaps Lucius Converse had smiled too often and too impartially, had said pleasant things too often and impartially. It was quite probable, indeed, that Lucius had smiled as pleasantly at the butcher as he had smiled at Catherine. But in her heart the smile had remained, like a rose pressed in a book of memory. Catherine could look at it, but she seldom did. She was entirely too sensible; moreover, she had not known that Lucius had not married. She did not know, that evening, until Maria spoke again.

"The butcher says he ain't never married," said Maria presently.

"Hasn't he?"

"No, he ain't. Mebbe he's come back to get Miss Elvira."

"Perhaps he has," assented Catherine. However, she remembered one evening when she was a girl, when Lucius had escorted her home from evening meeting. It was true that Elvira was visiting in Boston at the time; but on that evening, walking along the sidewalk upon which the hard-packed snow glistened under the moonlight, making it like a track of blue and crystal, Lucius had, if ever a woman could tell when she was made love to, made love to her, to Catherine.

Even now Catherine, bringing her hard common sense to bear upon the sweet old memory, told herself that it was entirely true: Lucius had made love to her. He had said things which could have only one meaning. He had looked at her with eyes which expressed devotion. He had not asked her to marry him, but Catherine, when she entered her house door, was convinced that he loved her, and not Elvira, as she had thought. She dreamed of wedding Lucius.

Then Elvira had returned, and appeared at meeting in a green-shot silk and a hat trimmed with roses, tied under her chin with white lutestring ribbons. And Lucius had never taken his eyes from that face of delicate, drooping loveliness. That evening he had walked home with Catherine and Elvira, had dismissed Catherine not ungently with a good night at her own gate, and had walked on with Elvira.

Catherine had sat on her front porch that evening and watched Elvira's house. It had remained dark nearly an hour. Then a window had gleamed out with light, and soon she heard a quick step. She had hurried into her own house and closed the door; but through a side light of the door she had seen Lucius falter and hesitate, as if he had a half-mind to enter. Then he had gone on, and the next day Elvira had come over and told her of his going West, and her rejection of his offer of marriage.

Now, after all these years, hearing that Lucius Converse had returned to Abbotsville and was still unmarried, Catherine wondered why he had come back. He had a married sister living in Boston; but there was nobody, apparently, to bring him back to the little village. Catherine was a shrewd woman, and she had come to estimate Lucius rather shrewdly, to understand him. He was a successful lawyer, and had made a considerable fortune. He had flitted from pillar to post in his wooing of women; but when the time arrived for him to settle for life, he would inevitably choose an harbor which he considered safe.

Catherine said to herself: "Lucius has come back here for a wife. He wants a wife and a home. He knows that neither Elvira nor I have married. Which of us does he wish to marry?" She considered Elvira's beautiful face. She considered her own—not unattractive—and her disposition, which was of a steadier, serener type than Elvira's and might appeal to an older man wishing for a peaceful and well-ordered household. She did not consider her superior financial state as an asset. Lucius had money enough of his own, and he had never been a fortune-hunter. Catherine, finishing her peach preserve, decided that she did not know which of them he wanted, Elvira or herself.

The next day was Christmas. Catherine heard early in the morning that Lucius had gone to Boston to spend the day with his sister. She said nothing about him to Elvira. She thought that Elvira also might have heard; but she decided that she had not, when they were working together in the church vestry over the tree. Elvira would have betrayed it, had she known. The nervous, high-strung creature could not hold a secret; it rasped her soul until she had rid herself of it. A woman of no mystery, except the inevitable mystery of every individual; one always knew, however one might disapprove, that there was nothing hidden in her for further disapprobation.

That day Elvira displayed all her weaknesses. It was Christmas. She was sad, almost pettish, because she missed for herself what would have made the day really Christmas. The lines between her blue eyes were strongly marked; her sweet mouth drooped at the corners. In the evening, when they were all assembled for the Christmas-tree, she did not look as pretty as usual.

Catherine regarded her uneasily. She had not told her about Lucius, because she feared to make her more nervous. Now she had a guilty feeling that if he should come to the tree he would not see Elvira at her best. Her hair was drawn back too tightly, her smile was forced. Her dress, even, was not as tasteful as usual. Elvira, although she had little money, managed her dress very well; but that evening her old black silk was shiny across the back, and gave her a bent appearance. Moreover, black never suited her. When her name was called, she went to the tree to receive her gifts, and returned with the same set smile.

The low-ceilinged vestry was aromatic with the odor of evergreen. The tree twinkled with lights, and its boughs were bravely festooned with strung popcorn. From all the settees looked eager faces, of youth, middle-age, and even age. There was an effect, to the imaginative, as of hands outstretched for the bounty of love itself. The children, although hampered by the uncouth fashions of their day—the girls with hoops, and starched pantalettes showing under crude-colored woolen gowns, with their childish locks pulled back from their candid brows; the boys in absurd jackets and trousers made by unskilled hands—were still beautiful with the unrivaled beauty and radiance of youth, which, having as yet had nothing, expects the whole earth.

Poor Elvira was as an introverted high-light of melancholy upon the festive picture. When people talked to her, she replied politely. Elvira was a lady, born and bred, but her face never once changed. She opened none of her packages while she was in the vestry.

Catherine walked home with her, along that track of snow gleaming with blue and crystal under the moon, waved over with lovely shadows from the trees bowing gracefully before the north wind. At first they were of a numerous company, which gradually dispersed, some entering home-doors, some turning into by-streets; and when they reached Catherine's gate, the two were quite alone. Then Elvira spoke, and her speech was at once tragic, absurd, pitiful. She railed, she raged, she gestured. Always she was graceful; never once did she lose the sweet undertone from her voice. Poor Elvira had an essentially sweet nature, but her highly-strung nerves quivered into discords under the strain of her life. Suddenly she tore the wrapping from a package. "An old blue head-tie!" said she, and gave the thing a fling.

Catherine stared, aghast. "Elvira, are you crazy?"

"No," said Elvira, in her strained, sweet voice, "I am not crazy. I am keeping from being crazy." She tugged at the cord of another package. "*Another* blue head-tie!" said she, and flung it.

"Why, Elvira!"

"Don't mind me, Catherine. I *must* do it." Elvira opened the next package. "A great green and white pin-cushion," said she. She gave that a toss, and it rolled like a ball.

"Why, Elvira!"

"I must, Catherine! Here is another pin-cushion, a red and white one." Elvira tossed that, and kicked it with her slender, pointed foot. "Here is another, and another! Just as I thought—all my Sunday school class has given me pin-cushions. I must have ten!" One after another, the pin-cushions dropped on the hard snow and were propelled by Elvira's lady-feet.

"Why, Elvira!"

"Catherine, they *knew* I did not want these things! They *knew*, and they did not care! We have things we do not want because nobody cares. It is awful; I am wicked, but it *is* awful!" Suddenly Elvira wept. She sobbed aloud like a child. The two were before Elvira's gate. "Somehow, this Christmas," Elvira lamented, "I have lost all courage, and all these worsted things seem to just make my heart break. I seem to look ahead and see nothing but worsted things that I don't want, on all my Christmas-trees, the rest of my life."

"You are not well, Elvira," said Catherine. "How much have you eaten today?"

Elvira hesitated. "We had a very good roast of pork," said she, with a show of defiance.

"You did not have chicken?"

"We none of us care so very much for chicken," Elvira said, but Catherine knew the truth: that her friend could afford nothing except the roast of pork, and that Elvira had never liked pork.

"They talked about having an oyster-supper tonight in the vestry, and I did not know they had changed their plans," said Catherine.

"Yes, they did talk about an oyster-supper," returned Elvira, in a hungry voice, "and they had cake and coffee. The cake was very nice."

Catherine knew that Elvira never ate cake. She gave her friend's arm a little pull. "Come home with me," she whispered. "There are oysters enough for a nice stew."

Then Elvira spoke lamentably. She never quite lost her dignity, her innate ladyhood; but she spoke as her friend had never dreamed she could speak. She revealed depths of her nature hitherto unsuspected. "It is not oyster-stews I want," said she, "neither do I want a lot of worsted things. I want the gifts of life that matter!"

"I don't think you ought to mind not being married quite so much," said Catherine calmly. She spoke with reason. At that time, spinster-hood was not usually voluntary.

Elvira turned upon her fiercely. "You think that is all? You know, and I know, that marriage is the crown of life for a woman, whether she owns to it or not; but women can live without crowns. It isn't alone being not married! It is everything else. I shall never, during all my life, have anything more than I have now. I have to give up my dreams, and I suppose I love my dreams more than I would the reality. I have to give up a real home. Sometimes I feel as if mother fairly hated me, because—with my face—I have this sort of life. Henrietta is more contented than I *can* be, although she has no more than I have. I know she is a better woman, but I am the way I was made, and I can't get outside of myself to make myself over. Of course, I know it is all my own fault that my life is not different, but that makes it harder. Catherine, I know you despise me, and I despise myself, but somehow, tonight, I have to tell what is in my heart. Somehow all those worsted things are the last straws. I can see nothing ahead of me but pin-cushions and tidies and head-ties, paving the road to my grave: all things I don't want." Elvira flourished another small parcel. "Here is another!" she cried. She tore the package open. "Nothing was lacking except a worsted lamp-mat," said she, "and now I have that!" She flung the fluffy thing down. Some beads on it sparkled tinily in the moonlight. She trampled on it.

Again it seemed monstrous to Catherine, who had never so lost control of herself. "Why, Elvira!" she said.

"Yes, I know how I seem. But perhaps I may be better for telling you, for speaking out just once. Ever since father died and mother got so nervous, Henrietta and I have just lived along like beads on a string, afraid to move lest we wear our string out. Henrietta has never realized that she was a bead on a string, but I have, and it is awful. Now I will go in, and mother will hear me. No matter how softly I move, she always hears me. She will scold me, and Henrietta will not say anything, and I shall go to bed and not be able to sleep, and— Christmas day will be over." Elvira flung her beshawled arms around her friend and kissed her cool cheek with hot lips. "God bless you, Catherine," she said; "I know I am wicked, but tonight I had to be wicked in order to be good."

"Well, go in now and be good," returned Catherine, with a soft, soothing laugh.

Elvira fled into the house.

Catherine turned and went her way. She did not fairly understand her friend, but she had strong convictions with regard to the oyster-stew, also reluctant convictions with regard to Lucius Converse. Catherine had a suspicion that he was at the root of it all: that Elvira had never forgotten him. She was surer because Elvira never mentioned his name. If Elvira, as frank as she was, was silent, her silence shouted.

Then Catherine met Lucius Converse—a big, blond-bearded man.

"Hullo, Catherine," he said, as if they had met but yesterday.

"Is it you, Lucius," said Catherine, and she also spoke as if they had met but yesterday.

The man looked down at the woman, and his face was tender. "As far as I can see, and the moon makes it as bright as day, you look exactly the same," said he.

"You look the same, only you have raised a beard."

"Yes, I raised a beard right after I went away. I weigh more than I used to."

"So do I."

"Well, I can't tell about that, you are so wrapped up in that shawl thing. What are all those bundles you are carrying? Let me take some of them."

"No, they are not heavy, and I am almost home. They are Christmas presents. I have been to the Sunday-school Christmas-tree in the vestry."

"I meant to get home for that. I thought I would see my old friends there, but I missed my train at the Junction, and the station was closed, and I have been three solid hours on the road, and I am cold and half-starved; but I thought I would look up somebody tonight, anyhow, as long as it is Christmas. Why are you headed this way? The church isn't back there."

"I went home with Elvira. You remember Elvira?"

"Of course I do, and you, too. I was going to make a call—" Lucius Converse hesitated. Suddenly he became not entirely sure whether he had been about to call on Catherine or Elvira. Catherine's face looked very good, even dear, to him, uplifted, with the moonlight flooding down upon it. She wore a white wool hood, and her calm face was framed softly in pale folds.

Catherine was thinking very swiftly, she who seldom thought swiftly, "If he goes to Elvira's now, he will get no supper, and the house will be cold." It also flashed through her mind that Elvira was not looking as pretty as usual. "You had better call on me first, Lucius," said Catherine, "and I will make you a hot oyster-stew. Then it will not be too late. You can still call on Elvira."

"A hot oyster-stew sounds good to me," replied Lucius happily. "Exactly what I want."

"And coffee?"

"That, too."

They entered the warm house. "This is comfortable," said the man. It seemed like home to him. Listening to Catherine stepping about in the kitchen, from which presently issued savory odors, he became almost convinced that he had intended to call at this house whose door he had passed. He was not essentially romantic, nor in the fullest sense a lover. He had returned to Abbotsville with the express purpose of seeking a helpmate. He knew that Elvira was still unmarried, and he could bring up the image of her lovely face quite distinctly to his memory. Still he knew, and also with interest, that Catherine was still unmarried. Now here was Catherine, in some respects more attractive than in her early youth; and more than herself was what she personified—the warm shelter and peace of Home.

And he leaned back in the haircloth rocker, and felt distinctly disinclined to make another call that night.

Meantime Catherine, preparing his supper, reflected and decided. She knew what she knew. She could have Lucius Converse for a husband if she chose. She knew that she was fond of him, and that he would be as fond of her, as the years passed, as of any woman. She had also a sudden illumination, this unimaginative, unromantic woman: she realized what the best of a marriage might be—the comradeship, the homemaking, possible only for the opposite sexes. She understood perfectly what she had to accept, or to resign. She loved Lucius with the best love that a good woman past her youth could give a man. She did not think of him as vacillating and swayed this way and that by the wills of women. She judged him correctly: he was of the type which, seemingly swayed by others, is swayed in reality only by themselves, never losing an osierlike foothold in their own interests. At the same time, no man would make a better and kinder husband. He was essentially a good man. This home-hunt, which the woman divined, proved it to her. It spelled more goodness than merely a wife-hunt. Catherine loved Lucius, but she loved him after the manner of a queen dignified before her own needs, and capable of foregoing them.

She had only one doubt: would Elvira make Lucius a good wife? Her whole faith clamored, "Yes." Elvira would probably be better for the man than she. Elvira loved him, and her dependence would arouse his strength. "The women who need men to take care of them are the women who make men able to take care of them," Catherine, forced into epigram by the strenuousness of the situation, told herself. Then she made her choice.

When Lucius was seated in the dining-room, with the steaming oyster-stew and the coffee, Catherine was flying across the field between her house and Elvira's. Catherine pounded on a side door, and Elvira came running.

"Hurry, and put on your blue silk," gasped Catherine. "I will put some more wood on the fire. Hurry! Lucius Converse is coming over to see you! He is eating an oyster-stew at my house. I ran over to tell you. Hurry!"

Elvira paled. Then a wonderful flush spread over her face and neck. She smiled a heavenly smile of a soul abashed by happiness undeserved, coming in the midst of complaints and ingratitude.

Her old mother had followed her to the door, her nightcap askew, grizzled locks flying around her face of a shrew. Now she smiled, and her smile was also wonderful before unexpected blessing. She called out to her daughter Henrietta, who occupied a room on the ground floor, "Elvira's old beau is coming to see her!" And the scolding old voice gave a chord of love and repentance and amazing gratitude.

Henrietta looked out of her bedroom door at Catherine, stirring the hearth fire into a blaze, at Elvira, fumbling with her hair. Henrietta's large, patient face, surmounting the frill of her nightgown, had a charming expression. She held forth a mass of shimmering blue. "Here is your blue silk, Elvira. It was in the closet here," she said. "Put it on out there where it is warm. If you go into a cold room to dress, you will get chilled. Here is a brush, too. Don't strain your hair too tight from your face!"

Elvira took the blue silk and ran to the old gilded pier-glass. The room, although shabby, was still stately, full of lovely effects of faded rose and lilac from ancient damask curtains and chair-coverings. The glass reflected, beside Elvira's face, the high-leaping flames of orange and violet on the cleanly-swept hearth.

Catherine hurried home.

Lucius had finished his oyster-stew. He gazed at Catherine with eyes ready to see in her face the fulfilment of his dreams and his longing.

But Catherine, seeing, would not see. She brought out pound-cake, and poured another cup of coffee. Then she said: "After you have eaten your cake and finished the coffee, you had better go, for it is really late. Elvira has not yet retired. There is a light in the parlor."

Lucius looked at her. He obviously hesitated.

Catherine held his overcoat ready. When he had finished his coffee, she touched his shoulder. "You must go," she said firmly, "or Elvira will retire for the night; and as for me—I must attend to making some ginger-tea for Maria. I have heard her cough since I came in."

Lucius looked longingly at her. He stammered. Catherine did not flinch. She held his coat. He shrugged into it, and went.

After the man was seated in the old parlor of the other house, with the other woman, beautiful as he had never known her, clad in shimmering blue, with her soft curls drooping over her crimson cheeks, with a dawn-surprise of happiness in her blue eyes, with the sweetest smile, as of a soothed infant, on her lips, Catherine stood gazing out

of a window across the moonlit field. She spoke aloud. A great loneliness was over her, and she wished to hear a human voice, even her
own. "Elvira has got the Christmas present she wants," said she.
There was in her voice the utmost womanly sweetness, and yet a high
courage, as of one who leads herself to battle. A peace and happiness
so intense that it seemed fairly celestial came over her. She could not
understand why she was so happy. She did not even dream of the truth:
that the gift of the Lord, the true Christmas gift, is, for some of his
children—the more blessed and the nearer Him—self-renunciation.
She did not know that, by giving, she had received a fuller measure
than she had given.

Then, smiling blissfully, all alone there in the moonlight, softly she
repeated to herself the beginning of the stanza she had written in
Elvira's album: "Friend of my heart—." And that friend of her heart
seemed standing before her, radiant, and blessing her.

Criss-Cross

Selma Wheelock sat in her accustomed place beside a front window. She swayed gently in her hair-cloth rocker. She leaned her head back and sidewise, and gazed out at the prospect with an expression almost absurdly tragic. Tragedy did not sit comfortably upon those mild features in that long, sweet face, softly curtained with folds of thin, blond hair which had not turned gray, although Selma was almost an old woman. However, tragedy, hawk-like, unswerving, did look from Selma's blue eyes. She might, from her expression, have been gazing at some scene of horror instead of at her own tidy, square front yard with its gravel walk bordered with leafless shrubs, with a leafless cherry-tree standing stark upon one side, and a leafless horse-chestnut on the other. Beyond the front yard with its prim fence was the main street of the village; opposite was Maria Hopkins's house. When Selma's eyes roved beyond her own front yard and the main street, and fastened upon Maria Hopkins's house, the tragedy deepened. It seemed about to swoop, fierce, beaked and clawed. There was seemingly nothing exasperating about the opposite house. It was a plain white structure with a door in the middle front and two windows on each side of the door. The house was raised upon terraces over which clambered rough stone steps. Upon each of the terraces were two trees—cherry upon the upper, horse-chestnut upon the lower. Two of the windows at the front displayed slants of lace curtains, two plain white shades.

As Selma gazed at the house an ugly frown came between her eyes. She set her mouth hard. Her face did not relax when a woman opened the opposite door. The woman wore a gray shawl and a white wool head-tie. She locked the door and put the key under a blind of the first window to the right. Selma frowned more deeply, but her eyes lit up.

The woman, who was Maria Hopkins, came down the rough stone steps. She trudged across the street. She carefully held up her black gown, although the wind-swept road was quite dry. Maria's skirts whipped around her advancing knees; her shawl-ends flew out; her head-tie fluttered. Maria did not bend her head before the icy blast. She came on, setting her large rubbered feet down squarely. Maria always wore rubbers in winter, whether it was wet or dry. She opened Selma's front gate, closed it carefully, walked up the gravel path, nodded to Selma in the window, and went through another gate to the side door on the south. She left her rubbers on the door-stone, opened the door, entered, crossed Selma's large, cold kitchen, and was in the warm sitting-room.

"Good afternoon, Selma," said she drearily. Selma responded as drearily.

"Good afternoon," said she. "Take your things off, Maria."

Maria removed the white hood and large gray shawl, and stood revealed—short, stout figure, with a face which had been pretty, but now was old and sagging and worried. She wore a black skirt and a purple waist and a white apron trimmed with knitted lace.

"Sit down," said Selma.

Maria took the chair at the opposite window. That was also a rocker. Both women swayed to and fro, and did not speak for some time. Now and then they exchanged glances of mournful understanding. Finally Selma spoke.

"We would have been most there by this time," she said.

"Yes, we would," agreed Maria.

"Well, we did what was right, anyway," said Selma.

"*I* did," said Maria. "Aggie is related to me. You hadn't any call to do anything."

"I had as much call as you."

"Aggie is no kin of yours. You had no call."

"I had a call to do my duty," said Selma.

"It is a good deal to do your duty when you ain't any direct call from relations. Aggie ain't related to you."

"No, she ain't, and I guess I can stand it," said Selma.

"Aggie means right," declared Maria, with half-hearted defense. Her eyes were condemnatory, even as she spoke.

"For my part, I am sick of folks meaning so well and not acting up to it," said Selma. "I would rather they didn't mean quite so well and act as if they meant a good deal better. Aggie always treated you as if you were the dirt under her feet, Maria."

"She did mean well," repeated Maria, but her eyes continued to condemn.

"She didn't *act* well," said Selma; "when she came to live with you after her folks died, she let you slave, and never lifted a finger."

"She had to practise, and give music-lessons."

"Fiddlesticks! She never had more than five music scholars, and she never played the piano well enough to teach, anyhow, and she only taught so as to be able to get fine feathers to catch Tom Willard. Well, she caught him, and she kept right on meaning well and working him for all she was worth. She was so extravagant he got in debt. I had it straight that she used six eggs in cake when the hens wasn't laying, and she used to leave all the draughts on the sitting-room stove open till it was so hot she had to fling up all the windows in midwinter to cool off, instead of saving the coal bills. Then, just when we had saved enough to go on that excursion to Washington, it had to come out that Tom was behind in his taxes and the house would be sold over their heads, and she had to come whining around you, all dressed up, too, with a hat with a long feather, and a silk dress, and we had to give up our money we had saved to take that excursion we had been lotting on so long."

"You never ought to have given it up," said Maria. "Aggie is no kith nor kin of yours."

"You don't suppose," replied Selma, with delicate hauteur, "that I gave that money to Aggie Willard? I gave that money to the Lord."

"I suppose we both did."

Selma brought her gentle swaying to an abrupt conclusion. She set both slender, pointed feet in their congress shoes firmly on the floor. "Yes, we both did," said she, "and it ain't becoming in women that call themselves Christians to complain, even if the Lord does send such a silly, extravagant thing as Aggie out collecting. What we've got to do now is just one thing—"

Maria stared. "What?"

Selma looked almost sternly at her friend. "Maria Hopkins, we have *got* to have a change."

"I don't see how, Selma. I haven't a cent except just what I need to keep going, and you haven't; and I haven't got anybody to visit except Aggie, and you haven't got anybody."

"Who said anything about visiting anybody? I wouldn't visit anybody if I had a town full of relations. Visiting was never according to my ideas, but you and I, Maria Hopkins, have got to have a change, and I have just found out how."

"How?"

"It won't cost a cent. It won't mean any traveling except crossing the street, but it will mean a change."

Maria was a little pale as she continued to stare at her friend. "I guess I don't just see what you are driving at yet, Selma," she said, feebly.

"It is as easy as the nose on your face. You stay here and live in my house awhile with my things. You are at perfect liberty to nose round the whole house, and peek into every closet and bureau drawer, and use my things just as if they were yours, and—I will go and live in your house while you are here."

Selma gazed at Maria with a defiant expression which gradually changed before the one of wondering delight on the other face. "It is complete," gasped Maria. "I'll admire to do it."

"Then," said Selma, "you can look out of my front windows at your house, and I can look out of your front windows at mine, and it will look entirely different. The Lord above alone knows how awful sick I am of sitting here day after day, and staring over at your everlasting front yard, and the same old trees, and the same old house, with two drapery curtains at two windows, and two plain ones at two. Sometimes I feel almost wicked enough to wish your house would burn down, Maria Hopkins. Seems as if I would admire to look over and see your chimney standing in a pile of ashes just for a change." Selma's eyes gleamed fiercely; then she laughed.

Maria laughed, too, after a little start. "You ain't a mite more tired of staring at my house than I am of staring at yours, if the truth was told, and its making me out wicked, too, but sometimes I've thought I smelled smoke, and—"

Selma nodded. "Don't blame you one mite. Then you and me can start in right away. You understand, whilst you are here this house is just as much yours as mine—more so. It *is* yours."

Maria nodded. "And my house is yours," said she. Then she looked a bit doubtfully at the other woman. "You know you mustn't give goldfish too much to eat. I will own I set a lot by that bowl of goldfish," said she.

"I have heard you talk about not overfeeding those goldfish enough to make me know," said Selma. "I shall look out after them just the same as I expect you to look out for my hens and see to it that they have their food warm on a cold day. There will be plenty of eggs. What you don't want to use you can trade to the grocer for his truck."

"Land, Selma! You don't mean you want me to sell your own hens' eggs!"

"Whilst you live in my house my hens is your hens," declared Selma, firmly, "and I shall feel the same way about that pig you're raising. He shall be my pig."

"He's fat enough to kill now," said Maria. "I calculated to hire Tom Simmons to do it. It's cold enough now to keep what pig-meat I want, and I always dispose of the extra easy enough. The butcher is always tickled to death to get my sausage-meat and headcheese and pork."

"I," said Selma, "will do the pig work."

"It's a big chore," said Maria.

"You can't teach me anything about pig work. We always kept a pig. Sometimes we kept two pigs. I'd admire to get a chance to try my hand at it again."

"I want to speak for some of the sausage," said Maria; "and a half a fresh ham, and half a salt, and some headcheese, and some of the salted-down pork."

"Of course," agreed Selma. "And you will find there's about six roosters of mine ought to be killed. But how about milking the cow?"

"If I can't milk a cow at my age, I'll give up beat," said Maria.

"I've got two steady customers for the milk, and some scattering ones."

"All right. I'll tend to them."

The two regarded each other with curiously child-like expressions. They felt like two children about to engage in a most exciting game.

"When," said Maria, with a fairly infantile grin, "shall we begin?"

"Right away. Why not?" replied Selma. "It ain't as if we had to pack up or anything. We haven't. All you've got to do is stay here, and all I've got to do is to cross the street. Land! It is the completest way of getting a change I ever heard of. We sha'n't even need to take our sewing. I'll get at any of yours I find round, and you can get at mine. And of course you know you are welcome to wear any of my clothes. If my skirts are too long, you can just baste tucks in them."

Maria began to laugh. "That part of it is going to be easier for me than for you," said she; "my skirts will all be too short for you."

"Land! I don't mind that. Of course I shall wear your petticoats, too; and I was reading the other day how short skirts were all the go. I ain't worrying about that part of it. I guess we might as well begin now. I am sick and tired of looking across at your house. Guess I'll run across the street and look at mine."

"I know just how you feel," said Maria. "I've felt real sort of rested since I came in here, being able to look out of the window and not see your house."

Selma rose. "Well," said she, "I'll put on your shawl and hood and be going. There's plenty in the house for supper. You can just hunt round and find it. You'll enjoy it."

"And you'll find plenty for your supper over there," said Maria.

"O Lord!" said Selma, "to think of the relief of going into your pantry and hunting up victuals and getting supper on another stove. My!"

"That is just the way I feel," said Maria.

Selma arose with no more ado. She went to the old-fashioned secretary which stood against the south wall. She rummaged under some papers, and took out an old wallet. "Here's some money," said she. "It will last awhile. When you want more, you hang a towel out the sitting-room window, and I'll see that you have some. It all depends on how long we stay before we get tired of the change."

"If," said Maria, "you go into my pantry and take the cover off the old-fashioned sugar-bowl on the second shelf at the right of the door, you will find some dollar bills, and there is some change tucked in the cracked pink cup on the lower shelf behind the tea-caddy. You hang out a towel, too, if you get short. You may, with hiring the pig-killing."

"All right," said Selma. She tied on Maria's white worsted hood; she wrapped Maria's gray shawl around her shoulders, which, high and thin, retained something of the grace of youth. Selma looked much better in the shawl than Maria did. She even put on Maria's rubbers. They were rather large, and she shuffled, but she was intent upon acting the rôle to the full. "Good night, Maria," said she.

"Good night," said Maria.

The two women looked at each other, and suddenly startled expressions appeared upon their faces. For the first time in their lives they meditated upon the unusual and the unconventional, and a quick tremor of alarm shot over both.

"If you get scared in the night, you set a candle in the sitting-room window and you ring the dinner-bell, and I'll be right over," said Selma.

"Yes, I will," agreed Maria. "And you, too."

"Yes, I will."

Then Selma went, shuffling in her large rubbers, across the street. Maria watched her find the key under the blind, unlock the front door, and enter; then she drew a long breath and looked about her.

"My goodness," said she. "I wonder if we are both plumb crazy!"

Maria actually turned around several times like a cat or a dog trying to become accustomed to strangeness. The primitive asserted itself, lifting its live head from the dust of the ages. After her turning around, Maria's face no longer looked bewildered. "Guess I had better see to feeding those hens, first thing before it gets dark," she thought. She found, with a revival of the delicious, childish joy of hide-and-seek, Selma's meal-bag. She mixed the chicken food with hot water and went out to the chicken-house. The fowls clustered around her greedily. Maria had never cared for chickens. Now she realized a certain fondness for the fluffy, pecking things. "They don't know a mite of difference betwixt me and Selma," she thought. Then she called, "Biddy, biddy, biddy!"

When she re-entered the house, she experienced the delight of a child rummaging about Selma's pantry. She also had a double delight from the reflection that Selma was rummaging about her own. "She won't find a thing out of order, and there's plenty to eat," she thought. She made daintily a pan of biscuits for her supper. She opened a can of peach preserve. She made tea. She cut a slice from a frosted cake.

She set the table in the dining-room punctiliously, and ate her solitary meal with relish. Across the street Selma was doing precisely the same thing. Each of the lone women was a guest at her own feast. Selma also had hot biscuits. She had also a bit of toasted salt codfish, and raspberry jam, and plum-cake, and tea.

She also ate heartily. "It is a real change from my own victuals," she said, quite aloud, and smiled happily. After she had cleared away the supper dishes she saw the light across the street from her own sitting-room window. It looked charming to her. She lit Maria's lamp, and Maria also looked across and realized that it was charming.

"Selma's been real quick. She has cleared away the supper dishes," she thought.

Presently Selma pulled down the white shades opposite, and Maria did the same. Then each woman could discern the silhouette of the other seated peacefully beside the evening lamp, moving a hand and arm regularly back and forth.

"Selma, she has found those napkins I was making out of the old tablecloth, and she's hemming them," thought Maria.

Selma was puzzled awhile about Maria's needlework, then she remembered the new dish-towels. "She is hemming them," she thought. Each woman saw a light later on in the cellar, and knew that coal was being got for the night. Then each saw the light in the other's bedroom. Selma's light went out first. "I do hope she sleeps well," she thought, as she lay looking across at Maria's light. Then that also went out, and both women lay thinking fondly of each other with drowsiness stealing over them.

The next morning there was a hard snow-storm. The visiting neighbors saw each other's faces at their opposite windows. Both nodded vehemently to give assurance of entire content and well-being. Each had her head tied up in a towel.

"She's sweeping," thought Selma. "Of course it's sweeping-day, but I don't believe she'll find half a dust-pan full."

Maria thought the same. Each felt radiantly happy. Later Selma wrapped herself up well and went out to interview the man about the pig-killing. Maria saw her go.

"She thought she wouldn't wait, because it is likely to clear off cold," she told herself.

Maria milked the cow and fed her, and dispensed milk to children

who came whooping through the snow with swinging pails; then she
went to one of the up-stairs bedrooms and dusted. She had previously
swept it. She had found it more in need of sweeping than many of the
rooms, since it was always unused, and Selma had had a cold, and had
neglected sweeping it longer than usual. Maria had entered the room
hesitatingly. She had stepped softly. Her middle-aged face had reddened, then paled. She had smiled almost a motherly smile. The
memory of the boy who had during his life occupied that room seemed
to her, in her settled state of life, like the memory of a departed child
of youth. He had been Selma's only brother, Henry. He had died
when he was only twenty-one. Maria had been a year older, and nobody knew what a torture of mortification that one year of life upon
earth had been to the girl Maria. How she had loved that dear boy,
who had died in one week of a fever! But she had not thought he had
loved her, although sometimes he had looked at her like a lover, and
Maria had trembled—that poor young Maria, who had been slim and
rosy-cheeked, with bright eyes, ready for wistful questioning and tears,
who remembered with shame that terrible additional year of earth-
life. When Henry had died, she had thought her heart broken. Now,
as she entered the room, the old pain came back, and she wondered,
not only how she had lived at all, but not even unhappily except for
a certain restlessness which at times stung her. It was that same restlessness which she could not outlive which had put the idea of the
excursion into her head. It was the outcome of that restlessness which
caused her presence in that room. It had not been changed since the
boy's death. She had seen it before, during his lifetime; she and Selma
had been girls together, and familiar with all the rooms in the Wheelock and Hopkins houses. But now it looked strange, with the sweet
and terribly pathetic strangeness of past youth which is not entirely
regretted, and seems to reproach because of it. Maria looked at the
dead boy's room which he had left; at treasures few and poor enough—
a shaving-mug lettered with gold on the bureau, a brush and comb in
a hand-painted tray, which he had bought at a church fair. Another
young girl had painted that tray, and young Maria had suffered tortures
of jealousy when Selma had displayed it, decorating Henry's bureau.
"Henry bought it at the fair. He paid seventy-five cents for it. Hattie
Loomis painted it," she had said, artlessly, and Maria had gazed at her

as if she had been an Inquisitor. Then Selma had calmly added that Hattie had painted seven trays just like that, and Henry had paid seventy-five cents when the others had brought only fifty, which she thought all they were worth; and Maria, comprehending the purely commercial nature of the transaction, felt her heart leap to heights of delight. Selma had been far from understanding. Henry was simply her brother. She knew just how many griddle-cakes and how little plain bread he could eat at a meal. She knew about the mending his socks required. She knew all the little homely details of his life and never thought of him in connection with love and romance. However, Selma thought little about love and romance in any case. She had not been a dreamer, even as a young girl, and moonlight nights had never quite rhymed with her moods. She was incapable of understanding Maria's tremors of pain and delight about the hand-painted trays. On the bureau stood, also, what the girls called vaguely "a fancy picture" of an ornate maiden mysteriously decked with roses, as far as the photographer had discreetly depicted her. Both girls thought it somewhat improper, and their maiden eyes took delicate shies at it. The picture was in a tarnished gilt frame. Selma had told young Maria that she guessed Henry had paid quite a price for it and got cheated. Maria had always feared lest the maid of the picture might prove to be some beauty whom Henry had mysteriously met and fallen in love with. Now, as she gazed at it, she smiled pitifully at her own young folly. The photograph was only that of some actress whom Henry could never have seen at all. There was a little brass ash-tray on the bureau. Henry, young as he was, had smoked. Maria had thought that delightfully wicked. On a little swinging shelf were two pipes. There was a dingy handkerchief-box on the bureau. Selma had given it to her brother one Christmas. She had also given him the fat pin-cushion worked in squares of red and green. On the table lay Henry's Bible and an ancient story-book bound in blue and gold. Maria took up the Bible reverently, and put it back. She took up the story-book. She remembered it so well—that dull old romance full of prosy sentiment. She opened the book idly, and there was a letter. Her name was on the sealed envelope in Henry's handwriting. Poor Henry had put it there and it had lain undiscovered all these years. Maria felt faint. She gathered up her broom, dust-pan, and dusting-cloth, and the letter, and went down-stairs. It was icy cold in Henry's room. Maria was not completely warmed by this unexpected flash of flame in the ashes of old love. "I will read the letter down in the sitting-room where it is warm," she told herself. "It is mine. I have the right."

Down in the sitting-room Maria read the letter, but first with a touching revival of youthful vanity she removed the towel from her head and looked at herself in the glass. She gave her hair a touch. Well, after all, a letter has no eyes. She sat down and read.

The boy in the old letter confessed his love for her; his adoration, which he spelled with two d's. He asked her to be his wife. Maria leaned back and closed her eyes. She realized that in some strange fashion she had received an answer to a question which she had asked, without really knowing it, during her whole life. She realized that henceforth she would know peace, the peace which she had seen on the faces of the aging and married women who had been girls with her. She felt utterly contented. "How could I have cared so much about that excursion?" she asked herself. Then she reflected what a blessing to her the caring and the disappointment had proved. It had given her the letter. It had given her peace and respite from restlessness. Maria suddenly felt a wish to go back to her own home. The need which had prompted her to this plan was over. "I hope nobody will ever hear of it," she thought. Suddenly the humor struck her— never the pathos. She chuckled to herself. "What old fools Selma and I are?" she remarked quite aloud. Then she heard a series of wild staccato yells of agony mercifully dying away soon. "Selma has had the pig killed," thought Maria, and laughed again. She looked at her letter, and remembered how Henry had loved sausage. "I could have cooked it just the way he liked," she considered with pride. She also considered how daintily his house would have been kept. She did not think of Henry as among the angel band of her childhood's teaching, but as of a banished youth whom she could have made warm and comfortable with the dear, homely comforts of earth. Maria had a pocket in her petticoat. There she stowed the letter. Then she went on with her tasks. She got the kitchen stove heated, and made a great fruit-cake. Selma always liked to have one on hand, and had none now. Maria worked away, all the time in her own atmosphere of perfect peace. It was tainted by no regret for what she had missed. That letter in her pocket proved that she had had the essential of life and love of the whole world. She was content and crowned with content. She now understood why her young cousin, Aggie, who had made apparently such a failure of her married life, could yet hold up her head, and, as some critical women said, "Walk like a peacock." Whatever the attitude of women in the wider world might be, the attitude of the women in this little village remained, however covertly, that of half a century ago. In their innermost hearts they were not, and never could be, emancipated from the old conception of the proper estate for woman. It was true that Maria's lover had died before his due time; that she had never been married to him, yet love had been hers; the dream in a man's heart had belonged to her. Death had taken him, but not before the love and the dream, and she was triumphant over death. Maria's voice was cracked, and she had never been able to keep to the key, and she sang horribly, yet with joy, while she worked.

The fruit-cake was a great success. Maria felt very happy over it, and also over the immaculate house. After supper, when she had milked the cow and fed the chickens and cleared the dishes away, she sat beside the window. Winter though it was, it was still not dark—Maria had worked rapidly. The snow had ceased. The window faced west, which glowed with pale gold through the dark interlace of the trees. The road and her yard and Selma's were pure expanses of billowing white. Presently a light flashed out in an opposite window, and Maria knew that Selma also had finished her tasks for that day and had sat down to rest. "I am glad she didn't work too long over that pig," she thought. Maria felt a great warmth of sisterly love for Selma. She, had Henry lived, would have been her sister. Maria was sure that Selma had never had any romance, that she had never been in love. She was right about that; Selma had never loved, but she also had had her lover, and the lover had been Maria's own old widower uncle, Aggie's grandfather. Maria had never dreamed of it. Selma had been ashamed. In her youth old John Hopkins with his married daughter, Aggie's mother, had seemed a ridiculous lover. Nowadays she sometimes thought of him with a mixture of indignation, of pity, and of a queer, shamed gratitude. After all, old John Hopkins had loved her, and a woman never throughout her whole life entirely despises even a scorned and rejected love. It has its diamond lights for her heart, which cannot be shut out for ever.

That day, Selma, making her queer visit in her friend's house, had

also made a discovery. When the pig-killing was in order she had fled
to the remotest corner of the house, to a little bedroom which old
John had occupied. It was a comfortable room, and evinced scholarly
tastes on the part of the old man. Indeed, he had received a collegiate
education, but had never entered a profession, preferring to work the
little Hopkins farm and live an isolated life aside from the struggle of
the world. A very gentle, mild man, but a man of deep thought, had
been John Hopkins. Poor young Selma, had she really understood,
had been honored by his love and by his seeking her for his wife, but
she had not understood. She did not now. Selma had been a beauty
in her youth, although of a type unappealing to the village young
men. She had been too tall and pale and still and stately for them.
She had always been a very simple village woman, whose life was
narrow and quite translucent, flowing over her path of fate with no
ripples of concealment. When she found herself in John Hopkins's
room she stood with fingers in her ears to drown out all sounds of the
tragedy being enacted behind the house; she looked about her and
remembered how one evening old John had crossed the street—all his
family and hers being away—and had declared himself, and she had
replied that she had no mind to wed, but thanked him. Then she had
watched him cross the street homeward bound, a slender, not old, as
she had then thought, but middle-aged man, with a slight stoop, but
a grace of motion. He had probably sought this very little room as
asylum, and nobody had ever known if in that little solitude a heart
had bled. Selma wondered a little. "I suppose he lit a candle and read
a book," she thought. The room was lined with dingy volumes. There
was a tiny hearth swept clean. There was dust like a silvery film over
the old mahogany. Selma went out and returned with a dusting-cloth.
She dusted everything with a sort of tenderness. After she had finished, some of the furniture still looked dull. She found Maria's bottle
of furniture polish and set to work. At last all the old mahogany glistened and showed its beautiful grain. Selma stood regarding the room.
She remembered so keenly its long-dead owner that she brought up
his face quite distinctly to her vision. He would have liked her to do
this service to his deserted room. He had been a most particular man.
She and Maria had used to laugh about him and call him an old maid.
He would surely have loved to see his mahogany shine. And—he had

loved her. Suddenly that love which had burned in the heart of the man who had lived in that room seemed as evident as a perfume. Selma smiled—a lovely smile. A gentle content with life stole over her. She was as one breathing incense burning to her, and to her alone. That old love which had never before meant much to her meant suddenly ineffable things. She bent her head. Her soul, even, bent before it as before a great radiance. The little room glowed with love of her like a jewel, and the woman saw it and smiled a smile of which she had never before been capable.

At last she went back to the kitchen. Her feet were cold. She opened the door of the stove oven and sat with her skirts gathered up, basking in warmth, and reflecting. "Poor man, he certainly thought a great deal of me," she told herself. She admitted at last her old lover to his place of dignity which true love owed him. She remembered him and she also remembered herself. She remembered how her face used to gaze back at her from her looking-glass. It had been certainly a very beautiful face. How the golden hair used to ripple over the pale, perfect curves of the cheeks; how serenely the great eyes had examined their owner! "I was like that," Selma thought. She valued herself as never before, and suddenly there came into her serene and monotonous existence a keen savor. She had missed that vaguely, just as Maria had missed something without knowing what. Both women had counted pitifully upon that excursion to Washington. Because of that now Maria would no longer miss anything; neither would Selma. Selma felt as if her life had been suddenly and pungently flavored with a most agreeable flavor. She withdrew her feet from the oven and began to work with wonderful zeal. Both she and Maria during one week did an incredible amount of work, each in the other's house. Neither stirred abroad during that time. They were too busy during the week-days, and Sunday there was an ice-storm which made it out of the question to go to church. It was clear, but the street was a glare of smooth ice. Selma looked across the road and hoped Maria would not venture out, and Maria did the same. Both breathed easily when they saw the other seated quietly beside a window, swaying back and forth and reading the Bible.

Maria had a roastchicken for Sunday, and Selma had spare-rib of pork. That week the visits ended. Maria was the first to go home. She

had the homing instinct of every woman to whom love, or the knowledge of it, comes. Ever since she had read that old letter of her dead
young lover she had longed to go home, although she had been extremely happy. She knew that she could enjoy more fully what had
come to her, in all its exquisite meaning, under her own roof. Nevertheless, until the week was up she flew about Selma's house, working
with vigor and full of delight. Then one afternoon she put on Selma's
shawl and head-tie; Selma's rubbers were too small, and as the ice still
endured she drew on a pair of old stockings. Then she tiptoed across
the road gingerly, toeing out carefully, like a pigeon. Selma saw her
coming and ran to the door. Selma's face looked much rounder, and
was broadening with smiles.

"Well, I never! So you have got home," said she.

Maria beamed at her. "Yes, I thought I might as well come," said
she. "I've been away a whole week."

"So have I," said Selma. "I'd just been thinking it was time for me
to be getting home."

Both entered the sitting-room, sat down, and giggled like two
children.

"Don't we two beat anything?" said Maria.

"I wouldn't believe it if anybody told me," said Selma. They giggled
again.

Maria took off Selma's shawl and head-tie, and pulled off the
stockings.

"Didn't you wear any rubbers?" asked Selma.

"I can't get my feet into rubbers just about big enough for a little
girl," laughed Maria.

"Well, I guess your rubbers must be over here," laughed Selma.

"I have brought over some chocolate-cake and fruit-cake and mince-
pie I baked," said Maria. "I thought we might have supper together
before you went home."

"Well, maybe I can stay enough longer for that," said Selma. "I've
got some biscuits most riz enough to put in the oven, too, and I've
made I don't know how many pounds of sausage-meat; and I've salted
down and tried out, and there's as nice a mess of pig meat as ever I
have seen. We'll have some sausage for supper, or cold spare-rib,
whichever you say."

"We might have a little of both," said Maria, briskly.

It was not long before the two sat down to supper. Both felt famished. Both ate almost greedily, and smiled at each other across the table.

"You certainly do look younger and fatter in the face than I've seen you for years, Selma," said Maria.

"You do, too," said Selma. "You look just as I remember you when you were a little girl and used to go to district school," said Selma.

Maria smiled happily. She felt exactly as if she were that little girl. She looked at her bowl of goldfish on the stand in the south window.

"Not one of them died," said Selma, proudly. "They are beautiful, swimming around. I guess I will have some, too."

The largest goldfish in the bowl flashed suddenly across its liquid world, a swift grace of golden scales. "I always have liked goldfish," said Maria. "I guess you will enjoy having some, and I can show you just how to take care of them."

When the moon was up after supper, Selma put on her own shawl and head-tie and rubbers. Maria had brought them over. The two women kissed each other when they parted in the doorway facing the street, which was a glorious track of silver under the moon. "I certainly am glad to see you looking so well," said Maria.

"I am well. All I needed was a little change," replied Selma, "and I am certainly glad to see you looking so well."

"All I needed was a little change," replied Maria. "I have been away a whole week, and it has done me good."

Both laughed aloud. They kissed each other again.

"Look out you don't slip on the ice," said Maria.

"Me slip? Why, I feel as young and spry as I ever did in my life, after such a nice change," said Selma. She went carefully down the steps. Maria stood watching her.

When Selma was half-way across the street she turned and waved her hand, and her laugh rang out. Maria laughed, too. She waited until Selma had closed her door. Then she closed hers, but the echo of the laughter was in the hearts of both, like the refrain of a glad song of life which can never be silenced.

Sweet-Flowering Perennial

Mrs. Clara Woods was in the bank, standing in front of the paying-teller's little window, having one of her modest dividend checks cashed. She was folding the crisp notes carefully when she was startled by the voice of a man who stood next in the waiting line behind her.

"May I speak to you a moment when I leave the window?" queried the voice.

Mrs. Woods, turning, recognized the man as the notable fixture of humanity in Mrs. Noble's very select boarding-house where she herself lived. The gentleman was wealthy, aged, and privileged, since for countless seasons he had been a feature of Noble's. The fact that Mr. Allston boarded there was Noble's best asset.

"Certainly, Mr. Allston," replied Mrs. Woods almost inaudibly, but emphasizing her agreement with a nod. She was a middle-aged woman, with nothing to distinguish her from a thousand other middle-aged women.

She stepped aside and stood by the high circular structure fitted out with paper, pens, and bank literature generally, and almost at once Mr. Allston joined her. At a slightly perceptible gesture—Mr. Allston, of course, never actually beckoned a lady to follow his lead—she went behind him toward the rotary door of the bank, where they were almost out of hearing. Mr. Allston, in his guarded voice, spoke at once.

"May I ask at what hour you left the house, Mrs. Woods?" said he.

Mrs. Woods, catching a vague alarm from his manner, replied that she had left quite early. She had been shopping, and was now about to return to the house for luncheon.

"I advise you not to do so," cautioned the old gentleman. Mrs. Woods gazed at him. She was frankly alarmed.

228

"Why?" she began.

"Noble's was quarantined an hour ago," said the old man. "One of the Sims children has scarlet-fever. They don't dare move it in this weather, so they have nurses, and the sign is up on the front door. Mrs. Noble is distressed, but she can't help it. You had better not return for luncheon, or you will be quarantined."

"I have not seen the Sims children for days and days," declared Mrs. Woods with an air of relief. "I have not even seen Mrs. Sims. Mrs. Noble told me yesterday that little Muriel was ailing and her mother was staying with her. It must have been the fever coming on."

"Of course," replied Allston. "I got out, luckily, just before the notice was put up. Then I met Dr. Vane, and he told me. He advised me not to go into the house, as it might mean being a prisoner there for some time. So I got away as fast as possible. I am going to a hotel. It is very inconvenient, but it would be more so being shut up at Noble's for days, perhaps weeks."

"I think perhaps I had better not return," said Mrs. Woods, hesitatingly. She was casting about in her mind exactly what she could do. Then Mr. Allston inquired if he could be of any service, and she thanked him and said no. He remarked that it would of course be very annoying and inconvenient for both of them, and went forth from the bank, while she went into the ladies' waiting-room. She sat down and remained quiet, but inwardly she was aware of precisely the sensations of a wandering, homeless cat.

It was, of course, rather obvious that she would either have to go to a hotel—a quiet hotel for those of her ilk—or return to Noble's and remain in quarantine. She was even inclined toward the latter course, as involving less trouble. She considered that probably the period of isolation would be limited, and that she would not seriously object to remaining housed in her own nest rather than settle even temporarily in a new one.

Then she suddenly reflected that little Muriel Sims was not the only child at Noble's. There were the two Dexter boys. She was almost sure that they had never had scarlet fever. There was the Willis baby. There was little Annabel Ames. Suppose all these came down with scarlet fever? Why, that might mean quarantine for months. Then, also, there was the noise of so many children confined to the house.

Probably none of them had escaped quarantine. The little Dexter boys were very boisterous children. They would probably slide down the banisters all day. Mrs. Woods again vibrated mentally toward the hotel.

Then Miss Selma Windsor entered. She did not notice Mrs. Woods. That was Selma's way. She was not apt to notice people unless she almost collided with them.

Selma entered and seated herself at one of the little writing-tables, took some papers from her black-leather bag, and began to examine them with as complete an air of detachment as if she were entirely alone in the world.

Mrs. Woods made an involuntary movement. She half rose; then she settled back. She was still entirely unnoticed by the other woman, who continued to examine her papers. She was probably about Mrs. Woods's own age. Mrs. Woods reflected upon that. "We went to Miss Waters's school, but Selma was in a higher class," she told herself. She wondered, quite impartially, whether that proved superior wits or superior age on the part of Selma.

She was not astute enough to realize that Selma had very few of her own ravages of time. Selma deceived people, though not intentionally. She had no desire to look older than she need. A woman who does that is almost monstrous. Selma simply considered that certain clothes were suitable for a woman of her age, and she wore them. She also considered that a certain invariable style of hair-dressing must be adopted. She adopted it. The result was that to most people she did look as old as she was.

Casual observers did not recognize the fact that there were no lines in her face; that her skin was smooth, with the ready change of color of youth; that her facial contours remained very nearly intact; that her hair had not lost its youthful thickness and warm color. Selma was regarded by most people, as she was regarded by Mrs. Woods that morning, as a woman over the middle-age line of life.

She generally wore black, and her clothes had always a slightly hesitant note as to the last mode. She wore small black hats, and her fair hair was brushed very smoothly away from her temples. None of it could be seen under the prim brim of her hat. She had removed her gloves. Mrs. Woods did not notice that the hands were as smooth as a girl's, and displayed no prominent veins. She did notice the flash of a great white diamond on one finger, as Selma handled the papers in a tidy, delicate fashion.

She reflected that Selma was a rich woman, and how very fortunate that was, since she had never married. She remembered that Selma lived in the suburbs, in a very wealthy town. She had never visited her there. She had seen but little of her—and that little had been through chance meetings—for years. They always exchanged cards at Christmas. They were on an even level of friendship which both acknowledged, but there was no intimacy.

Mrs. Woods did not feel at liberty to interrupt the other woman in her scrutiny of her papers. Selma scrutinized very leisurely. Evidently something was perplexing her a little, but she did not frown at all. She simply examined and considered, with a serenity which was imperturbable. At last she seemed contented. She refolded the papers, slipped the elastic band around them, put them in her leather bag, fastened it, and began to put on her gloves.

Then, for the first time, she glanced about her as if she were capable of sensing anything or anybody outside her own individuality. She saw Mrs. Woods. Evidently not expecting to see her in that particular place, she did not at once recognize her. However, she was aware that here was a woman whom she knew. She calmly regarded the other's large, rather good-looking, obvious face. Then she rose. She extended her right hand, upon which the glove was now smoothed and buttoned. "How do you do, Clara?" she said, composedly, addressing Mrs. Woods by her Christian name.

Then the two women sat down together on the little leather-covered divan and exchanged confidences—or rather, Clara Woods volunteered them. There was scarcely an exchange, except for the trifling inevitabilities of health and weather. Clara Woods told Selma Windsor about the scarlet fever at Noble's, and how she was as one shipwrecked without the necessities of life, or compelled to return to indefinite isolation of quarantine.

Selma disposed of the situation pleasantly and gracefully, and finally. "You will, of course, return with me to Laurelville this afternoon," she said. "I can supply you with everything you need. I shall be glad to have you with me until the quarantine is raised."

Clara Woods made only a faint demur. The proposition seemed to her fairly providential. She had not known how to afford that quiet, exclusive hotel. Her income was very limited. Then, too, there had been the apparently insurmountable problem of her belongings quarantined at Noble's.

Clara Woods was a pious woman, and humbly inclined to a conviction of the personal charge of the Deity over her. Visions of shorn lambs, and sparrows fluttering in search of suitable sites for nests, floated through her mind, which was really that of an innocent, simple child in spite of her ponderousness of middle-age. There was something rather lovely in her expression as she looked up into Selma's face. Clara's eyes were shining with vistas of gratitude. Selma, who was imaginative, realized it. She smiled charmingly.

"I am so glad I happened to come in here to-day," she said.

"It seems like a special providence," returned Clara, ardently; and Selma heard herself practically called a special providence, and rose above her own sense of humor because she understood what was passing in her friend's mentality.

The two lunched together; then Selma had some shopping to do in one of the big stores before they took the four-thirty train to Laurelville. It was probably that little shopping expedition which started queer after-events. At least, Clara Woods always considered them queer, although sometimes she was divided between the queerness of the events and the possible queerness of herself for so estimating them.

Whenever she met Selma, after what happened, she looked at her with a question in her eyes which, if Selma understood, she did not attempt to answer. Whenever Clara Woods endeavored dizzily to understand, she always got back to the ready-made frocks displayed in that great store on the day of her meeting Selma in the bank.

Clara Woods, when she stood with her friend in one of the departments, had something of the sensations which one might have had in the company of royalty—if royalty ever went shopping for ready-made clothes! There was something about Selma Windsor— It was difficult—in fact, impossible—to say what that something was. She was well and expensively clad, though with that slight flatting of the fashion key; but there were hundreds of women as well clad. She had a perfect poise of manner; so had other women by the score. Clara decided that it was impossible to say what it was that awoke to alert life and attention the groups of saleswomen. Selma had no need to stand for a second hesitating, as Clara always did in such places, feeling herself in the rôle of an uninvited guest at some stately function.

Selma was approached at once. There was, apparently, even some rivalry between the trim saleswomen. Clara wondered if Selma was known to any of these. She afterward learned that it was the first time in her life that Selma had entered that department of the store.

"Anything I can show you to-day, madam?" inquired a voice, and the other women fell back.

Selma expressed her wishes. She and Clara were deferentially shown to seats among the grove of dummies, clad in the latest modes, and resembling a perfectly inanimate afternoon-tea style. Clara felt a reflected glory, as one thing after another was displayed to her friend, not with obsequiousness, but with really fine deference to that mysterious something. Finally the purchase was made, and then Selma and Clara were in a taxicab on their way to the station.

They reached the suburban town where Selma lived about five o'clock. Selma had a limousine waiting for her. Clara experienced an almost childish sense of delight when she sank into the depths of its luxurious padding. Again the innocent, if perhaps absurd, conviction of the special providence which had her in charge that day illumined her whole soul.

"Well, I must say I never dreamed this morning that to-night I would be here," she remarked, happily.

Selma laughed softly. "We are both encountering the very delightfully unexpected," she replied.

"But when I think of coming entirely without baggage!"

"My clothes will fit you perfectly," said Selma. "I have a new black chiffon which I have never worn, which you can wear at dinner to-night."

"You dress for dinner?" asked Clara with an accession of childish pleasure.

"Sometimes. When I am entirely alone I make no change," said Selma, "but to-night I am entertaining—a very unusual thing for me—two guests, my lawyer and his cousin. We have some business to discuss, and I thought we might combine a little festive occasion with it. Mr. Wheeler is a charming gentleman. His cousin I have never met. This cousin is a Southerner, visiting him, and I included him in the invitation. I wished at the time I had another lady, and here she is, provided most providentially."

"Are they young men?"

"Mr. Wheeler is not. He is of our age. He has an invalid wife. I suppose his cousin is also middle-aged. I did not inquire."

By some law of sequence not evident on the surface, Selma immediately began to talk about the costumes which they had seen that afternoon. "It is very strange how the fashions have turned to ante-bellum days," said she. "How much at home the few survivors of the Civil War would have felt in that crowd of dummies dressed in flounces and fichus and full petticoats!"

"Yes; they even wore plaids," agreed Clara. Then she added that she supposed there must be many wardrobes in which hung duplicates of those very gowns which they had seen that afternoon. "I remember my aunt Clara showing me one exactly like that flounced plaid taffeta, except hers was a purple-and-green plaid, and the one in the store was blue and brown," said she.

Clara noticed a queer expression on the other woman's face, which in the light of after-events she remembered. Selma nodded.

"Yes," she replied. "I dare say you are right."

Her blue eyes were fixed upon the leafless trees against the sky. They had such a curiously childish expression that the other woman laughed softly. Selma looked at her inquiringly.

"You had a look in your eyes which carried me back to our school-days, then," said Clara.

"A look in my eyes?"

"Yes; there was a sparkle in them."

Selma herself laughed. "I wonder sometimes if the sparkle of life is really all over for me," she said. "I cannot accustom myself to being old."

Then the limousine drew up in front of Selma's rather splendid house, set back from the road in a lawn full of straw-clad rose-trees. Clara looked about her with enthusiastic interest.

"What a beautiful place! And you still like roses as much as when you were a girl," she exclaimed.

"Yes, I think the place pretty good. I did not hesitate much about buying it. I had always planned some day to have a country place for the sake of the roses."

When Clara entered the house her delight was increased. Had it not been sinful, she could have blessed the Lord for the disease of scarlet fever which had been the cause of her coming. Clara had, although she was commonplace, a love for the beautiful amenities of life, whose lack had irritated her. She was not a woman to say much concerning her emotions. Fairly hugging herself while gazing about at the soft richness and loveliness, she thought, "After Noble's!"

Selma gave her a beautiful room at the front of the house. Its great windows commanded a view of the drive and the road behind the rose-trees. Clara thought afterward that Selma could have had nothing planned at that time, or she would not have given her that room, from whose windows she could see—well, what she did see.

Clara Woods took a bath, with a secret awe before such luxury. The bath-room belonged to her room, and was all pink and white and silver. Clara had for years been obliged to watch her chance to sneak into the one repulsively shabby, although clean, bath-room at Noble's, and she had always an uneasy impression of publicity in using it. Here it was perfect. Everything was perfect. Her room was done in dark blue with pink roses. She had a long mirror in which she could survey herself when arrayed in Selma's black chiffon.

Selma's maid assisted her to don the gown, and, although she was stouter than her hostess, it fitted her well, because Selma's gowns were always very loose. Clara Woods fairly peacocked before the mirror. The maid surveyed her approvingly. She appreciated the guest's attitude. She had not entirely approved of the loan of the elegant black chiffon which her mistress had never worn; but, once the deed was done, she gloried in it.

Selma's maid had been with her for years, and fairly worshiped her. She gazed at the commonplace guest's reflection in the mirror, made for the time uncommonplace by the elegant costume and a little touch which she, the maid, had given her hair, and beamed with admiration at the effect of her mistress's kindness.

After Clara had gone down-stairs she hung up the visitor's street gown, and considered within herself how Miss Selma was too good to live, almost. How many women in the world would despoil themselves of their fine feathers to deck another poor feminine fowl who lacked them? However, Jane triumphed in the knowledge that not all the fine feathers could make another such lady-bird as her own mistress.

That evening Selma in black and silver was adorable. She had failed to make as little of her natural advantages as she had innocently attempted. What if her fair hair were brushed so severely back? Her delicate temples were worth revealing. The high collar concealed her long, graceful throat, but did not deform it. Selma, in a high collar of silver, with a silver band around her head, was really lovely.

The two gentlemen evidently admired their hostess. The cousin, Ross Wheeler, from Kentucky, did not meet the expectations of either Selma or Clara. He was much the junior of his cousin, William B. Wheeler, who had charge of Selma's affairs. However, he had been recently made a partner in business by William B., and in spite of his almost boyish look and manner he was supposed to be taken quite seriously.

The dinner, which was perfect, passed off triumphantly. Even poor old Clara Woods, in her elegant black chiffon, shone in her own estimation. Years ago dinners like that had not been infrequent for her. She felt as if she were taking a blissful little trip back to her own youth.

When it was all over, and the gentlemen had gone, and Selma was bidding her good night in her own room, Clara waxed fairly ecstatic.

"Oh, my dear," she exclaimed, fervently, "if you knew what this means to me after my years in a boarding-house since my little fortune was lost and my poor husband passed away!"

Selma regarded her with self-reproach. She reflected how easy it would have been for her to give the poor soul the little change and pleasure before. It was true, though, that she had not lived long in Laurelville—only since her mother had died, some three years before.

"I am glad, Clara," Selma replied. "Now that you have found the way, there is no reason why you should not come often."

"Oh, thank you," responded Clara. "I am enjoying myself as I never thought to enjoy myself this side of heaven." She sighed romantically and reminiscently. "What a very charming gentleman Mr. Wheeler—the elder Mr. Wheeler—is!" said she.

"Yes, I like him," agreed Selma. "I have never regretted employing him. He forgot some papers to-night, though, and we could not settle a little matter of business for which he really came out. The dinner was hardly more than incidental, although he did wish to introduce his cousin."

"His cousin is a beautiful young man," declared Clara.

"Yes; and he must be clever in spite of his youth, or Mr. Wheeler would not have taken him into partnership," replied Selma.

Suddenly a change came over her face. Clara started.

"What is the matter?" asked Selma. The change had vanished.

"Nothing, only you—looked suddenly—not like yourself."

"Did I?" responded Selma, absently. She said good night, hoped Clara would sleep well, and trailed her sparkling black and silver draperies out of the room.

Clara Woods stood still a moment after the door was closed, thinking. "She looked exactly as she did when she was a girl, for a minute," said Clara Woods to herself.

Clara was almost asleep when she heard the ring of the telephone, the up-stairs one, in Selma's room. She heard Selma's voice, but could not distinguish a word. She did not try to. Clara Woods had a scorn for curiosity. She felt herself above it, and her high position was about to be sorely attacked.

At breakfast the next morning Selma announced that she was very sorry, but she would be obliged to go to New York on business on the noon train. Mr. Wheeler had telephoned, she said.

"I heard the telephone ring," returned Clara.

Selma started. "I fear the talk kept you awake," she said. "I held the wire quite a time."

"Oh no," said Clara; "I could only distinguish a soft murmur of voices. It did not disturb me at all. I fell asleep while you were talking."

Selma appeared strangely relieved. Clara noticed with wonder that the look at which she had started the night before was again upon Selma's face. Selma, in her pale-blue house dress, was rather amazing that morning. It was not so much that she looked young in color and contour, but the very essence of youth was in her carriage and her glance. She looked alive, as only living things which have been a short time upon the earth look alive. Her blue eyes were full of challenge; her chin had the lift of a conqueror; her very hair sprang from its restraining pins with the lustiness of childhood.

Selma and Clara sat together lingeringly over their breakfast, then Selma excused herself, and Clara settled herself happily in the library with newspapers and magazines. She was conscious, half fearfully, of being in a state of jubilation that she distrusted. She was of New England parentage, and involuntarily stiffened her spiritual back to bear reverses when in the midst of unusual delights. It did not seem to Clara Woods that this could last long. It seemed to her entirely too good to be true.

It was not a great while before her perturbation of soul began. It was, in fact, that very noon. Selma had told her that she was going to New York on the noon train, and had apologized for the necessity of leaving her guest to lunch alone. Clara was in her room about fifteen minutes before train-time, when she heard the whir of Selma's car in the drive. She saw a figure step lightly into the car, and she gave a little gasp.

That was surely not Selma Windsor! That was a lightly stepping girl, with a toss of fair hair under a blue hat, over which floated a blue chiffon veil. The girl was clad in ultra style. She was a companion, as far as clothes went, of that notable company of dummies in the New York store where they had been yesterday. Wide blue skirts floated around that slender figure. A loose coat of black velvet, of the antebellum fashion, was worn over the blue gown.

The girl seated herself. Clara could not distinguish anything of her face under the loose wave of her veil, except a vague fairness of color and grace of outline. The car whirred, and Adam, smart in his chauffeur's costume, drove rapidly around the curve of the drive. In a second Clara saw the car in the road. Then it was out of sight. She wondered who that girl was. She looked at her watch and wondered how Selma could make her train, since she was so delayed by a visitor. Clara never doubted that the girl was a visitor whom Selma had sent home in her car. Selma must know some people in Laurelville, although she had heard her remark that she had made few acquaintances, and no friends, there. This girl must be one of the acquaintances.

Clara watched very idly beside her window for the return of the car and Selma's departure for her train. Presently the car returned. Adam drove directly past the curve of the drive to the garage. Clara looked at her watch. There were now only three minutes before the train was due.

When Clara heard the broken, hollow music of the Japanese bells which announced luncheon, she went down-stairs, expecting, of course, to find Selma in the dining-room, and hear her announce the change of programme which had kept her at home. There was one plate laid in Clara's place on the table, and Jane stood there ready to wait. She had, somehow, the air of a sentinel on duty when Clara entered.

Clara Woods was in one respect rather a remarkable woman. In spite of what she had seen, she said nothing. She ate her dainty luncheon, with not as much appetite as she had eaten her breakfast. She asked nothing. She said nothing, except to make the usual remarks due from guest to servant. Then she returned to her room. Therein she sat down and looked rather pale.

"Who," demanded Mrs. Clara Woods of her own stuttering intelligence, "was that girl?"

For some cause Clara Woods avoided her front windows that afternoon. She remained in her own room for some time, writing letters at the inlaid desk between the other windows which did not command the road. Then she heard the telephone-bell in Selma's room, and Jane tapped at the door and informed her that Miss Selma wished to speak to her on the long-distance from New York.

Selma's room was beautiful, but rather strangely furnished for a woman of Selma's apparent character. It was something between a young girl's room and a bachelor apartment. One surveying it— knowing nothing of its occupant—might easily have conceived that either a young girl had married a bachelor settled in his habits, and brought him home to live with her people, or that the old bachelor had yielded to a young wife's girlish preferences. Certainly, white-silk curtains strewn with violets, looped back with that particular shade of blue which suits the flowers, white walls with a frieze of violets tied with blue ribbons, and a marvel of a dressing-table decked with silver and crystal were fairly absurd combined with a great lion-skin in front of the fireplace, a polar-bear skin in the center of the great room, and heavy, leather-covered divan and easy chairs.

"What a queer room!" thought Clara. The telephone was on a little table beside Selma's bed. The bed had a leopard skin flung over the foot, and the counterpane and pillows were of heavy yellow satin.

Selma's voice came clearly over the wire. "I am so sorry, Clara," said Selma, "but I find I am detained. I cannot be home in time for dinner. I probably cannot be home until the ten-thirty train. Jane will take care of you. I am sorry, but you will not mind."

Clara replied that of course she would not mind, assured her that she was being very well cared for, bade her good-by, and hung up the receiver. She kept on her own dress, which was a good one, for her solitary dinner. Jane waited on her, as at luncheon, and she made no attempt at satisfying any wonder or curiosity which she might have felt. Jane at times cast an apprehensive glance at her. Clara felt the glance, but never met it.

After dinner she sat in the library and read the evening paper. Then she found a book which interested her, although she felt nervous and uneasy, and from time to time thought of her own humble nest at Noble's. The hours passed. She heard the automobile go out of the yard, and at the same time Jane entered the room. She asked Mrs. Woods if she could do anything for her, and looked so disturbed that Clara understood. "She wishes me to go up-stairs," she told herself. With a stiff subservience to all wishes of that kind, she rose and went. She realized that it was not judged by Jane as advisable that she should be down-stairs when that motor-car returned from the station.

She heard it as she sat in the dressing-gown which Selma had provided, continuing her letter-writing (Clara had a large circle of feminine correspondents). She expected to hear voices. She heard none. She wondered if Selma had not returned on the ten-thirty train, then dismissed the wonder as unworthy. It was none of her business.

She waited a long time before she returned to the library for the book which she had been reading. She considered that there had been time enough for all mysteries with which she had no concern to settle themselves, when she stole down-stairs and got the book. Some of the lights had been turned off, but many were on. It was quite evident that Selma had not returned. Jane looked in at the library door and asked if she could do anything. Clara replied, in an almost apologetic voice, that she had come down for a book. Then she heard a car speeding up the drive.

Jane's face became almost agonized. Clara sped out of the library. It was years since her middle-aged feet had moved as swiftly as they did along the hall and up the stairs. She gained her own room, opened the door, turned to close it, and saw the face of the girl coming up-stairs. Clara could not help that one glimpse, but it was so fleeting that nobody on the stairs—Jane came after the blue-clad figure—saw anything but the flirt of the closing door.

Clara sat down helplessly. Always before her eyes was the face she had seen, the face of the blue-clad girl ascending the stairs. The face was fair and sweet, so sweet of expression that it compelled admiration for that alone. It was smiling radiantly. Soft, fair hair tossed over the forehead, as innocently and boldly round at the temples as a baby's.

Clara Woods remembered Selma Windsor when she looked like that, exactly like that. The likeness was uncanny. Clara had little imagination or she would then have gone far in imaginative fields. She did tell herself that the girl looked enough like Selma to be her own daughter. She went no further.

Clara went to bed. She could not sleep. She rose early, and after dressing sat in her room waiting for sounds in the house to denote that other people were astir. At the breakfast-hour she went down-stairs. She was aware of a queer unsteadiness. She could not analyze her perturbation, but felt helpless before it.

When Clara entered the breakfast-room Selma greeted her from a little conservatory beyond. She had been tending a few blooming plants which she kept there. Selma said, "Good morning," and there was nothing unusual in her manner. There was nothing unusual in Clara's, although she looked pale. Breakfast was served, and she and Selma partook of it, and the mysterious girl did not appear, and was not mentioned.

Selma said nothing about her trip to New York, except to express regrets that Clara had been left to dine alone. Selma, eating breakfast, did not look in the least tired. On the contrary, Clara thought she looked, in some strange, intangible fashion, younger and fresher. Her voice rang silvery. She laughed easily and delightfully.

"You seem just as you did when we were girls together at school," Clara exclaimed, involuntarily. Then Selma gave a quick start, but recovered herself directly.

"Those were the happiest days of my youth, those days at school," she said, and there was a sad note in her voice.

Clara did not reply. She had known very little about Selma, except through those days at school. Selma began to talk more freely than she had ever done. She told how her home life had been saddened, even embittered, by an older sister who was an invalid; one of those kickers against the pricks who drag all who love them into their own abyss of misery. Selma and her father and mother had been as beaten slaves under that sore tyranny, which had endured until the sister died, long after Selma's youth had passed.

"I never," she said, "could have company of my own age. I never could go like other young girls." She flushed slightly. "I could not have a lover on account of poor Esther," she said. Then she added, with a curious naïveté, "I have always wondered what it would be like."

Jane brought in hot waffles, and the personal conversation ceased. After breakfast the two women went up-stairs. It was a windy morning. Selma's door was blown open as they reached it, and a sudden puff of wind caused a skirt to flash out with a sudden surprise of blue, like a bird of spring, from an open closet door. Selma did not act as if she saw it. Clara again felt shaken, and proceeded to her own room, telling Selma she had some letters to write.

In her room she sat down and pondered. She might not own to curiosity—other people's affairs might be sacred in her estimation— but she could not ignore, in the privacy of her own consciousness, the blue flirt of that skirt. After a while, however, she gained command over herself, with her usual incontrovertible argument that it was none of her business. She went down-stairs, and Selma provided her with some fancy-work, and the two visited serenely all the forenoon.

After luncheon they separated. Clara had a habit of lying down for an hour. This afternoon she fell asleep—the effect of her wakeful night. She started up about four o'clock. She had heard a motor in the drive. Against her own will she slipped down from the divan and peered out of a window. There was a great touring-car and a magnificent chauffeur, and Mr. William B. Wheeler's handsome young cousin was assisting into the tonneau the girl—*the girl*—clad this time in fawn-color, ruffling to her waist, with a quaint velvet mantle to match, fitch furs, and a fawn-colored poke bonnet with a long feather curling to her shoulder.

The car sped away. Clara really felt faint. She lay down again on the divan. It crossed her mind that she might go in search of Selma and see if she were in the house; then she dismissed the thought as unworthy. A very soul of small honor had Clara Woods. She immolated herself upon that little shrine, which most women would not have considered a shrine at all.

Clara finally dressed herself and then hurried down-stairs to the library, whose windows did not command the drive. There she read conscientiously. Finally Selma came in smiling. Clara noticed guiltily that her cheeks were flushed as if by coming in contact with cold, outdoor air. It was curious that Clara was the one who felt guilty before all this. Selma seemed entirely unruffled until Clara inquired if they were to dress for dinner that night, if guests were expected. Suddenly Selma flushed. She looked for one second like a young girl trapped with some love-secret, then she answered composedly that she expected nobody, and it was not necessary to dress.

There was a tap on the door, and Adam entered. He wished to see his mistress with regard to preparing a new garden-patch. Selma excused herself. When she returned she was smiling happily.

"I shall have a lovely new garden this year," she said. "I have bought half an acre at the left of the house, and I am to have a flower-garden—a flower-garden with a stone wall around it, a wonderful flower-garden!"

"What kind of flowers?" inquired Clara, and was surprised at the intensity and readiness of her friend's reply.

"Perennials," she exclaimed with force. "Always perennials. Always the flowers which return every year of their own accord. I like no other flowers. Always the returning flowers—roses and lilies and hyacinths and narcissi and hollyhocks. There are plenty of them. No need for us to trouble ourselves with flowers which demand taking up and gathering and replanting. It is always a perennial flower for me! I love a rose which has returned to its own garden-home year after year. There is faithfulness and true love and unconquerable youth about a flower like that!"

Clara stared at her. "I suppose so," she assented rather vaguely. Selma puzzled her in more ways than one. However, a perfectly pleasant little conversation ensued. Selma asked about some old school friends of whom Clara had kept track through the years.

The solitary dinner passed off happily. The two separated rather early. Selma owned to having a slight headache. Clara read awhile, then went to bed. She was just beginning to feel drowsy when she heard a motor in the drive, and simultaneously she noticed a thin line of light across her floor. She had not quite closed her door. Somebody had turned on all the hall lights, and they shone through the crack. It was too much for Clara Woods. Curiosity raged and would not be subdued.

She slid noiselessly out of bed and stood behind the door. She peered through that slight opening and saw—the girl, all clad in rose-color, a full skirt blossoming around her, ribbons and laces fluttering. She beheld the girl fairly dancing on slim, pointed feet along the hall toward the stairs. At the same time the fragrance of roses came to her, and she remembered how fond Selma used to be of that perfume, and how the other girls used to make fun of her for using it in such quantities. All the hall was now scented with roses. There might have been a garden of them.

Clara closed her door noiselessly and went back to bed. That night she was so tired that she slept. The next morning she wondered if the girl would appear at the breakfast-table, but there was only Selma in a lavender morning gown, sweet and dignified and serene as ever.

Whatever there was to conceal, Selma was careless, for again when Clara went up-stairs—Selma had gone out with her gardener to give directions for her garden of perennials—Selma's door was open, and over a chair lay a fluff of rose-pink and lace and ribbons.

Clara shook her head. She went into her own room, and she thought of Noble's. She had lived there over ten years, and nothing in the least mysterious had happened. She wished herself safely back, but again she stifled her curiosity. She stifled it, and in fact never quite knew if it had been gratified—if she ever found out the truth of the case. Clara had always a mild wonder if a cleverer woman than she might not have known exactly what had happened, what did happen. For the climax of the happening came very soon. And it came in an absurd sort of fashion.

Selma had been busy in her own room all the afternoon. Clara had not seen her since luncheon. Finally she dressed in one of the costumes which had been placed at her disposal—a pretty black net trimmed with jet—and went down-stairs to the library. After trying a book which did not especially interest her, she settled herself comfortably in a long lounging-chair beside a window. Although the day was far spent, it was not dark.

Clara lay back, gazed out of the window at the grounds, and reflected. Where she sat she could see, mirrored in a picture facing the large drawing-room into which the library opened, the two actors in the little drama of mystery. She could not help seeing them unless she moved, which was quite out of the question.

Clara stared at the reflecting surface of the picture facing the interior of the drawing-room, and she saw Mr. William B. Wheeler's cousin—that charming young man from the South—enter and seat himself. She saw in the picture that he was very pale and evidently ill at ease. Then Selma entered. To Clara she looked much older than usual. Her black-satin gown was very plain; her fair hair was strained back very severely from her temples. She also looked pale and worn.

Clara saw Selma and the young man shake hands; then, with no preamble—he was hardly more than a boy—he sank down on his knees before the woman, buried his face in her black-satin lap, and his great, boyish frame shook. Then Clara heard the boy say, chokingly: "Forgive me, Miss Windsor. I am—hard hit."

Clara saw Selma's face bent over the bowed, fair head pityingly, like the face of a mother. The young man went on:

"You must know that I understand how very odd this may all seem to you. I have only seen her those few times. But from the very first minute she entered Cousin William's office that morning after we dined here—when he had telephoned you, and you had sent your niece to represent you because you were ill—from that very first minute it was all over with me. She was so sweet and kind. She stayed and went to that concert with me, although I know she feared lest you think she ought not. Everything happened so very quickly. She was not at fault. She never encouraged me, led me on, you know. You surely don't think I am such a cad as to imply that, Miss Windsor?"

Clara heard Selma's reply, "No, I certainly do not think you mean to imply that."

The boy went on. "I know I was terribly headlong. I have always been headlong. It is in my blood; and I was so sure of myself. She was so wonderful. Then I wrote her that note. Did you see it? She showed it to you, didn't she? I expected of course she would."

Clara saw Selma bow her head in assent.

"Then she sent that special-delivery note of refusal. You saw that?" Selma again bowed her head.

"Do you think it was—final? Will there never be any hope?" cried the young fellow with a great gasp.

Clara heard Selma say "No," in a strange voice.

"There is no use in my asking to see her?" pleaded the boy, pitifully.

"She has—gone," replied Selma.

"And she is not coming back?"

"I doubt if she ever comes back."

Clara saw the fair head of the young man on Selma's black-satin lap. She saw the broad young shoulders heave. She saw Selma Windsor put her hand lovingly on the fair hair and stroke it, and murmur something which she did not catch. But soon the young man stood up, and his white face was lit by a brave smile.

"Oh, of course, Miss Windsor," he said, "it is all the fortune of life and love and war. Of course I have courage enough to take what comes. Of course I am not beaten. Of course I am young, and shall get over it. I am not a coward. I simply did love her so, and it is the first time I was ever so hard hit. It is all right. I am sorry that I have troubled you. It is all right, but—I am going back to Kentucky to-night. I am going into business with a fellow of my own age. I have told Cousin William. He was upset, and I did not tell him why I was backing out of the partnership so soon. He did not like it very well. I am sorry, for he is a mighty good sort. But I have to go. I have plenty of fight in me for everything, but a fellow has to choose his own battle-field sometimes. I am ashamed of myself, to tell you the truth, Miss Windsor. Your niece is wonderful, but I never thought any girl living could settle me as soon as this. She is wonderful, though."

Clara saw in the picture the young man gazing intently at Selma Windsor. "You must have looked much like her when you were a girl," he said.

"Yes, I think I did," replied Selma.

Then Clara saw the two make what was apparently an involuntary movement, and Selma had kissed the young man, and he had held her for a second like a lover.

Then Clara did close her eyes. She remembered when it was all over except the fervent good-byes and kind wishes which the two exchanged. Clara heard the door close behind the boy. She heard Selma leave the drawing-room, and soon, in the now fast-fading light, she saw her talking with Adam over the flower-garden in which she was to have her perennial blooms when spring and summer came again.

Clara seized her opportunity. She made her retreat, all unseen, to her own room. When later she and Selma met at dinner everything was as usual. After dinner they had a pleasant evening. The two ladies played a game of Patience.

Nothing more which savored of the mysterious happened during Clara's visit. She remained until the quarantine at Noble's was lifted. She enjoyed herself thoroughly.

She visited Selma again rather often, spending week-ends. They were closer friends than they had ever been, and Clara never knew the explanation of what she had unwittingly seen and heard. It suited her obvious mind better to believe that a niece of Selma's had really been in the house and had a love-affair, and for some unexplainable reason had been concealed from her. She had not the imagination to conceive of the other possibility—that some characters, like some flowers, may have within themselves the power of perennial bloom, if only for an hour or a day, and may revisit, with such rapture of tenderness that it hardly belongs to earth, their own youth and springtime, in the never-dying garden of love and sweet romance.

The Cloak Also

All his life Joel Rice had cherished what may seem a humble ambition. Exactly why Joel had considered the ownership of a little retail dry-goods store in a country town the apex of his ambition was puzzling. As a child he had played at keeping store, with a soap-box for a counter and pins for the currency of the realm. His lack of success in that juvenile venture ought to have warned him of his entire unfitness for carrying out his scheme, but it failed to do so. Even when he had disposed of countless stocks of cups of sweetened water, of bits of broken china gathered from back yards, of green apples and the cores thereof, and his customers had not only defrauded him of pins, but had mocked him from vantage-points of safety, he remained sublime in his determination that when he was a man he would "keep store."

However, he was made to take a course in bookkeeping, by his mother, who was of a less sanguine nature than he, and understood much better his capacity.

"Poor boy!" she had observed to his father, after repeated bankruptcies of the soap-box store, with its currency of pins—"poor boy! He will never make a storekeeper. He would be cheated out of his eye-teeth in a month."

Joel's father, a saturnine man, with much confidence in his wife's judgment, had nodded assent.

It was thus settled, even while Joel, in his dauntless ambition, was starting another store on the soap-box, and inviting bankruptcy to call again, which invitation was promptly accepted. Joel kept all the neighborhood children in green apples and broken china for seasons, without a pin's worth of profit to himself, but his faith in the enterprise remained beautiful and serene.

A year after Joel left school his father died. His mother owned the home, and there was a small life insurance. Before her marriage she had been a dressmaker. She took up her old employment, and kept herself and Joel in comfort, while he attended a business college in a near-by city.

When Joel graduated he obtained a position as bookkeeper in a factory. His pay was moderate at first, and the hours were long. Joel did not marry when he was young. His mother had died and he was nearing middle-age before his salary was raised, and he asked a girl—hardly a girl by that time—to marry him. Both of them had had expectant eyes upon each other for years. The girl whom he married brought him enough money to pay off a mortgage on the house, which had been necessitated by his mother's long illness. She insisted upon doing so with the savings of her work as a music-teacher.

They lived together happily enough, and a little girl was born. She was a delicate, sweet, little creature. Joel's wife was contented. She reveled in her motherhood and her little home. She did not dream of Joel's state of mind. He was secretive as to his inmost emotions. He was happy, but always at his heart teased the old ambition. He was tired of bookkeeping. He longed for the store of his boyish dreams. Joel had never actually grown up. In his increased stature lived still the naïve, trusting, boy who had kept the pin-store on the soap-box and risen from bankruptcy with a perennial courage worthy of something larger.

Of course Joel's wife, Susan, knew her husband would like to own a store; he had told her that much. Perhaps three times since their marriage he had spoken of his ambition.

Susan had not paid very much attention. She considered that her husband had a good position and she was entirely satisfied. She failed to grasp the fact that Joel was not.

However, she glimpsed facts when her aunt out West died and left her five thousand dollars. She opened an account in the local bank while she deliberated what disposal to make of the money.

One evening Joel regarded her with a look like that of a good, faithful, starved dog as she talked of it.

"I feel as if it ought to be well invested," said she. "It will be good to know that we have a little nest-egg, especially as Vivien grows up."

Vivien was the little girl. Her mother had allowed herself one lapse into the romantic when she named the child Vivien. "I wish I knew what to do with that money," she said.

In Joel's eyes the look of a faithful, intensely loving, wistful dog—wistful beyond the reach of humanity—remained.

"What is it?" asked Susan.

"Nothing," said Joel. He sighed.

Susan eyed him sharply. "What is it that you are reading so intently in the paper?" said she.

"Nothing."

"Let me see."

Susan took the paper from him. He looked pitiful while she looked it over. Susan was a delicately pretty woman. Her forehead furrowed when she was disturbed in mind. It furrowed as she looked at Joel after she had read what she knew had caught his attention.

"This advertisement for a man with a little capital to buy a dry-goods store, stock and interest, in Racebridge, Maine, is the item you wished me to read?" said she.

Joel nodded, still with those eyes of wistfulness on her face.

"I thought so; it is just what I thought," said Susan. She looked keenly in her husband's face. "You can really tell little or nothing about it from this," said she, finally, scanning the advertisement again.

"Abner Scott's wife has a cousin who used to live there," said Joel.

"It doesn't seem much to go on," remarked Susan. She knew perfectly well what that look in Joel's eyes meant. He would die before he would put the look into words, but she interpreted it with her loving insight. Joel wanted her, as he had never wanted anything before, to offer him her legacy to invest in that store.

Finally she did. She made a few inquiries. The results did not satisfy her. Susan had a good head for business, but her heart weakened it. It was as if she said to herself, "I will gamble for once."

"You can have that money, Joel," said she.

"Perhaps I ought not to take it," said Joel, pitifully, "but I have wanted this chance all my life, and I don't see any possibility of another."

Susan laughed pleasantly. "Then take it, and don't say anything more, Joel."

Joel looked at her with adoring wistfulness and a little shame. "I wouldn't take it if I didn't think I could do better for you and Vivien," said he.

"Of course you wouldn't. Now we'll take up with Henry Nason's offer for this house, and the money will buy us one in Racebridge. We had better sell most of our furniture and buy new."

"There are splendid stores in Racebridge," said Joel, with an air of pride, as if he owned the place.

Within six weeks they were settled in Racebridge. Susan's suspicions were awakened the instant she looked about the store. She knew. She said nothing, but her nesting, feminine instincts stirred fiercely. "If my money is gone I will at least have a home," she thought.

She found a house. It was bought in her name. She suggested that, but Joel did not know. He thought he suggested it. He did not yet dream of his bad bargain about the store. He was pleased. He went about better clad than formerly. He felt himself, now that he was proprietor of a store, quite a gentleman.

He was a handsome man, although worn and nervous. Susan regarded him, in his new light suit, moving with a slight swagger, and admired him in spite of her dismay. She had appraised the stock of that store. She had said to herself, "Not one-tenth of it but is out-of-date. It means buying new if there is to be any store. Poor Joel has been cheated, cheated!"

For all poor Joel knew, those obsolete fabrics on the shelves might be the latest vogue in Paris. For all he knew, women went "clad in white samite, mystic, wonderful," or in Tyrian purple.

Poor Joel knew absolutely nothing of the simplest requirements of his new business. Susan reflected with horror that he did not know how to buy a paper of perfectly good pins. When he made his first trip to New York, to buy for the spring trade, Susan almost asked to accompany him. If she had known anybody in that strange place with whom she could have left the child, she might have gone. As it was, she remained, and trembled. Joel had asked her, with a frown of boyish perplexity, what was the voile the women were wearing, and what was the crêpe de Chine, pronouncing the words in such strange wise that Susan wondered what would be sold him in their stead. She tried to coach him in the proper pronunciation, although she could see that her effort hurt his pride. He colored and said he guessed the merchants would know what he meant, but all the same she heard him out on the front piazza, repeating the words over and over.

Susan felt in a chill all the time he was away, but he returned radiant, bringing gifts for her and the child. "You needn't have worried, Susan," he said, "They knew what I wanted before I spoke. Those great wholesale dealers know what they are about."

Susan reflected ruefully that they undoubtedly did, but she thanked Joel for his gifts and gave him hot biscuits for supper.

When the purchases arrived she was surprised to see any voile or crêpe de Chine, but there is some good in Sodom. Joel had chosen some slightly obsolete muslins, of course, and even some figured light wool stuff which looked, and probably was, somewhat historic, but she said nothing. After all, Racebridge was provincial and the fabrics were pretty. Joel might sell them.

He did sell more than she had expected, but—his customers ran bills. Joel was naïvely pleased at that. "Don't believe there's another store in town with so many charge-customers," he said.

Susan tried to smile, but she sighed.

Joel looked at her in perplexity. "Ain't you pleased to have me get so many charge customers?" he asked.

"Of course."

"Any store that *is* a store has charge customers," said Joel. He eyed Susan.

"Why, of course I know that," said she.

"I shall send out bills the first of every month," said Joel. "And I am always going to give you half, Susan. I want you to feel sure of something. It is your right, because it is really your money that is in the store."

"That is real nice of you, Joel," said Susan.

The conversation had taken place during the noon dinner. Shortly after, Joel set off to the store. Susan watched her husband, looking more erect and much younger than when he had been only a bookkeeper in a factory, walking smartly down the street under the spread of the maple-trees which bordered it. She looked troubled, but she forced smiles as she bade Vivien good-by when the child set out for the afternoon session at school.

When she had gone Susan washed the dinner-dishes. Then she

changed her dress. Then she sat down and wept. She did not dare weep long, because callers were apt to come of an afternoon. Racebridge women were friendly, and welcomed strangers in their midst. Susan bathed her eyes in cold water and sat down beside a window with her needlework.

Presently two women in fine silk dresses appeared under bobbing, ruffled parasols. They were coming to call. Susan admitted them, and the three sat in the parlor and talked. Everybody who called said exactly the same things. They all asked Susan where she had lived before she came to Racebridge, if she was homesick, how old her little girl was, and if Vivien had had the mumps, because the mumps were going around.

These ladies were no exception to the rule at first. But when they took leave, one, who had a sharp tongue, and was feared because of it, said something radically different.

"How does Mr. Rice like his store?" said she.

"Very much, I think," replied Susan.

The lady had a fine, shrewd face with a peculiar expression compounded of bitterness and mischief. "It is an experiment for any man to go into business in Racebridge," said she. She regarded her hands encased in immaculate white kid gloves. She did not touch them to smooth them, as did most ladies. Miss Eliza Bangley never crossed the threshold of her own house door without being as completely adjusted as possible in every detail of her attire. She emerged, as it were, in full plumage, with every feather in its exact place.

As she made that remark to Susan she stood complacently, with the soft flare of her nice skirts around her, with the crisp rise of white ruche at her neck, with the tuft of violets in her toque, one hand clasping a card-case, the other held away from her skirt, with the little white kid finger slightly curved outward.

Susan changed color. "You mean—" said she.

"I mean," repeated Miss Eliza, "that it has always proved experimental for a man to go into business in Racebridge."

Susan regarded her with an expression of alarm. The other woman fidgeted. She was large and handsome, richly, although not carefully, dressed. She smoothed the fingers of her gloves and murmured something about other calls.

"Please tell me what you mean, Miss Bangley," said Susan.

Miss Eliza did not even glance at her companion, who now determinedly walked out. Susan could not dream that a fine and subtle revenge was being wreaked upon the large, handsome woman, Mrs. Morse, because she had invited herself to accompany Miss Eliza Bangley, who considered herself of a quite superior caste, on a round of calls.

"I mean," said Miss Eliza, distinctly, although with the gentlest of accents, "that often the people of Racebridge attain a spiritual plane above bills."

Then she also passed through the door with a "Good afternoon."

Susan sat down and reflected hard. She was a simple woman, although a shrewd one. She failed at first to grasp the entire meaning of Miss Eliza's remarks, but she was very uneasy.

"She means," said Susan, finally, "that people in Racebridge are bad about paying their bills."

That evening she declared to Joel that she thought it would be wiser to have cash customers than charge customers. Joel stared at her. "Why, Susan," he said, "who ever heard of a business without charge customers? Three more opened accounts today."

"I should much prefer cash," Susan said, firmly.

"Cash? Why, a good charge is better than cash. There was a drummer in the store to-day talking about it. He was a real up-and-coming young man. He said if he were keeping store, give him a woman charge customer, instead of a cash one, every time. He said a woman with cash would squeeze a dollar until the eagle squealed, but a woman with a charge account never knew where she was. She'd go right ahead and buy everything in sight and never know she'd bought anything. He said a woman with a check-book was as bad as a thousand prodigal sons boiled down into one."

"I wouldn't act like that if I had a check-book," said Susan, with a show of spirit.

"Of course you wouldn't. I told that drummer I would trust you just as much in a business deal as I would myself."

"Thank you," said Susan.

Joel started and looked at her. "Why, what's the matter?" he asked, anxiously.

Susan controlled her facial muscles with a strong effort. "Nothing," said she. "Why should there be?"

"I thought you looked sort of funny, and your voice sounded funny."

"All imagination," said Susan, briskly. "You have a powerful imagination, Joel. I must go and see if the corn bread is done."

Joel did not even reflect upon the conversation after Susan had left the room. He was entirely self-satisfied. His list of charge customers looked to him like an orderly pile of gold coins. Later it was different. Joel sent his monthly bills a second, and third, and even fourth time. When no remittances were forthcoming he began to look worried. He haunted the post-office. He lost flesh and did not sleep well. It seemed as if from the first Joel, with his expert knowledge of bookkeeping, might have realized something of the state of affairs, even with his profound ignorance of his stock. He may have been more suspicious than his wife knew. He may not have dared to fully investigate the books in which the store accounts had been kept for many years. The poor man was so pleased and proud that he may have trembled before his own happiness. Sometimes people are afraid to touch their good fortune lest they find a soft spot of rottenness, especially people like Joel, to whom good fortune has been so long in coming.

It was Willie Day, a nephew of his wife's, who forced Joel's reluctant knowledge upon his mind. Willie had a little money, and he came to clerk for Joel, a year after the latter bought the store. Willie was a pretty boy. At first Joel thought he was greatly increasing his custom. His former clerk had been a sober, rather testy, middle-aged man. When he died suddenly, Joel sent for Willie. Willie was very naïve and not at all shrewd, but he had a vein of curiosity. He poked around between hours in the storeroom behind the main store, and he made discoveries.

"Seems to me you've got a lot of queer goods packed away out there, Uncle Joel," he said one day. It was raining and the two were alone. It was raining so hard that the great voice of the river, which ran behind the store, was drowned out, as a shrill soprano drowns out accompanying chords.

Joel paled and started: "What d'ye mean?" he asked, gruffly.

"Haven't you ever looked into those big boxes out there?" Willie indicated the store-room by a nod of his head. A long streamer of cobweb, acquired during his search, floated from his right arm.

"Not so's to say I have," replied Joel.

"I don't know much about the stuff women folks are wearing," said

Willie, who had previously clerked in a grocery, "but it seems to me a lot of the goods packed away out there are older than the old goods you told me you couldn't sell here. Why don't you get Aunt Susan to look at them? She's a woman, and she ought to know the styles."

"I don't believe in having women folks mixed up with men's business," replied Joel. "I guess the goods out there are all right."

"Suppose I bring some in and fill up those shelves," suggested Willie, eagerly. He was quite ready to be convinced, and he was an industrious boy. Joel hesitated.

"Don't you want me to?"

"All right, go ahead," said Joel, but he looked positively terrified.

Willie delightedly began going to and fro between the store and back room, his arms piled with goods. "After all, they look pretty nice to me," he announced, after he had neatly filled the shelves. "I didn't just know about the plaids and spotted things and bright shades of red, but they look all right."

"Of course they are all right," said Joel, sharply. "Do you suppose I bought out this stock unless it was all right?"

"Don't know why I did think they were old-fashioned," admitted Willie. "You see, I don't know anything to speak of about dry-goods."

"Then you had better wait till you do before you criticise," said Joel.

Willie was meek before the reprimand. But the next evening he came to Joel and made a whispered report. He was careful that his aunt should not hear. There was the making of a man among men in young Willie, and he instinctively excluded women from councils of such import.

"Say, Uncle Joel," he began, with a wary eye on the kitchen door, where Susan and Vivien were washing the supper-dishes.

"Well?"

"When you were out this afternoon the Lindsay girls came in; they laughed till they cried over those goods I brought out; then that pretty Maud Willet came in, and the Adams girls and their mother, and Mrs. Adams said those goods dated back to her grandmother, but the girls, they said—"

"Said what?"

"They said Noah and his family was dressed up in just such things when they went into the ark, and it was a pity they couldn't have had the remnants."

"Then they didn't buy any?"

Willie shook his head. "They all went off laughing. They acted dreadful silly."

Joel's face was pale. Willie looked at him lovingly. "Guess we shall have to buy some new goods, Uncle Joel," said he.

Joel shook his head with a strange, numb gesture. Willie knew his uncle had no money. "Take my money, uncle," he whispered eagerly.

"I've took enough money to lose. I've lost about enough for your poor aunt."

"You won't lose mine, because you know how to buy now."

Joel regarded his nephew eagerly, "I rather guess I do."

"Of course you do, Uncle Joel. Didn't the things you bought in New York sell?"

"Sold like hot cakes, but—"

Willie looked expectantly at his uncle. "They're most of them charged, but I guess the customers are good. I guess they'll pay sometime. They live as if they had money."

"Of course they'll pay. Let's go down to the store this evening and make out some more bills. Then you can take my money and go to New York and buy new goods. When the money begins to come in for the others you can go again."

Of course it ended in Joel's taking Willie's money. The boy was eager to lend it, and very proud to be left in charge of the store while his uncle was in New York buying. Susan did not know of the loan until long afterward. She had begun to face the situation with courage, although with deep sadness. She retrenched in every way. She began practising faithfully on her old piano, and it was in her mind that she could give music lessons again, if necessary.

When the stock of new goods was in, business improved. Joel became uneasily cheerful. "The things are going like hot cakes, uncle," Willie said.

Joel sighed.

"What is the matter, uncle?"

"Not many of the customers pay cash, but I guess they must be good. We have had a big trade this last week."

"Of course they are good. Look at the way they live," said Willie.

But the new stock of goods was soon exhausted and very little cash had been turned in for them. Joel began to return to the store after supper and pore over his books. After a while Willie accompanied him. They sent out beautiful bills, and spent much time on the road to the post-office. Their hope waxed and waned like the moon, month after month. When the first of a new month came, more bills were sent out, and the moon of financial hope waxed and waned again.

Susan had secured a few music pupils. She was barely able to supply the meager table and pay for the coal. The taxes remained unpaid. The tax bill lived like a terrible ghost in a pigeon-hole of the sitting-room desk. Vivien went to school in a gown made of Royal Stuart plaid, from her father's ancient stock and came home looking old. The other girls had made fun of her costume, but she did not tell her parents. She was a delicate little thing, but she had moral courage. Her other clothes were worn out and outgrown. It was either things made from those obsolete fabrics or staying home from school. But Susan knew without being told. She suffered more than her daughter. She worked beyond her strength and grew thin. All of them grew thin. Even Willie's rosy cheeks lost their color and curves.

Then suddenly came a rumor that Joel's wife had a fortune left her. It transpired later that it was a legacy of seven hundred and fifty dollars from a distant cousin, who died intestate and had spent all she had in the world except that.

People believed in that fortune. Joel, without a question, took the money and made another trip to New York to replenish his stock.

When he returned, customers fairly crowded the store. Poor Joel had become wise concerning desirable fabrics. It was announced in the Racebridge *Chronicle* that Mr. Joel Rice had returned from New York, having purchased a stock of goods equal in style and exclusiveness to any in the great metropolis. There was such a rush of custom that Joel was obliged to hire an extra clerk. In spite of his ulterior forebodings, Joel began to take heart. He added more charge customers to his list, and twice he had an unexpected cash payment. Even Susan began to wonder if the tide had turned, and relaxed her stern efforts for a little.

It was soon enough she knew the truth. All the beautifully made out bills were disregarded. Even Willie was not ready with his jokes for the pretty girls, and his face fell when they tittered, "Charge." Poor Joel went about with a wistful, questioning expression. He became almost painfully obsequious, he was so terror-stricken lest customers desert him for another firm before they settled their accounts. That was what happened when the last fine new stock disappeared, for people thought so little of the obsolete goods, that they did not even buy on credit. Day after day passed with hardly a customer. Joel's wife had obtained all the music scholars possible, then she resorted to other means of gaining extra pennies. She answered one of the advertisements advising women to make fortunes, with elegant ease, in their own homes, and sunk a little money in the venture. It was quite a task which she had undertaken. Susan toiled at it, sent it off, and that was the end. She tried to get sewing to do, although that had to be kept a secret from Joel. Even in his tottering estate of storekeeper he would not have brooked knowing his musical wife was taking in sewing. People gave her work readily enough, but they did not pay her. She became almost vicious then. She refused to even see the women who flocked after her like harpies.

When her music pupils' parents became lax in payment Susan was relentless. She gave up teaching the non-payers. Finally she had just two pupils left. One was the daughter of a clergyman, the Reverend Silas Blake, the other was the daughter of Judge Lincoln Ormsbee, the richest man in the place.

Things were at this pass when winter set in, an unusually cold one. The Rices had little to live on except the pay for those two little girls' music lessons. They actually suffered for some of the merest necessities of life, but nobody knew it. Nobody made it his business to know. People loved to dwell upon Susan's fortune which she had inherited. They loved to think it was pure parsimony which made Joel wear his thin overcoat of black, turning green, and made Susan dress her little girl in such uncouth fashion, and buy so very little at the butcher's and grocer's.

"The Rices are saving people," they said.

They knew how Joel's store custom had dwindled, but they attributed that to Joel's failure to spend money on new goods.

When Willie got a job for a short time in a store in another town, they said Joel was too miserly to keep a clerk. The young girls missed Willie. When he returned, being sick with a fever, they used to go, giggling and pushing each other forward into the store, to inquire of Joel how he was.

Finally the Rices were obliged to call in the doctor, and Susan sold, in an adjoining town, her pearl pin, to buy medicines and luxuries. At last the doctor understood how matters were. He sent fuel and provisions and, when Joel received them grudgingly, told him that the boy's life was at stake.

The doctor was a bachelor, and target for all the unmarried women in the village. How he contrived to steer a clear course, and awaken no jealousies to interfere with his practice, was marvelous. He did so contrive. He also contrived that his bills should be paid. He had many conferences with Joel about his lack of business ability when he found out the latter's circumstances.

"Why do you let a yard of goods go out of your store without the cash in hand?" he demanded. "Why did you ever do it?"

Joel regarded him helplessly. "I thought all business was conducted in that way," he replied, feebly.

"Well, I can tell you right here it is not," said Dr. Frank Hapgood. He was a handsome, middle-aged man, smooth-shaven, and decisive in manner.

"How do you manage? You can't possibly ask the folks you call on to hand out your fee every time."

Doctor Hapgood laughed. "Of course not, and I do pay visits and take the chance of never collecting a cent, but—" He hesitated and laughed again. Joel eyed him inquiringly.

"Oh, I have my methods," said Doctor Hapgood. "They differ, with different people, of course, but I collect very well. If I found too much difficulty in collecting, I should set up practice elsewhere," he concluded, dryly.

"Willie always hated to ask for cash, just as I did," said Joel.

"Of course. Well, you make up your mind to one fact before you are a day older, Mr. Rice. Life is strictly a cash business for all of us, and we can't live, or practise medicine, or keep dry-goods stores without a cash basis. And you can make up your mind to another thing; cash always exists and somebody gets it."

"I can't pay you cash," Joel said, miserably.

"Who said anything to you about cash. You'll pay me when you can. I'm not a heathen." Hapgood packed up his bottles in his case. "Glad that boy is out of the woods," he said, with a jerk of his head toward the ceiling.

Suddenly Joel turned deathly pale. "I have lost every dollar he had in the world," he said, hoarsely.

"Well, he's young. He can go to work. Don't fret."

"I have lost all my wife's money, too."

"See here, Rice, you are tired out. You have lost a lot of sleep over your nephew. You had better go up-stairs and lie down and keep quiet. I will give you something to—"

Hapgood began opening his medicine-case, but Joel stopped him.

"No, I don't want anything," he said. "I've got some business to attend to."

Hapgood eyed him sharply. "All right, but don't overdo it. Go slow," he advised. "Nerves and brains are queer things, and yours are a bit over-strained. Go slow, Rice."

Joel nodded in a queer, absent way. Again the doctor made a motion as if to open his medicine-case, but checked himself, repeated his advice to go slow, and went out.

The next morning Joel slunk out of Racebridge laden with two suit-cases filled with samples of his antiquated goods. He had made up his mind to turn peddler, and had gotten his license.

Poor Joel was absent for days at a time, and returned looking worse and worse. He always told Susan that he had been away on business. She never dreamed of the true state of affairs. Joel persisted in his hopeless venture. Once in a while he sold a few dollars' worth, and then he would return elated, with mysterious hints of future success, which did not in the least reassure Susan. She had no doubt whatever that her poor, honest, innocent husband was engaged upon some perfectly legitimate venture, but she also had no doubt of his failure.

After a while she got one more music pupil, through Doctor Hapgood. She never knew that the doctor himself paid for the lessons. The little girl was rather talented, and he had taken an interest in her; besides, he had an enormous respect for Susan herself, as one of the fighters of the world, in an unrenowned battlefield.

About the time that Joel Rice started out in his futile efforts to redeem his fortunes the Great War broke out, but neither he nor Susan felt much vital interest in it. Their tax bills, and the problem of their daily food forced them into narrow ruts of self-interest.

After a while, however, Joel got a certain comfort from attributing his failure to succeed, as a peddler of shop-worn and antiquated goods, to the war. Of course he only made vague allusions to it at home.

"When that dreadful war is over we may make good," he would say to Susan, then would add, "All the little dogs go under when such a world-wide crisis occurs." He had heard a man say that to another on a train, and repeated it often.

Joel made his desultory trips for some months. Then came the spring, and his courage for anything except resentment had failed.

That year the spring came upon Racebridge with a rush of sweet violence. The heat, the terrible, virile heat of spring, attacked the world with a force which was overwhelming. The buds on the trees burst so suddenly it seemed as if one must hear explosions. The branches were clouds of crimson and emerald and gold, floating low under the brilliant blue of the sky. Suddenly bushes in full bloom stood out in dooryards, like radiant visitants. One expected them momentarily to spread their flower-wings wider and fly away. They did not seem real. Bird-calls were everywhere, and the air was sharply clipped by wings. All the brooks were in full chorus. The earth was vocal with the song of running water.

Then came a strange, weird day. For, during those few days of early, triumphant spring, when a whole town sang with voices of tree-branches and streams, with laughter of children and whistles of birds, the great, rapid river, which bounded Racebridge on the west, had not broken up. It remained ice-locked.

The night before the local paper had come out with an invitation marked by big headlines:

To the People of Racebridge

You are, one and all, invited to the dry-goods store of Joel Rice at 1 P.M., April 24th, for the purpose of a spring festival upon lines heretofore unprecedented in any community. A wide attendance is expected, for great delight over the distribution of gifts exemplifying Scripture is predicted, with a certainty of fulfillment.

People read it, and looked askance at one another. Many said it sounded crazy, but they planned to go.

The next day was chilly. There had been a drop in temperature during the night, and a breath of northward snows was in the air. And on that strange day came the breaking up of the river. The people crowded to the banks that morning to see the spectacle. The river on that day was like the rush of a herd of yellow-maned lions. People saw their heaving backs and tossing manes, the foam from their gaping mouths of flight, and heard their roar. The river on that day became more like a multiple wild beast, in a fury of raging flight, then anything else. The whole scene was magnificent and terrible. It might have been one of the seven days of creation, from the sensation of tremendous forces let loose toward infinite change and progression.

Poor Susan Rice, that morning, was unusually sad. She heard the roar of the river, like a dreadful accompaniment of adverse fate to her little, insignificant solo of woe. Over her was a premonition. She said to herself that she felt as if something was going to happen, but she did not say it to Joel nor her little girl.

Beyond that dull mental cowering, as before a blow, she felt nothing. She had no gleam of the brightness which was afterward to come into her life, alleviating even her terrible loss. That she could not see. She only cowered before the certainty of impending tragedy. Joel had not shown her the local paper. She had asked for it, and he had made some evasive reply.

At noon that day Joel asked her to go with Vivien to the store, but when she inquired the reason he would not tell her. Susan and Vivien arrived a little late. Susan had shrunk before her husband's bidding, without knowing why. The store was half filled when they got there. Susan went close to her husband, who stood, looking strangely solemn and important, in the center of the floor.

"What are you going to do, Joel?" she whispered.

Joel looked at her, then suddenly, before them all, he bent and kissed her. "You poor woman!" said he.

"Joel!"

"Don't you worry, Susan. I am going to do what the Lord has appointed me to do."

Susan stared about her. Joel had gotten evergreen and trimmed the store. He had brought down the little girl's canary-bird. The cage dangled overhead, and the little golden thing shrilled above the awful roar of the river.

"What did you bring Dicky down here for? Oh, Joel!"

Susan did not ask any more questions after that. She lifted Vivien to a stool, and the child, with her shock of fair hair and her white face, seemed to focus all the light in the dim place. It was dim, for the clouds were heavy and it was beginning to rain.

Presently the store was filled with people. Some of them, after they had entered, made as if to retreat, but they stayed.

Then Joel began to talk. His wife stood close to him. She even clung to a corner of his old coat, but she shuddered so at every word that it did not seem possible that she could remain standing. Judge Ormsbee got a chair and forced her to sit down, but she was up again in a second, as if propelled by a spring.

Joel began quietly and slowly. He did not hesitate, but his voice was weak. It was at first difficult to hear him, on account of that and the roar of the river, and the singing of the canary-bird.

He began in the stilted, old-fashioned manner of speech-makers:

"Ladies and gentlemen, I have summoned you here to-day for the purpose of saying a few words to you. I have long planned to do this, but have only now found my mind firm enough to carry out my plan."

Then there came a pause. Joel's wife fairly crouched, and one could see the whites of her frightened eyes as she stared up at her husband.

"Two and two and three and four make eleven," went on Joel.

Everybody jumped. Then he repeated it. And after that it was repeated once in a while like a refrain. Doctor Hapgood always had a theory that Joel had acquired the habit of going over that little mathematical statement for the purpose of steadying his poor, tottering brain.

Then Joel went on. It sounded reasonable enough at first.

"It took considerable time for me to realize the exact situation," he said. "I was brought up to believe in the honesty of all men and women not behind prison bars. I have been honest, as honest as I knew how to be, according to my lights."

Then he paused and again repeated his little mathematical statement. Some of the women began to look frightened and turn to the door, but their curiosity held them. With so many men there they could not be exactly afraid, especially when a man was so very thin and weak and worn as Joel was.

He went right on. "I never thought I was any better than other people. Now I know I am. It is a terrible knowledge to come to a man who loves God and tries to walk in His path. It is terrible to know yourself better than others because you cannot help but disobey Scripture. You know that you fail in humility, and yet what can any man do against facts?"

All of a sudden he turned like a flash and his eyeballs gleamed red. He pointed to a woman standing near him. She was a pretty, well-dressed woman, the wife of a well-to-do man. She wore an outer garment made of a soft shade of gray, decorated with fur. Joel pointed straight at that garment, and the woman turned pale and shrank. Then he shouted, and after that there was no trouble about hearing him above the roar of the river and the pipe of the canary-bird.

"Mrs. Lester Weeks," he screamed, "I am here to-day to obey the precepts of the Holy Bible. That coat you have on was made of cloth at three dollars a yard, that you bought of me. You have never paid for it. You have taken my coat; now take my cloak also!"

He pointed with a gesture worthy of a tragedy star at a roll of old cloth on a counter. "Plenty there for a cloak," said he. "Take my cloak also."

Then he glared at her. The woman started to leave the store, but her husband elbowed his way up to her. "Do you mean to say you have never paid for that cloth, Alice?" he said.

His wife looked at him and nodded.

"I have given you plenty of money, Alice," said Weeks. "There is no excuse for this. No, you can't go. You stay right where you are."

Joel pointed next to a man. He was the proprietor of the Racebridge House, and was called rich.

"You!" shouted Joel. "You, too! Take the cloak also. You bought table linen and sheets for your hotel the first year I was here. I have sent you bill after bill. You have never taken the slightest notice. There is some more sheeting; there is some table linen. Take my cloak also! Take my cloak also, John Woodsum!"

Woodsum had a terrible temper. He swore and made for the door, but Judge Ormsbee and some other men shut it and stood guard before it. They had begun to see light in darkness, and they were determined that nobody should get out of that store scot free, who needed to hear the truth.

"Let me out, damn you all!" shouted Woodsum. "I'll have the law of ye!"

"Better keep still," advised the judge, in his deep voice. "Joel's got the right of it."

Well, Joel went down his list. He had a good many names on it, and he did not spare one. The goods for which they owed him were specified, and they were ordered to take his cloak also. Now and then he stopped and reeled off his little mathematical formula, then he was off again.

Some of the women cried, some looked mad, and some frightened. The men appeared mortally ashamed.

At last Joel's list was finished. "God help and pity a poor man," he cried, and his voice was something dreadful, and yet at the same time it trembled, as if he were spent and about at the end of his strength. "God help and pity a poor man who came here thinking he was going to realize the hope of his lifetime, who trusted every one to be as honest as he was. All my money has gone, the seven hundred and fifty dollars my wife had left her is gone, and her nephew's money is gone. You have made me a thief, you people whom I came among so happy and trusting. You made me rob my own flesh and blood. You made me a thief, as you are thieves! Oh, my God! How beautiful I thought the whole world was when I came here! You have spoiled God's world for me! You have made me see the wickedness of my own kind! You have done me the worst wrong that human beings can do one another. You have made me know myself better than other men, so I shall be set among those who are not elect at the Judgment Day. How can I say, after living here these years and finding you out, that I am unworthy and you are worthy, and not lie to God himself? You have robbed me of my coat; I have given you my cloak also!"

Then he fell. Doctor Hapgood, who had been gradually edging nearer, caught him. He worked over him until he had regained consciousness, and, the people having slunk away, walked home with his poor trembling wife and his little girl, who cried aloud for sheer fright as she went along.

Nobody ever saw Joel alive again. There was good evidence that he had stolen out while Susan was trying to quiet the poor, nervous child, and had thrown himself into the death-drive of the river. His body was never found, but a man had seen something drifting past.

Afterward the debts were paid in like a stream of gold. Soon Susan had enough in the bank, with the now certain proceeds of her music class, to keep her and the child in comfort. She settled down into that peace of negation which sometimes comes, like a dew of blessing, after a tragedy.

Doctor Hapgood auctioned off the forlorn stock of the store. People bid against one another as if they were fighting for the acquisition of rare bargains. They were a mean people, the people of Racebridge, but in the end their own meanness shocked them into a sense of it, and they were at that auction of the man whom they had all wronged, a grand people, with hearts of love and fire. There was a breaking up of human meanness and dishonesty greater than the breaking up of the ice in the great river.

Mother-Wings

Mrs. Bodley's two married daughters, Isabel and Clara, were in Isabel's sitting room, sewing. The winter sunlight filtered through a window filled with beautiful potted plants.

"Mother," said Isabel, "is exactly like a hen."

"Goodness!" responded Clara.

"I mean about poor little Ann. She wasn't in the least like a hen about us. She didn't think your Sam and my John were quite good enough for her daughters, but she didn't take to scratching violently for better husbands. She just let us go and devoted her whole soul to Ann."

"Why, Isabel, you can't say mother hasn't been good to us!"

"Oh yes, she has been a good, normal mother, all right. I am not finding any fault with poor mother, as far as we are concerned. But about Ann she is exactly like a hen. Do you know Ann is coming home to-night?"

"Does that mean she has failed in her kindergarten teaching?"

"Oh, I suppose so! Poor little dear! She has failed in everything, and not her fault, either. Ann is a darling little old-fashioned dove of a girl, and mother has been trying to make goodness knows what, peacocks and birds of paradise, out of her. Ann could not paint any more than a cat, and mother made her take all those lessons; and she could not sing, and mother made her study singing until she nearly cracked her poor little throat; and now the kindergarten. It has been awfully hard, and anybody might have known Ann couldn't teach. All Ann is fit for is to marry and settle down, but mother wanted her to be in the front rank of the advance woman movement, and she simply can't."

Clara looked reflectively at her sister. "Do you think Ann has ever really had a chance to marry?" she almost whispered.

"Who is there in Barr-by-the-Sea for her to marry?"

"I must confess, after we had snapped up Sam and John (and mother wouldn't have been satisfied with them for her) I don't know."

"She has met men outside, I suppose."

"She must have. Oh, I don't know. Ann is pretty and a darling, but there never is any accounting for men."

"I wish mother—"

"Hush!" whispered her sister. "Mother is coming."

Mrs. Bodley immediately entered the room. She was a very erect little woman, well dressed, carrying her chin high. Her daughters stared, pale-faced, but not at her. They stared at the blue-eyed baby she was carrying.

"What in the world!" gasped Isabel.

"Mother, whose baby is that?" cried Clara.

Mrs. Bodley sat down and took the child in her lap, and loosened her little white coat and hood. "I left the carriage outside," said she. "She is not quite old enough to walk. I am afraid of her little legs getting crooked if she tried. She can walk, though. Can't you, darling?"

The baby smiled deliciously at Mrs. Bodley, then at the other women. She was a lovely baby, curly-haired and pink-cheeked.

"What is her name?" asked Isabel, in a faint voice.

"Her name," said Mrs. Bodley, in a stately manner, "is Bessie Wright."

"Where did she come from?" asked Clara, as faintly as her sister.

"Ann is coming home to-night," said Mrs. Bodley, by way of answer. She regarded her two daughters with an air of defiance.

"Poor little Ann! We are so sorry," said Isabel. Clara nodded acquiescence.

"I don't know why you are so sorry."

"Why, we are sorry because she has made another failure, teaching kindergarten."

"Who said she had made a failure? There are other reasons why girls give up teaching and come home." Mrs. Bodley cuddled the baby close to her. She looked rather pale.

"Mother, you don't mean—" said Isabel.

Mrs. Bodley was silent.

"You don't mean Ann is going to marry a widower, that baby's father?"

"Hush!" said Clara.

"She's too young to understand," said Isabel. "Is she, mother, after all?"

"Ann," said Mrs. Bodley, "is only twenty-seven. That, nowadays, is young to be married."

"Is she?"

Mrs. Bodley was silent.

"Why don't you speak, mother?" asked Isabel, in a subdued way. She felt a little frightened. She could not have told why.

Mrs. Bodley's daughters did not talk more about Ann. They petted the baby, and after a while Mrs. Bodley adjusted the warm little white wraps and took her leave.

The daughters, screened by folds of window curtains, watched her pushing the perambulator down the street.

"I feel stunned," said Isabel.

"So do I," said Clara.

While Mrs. Bodley was out Carry Munn, the middle-aged woman who worked for her, had gone over to Doctor Dickerson's, next door, and told her unmarried cousin Maria, who worked there, the news.

"Mrs. Bodley was away all day yesterday," said she, "and when she came home she brought a baby."

Maria, who was stout, gasped, "A baby!"

"What baby?"

"I can't make out. Ann is coming home to-night, and I sort of guess, from something Mrs. Bodley said—no, she didn't say anything, but she looked funny when I asked her—that Ann Bodley is going to marry that baby's father."

"Then he's a widower?"

"Of course he is. How could she marry him if he wasn't?" said Carry Munn. Carry Munn had a rasped, melancholy face, but she spoke with force.

Maria changed the subject. "I've got to get dinner," said she. "Doctor Dickerson's nephew is coming to-night. He's going to be assistant doctor."

Carry Munn went home. Mrs. Bodley was just entering the yard with the baby. In an hour Ann came. She seemed as astonished at the baby as her sisters had been.

"Where did you get her?" she cried.

Mrs. Bodley, with the baby cuddled against her shoulder, led Ann into the parlor where Carry Munn could not overhear. "I did not tell your sisters, but I am going to tell you, on one condition," said she. "You must promise me solemnly not to tell."

Ann stared at her mother. "Why, of course I will promise!" she said.

"Well, this is your poor second cousin Emma's tenth child. She wrote me about it. Her husband can't earn enough to half keep the others, and Emma is out of health. I took the baby. But Emma is proud. You know how proud Emma is."

Ann nodded. She began to fondle the baby. "Precious little darling!" said she. "I am glad, mother. I'll do all I can to help with her, and I will never tell. Poor Emma! It must have been awful for her to give up such a beautiful baby."

"She did seem to feel badly, but she has nine besides," said Mrs. Bodley.

That was on Saturday. The next day Ann, coming out of church with her mother, was repeatedly stopped and congratulated. Ann was a sweet-faced young woman with a great mass of reddish-brown hair. Her eyes were brown, and her high-arched brows gave her an expression of wonder. It might have been because of those wondering brows that people did not notice her bewilderment when she was congratulated.

When she and her mother were walking home alone she looked very pale and grave. On one side of the road tossed the sea; on the other were the closed residences of the summer colony.

Ann did not speak until they had nearly reached their home in the all-year-round part of Barr-by-the-Sea. "What did they mean, mother?" she said then.

"What did who mean?"

"Why, all those people congratulating me! What were they congratulating me for? Because I had made another failure? I did not know the people here could be so cruel."

"I guess they didn't mean to be cruel," replied Mrs. Bodley, in a smothered voice.

"Clara and Isabel congratulated me, too. They did last night when

I ran in there; and Brother-in-law Sam asked me who the happy man was. What happy man? What did he mean?"

"I guess he didn't mean much of anything," replied her mother.

The next day was very pleasant, and Mrs. Bodley proposed to Ann that they drive over to Barr Center and do some shopping. "I've got to buy some napkins and a tablecloth or two," said she. "Carry Munn can look out for the baby."

Ann stared at her mother. "Why, mother, I thought you had more table linen than we could use!"

"That was two years ago," said her mother, sharply. "You act as if tablecloths and napkins had entered into eternal life."

"Why, mother!" Ann looked shocked.

Carry Munn, bringing some biscuit in for breakfast, stopped short. "I didn't know you swore, Mis' Bodley," said she.

Mrs. Bodley colored.

"Mother wants some fine linen to sew on," said Ann extenuatingly.

"Yes, your ma always did like to sew on nice fine linen," said Carry Munn. She cast a look at Ann which the girl utterly failed to understand. Carry Munn flushed suddenly and giggled as she went out.

"What ails Carry Munn, mother?" asked Ann, wonderingly.

"Nothing, I guess," said Mrs. Bodley. "You had better get ready."

"Does Prince shy at automobiles as much as he used to?" asked Ann, rather wearily.

"No; he has almost stopped."

Ann dressed herself reluctantly. She did not want to drive to Barr Center. She hated driving, anyway; horses made her nervous, and she did not anticipate any pleasure from the shopping. She looked very pretty as she came downstairs. Ann wore brown, with a touch of cherry velvet in her hat which brought out the color in her soft, fair cheeks. Her mother drove, and Ann sat beside her quietly, with rather apprehensive eyes on the horse. He was old, but capable of doing youthful mischief under provocation. They met three automobiles, one after another, immediately after they started, and Prince did not even prick up an ear.

"I told you so," said Mrs. Bodley. But after driving several miles without seeing a car, one shot by with a warning toot from the klaxon, and then old Prince certainly shied. Mrs. Bodley clung to the lines.

"Don't you be scared, Ann," said she. "It's only when one automobile all alone comes along that he notices at all."

It happened very quickly. The lines snapped, and the buggy was tilted into the ditch, and Prince stood in an attitude of panicky, ready-to-do-more attention, perfectly still.

The car ahead stopped. The driver had seen the accident in his little mirror. A young man came running back along the road. He carried a small medicine-case. Ann and her mother were out of the buggy. Mrs. Bodley was at the horse's head, and Ann stood helplessly doing nothing at all.

The young man came alongside. "Anybody hurt?" said he, solicitously.

"No, we ain't hurt," replied Mrs. Bodley, sharply, "but we might have been. You hadn't any right to go so fast."

"I was running only about eighteen miles an hour," said the young man. His voice was boyish and aggrieved. "I did not know your horse was afraid of cars," he pleaded.

"He ain't," said Mrs. Bodley.

"But he acted as if he were."

"He ain't afraid of cars, but he's mortal scared of *a* car," said Mrs. Bodley.

The young man looked bewildered. He glanced at Ann. She was pale and trembling, but she could not avoid smiling slightly. "My mother means that Prince, when there are a number of cars, doesn't shy, because he can't make up his mind which to shy at; but when there is one he does."

"Oh!" said the young man. He continued to regard her. "You were frightened?" said he.

"Yes, I was."

"Ann was always afraid of a horse," said Mrs. Bodley. Her eyes upon the young man were suddenly very sharply speculative. "Ann is delicate," said she, as if she were complimenting Ann.

Ann colored. "Nonsense, mother!" said she. "I am not delicate at all, and I realize I am a fool to be afraid of an old horse like Prince."

"Some people can't help it," said the young man. He surveyed Ann admiringly. "May I inquire where you were going, madam?" he said to Mrs. Bodley.

"To Barr Center, if I can ever get those reins mended," said Mrs. Bodley. Her words were rather aggressive, but her tone was not. The young man hesitated.

"Why can't I tie your horse here and take you two ladies to Barr Center in my car?" he propounded, finally.

Ann started and flushed. "We have some shopping to do," said she.

"That's all right. I have time enough. You can do your shopping while I make my calls. I am Doctor Dickerson's nephew, Frank Dickerson, and I am his assistant, and he sent me to Barr Center to make five calls."

Mrs. Bodley looked at him with veiled eagerness, but she spoke hesitatingly. "Well, I don't know," said she.

"Oh, mother, it is very kind of Doctor Dickerson, but we had better mend the reins and go on in the buggy," said Ann.

"I don't see how the reins can be mended so as to be safe if Prince shies again," said Mrs. Bodley. "I guess we had better give up going to Barr Center."

The young man examined the reins and then whistled. "They are in rather bad shape," said he. "I don't quite see, myself, how we can mend them enough to enable you even to drive back to Barr-by-the-Sea. But if you will only accept my invitation and get in my car, we can find something in Barr Center to mend the reins with when we come back."

Ann looked distressed. "Mother, you wouldn't leave Prince and the buggy right here by the road, without a house in sight?" said she.

"I don't see how anybody can drive Prince off, with the reins broken, any better than we can," said Mrs. Bodley, and Frank Dickerson recognized her as being distinctly on his side.

"They could hitch Prince and the buggy on behind another team," said Ann. Frank wondered if she really did not wish to go in his car.

"Prince never would go hitched on behind anything," said her mother, grimly. "I remember when Sam Johnson tried it, and Prince kicked in the back of Sam's new carryall."

Frank Dickerson, in spite of himself, burst into a peal of laughter. The exploits of the defiant old sidewise-poised horse did seem incredible. Ann laughed, too, after a second. Mrs. Bodley did not laugh. She wished very much, for many reasons, to accept the young man's invitation; besides, she was always serious in her statements.

"It is true, even if Prince does look as if he wouldn't," said she. "It is as safe to leave him hitched here as if he were a tiger. You know he always tries to bite strangers, too, Ann. You can't laugh at that."

It ended in Prince being tied fast to a fence post, and Mrs. Bodley and Ann spinning off with young Doctor Dickerson in his shiny car. Frank Dickerson had wanted very much to ask Ann to sit in front beside him, but had not dared. He had, therefore, been surprised and delighted at Mrs. Bodley's suggestion, "You had better sit in front with Doctor Dickerson," as Ann was following her into the tonneau. "Maybe you can get a little idea about driving a car," she added.

Ann looked at her mother and gasped.

"I have been thinking for quite some time of selling Prince and the buggy and the carryall—Prince is so afraid of an automobile—and buying one," declared Mrs. Bodley, coolly.

It almost seemed to poor Ann Bodley that her mother must be lying, the whole appeared so preposterous. She had never heard her mother speak of cars with anything but disapproval, and the idea of her, Ann, driving one, was fairly beyond imagination. She rolled a soft brown eye over her shoulder at her mother, who met her gaze defiantly. It actually occurred to Ann that her mother might be losing her wits. It was simply monstrous, the mere thought of herself, little Ann Bodley, driving an automobile. Ann realized that this ought not to be so. She felt herself quite evidently anachronistic. She lived in an era of automobile-driving girls, of golf and tennis girls, but unaccountably she had failed to make her title clear in her own age and generation. She was, nevertheless, rather keen-witted. She really sensed, as probably her mother did not, the reason for the older woman's ceaseless driving of her before her almost juggernaut wheels of ambition.

Poor Mrs. Bodley felt instinctively that her daughter was not keeping the pace of her day; she was mortified, and hence the tireless spur of the maternal will. Mrs. Bodley had advanced ideas. Her other daughters had married, as she considered, not to their great advantage. She wished her darling Ann to dance through life in a strictly modern fashion. The idea of her marrying a commonplace man had secretly antagonized her. Still, if there were nothing else—it was out of the question that her Ann should live the life of a spinster, with limited means, in her own home.

"I doubt if your daughter would like driving a car," said Doctor Dickerson.

Ann regarded him gratefully. Her mother did not hear the remark.

"Driving a car is quite a strain on the nerves," said Doctor Dickerson.

"I suppose it is," agreed Ann. Then she added, apologetically, "I am ashamed if I am not equal to it, now women do drive cars so much."

The young man laughed.

"And they do drive well," said Ann, a little resentfully. After all, if she could not live up to the standards of her time, she was jealous of their admission. She fancied there was something a bit scornful in the young man's laugh.

"Oh yes, they drive all right, lots of them," he said, "but, after all, there are survivals of the species, and I guess you are one."

Ann colored a little. "I have always been ashamed that I could not do things as well as other women," said she—"that is, the things all the women did not do years ago, and do now."

Doctor Dickerson laughed again. "I don't even know your name," said he, changing the subject abruptly.

Ann started. "I am Ann Bodley," said she, "and my mother was driving when the horse shied. I forgot. I beg your pardon."

"Oh, that's all right! I simply thought I ought to have some name in mind when I thought of you."

Ann started again. She had never had anything like that said to her, at least not in that tone. She looked away at the sere fields past which they were flying. Her heart was beating fast.

"Must be a pretty country in the summer," said Doctor Dickerson.

"Very pretty," whispered Ann.

"It is pretty now, for that matter." The young man eyed a field, and wondered if the girl saw that it was pink and gold and mauve.

"Really the colors are prettier than in midsummer," said she, unexpectedly, and he beamed.

"You are right there," he agreed.

Soon they were approaching Barr Center. Mrs. Bodley leaned forward.

"It is wonderful how fast you get to places," said she. She was clutching her wayward bonnet fast; her gray hair stood out in stiff locks before the rush of the wind, but she looked positively gay.

"Then you find you like the car?" said Dickerson.

"I'd be a fool if I didn't," said Mrs. Bodley.

"Most people feel that way after they have taken the plunge."

"I, for one, don't mind the plunge after that old horse," said Mrs. Bodley.

Ann cast an apprehensive glance at her. Was it possible that she would really try to have her drive a car? Dickerson relieved her inexpressibly.

"If you do get a car I advise you to drive it," he shouted back at Mrs. Bodley. "Some women are born drivers, and you look to me like one. Your daughter might drive all right, but she is not one to take to machinery like you."

Mrs. Bodley nodded. "You are right about that," said she. "My daughter can't even manage the sewing-machine, but I should like to have her learn a little if I do buy a car. Suppose I were to have a fit, or anything."

"Oh, mother!" gasped Ann.

"You are very wise," shouted back the young man, and forthwith proceeded to explain carefully to Ann how to shut off the power. "That is really the most important thing for you to know," said he.

Before they reached Barr Center, Ann had tremulously moved the emergency brake and been inwardly thankful that there was no explosion.

Dickerson left the two women in the principal shop in Barr Center, and Mrs. Bodley astounded her already astounded daughter by purchasing table linen in considerable quantity. She also bought other things which Ann did not consider were needed. She wondered at the purchase of nainsook, lace, and embroidery.

"Why, mother," she ventured, when the saleswoman's back was turned, "we have so much underwear already."

"I want a half dozen extra of everything," said Mrs. Bodley.

Ann looked at her mother, and her eyes were almost wild. It occurred to her that Mrs. Bodley might be going to marry again. Ann was frightened. She said no more about the purchases, but she wondered painfully when Mrs. Bodley bought some delicate blue material and told the saleswoman she wished to use it for a negligée. The thought of her mother in a wedding negligée of that infantile blue was almost too much for the girl. She felt hysterical.

Ann was thankful when the shopping was over and the parcels were carried out to Doctor Dickerson's car. She obeyed meekly her mother's command to occupy the seat beside the young man.

"You get right in there, Ann, and learn how to work that thing when I have a fit," said Mrs. Bodley, with grim humor.

Mrs. Bodley felt very grand, having her parcels deposited in the car, and sitting there in state.

That very night young Dr. Frank Dickerson, telling his uncle about the very pretty girl and her very amusing mother, whom he had rescued from an untoward combination with a buggy and a scared, side-wise, ancient horse with bad habits of kicking and biting in spite of age, was informed of the news which Maria had divulged after hearing it from Carry Munn.

Old Doctor Dickerson looked shrewdly at his nephew. "Mustn't poach on another man's preserves," said he.

The young man was talking so fast that he paid no heed. "It was all true, too," said he. "That old beast tried to take a nip at me when we got back to the place where he was hitched and I made an effort to re-establish the original traveling *cortège*. I had to get in my car and drive off, and leave the old lady to unhitch her remarkable steed. The girl was afraid of him. She looked up at me and I declare I hated to leave her. She is one of the gone-out-of-date young women who rather appeal to me."

"No use, Frank; she has appealed to another man before you," said the old doctor.

This time the nephew heard. He stared with a shamed, taken-aback expression at his uncle.

"You mean—?"

"You drove them over to Barr Center on a shopping expedition for the young woman's trousseau. She is going to marry a widower with one child, who is staying with her prospective ma now."

"How do you know?"

"Surer information than telephone, mail, or cable. Servants. You don't mean to say you are so anacreontic as to fall in love at sight?"

Frank Dickerson colored absurdly. "What do you take me for?" he demanded. "Of course she is a pretty girl, and one somehow that makes you realize you are a man, and that is subtle flattery in these days. That girl could no more drive a car, and I know she never rode a bicycle; and she is charmingly afraid of a horse, and makes a fellow feel like a knight of old. But in love? Good Lord! She seemed just a variety which pleases because it is out of date. Hope she's got a good man. A widower with one child. How old?"

"Only a baby. I don't know who he is. I suppose he is somebody she met while she was away. I never heard of anybody here paying her the slightest attention. Guess the young men here like the prevailing mode in girls. I have noticed her. She is a nice little thing, and one of the sort who used to surprise me by being a darned sight smarter than they looked, in an emergency."

"That is just the way I feel about a girl of that type."

The result of that conversation was that young Doctor Dickerson did not call on Ann Bodley, although he had been cordially invited to do so by her mother. For several evenings Ann herself changed her gown for a blue one which was becoming, and took extra pains with her hair. Then she would have stopped, but her mother drove her on, and she continued with the docility which she had in all little things. She was not quite so docile in the large affairs of life, and her mother realized that, and endeavored very cleverly to present them as small ones.

"You are foolish not to wear that pretty blue dress while it is in style," she said, and the girl continued to array herself in it. Had she once suspected—but she did not. She sewed obediently on the linen and cambric, too. She was rather fond of sewing—setting nice little stitches seemed to her like a sort of lady rhythm of life—but not one would she have set had she known. As it was, she finally became rather melancholy about the delicate work. She could not help associating it with the lot of other girls, a lot which she was confident would never be for her. However, the baby was a great resource. She could not be entirely unhappy with the baby.

She thought sometimes of the young man who had driven her and her mother over to Barr Center. She saw him every Sunday in church, and he always bowed politely. She was not foolish about him. There was in Ann Bodley a firm ground-work of common sense, but she realized, when she thought of him, a sense of something slipping away which might, if it remained, count. When he did not call, she made the best of it. Then he came. She was all alone that evening. Her mother had gone to prayer meeting, and Ann, who had a slight cold, had remained at home. She wore the blue dress, and sat sewing, after she had put the baby to bed, before the fire when the bell rang. Carry Munn had also gone to church, so Ann went to the door. She started a little when she saw Frank Dickerson.

"Oh, good evening!" she said, hoarsely.

"You have a cold. Go right away from the door," ordered young Dickerson.

Ann fluttered before him like a blue flower, and the two sat down before the hearth fire.

Dickerson looked at her smilingly. "Not much of a cold, eh?" he asked.

Ann shook her head. "Nothing at all," she said, quite clearly. "I am better than I was yesterday, but mother thought it rather damp for me to go out this evening. Mother has gone to meeting."

"Yes, I was on the street and I saw her go into the church," returned Dickerson, quite frankly. Then he colored, and Ann colored, too. She could not possibly avoid thinking, "He came because he thought I would be alone," and he knew that she thought that, and also knew that it was true. The girl had, in reality, made more of an impression upon him than he owned to himself. He still believed she was to be married soon to another man, but he resented it.

After they had talked a little while he glanced at the pile of dainty white stuff in a work basket, and the resentment grew. Frank Dickerson knew that this delicate, reverting-to-type girl could not possibly be going to marry a man who was worthy of her. He knew men. He felt that he wanted to shake Ann by her blue shoulders and tell her brutally that she was a little fool to marry the fellow, whoever he was.

After a while, Ann, by sheer force of habit, because her fingers yearned for their accustomed task, took up her work. Frank Dickerson looked at her admiringly, even tenderly. He loved to see the pretty, feminine thing at her feminine employment. Then he set his mouth hard.

After a while Ann glanced up at him and wondered at his expression. His eyes met hers defiantly. "I suppose you are very happy?" he said, and his tone was unwarranted.

Ann looked bewildered. She did not dream what he meant. "I have a great deal to make me happy and thankful," she said, tritely, after a pause.

"Of course," said the young man, quite viciously. Ann was startled.

However, after a bit he began talking quite naturally again, and it was not until after he had gone that she thought of it all with wonder. When Mrs. Bodley came in she sniffed. She smelled cigar smoke.

"Who has been here?" said she.

"Young Doctor Dickerson," replied Ann, flushing softly.

"He smoked?"

"Yes. He asked if he might."

"How long did he stay?"

"You hadn't been gone long when he came, and he went away a few minutes ago. He had a call to make."

"I suppose he was in his car."

"Yes."

"I am thinking about getting a car in the spring," said Mrs. Bodley.

"Oh, mother!"

"I guess you'll find you like a car when you have one," said her mother, and smiled subtly.

The next week Mrs. Bodley went again to prayer meeting, and insisted that Ann was still not well enough to accompany her, although the girl was sure that her cold was cured. When Mrs. Bodley came home she smelled cigar smoke, but she said nothing. She was an astute woman. Finally it happened that two evenings of every week Mrs. Bodley was either away from home or out of the parlor of an evening, and smelled cigar smoke on her return, and poor little Ann began to sew with more zest.

It was nearly spring when the climax came. Frank Dickerson called, and it was too much for him. He did not stay as long as usual, but when he took his leave he clasped Ann's two hands in his and said, abruptly: "It is good-by, dear. I am not coming again."

Ann turned white. "Are you going to leave town?"

"After a little. Begin to think I must. I can't leave just yet, on account of my uncle."

"Why—?" began Ann, then stopped, for Frank bent and kissed her.

"Why do I stop coming?" he said, quite fiercely. "What do you take me for? How can I keep on coming?"

He kissed Ann again, and, before she got her breath, was out and she heard the whir of his car starter.

Ann went back and sat down. She felt faint. Presently her mother came in. She had made an errand over to her married daughter Isabel's. She smiled when she smelled the cigar smoke, then she noticed Ann's white face.

"What is the matter?" she asked.

"I don't know, mother," replied Ann. Her voice sounded strange in her own ears. She left the room and ran upstairs. Mrs. Bodley sat down and thought.

The next afternoon Ann went over to her sister's and soon came flying home. She rushed into the room where her mother was hemming a tablecloth. She flung up a window, snatched the web of fine linen from her mother, and bundled it out into the dead garden; then she slammed the window down.

Mrs. Bodley gasped. For a moment she thought the girl had gone suddenly mad. This was no Ann whom she had ever known, this creature with angrily flaming cheeks, flashing blue eyes, and vociferous tongue.

"Now I know!" almost shouted Ann, in a high voice of indignation. "Now I know!"

"What do you know?" asked her mother, feebly.

Ann faced her mother, and her little, gentle countenance was fairly terrible. "Mother," she said, almost solemnly, "you have—lied."

Mrs. Bodley cowered before the look and tone. "You tell your own mother—that?" she said, but her voice was a mere whisper.

"Yes, I do. You have been making everybody think I was going to be married. They congratulated me, and I didn't know why. You made a fool of me. You have tried and tried to push me into everything else, and I have submitted. I have acted like a fool about the other things. I knew I couldn't sing or paint or teach kindergarten, but you talked so much, and finally I got not quite sure of myself. But to try to push me into marriage! To tell people such a shameful lie when all the time he has never said one word about marrying me! And the last time he bade me good-by and said he was never coming again."

Mrs. Bodley started violently, and regarded her daughter with a queer expression. "Who do you mean by 'he'?"

"Young Doctor Dickerson. He has seen right through it all. He knows how you have fairly flung me at his head, making me sit on the front seat of the car with him and pretending you were going to buy one. He knows all about it. He has even seen me sitting here—sewing things. He must think I am as bad as you are—telling everybody I was going to marry a man who has never asked me, shaming me so I never want to look anybody in the face again."

Mrs. Bodley's countenance continued to wear a thoughtful, slightly relieved expression as the girl stormed on. Once she interrupted: "I never told anyone right out you were going to marry anybody," she said. "I never mentioned young Doctor Dickerson's name."

"You might just as well. Isabel has told me everything you said. It was a lie you told, mother, and you a church member! Oh, I don't see how you could! I must go right away from Barr-by-the-Sea and live somewhere else, where people don't know me, where I shall never run any chance of—seeing him again."

Ann was rushing out of the room when her mother arrested her. "Stop right where you are, Ann Bodley," she said, in a voice of mixed shame and triumph. "You accuse your own mother of lying when folks only jumped at their own conclusions, and you think yourself a lot brighter than you are. Young Doctor Dickerson never once thought I was talking about him. If you think a minute, instead of talking so much, you will remember that folks congratulated you coming out of church that Sunday, before he'd even come to town. He never thought for one minute I was telling people you were going to marry him. He thought it was a widower who was the baby's father. I own I didn't deny it, and if ever a man is dead in love with a girl, he is with you; and maybe he wouldn't be if he hadn't thought some other fellow had got ahead of him. Men are built that way, and you may have your mother, that tells lies, to thank for making you happy, after all, and—and . . ."

Mrs. Bodley stopped short, frightened. Ann's face had turned a dead white. She knew that what her mother said was true, but she grasped complexities of the situation which her mother did not.

"If—that is true," she said, in a thick voice—"and—maybe it is, then—it is all over. He will have to go away from town thinking it is somebody else, for, however I tell you you have lied, I will not tell him my own mother as good as lied to get me a husband. It is— all over."

"O my Lord!" said Mrs. Bodley.

She did not stop Ann when she left the room. She heard the girl sob as she went upstairs. "O Lord!" said Mrs. Bodley. She sat motion- less a long while. Shrewd little woman, with will of iron for her own purposes, she knew it was a deadlock. She agreed with Ann that she could not possibly tell Frank Dickerson.

"Might think it runs in the family," Mrs. Bodley said to herself, with grim humor.

Ann did not come down to supper. Mrs. Bodley herself made a special kind of toast which the girl liked, and fitted up a tray and set it outside Ann's chamber door. It was unlocked, but the mother did not dare open it. She called out: "Here is your supper. You had better eat it." When she went to bed the tray was still on the floor and had not been touched.

"I don't blame her," Mrs. Bodley said to herself in a harsh whisper. It did not occur to her to acknowledge her sense of her wrong-doing to Ann. It really seemed to her that she had acquiesced in the girl's judgment of her.

In her own room, Mrs. Bodley sat down beside a window and gazed out at the moonlit night. It was warm for the season, and the window was open, and a faint breath of returning spring came in. Mrs. Bodley talked to herself almost inaudibly. "I meant it all for her good," she said. "Goodness knows I did. But I realize now I ought not to have let people go on thinking she was going to be married, when I didn't know for sure, and now I wish I hadn't. O Lord!"

"I don't blame her," she said. "Poor child! I don't know what I would have done if my mother had acted the way hers has. I meant all right, but I got in the path of divine Providence, and now I'm paying for it, and I'm afraid she will have to."

The next morning Ann came down to breakfast. She looked tired and wan, but she spoke as usual, and ate her breakfast. She was a good girl. It seemed to her that she had no course open to her but to treat her mother kindly, forgive her, and live her life as it was ordered. She tried not to think of Frank Dickerson.

After breakfast Mrs. Bodley announced her intention of driving over to Barr Center. She did not even ask Ann to go. Both mother and daughter were shy of each other.

Ann, after her mother had driven out of sight, took up the baby and petted her and played with her. She could not sew. It seemed to her that she could never touch needle and thread again. She had an east window open, it was so warm, and the sweet air came in. She noticed that the tree branches were faintly rose-flushed, and reflected that it was almost spring and that her life might be harder when it was come.

She did not see Carry Munn hustle across the yard to the Dickersons', leaving her dishes unwashed. Carry Munn fled with the spring wind, her calico skirts lashing, her straight-locked hair stiffly leaving her aggressive forehead. She was met by her cousin Maria at the Dickerson door.

"Anybody in there to hear?" demanded Carry Munn, breathlessly.

"Not a soul. Young Doctor Frank has gone out making calls, and the old doctor is down for the morning mail. For the land sakes, what is it?"

"Ann wa'n't goin' to be married, when I told you she was."

The other woman gasped. "You said her ma told you so."

"I didn't tell you no such thing. Mis' Bodley ain't given to tellin' lies, and she a professin' Christian. I understood from somethin' she said that Ann was goin' to be married, and told it from Dan to Beersheba, and there wa'n't one word of truth in it."

"Then Ann ain't goin' to be married?"

"Not unless somethin' new has come up," said Carry Munn.

"Young Doctor Frank said last night he was goin' to leave town," said Maria.

"Hm!" said Carry Munn. Again they eyed each other.

"Whose baby is it?" demanded Maria.

"I know. I own I listened. It's all right about her."

"You won't tell?"

"Never; but it's all right."

They eyed each other again. Then Carry Munn flew home against the wind, and her hair stood out over her eyes like a thatched roof, and Maria went into the house. She started, for old Doctor Dickerson stood in the kitchen.

"What are you jumping so for?" said the old man, with a grin.

"I thought you was gone, Doctor Dickerson."

"No, I was here. All a piece of gossip, was it?"

"Ann Bodley ain't goin' to get married. Carry Munn always did jump at things," said Maria.

That same afternoon Ann, sitting alone with her book—she loathed her sewing—started at the sound of a motor car. She answered the doorbell, and Frank Dickerson stood there. He could not wait to come in before he spoke.

"See here. I thought you were going to marry somebody else," he cried. "I heard so. I heard it came straight from your mother. Now I want to know, is it true?"

Ann stood before him, pale and trembling.

"Tell me, dear."

Ann was silent.

"Ann!"

Mrs. Bodley came down the stairs with a swoop of black silk, like a bird.

"She will never tell you!" she said, in a desperate voice. "She will never tell you her own mother as good as lied. She is not going to marry any other man. She never was. I adopted the baby. Her father is alive. You needn't have anything to do with *me* if you don't want to. Ann never told a lie in her life."

Ann began to cry. "Don't, mother!" said she, pitifully.

Frank Dickerson took her in his arms. Then he looked over the bright head at Mrs. Bodley. He was blushing like a girl, and laughing.

"Strikes me the biggest truth-telling in creation is telling that you haven't told the truth," he said.

Mrs. Bodley gasped. Her face became incredibly tender. "You look at it that way?"

"I certainly do."

"My Lord!" She said it reverently, and she looked at the young man as if he were her own lover. Her face at that moment was wonderfully like Ann's, and a charming prophecy of her daughter's own future loveworthiness.

The Jester

She lay on her day-bed, long, thin, exquisite, an old woman in fact, but always and forever while she drew mortal breath a thing of beauty.

She wore a dressing gown of heavy lavender satin, disposed in the most charming folds. Blue lights and rose lights were in the depths of those folds, and not one but Almira Clapp, with her eyes of fadeless radiance, saw with delight. She was a beauty-worshiper. Her pose was studied. One slender leg partly raised the knee, disturbing the level of the lavender satin; one slender milk-white arm lay along the satin, in a curve of utmost grace.

One side of Almira's face was superior to the other. That side was exposed, a profile of perfection in age, on a pillow of black satin. Her skin was unbelievably smooth and white, blue veins showing on her temples under the lace frill of her rose-coloured cap.

Almira's whole soul was always in revolt against her white hair, which was not in the least suited to her. Years ago she had given up mild colouring tonics in as much of a rage as she allowed herself. After that she darkened her pale eyebrows and shaded her eyelids, and displayed her white locks defiantly when obliged.

She affected as much as possible the frilled boudoir caps.

"Lucky these caps came in my day," she often told her cousin Lois, who lived with her, subsisted on her bounty, and saved her immortal soul by patience with her lot in life.

Almira Clapp's bounty was so highly seasoned it would have choked a less patient, less proud stomach, for extreme patience is a synonym for extreme pride.

Almira never lost her temper, but she never lost her almost super-human consciousness of self which made of her personality a weight for the smothering of all about her. Lois Hemingway, the cousin, was not subtle enough to understand her. All she dimly sensed was an effect of burden, vague, unexplainable, which at times almost smothered.

All the women who knew Almira, or rather did not know her, said: "She is so sweet."

Lois herself said: "She is so sweet," and never knew she lied to her own soul.

Almira was not in the least sweet, but she was that unusual thing, a consummate actress before an audience of self alone. She was in reality an unclassified genius.

She had perfect health, the health of youth in her old age; but except for her histrionic genius which never slept, even when her body slumbered, she was one of the idlest of mortals. That is, apparently. She would lie for hours perfectly still so far as her body was concerned, but her brain was a radium brain. It gave out wasteless energy, endless light. She was marvelous. She accounted for her son Jonathan, who was also marvelous, in an inverted way. It was said of Jonathan Clapp that it was quite wonderful how well he had turned out, considering all he had against him. This was the sort of praise that damns; but Jonathan, when he heard it, and he heard it often, it being the sort of compliment which people do not grudge handing on, laughed.

He had undoubtedly been handicapped from the start, and no matter how well a race is run, the wonder remains, what if there had been no handicap? What marvel of speed exceeding all records might not have been attained?

Jonathan's handicap was a vague thing. It existed, but indefinitely. After all, the boy and man was not crippled, deformed, or ill, either in mind or body. There was about his whole personality that curious quality termed insignificance. He was not unduly short nor tall. He was of good average height.

He was neither too stout nor too thin. He had not one noticeable bad feature, nor noticeably beautiful one, with the exception of his eyes. They were blue, and it is seldom that blue eyes achieve true beauty.

One blue is too cold, too much of the surface; or the blue jewel is too small. Jonathan's eyes were a blue of whatever emotion Jonathan wished.

Generally Jonathan wished humour. Humour was his long suit, his long trump suit of life. Instinctively he had known that when he was a mere lad.

Jonathan had his mother's histrionic genius. He had apparently inherited nothing whatever from his father, beyond his mere physical fact. The elder Clapp must have been as near nonentity as possible.

Nobody ever even mentioned him. He had died suddenly when Jonathan was a baby. Nothing remained of his existence except his name on the monument in the Clapp burial plot in the Fairlawn cemetery of Bloomfield.

When Jonathan was a child, he had always been taken by his beautiful mother on Memorial Day to the cemetery, where a queer, decorous sort of festival was held by the inhabitants of Bloomfield and their visiting friends and relatives.

People who had ever had any connection with Bloomfield made it a point to be present at the cemetery reunion on Memorial Day.

Almira always had the lot carefully decorated. Young Jonathan assisted the night before. Laden with wreaths and flower-baskets, trailing with vines like a young Pan, he tagged his mother, herself laden with floral booty, and together they decorated the Clapp lot.

There were not many graves there. It had been a small family. Grandfather Eliphalet Clapp, of course, and his wife Marie, their graves long since sunken; the more recent grave of a spinster Clapp whom Jonathan could dimly remember; his father, Arthur Clapp's, and a tiny mound for a baby sister.

Jonathan's father's grave had always the best of the decorations. An urn blazing with geraniums, overflowing with graceful vines, stood before the headstone, the grave covered with pansies in a royal arabesque of colour.

Jonathan was so young, his mind became confused. He confessed in later years to hilarious friends, that he had been led to think of his defunct sire as a perpetually blooming, gigantic pansy.

He never told his mother of his impression. He had been a very quiet youngster. He thought a great deal. He recorded impressions upon his receptive mind. The only sign of emotion he evinced was a sudden humorous upward quirk of the upper lip, the right corner, and a twitch of his thin nostrils. His blue eyes remained as always, perfectly clear, beautiful and serene, betraying nothing.

His mother could not have understood him, else his silence might not have been so persistent. She had not the ability to recognize the glitter of the merest spark of humour. She laughed at times, of course. That was obligatory, to maintain her rôle, but her laugh was simply a facial affair: an upcurving of the lines of her mouth. Her eyes above the lines remained unmoved, even stupid, because of the contrast between her real mental attitude and her expression.

Jonathan never loved his mother, during his youth. He was never sure, upon later mature reflection, that he had loved any living thing except an absurd little mongrel dog, which had come yelping and tin-kettled to the kitchen door of the Clapp house.

Jonathan had displayed the first insistent mind of his own, regarding the keeping of that ridiculous dog. He named him Lazarus, and he made a face at his mother behind her back because she mocked at him.

"I will buy a really good dog, a thoroughbred for you," she said.

But Jonathan clutched the mongrel with such fierceness that the dog, only a puppy then, yelped with alarm at the cruelty of love.

Lazarus remained. He was not even banished from Almira's presence in the living-room. She in time reconciled herself to him by fastening an enormous bow of orange ribbon on his collar. For some undefined reason, that enormous orange bow conferred the grotesque distinction of a gargoyle upon poor Lazarus. He, a composite of many breeds, became definite. He was hideous, but markedly so. Almira, who was clever artistically, immediately perceived that.

"I have made Lazarus possible with a bow of orange ribbon, and he may remain on the hearth on the black satin cushion," she told Jonathan.

Jonathan nodded silently. Lazarus lay coiled on the black cushion, his orange bow a strange, unearthly colour in the firelight. His eyes gleamed like jets. There was a faint movement of his stumpy tail. There was not enough of it for an actual wag. If he had been a cat he would have purred.

Jonathan had happy hours watching Lazarus on the black cushion, warm and contented in the light of the hearth fire.

Two years before he went to college, Almira sent Jonathan to an inexpensive school. Her luxuries were costly, and her income was limited.

Jonathan had rather a brilliant record in college. However, that was more because, while there, he discovered what his real asset of power in life was, than because of exceptional mental ability.

While in college, during the latter part of his freshman year, Jonathan discovered that he had the rarest type of genius. He could make the world laugh. He did not even need to say anything funny. He could force laughter from embodied sorrow and despair, by a look, a motion.

Jonathan had Lazarus with him in his college rooms. He had always a feeling that the absurd dog had in some occult fashion revealed him to himself. The combination of Jonathan and mongrel dog became the inverted pride of the college.

Jonathan and Lazarus eclipsed in a subtle fashion everything else. They had their own honour, so strange that it commanded first attention.

Even the stroke oar and the football captain retired, if only for the time, into the background when Jonathan, his Lazarus at heel, appeared.

"Here comes Jonty, and the Beggar at the Gate," the shout went up.

Everybody stared, and hilarity appeared like a rainbow. Even the faculty lost dignity.

There was no doubt that Jonathan and Lazarus were the high lights of the young man's last collegiate year.

Jonathan had no need of class honours on Commencement Day. It was enough to be himself when he graduated.

Honours conferred would have been like crowning the already crowned.

He was the real delight of the whole affair: of the weary grind at useless mental tasks, of the enthusiastic games, of the rebellions against authority. He was sheer delight, the promoter of innocent mirth. They could better have given up electric lights in the college buildings, than Jonathan.

But with all this, nobody loved the boy, except as they loved themselves. When they laughed with joy, there was not the slightest love in their hearts for him. They would have lamented had Jonathan been taken away; they would have grieved; but not because they loved him, because they loved themselves and their own joy of life which he, and he alone, had the power to awaken in them. Jonathan was perfectly well aware of that. He did not admit to himself the slightest repining because of it. He told himself gallantly and gayly, that it was a great feat for any man: to like to make his fellow beings laugh and forget sorrow, and have them ready to forget him, as they would any spectacle of amusement.

"I am a sort of jumping-jack for the gods and men," he said to a man once, a man who was the nearest to a friend he had found.

The other looked at him, startled for a minute. Was there, or did he imagine it, a faint inflection of sadness and bitterness in Jonathan's tone?

But Jonathan laughed: a long ringing laugh. "Tell you what it is, Sam," he said. "When you are a joke on yourself, you are the biggest joke in existence."

Sam looked doubtful, then he also laughed.

"See here, old man," he said. "It isn't altogether because you are so damned funny that I like you."

The sweetest smile curved Jonathan's mouth. Then he laughed again. "But," he returned, "you might as well own up, if I hadn't made you laugh you would just have gone your way, just gone past without even noticing me."

Sam, who was the brightest scholar of his class, the one out of the whole college destined to live in the history of his country, was honest. His honesty was, in fact, his asset of success.

"Of course, you are right about that, I suppose," he admitted; "but now—."

"Now, you wouldn't turn your back on me, if I failed to make you laugh at all," Jonathan said, and looked with love in his eyes (love for the passing second, he allowed himself no more: the aftertaste was too bitter), at his friend. "Well," he added, "you are not likely to be put to the test. I shall make everybody, myself included, laugh till I die, and then I reckon I shall contrive to be somewhat ludicrous in a ghastly fashion. It is a component part of my personality; I am proud of it, old man. If I didn't have that, what on earth would I have to be proud of?"

Sam regarded him thoughtfully. "After all, it is a rare gift," he said hesitatingly, for suddenly the savour of terrible pathos was strong in his nostrils. "You are the one man here who has it," he added.

"To waken laughter in this world is better than to waken love,"

Jonathan said, a bit cryptically. "I think the memory of love is shorter than the memory of a laugh," he continued. "Most people remember a good joke. It has immortal youth; but whose sweetheart has? Not a man-jack but will pass the lass to whom he swore eternal devotion, without even recognizing her, twenty years later; but never will he pass a good joke twenty years later, without feeling his heart warm."

"Dare say you are right," Sam returned, but he looked puzzled.

When Jonathan was alone in his room, he stood before his mirror. Every line in his face was downward. His whole face was a mask.

"Needs this sort of thing for a jest foundation," Jonathan said, quite aloud. "Well, I must have something out of life, and this is better than nothing at all."

Jonathan's mother, old and exquisite in her triumphant age, was rather proud of her son's unique talent. She laughed with the rest. When Jonathan was at home, not a word or pose but was for the sake of his mother's laughter when he was with her. And this although he was well aware that her laughter was only perfunctory, the only laughter possible to a woman of her type.

However, that left the boy unmoved. He did not in the least love his mother. He saw no reason for gratitude that she, presumably not considering his welfare at all, had brought him into the world. It did not seem to him reasonable to be grateful for anything like that—for a life such as his.

He admired her only coldly and impersonally. When he had aroused her vain laughter, he felt that he had been purely filial.

"Mother is so proud because she thinks she has a sense of humour," he told himself.

Once the old cousin Lois waylaid him. She put her hand on his shoulder. "You poor boy!" she said.

The meek, involuntary butt had grasped the situation. She had steeled her heart against affection. It was too costly a commodity for her, but she had grasped the situation. He looked at her astonished. A tear was rolling down each withered cheek, although she kept her patient face immobile.

Jonathan had never seen love for himself enough to know it; in reality, he had not seen more of pity, but he did recognize that.

"Look here, old lady," he said. "Tears make me own failure. No tears. Lord, life is one immense joke. Look here, life is your joke as well as mine. If one has nothing else, there is always the joke. Laugh, for God's sake, laugh, old lady!"

Lois, ancient, bent, weazened, her black silk gown crinkled on her flat chest as with a grotesque mirth of fabric, laughed.

"You are the funniest boy that ever lived," she chuckled, and dashed a little wrinkled hand across the streaming tears.

"And isn't that distinction for one boy?" Jonathan laughed back. "Laughter is good for the souls of men. It makes them glad, and as yet the Government has nothing to say against it. Laugh, old lady, laugh, for God's sake!"

And for inexplicable reasons, old Lois laughed, until tears of mirth instead of pity drenched her cheeks.

Jonathan laughed too, but not to tears.

Almira, in her lilac satin, heard, although her door was closed, and laughed also.

"What were you and Jonathan laughing at?" she asked Lois when she entered.

"I don't know," Lois said, still laughing helplessly. "Just Jonathan."

"I have never seen any human being with such inexhaustible spirits," Almira said complacently.

"He would laugh at that," Lois said.

"At what?" Almira stared.

"Inexhaustible spirits—just now—you know."

"I do not understand," Almira said. "For goodness sake, don't you try to be funny, Lois. Leave that to Jonathan. He has a perfect genius for it. As I remember perfectly, he was always laughing when he was a mere baby."

"He needs to," Lois replied with unexpected force. She looked at the other, beautiful, prosperous woman, defiantly.

"What do you mean?"

"He has always had to laugh to keep from crying," Lois said.

"There you are, trying to be funny again, and you are simply stupid. Leave it to Jonathan," Almira said.

She lay on her chaise lounge, reflecting. "On the whole, Jonathan is turning out much better than I expected," she murmured. "Of course he is handicapped. I am his mother, but I have always faced the truth that he is handicapped."

"Not as long as he can laugh," Lois said again with her unusual defiance. "A man who can laugh can take all the fences of life."

"There you go again, trying to be funny. You can't. It is not in our family. Jonathan is a throwback."

"Perhaps he is a throwback to a jester of some old king."

Almira stared at Lois icily. "Your hair is growing grayer very fast," said she, "and the lines on your face are deeper. I will give you some of my skin tonic."

"Thank you," said Lois.

Jonathan, after he had transformed his old cousin's tears to laughter, went out to the garage. There was one car there: an old model of a good make, in perfect order. The man who worked about the place for his mother was rubbing its glittering sides.

He looked up and saw Jonathan and began to laugh, without a word being said. It was not the least of Jonathan's genius that he could arouse paroxysms of laughter, and do absolutely nothing except present himself to view. In the face of the fact that no mortal could specify one distinctly humorous feature of his, it was almost uncanny. Jonathan did not even need to change a muscle. He was as a god of hilarity commanding laughter with no perceptible action.

"What in the name of common sense are you laughing at now?" Jonathan inquired. And the man bent over double with mirth. He glanced up at Jonathan's unmoved face, and was off again, fairly choking. Jonathan stood by with absolutely unmoved face. However, although unmoved as to muscle, his features wore an expression of gravity, even sternness, before the other man's laughter, which in some strange paradoxical fashion was the extreme of comedy, at least for an untrained mind.

The man sat down on the running-board of the car; he was fairly weak with his unrestrained mirth.

Jonathan, without a word, got into the car, and took the wheel.

Dickson, the man, slid off the running-board, and stood out of the way. The last thing Jonathan heard as he drove off was the echo of his silly laughter. Then he frowned. "Lord, if there only was something funny," he said. He put on more speed. A girl crossing the street gave a quick, graceful leap to the sidewalk. Jonathan saw her looking back over her silken shoulder, and an old twinge of pain to which he was accustomed, shot over him. It seemed to completely fill his whole consciousness of body, soul and mind.

Years before, when in fact he was very young, Jonathan had taken his fixed attitude of life toward girls and women, and what they could mean to him, or rather what he could mean to them.

It was strange that, without any actual deformity or physical fault, a man could have been so physically repellent toward women; but he was. Jonathan, when he first fully realized it, had felt heartbroken. He was, after all, in spite of his strange gift, as other men. He had his dreams. A youth without dreams would be a spiritual and physical monster. Jonathan had loved his dreams. He had not only to relinquish all hope of happiness,—that natural food for the starved yearning of his kind,—but he had to smother his dreams.

Then he gained greater power in his one talent; but while the laughter swelled louder around him, he knew for the first time the terrible loneliness of his own heart. He knew it must exist while he walked the earth. He would be alone as long as he lived. Sometimes the boy wondered if it would not be better to be alone with openly confessed sadness, than with roaring mirth.

He knew only gradually the dreadful under-note of the born jesters of the world—that compelling endurance of despair which alone makes possible their superhuman mirth and power of awakening mirth.

He was fully fledged in his knowledge, in his development of what is fortunately a rare gift, as he drove down the principal street of his native town.

He had graduated the year before. He was studying with a lawyer who was an old sweetheart of his mother's. Who was in a way her sweetheart still. Peter Saunders had survived his love's marriage with another. He had not attempted, when death had freed her, to renew their old relations and marry her.

Still he clung to the old romance, and Almira was a faithful obbligato.

Both of them enjoyed the situation. Almira did not wish to marry again. She was rather a clever woman. She understood perfectly that with years she had lost her power of creating illusion, when in close daily communion. Not always could she maintain her lovely poses, her charming acceptance of situations with a husband. No mortal woman could at her age.

She knew also that, while it would not have mattered in the least to some men, it would seriously matter with her old lover.

The romantic strain which more properly had belonged to a woman, when she was a girl, had made her turn from him as a husband.

She recognized his perfection as a lover, but she recognized her own inability to keep it green, and his inability to maintain the married pace without actual dislike for her. She had married a man to whom romance meant nothing, but whom she could hold, and did hold until death did them part.

Then, although she was not inconsolable, she was not of that caliber; she had no desire to marry again; and she did regard the return of Peter upon his old footing, as adorer, as perpetual lover, with gratitude and pride.

She thought of him secretly as another Petrarch, although out of his romance he could weave no songs, and of herself as another Laura.

She was aware that this perpetual homage kept her young beyond her years.

She dressed for Peter, she cold-creamed for Peter, she kept her hair wonderful for Peter, and secretly, in the recesses of her terribly feminine mind, knew him for what he really was: a tonic for the preservation of her youth.

There was never any scandal, never any gossip as to their possible marriage. It was the most graceful, properly conducted elderly love-story possible, and was considered very charming.

Peter was the faithful lover, she the accepter of love, holding it to her soul like a sacred chalice. Occasionally she intimated to some other woman that she could not dream of ever marrying again, because of her son.

That absurdity was credited to her account of womanly perfection. Jonathan never heard of it. He would have laughed the most genuine laugh of his life if he had.

He accepted Peter as he accepted the best easy chair in the library, one covered with red leather and worn to ultimate intimacy with the weary curves of the human anatomy. It was there Peter sat, while he paid his calls of faithful and poetic love.

Strangely enough, considering this side of his character, Peter was a lawyer, and rather an astute one. He had inherited wealth, and his legal energy must presumably have been for some motive other than acquisition.

When Jonathan had completed his college course, he naturally studied law with the man who might have been his father. It seemed really all in the family.

Strangely too, as strangely for Jonathan as for the older man, he also promised from the first to be rather more than a moderate success in his profession.

As time went on, he won more than one case by his rare natural gift, instead of his acquired knowledge of the law.

It was as good as known what the verdict would be when the jury went out shaking with suppressed laughter. Jonathan successfully de-fended one ghastly murder case with that queer power of his. He could make the dreadful swing over the crossbar into the irresistibly funny.

It was against all reason, and the press criticized, but he succeeded.

Jonathan had been practicing law two years, and Peter had gradu-ally played his part of perpetual lover to the usurpation of his business, drinking tea every afternoon, and smoking as his old sweetheart gra-ciously allowed. Peter was a handsome man, fastidious about his dress, peculiarly fastidious, for a man, with regard to coming in contact with the unclean and unkempt.

A distaste for the close fetidness of court rooms had increased with him, as had also an actual loathing which dangerously disposed him to unfairness toward a client whose status in society was below his own.

Jonathan had no such scruples. In fact, he liked very well to have his senior seated metaphorically at his charming mother's feet, drink-ing tea, and playing with the shadows of a past love.

Privately, he considered Peter better fitted for that than for the law.

"No man has a right to be where he is apt to see a horrible mess any minute, if his stomach is so damned delicate," he told himself.

He was not unhappy, although he had foresworn, or rather been forbidden by fate, the sweets of life which hung too high over the wall of situation for him. He was proudly conscious of never endeavouring to reach for them, and of seeing them grasped and swallowed by others, with a kindly jest upon his own part.

That day when Laura Wayne made her swift graceful leap out of the danger which he had created for her, was destined to mark an epoch in his life.

Two days later Jonathan met her at a little dinner.

Jonathan's home town, although not large, was rather unusually smart at aping city fashions. Except in rare instances, it betrayed no provincialism.

Jonathan was a popular guest at dinners. He could eat his dinner and scarcely speak, and be credited with the social success of the whole affair. Jonathan grinningly admitted to himself that a man might be worse off than being perfectly able to eat a very good dinner, and not pay for it with a single word, and yet receive the credit.

However, it happened this time that he was to take out Miss Laura Wayne.

She was a beauty, although in a subtle fashion which sometimes flung doubt upon the fact. She was very tall, almost too tall, taller by an inch at least than Jonathan; but somehow she contrived to make little of her height, as some women contrive to make much of their lack of it. The subtlety of her beauty consisted mainly in the fact that men in a great majority recognized it, women in a small minority.

Women generally admitted that Laura Wayne had a good complexion and good features, but as for beauty, or the indefinable combination which makes for that, they failed to see it.

Men saw it.

Jonathan could scarcely command himself sufficiently to look squarely in her face when he offered her his arm to lead her to the dining-room—Jonathan, one of whose chief assets of popularity was his entire lack of self-consciousness.

As they sat at table, Jonathan for the most part addressed remarks to the smooth cold curve of her bare shoulder, surmounted by a silver strap which held her black velvet dinner gown in place.

Jonathan had not the slightest idea what the beauty wore. He had a confused perception of soft dark depths of fabric, confining her tall slenderness like a sheath. He could not have told if the shoulder straps were of gold or silver. He was, however, aware of a long platinum chain, from which swung a diamond cross. The thing glittered obtrusively.

He felt curiously confounded before it. Sometimes, when he essayed to make a remark to the girl, the dazzle of the cross seemed to make him stop dumb, to lose entirely the thread of his contemplated speech.

Once Laura laughed. "What is the trouble, Mr. Clapp?" she asked.

"Trouble?"

"Yes, you seemed about to say something, but then you checked yourself so abruptly. Was it something shocking?"

"I quite forget. I beg your pardon," Jonathan said. He felt himself a burning crimson. His lower lip almost dropped.

Laura laughed again. The girl's laugh, at once mocking and caressing, rang in the man's ears all night long. He could not sleep. Such love had entered his soul that he was too alive for sleep. Every nerve in his body was like a thread of fire. The whole man flamed with the utmost divinity of love, that which gives and does not ask.

Poor Jonathan never dreamed of asking. He never dreamed of the possibility of his love being returned. It is doubtful if he could have done that and loved. Love in its fullest sense means, for a rare soul, giving only, never receiving, and the man had a rare soul. His love was worth more, a minute of it, than another man's love of a life.

Jealousy was not in Jonathan. Laura's name was coupled with that of another man: a handsome, graceful fellow, with wealth and charm. Jonathan even thought of him with a queer sort of affection tinctured with doubt. He wondered was he worthy. He sought his company, he studied him. Finally he took the purest delight in finding him of rather exceptional merit.

Jonathan, convinced of that, thought of the girl as already married, placed beyond his honourable reach. He realized no suffering because of that. He had not even wanted her for himself in the sense that the other did. She was his butterfly wing of existence. He could scarcely venture to touch her with the antennæ of his thought. Possessed by him, she would have lost her value for him.

No man could ever possess her, as he already did for time and eternity, not even himself.

In those days Jonathan came near losing his insignificance. He appeared taller, almost imposing. Sometimes Laura looked at him with dawning wonder, but he did not realize it. He realized nothing except the rapture of utterly selfless love which ennobled him past his own understanding.

The true hero cannot escape his pedestal. Worship raises, as by some divine lever, the soul above itself. Peter Saunders noticed the change in him, but it assumed in his estimation a perfectly natural advance along the lines of the young man's rare gift.

Jonathan was more successful than ever in his profession. More and more he compelled the adoration of laughter, and won his way through all obstacles.

His mother was proud of him because he was her son. Her laughter at his jests had a ring of genuine fondness in it.

Jonathan was mentioned as a possible factor in politics. A high position was hinted at as not being beyond his reach.

"A man who can hold an audience like that can hold the reins of power," it was said.

When Laura heard that she looked reflective. Still, Jonathan's possible elevation did not move her. She had not thought of him as a lover; she did not then. That came later.

There was a benefit play to be held in the town for a new hall. A celebrated stock company with a Broadway success was engaged.

Strangely enough, the play had for one of its cast a queen's jester, and the jester died suddenly just before the date of the performance.

He had been in reality the star of the cast, although the playwright had not so intended.

The man had gained, almost without his own connivance, undue prominence. The jester made the play.

When he died there was consternation, for there was nobody among the professionals to take his part and not let the whole play down.

Then Jonathan suddenly came into his own.

He was besieged, first by his fellow-townsmen, then by the manager.

He did not hesitate long. The thing appealed to him. It was, and he instinctively knew it, the right footing after many days. The peg was to be fitted to its own niche.

Laura was out of town. She returned the night of the performance.

She was amazed when Jonathan appeared in the traditional cap and bells.

"Why, that is Jonathan Clapp!" she whispered to a woman beside her.

"Yes, didn't you know? The professional dropped dead, and Jonathan Clapp is taking his part." As she spoke, the woman's face was creased with mirth.

The audience went mad with delight over their own jester. Every movement, every word was applauded, and the laughter rose and fell like waves of the sea.

Until the last.

Then the poor jester, on his knees before the queen, confessed his love. Suddenly a silence like a shock was over everything. The people sat still and held their breaths. This was something new. They had not expected it.

The tremendous pathos which alone can make great comedy, was before them, made known to them.

When the curtain went down the house rose with one accord. Something almost like hysteria swept them. Jonathan appeared again and again.

The next day it was known he had refused the most flattering offers to continue with the company. They said he was greater than the dead comedian had been—that a career was open to him.

That evening Jonathan went to a dinner in his honour. He was made a hero. Laura, who was there, did not approach him with the rest.

After dinner she beckoned him into a little conservatory off the drawing-room. She stood half-concealed behind the tall palms and motioned to him.

He shook his head slightly. That simple motion awakened laughter among all who saw and did not understand.

She was insistent. He saw a flash of emeralds on her finger.

After a time he stole away and joined her.

The girl did not hesitate. She was bold, out of herself.

"Jonathan," she whispered. "Jonathan."

He knew that she understood herself as being in the place of the queen in the play. He knew that he had betrayed himself. He knew that at last it was possible for him to take as well as give, but the taking had no savour for his soul. He knew that if he took, love would go, both from his own soul and hers.

What had moved her was the jester in the consummate climax of all jest. Not even for her could he accept as his own the sad underlying fact. He could not all his life play a part not his own birthright.

When she whispered again and laid a hand on his arm, he only laughed.

He flung back to the people in the drawing-room. "Another bouquet for the fool," he called out gaily.

There was a roar of laughter. The girl's face blazed, then went white. Then she too laughed of her brave spirit.

Nobody could have said those five words as Jonathan said them.

Nobody could have made them so unaccountably funny.

When Jonathan got home that night, the lights were on. The perpetual lover had not gone, and old Lois was waiting for Jonathan in the little room near the door. The servants had gone out. She let him in before he could take out his latch-key.

Old Lois pulled him gently into the little room gleaming with light. "Jonathan," she said in very much the same manner that the girl had.

"Well, old lady."

"I know," said old Lois.

"Then you know why I laugh," Jonathan replied.

She gazed up in his face, tears streaming over her cheeks, her mouth twitching.

"Laugh, old lady, Life can be met by you as by me, only with a laugh—or we shall both go down under it. Laugh, old lady."

Lois laughed. Jonathan's laugh rang out. "It is a duet," he cried gaily, and they laughed again.

The White Shawl

"Susy?"

"Yes, Willy."

"Where are you?"

"Right here, Willy."

"Sort of dark."

"Yes, it is rather dark."

"Don't light the lamp yet."

"Don't worry. I won't light the lamp till you want it."

"I—can't see out of the window. I bet I ought to stand the other way. Want—to see out the window facing the tracks."

"You'd be right in a draft then. I'll see out the window for you."

"Can you see the signals?"

"Course I can."

"See the gates?"

"You know I can." The old woman laughed sweetly, even gayly. She was spent and sad, yet there was a ring of real humor in her laugh.

Susy Dunn had a gallant soul. All her life that gay acceptance of adversity as well as joy had cheered her on like a soldier. Always before her mental vision was something like the wave of a captain's hand, the flash of a flag.

"See 'em without glasses, too," she added, "spite of all the doctors telling me I ought to put 'em on years ago."

"Susy, little tired," the broken-hearted woman laughed again. She knew what she knew about the track, but kept her knowledge to herself.

He did not dream of the real seriousness of the situation, this old dying keeper of the crossing-gates.

That morning the doctor who was attending him had told Susy that the man who had charge of the signal tower had died suddenly. There was not a man in the village who could fill his place, and there was the worst north-easter of the winter raging.

One of the directors of the railroad lived in the village and Doctor Evarts had just seen him. "Little Sloane girl has tonsilities, and I was in there this morning," he told Susy. "And Sloane was near out of his mind about this signal tower here. He says it's one of the nastiest little danger spots on the road with those tracks crossing the way they do. The Corporation ought to fix it. Sloane says it has been brought up time and time again, and he's said and voted all he can, but some of them are waiting for an accident to get a move on. Sloane had wired to Oxbridge for a man and got a reply that he'd come. I guess it's all right if he can get here. It is one of the worst storms I was ever out in, and that road to Oxbridge drifts enough to stall a train when every other road is clear."

Susy looked at him with quick anxiety. "Willy knows about the signals as well as the gates. If he knew he would be out there if he was dying," she said.

"Musn't let him know, whatever you tell him."

Susy watched the doctor's car hump and slide out of the yard and down the road. "He can't get here again to-day," she thought.

Then she had begun to watch the signal tower and the gates from the window. She had not seen one signal; the gates had not gone down. Only two trains had gone through after the doctor left, a passenger and a short freight.

Every moment which she could snatch, she had spent in watching the signal-tower seeming to veer and slant before the fierce drive of the snow-packed gale. She knew that the boy who had taken Willy's place at the gates was not there. She had wondered if possibly the boy might not have taught him. But she knew, as the hours wore on, that there was no man for the tower, no boy for the gates, and the earth like an ocean in a hurricane, heaving up mountains of deadly fury, in gulfs of despair.

Willy questioned her continually and she lied those lies which the unselfish lie to spare pain.

"Jimmy tending the gates?"

"Yes, Willy."

"See him?"

"Yes, Willy."

"Hope he holds out. He ain't anything but a boy. It would be pretty hard for Tom minding the tower and the gates too. Hope he holds out."

"Don't you worry. He'll hold out."

"The snow ain't drifted, is it?"

Susy laughed her gallant laugh in the face of a dreadful world. "I guess a canary bird could hop over all the drifts I see."

"Tom tending the signals all right?"

"Didn't you see the green light yourself on the wall at the foot of your bed when the last train went through?"

"I don't know. My eyes seem sort of dim."

"I guess you forget seeing it."

"My eyes are dim. Susy, is the wind blowing just as hard?"

"Wind must be going down."

"I can't hear any too well. Half the time can't tell whether a noise is in my head or outside it," Willy sighed wearily.

"You hear all right."

"I wish I could go out and see for myself that the signals and the gates are being tended to."

"Now Willy, you stop worrying. You'll get so you can't get out to tend the gates for a month if you worry. You'll make yourself worse. You must stop it. It's wearing on you, and it's sort of wearing on me too."

"I don't mean to tire you all out, Susy."

"Of course you don't. You're my blessed old man. I speak so just on your own account. The signals will be tended and the gates kept. I promise you that and you know I never promise you anything that don't come true."

"You mustn't try to go out, Susy. You are too lame."

"Who said anything about my going out? There's the three fifty-seven now; it is almost fifteen minutes late. Hear it?"

"I can't seem too," the old man replied patiently. "Gates and signals all right?"

"See the green light show up on the wall there and winking in the looking glass over the shelf?"

"Mebbe I do see it."

Willy lay in his bed, very flatly, the patchwork quilt drawn up under his sharp, bristling old chin. Through his beard-stubble his skin gleamed ghastly white. His eyes were still bright with a strange questioning brightness, seeming to demand information concerning the destination of a little unimportant, unknown old man. Old Willy Dunn's eyes, as he lay there dying, asked terrible questions.

Susy seemed to hear them. They shouted, unanswered in her own heart, stirring it to rebellion, because of the love of an old wife, which passes the love of a mother, for her old man, as the time of parting drew near.

The angry love and pity, which filled her heart, as she watched over her dying husband, expanded it to almost breaking point. Her small old face was beautiful with fadeless romance and endurance of youth.

Willy had always thought his wife very beautiful, never dreaming that it was the love for him shining from her whole face which made her seem so. Always when a man sees himself reflected as a god in the eyes of a woman, he sees the mystery of beauty and does not understand.

Before the day quite faded Susy prepared Willy's supper. The light in the room was now ghastly, a snow-light streaming through the windows like the effulgence from a corpse. The wind blew fiercely, many miles an hour. Great waves of snow sprayed against the windows, with every departing gust leaving always a delicately frozen spume.

Susy was thankful that her husband could not hear the roar of the wind, could not see with his failing eyes the up-toss of the storm. Now and then she drew the quilt over his face, opened the window giving on the railroad crossing, and brushed away the snow. She kept that one window clear enough to enable her to see the gates and the tower.

Susy placed Willy's little meal before him and tugged at his sinking shoulders with her skinny arms. "Try and lift yourself up a little mite, pa," she said. Ever since they had lost their one child years ago, she had sometimes called Willy "pa." It pleased him.

Poor old Willy tried, but he was very feeble. His thin shoulders heaved upward then sank down helplessly. "I—don't—seem to— want anything to—eat," he gasped.

"Just take a swaller of this nice hot tea and a mouthful of this milk toast."

Susy kept her arm under Willy's neck and fed him. His mouth gaped like a sick bird's. He swallowed pitifully obedient, but with great difficulty.

When Susy took the tray away, tears were streaming over her face. "You shan't be pestered any longer, pa," she said.

She carried the tray into the kitchen and set it on the table. She leaned her head against the wall, and shook with great sobs. "Sometimes being deaf is a blessing for them that can't hear," she wailed out.

All her little body was racked with terrible grief. The black and white cat came rubbing against her, as animals will do when their beloved humans are in grief. His back arched, his tail waved. He made little affectionate leaps against her knees. Susy caught him up and wept into his soft fur until it was sodden.

Suddenly she heard Willy call. She put the cat down softly and hurried into the next room.

"Is it—time for—the express?" Willy gasped wildly.

"Wait a minute. I'll see." Susy went close to the loud-ticking clock on the shelf. "Not quite time."

"How long?"

"Oh, a good twenty-five minutes."

"Has it stopped snowing?"

Susy gazed out at the gray drifting violence of the snow and lied again. "Yes, Willy."

"Has it drifted? I wonder if Jimmy will have grit enough to stay all night with Tom if the snow is deep on the tracks and he has to be extra watching. Pretty hard on Tom to see to the tower and gates both on a bad night. Wonder if—Jimmy has got—grit enough."

"Course he has. Boys always have more grit than grown men. Don't know enough to be scared."

As Susy spoke, she knew in the depths of her agonized heart that Jimmy, little fair-haired, mother's boy, had not had grit enough even to face the elemental odds of the day, for his coming, much less for staying. She knew that the Oxbridge train had been stalled, that the man for whom Mr. Sloane had wired had not arrived. She knew of Tom, stark and dead, released from all tasks of earth. She knew that not a human being, man or boy was there to tend signals or gates. A night of awful storm was closing in. It was nearly time for the express; another train, a local, was due seven minutes later. If either or both was off schedule! Off schedule in that blinding fury of white storm, what then?

Susy said she would go down cellar for more coal before it got darker. When she was down cellar she began to pray. Susy came of a God-fearing race. All her life, she had read the Bible, she had attended church, she had prayed—now she *prayed.* For the first time in her life in the cold, gloomy cellar, knees on stones, prostrate before a mighty conception of a higher Power, cut off from all human aid, she realized some Presence while she prayed. Great waves of love and awe, also a terrible defiance born of despair, swept over her.

"God Almighty," prayed Susy in her wild voice of accusation and terror, and the greatest love of Humanity, the love for its Creator, despite the awful suffering of enforced life. "God Almighty, show me how to keep the gates. You sent the storm. You call[ed] Tom from this world. You know. Lives will be lost, lives not finished. Help me to keep the gates."

Susy carried the scuttle of coal upstairs. As she entered the room Willy stirred. "The express."

Susy heard a swiftly swelling roar. She ran to the window. A green light flashed out, a slanting shaft of green light; the gates clanged down.

"The express has gone through," she proclaimed in a loud, strangely clear voice.

"The signals? The gates?"

"The green light came on; the gates went down."

A gasp of relief came from the little mound of humanity in the bed. "Tom—Jimmy, there?"

Susy said nothing. She was trying to light the lamp. Her hands were cold and stiff.

"Why don't you speak, ma?"

"Everything was all right, pa."

"Both there," Willy murmured peacefully. The shadow of a smile was over his gray face.

After the lamp was lighted, Susy looked at the clock. It was time for the local, overtime by two minutes. The express had been late. Susy stood out of sight of Willy. She seemed as if in a closet of sacredly isolated self, alone with her new conception of God.

She prayed again with a terrible silent shout of her whole being. "The gates, the signals. God, show me how to keep them."

"Susy."

"Yes, pa."

"Blow out the lamp and watch for the next train."

"Yes, pa."

Susy blew out the light and sat down beside the window. It seemed to her that the whole room was vocal with her prayer. It drowned the roar of the storm for her.

The man in the bed breathed heavily. She knew that his dying eyes were strained toward the window.

Susy saw or thought she saw the green light flash out like a living emerald; the gates swing majestically down. Then the train labored past after a short stop. No one got off the train. "No passengers to-night, pa," she called out loudly.

The engineer was visible leaning sidewise from the cab in a cloud of rosy smoke. The gates reared up, the train chugged out of sight, the red light disappearing through the drive of the snow.

"All right, pa. There was the green light, then the gates went down, the train came and stopped, no passengers; saw Mike Kelly leaning out the engine. Then the train went on, now the gates are up. Don't you worry one mite more pa. A higher Power than us looks out for things sometimes."

"Jimmy is an awful smart boy to be tugging at the gates such a night as this," the old man said, almost sobbing.

"He wouldn't be so smart if there wasn't some higher Power back of him." Susy's voice had a noble quality, also a curiously shamed one. She could not show even to her dying husband more than a glimpse of her stunned faith.

"Light the lamp now, Susy."

Susy lighted the lamp. It stood on the table in the centre of the room, the table with a fringed cover. Susy looked at the old man in the bed. He was changing rapidly. He was so sunken upon himself that he seemed disappearing. His face was sharped out with the death-rigor. His mouth was open ready to gasp.

"How do you feel, pa?"

"I—don't know, ma."

"You'll be better in the morning."

Willy made a slight movement with his head. A ghost of a smile, half sweet, half sardonic, widened his face. He said something which Susy did not catch.

"Anything you want, pa?"

Susy placed her ear close to the poor gaping mouth, struggling into speech. She heard one word and understood.

It was Sunday night, and always on Sunday night, she and Willy had been accustomed to a chapter in the Bible, which Willy read, and he afterward repeated the Lord's Prayer. Susy got the Bible from the centre table, put on her spectacles, and read the Twenty-third Psalm. Willy could not hear at first. Finally she raised her voice to a shout. Then she knelt beside the bed and said the Lord's Prayer, also in a very loud voice.

After the Amen, she did not rise. She still knelt, her face buried in the bed-clothes. She was then praying her own terrible, almost blasphemous prayer about the signals and the gates. Susy felt a feeble touch on her bowed head, an inquiring, wondering touch. She rose.

"I didn't hear the—Amen."

"I said it."

"Blow out the light and look at the tower and the—gates—ma."

"They will be all right."

As Susy rose a red light shone out on the opposite wall. The old man raised himself in bed with an awful cry.

"Danger!" cried old Willy, whose dying body kept his faithful soul from duty. "The red light! Danger!"

Susy sobbed dryly. She ran across the red light, laying like a flag over the floor, into her bedroom. It was icy cold. The room was not quite dark because of the dreadful corpse-like pallor of the storm, driving in full fury against the one window.

Susy sank on her knees beside the white-mounded bed, hearing as she did so, poor Willy's feeble cry of "Danger!" Susy prayed again. She was there only a second, but in that second was concentrated the mighty impulse of a human heart toward the Greatness from which it came, toward which it went.

Susy hastened back to the other room. It was full of golden light. "Tom's onto it," whispered Willy, "Tom and Jimmy. That light's caution. They're lookin' out. Yellow light—Caution."

Suddenly instead of the yellow light flashed the splendid green.

"Track clear!" Willy shouted with incredible strength. "Susy! Window!"

Susy looked out of the window, shading her eyes from the light in the room with her curved hand.

"Green light," she said in her voice of strange awe and triumph. "Green light, train through."

Willy lay still.

"Hear the train, pa?"

Willy did not reply.

Susy left the window and bent over her husband. He seemed fairly melting into the bed so complete was his collapse. Obviously nothing had kept him alive so long except his anxiety over his unfulfilled duty, acting like a stimulant to his passing soul.

Susy sobbed, a little meek, dry sob. Her husband paid no heed. She went again into the freezing bedroom. When she came out, her face was pitiful but stern. She brought clothing and sheets, and laid them in neat piles on a sofa.

It was time for Willy's medicine. She held the spoon to his ashy parted lips. "Try and swaller, pa."

Willy moved his head slightly in meek protest. He rolled his eyes pitifully at his wife. He could not swallow.

"You shan't be pestered any more, pa," Susy said.

She put away the medicine. Then she sat beside the bed and waited. Her stern, pitying, loving eyes never swerved from her husband's face. She saw him in the past, the present. She saw him obediently dying there, an old spent man; she saw him in his strong middle-age when he had held a responsible position in connection with the railroad. Mr. Sloane had obtained it for him. He had always been a good friend of Willy's.

After Willy's fever which had prematurely aged him, Mr. Sloane had placed him in the only post for which his strength was fitted, gatekeeper, and paid him liberally. She saw Willy in his youth when he had come courting her. He had been a gay, laughing, handsome boy. All the girls had envied her.

The old wife, sitting beside her dying man, loved him with a comprehension and memory of the fullness of love as she had never loved him before. Through the hours the storm howled and drifted, the signals never failed, and the crossing-gates clanged up and down amid the chugging roar of the laboring trains, and no disaster befell.

When the weak new day was born, the storm was over, and the man in the bed had begun his dreadful stertorous last breathings of mortal life. Susy raised his lopping head in an effort to ease him. She had seen people die. She knew that Willy was dying.

It was past three o'clock. She thought dully that Doctor Evarts would not come now until daylight. "Most likely his car got stalled trying to get here," her thoughts spelled out. Susy was anxious about the doctor. He was not young, he was overworked, and such a storm was a man-killer like a beast of the jungle. She reflected that his coming could do no good here. Her poor old man was past medical science. Doctor Evarts was to have brought the district nurse with him on this call. The nurse would have been a comfort, a good, middle-aged woman who had buried her own husband.

Susy hoped the nurse, if she were with the doctor in the stalled car, was well wrapped. It was clearing cold. Willy continued to breathe those shocking breaths which mark the passing of a soul from its body of earth. Susy spoke to him now and then, but he did not seem to hear her.

She sat still and watched. The breaths seemed to shake the house. Suddenly they stopped. It was still, and the stillness seemed to smite the ears like a cannonade.

Susy was stunned for a few moments. Then she rose and went about her last duty to her husband, her little wiry body and frail arms doing apparently superhuman tasks. She was lame, too. She had fallen and injured her knee the winter before and had never fully recovered.

She limped about, performing her last duties to her husband slowly and painfully, but thoroughly. At last the little dead man lay peacefully in his clean smooth bed, his upturned face wearing an expression of calm rapture.

Susy crept across to the window. The storm was over. At the last it had rained and frozen. The earth looked like a white ocean suddenly petrified at the height of the storm. The trees were bent stiffly to the icy snow and fastened there. The telegraph wires sagged in rigid loops. Everything gave out blinding lights as from sheets of silver and gold with sudden flashe[s] of jewels. Susy gazed out dumbly for a few min-

utes. Then she collapsed. She lay quite still on the floor, a little help-
less bundle, until Doctor Evarts and the nurse found her.

Following them was a tall, fur-coated man, Sloane the railroad di-
rector. His high-powered car had made it possible for the doctor's
small one to get through the drifts, had in fact towed it. The doctor
and the nurse lifted little Susy, carried her into the bedroom, and
worked over her.

Sloane bent over the dead man, his face very grave. He had been
Willy's friend. The two had been boys in school together. Sloane sat
down beside the window which gave on the station. He looked both
sad and puzzled.

The doctor and the nurse went back and forth between the bedroom and the warm kitchen. The fragrance of coffee filled the air.
Sloane stopped the doctor. "How is she?"

"All right. Little determined women like her have terrible tenacity of life. She only dropped because for the moment she was down
and out."

"Who laid him out?"

"She."

"How?"

The doctor laughed grimly. "I don't know, suppose I might say
reserve strength. No mortal, man or woman, knows how much is
owned, until a test comes."

"I cannot understand."

"Neither can I. It is physically impossible apparently of course, but
there you are, no one else was here. She did it. Women of her sort are
almost terrible when a demand is made on their love and strength,
and there is no one else. Sometimes it has seemed to me they can
work miracles."

"She is a good little woman. I shall see that she is provided for all
the rest of her life in comfort."

"Glad to hear that. Come out in the kitchen and have some coffee.
Wait a minute. Come to the door with me first."

The men stood in the doorway looking out at the blinding, glittering morning. The crossing gates upreared, [a] splendid slant of ice.
There was a little chimney in the tower. It was plumed with violet
and rosy smoke.

"The line to that tower there, the telephone line was open all night," Sloane said in a curious, dry voice.

The doctor turned sharply on him. "Open? Thought the telephone lines were all out. Mine was and is."

"That line to the tower, special line, was open all night. Kept calling up, always got an answer."

"Who answered?"

"I don't know. Didn't know the voice. It was thin and low, but very clear, almost like singing."

"You see there is not one foot print to that tower. Foot prints would show in the crust."

ENDING I

The doctor nodded.

"Wait a bit. I am going over there."

The doctor stood waiting while Sloane went crunching through the frozen snow-crust. He was not gone long.

The nurse came and told the doctor about Susy. "She is coming to," she said softly. "She wants her little white shawl. I can't find it."

"Well, put something else over her, I will be in directly."

Sloane returned, a fluffy mass over his arm. He was obviously agitated.

"What is it?" asked the doctor.

"Looks to me like a woman's shawl, found it right beside the telephone."

The doctor paled slowly. "It is Susy's shawl. Have seen her wearing it dozens of times. She has just asked for it. The nurse told me."

The doctor took the shawl into the house.

"Coming out all right," he said to Sloane when he returned. "That was her shawl."

"Did she remember?"

"No, and she must not be told. She is cast on simple lines."

The men stood staring at each other in a sort of horror.

"How in Heaven's name do you account for it?" Sloane gasped.

"Don't account for it. This is not the first time I have been at a loss to account for them. Maybe there is a thinner wall and a door into the next dimension for loving women that men never find. Love like that woman's is an invincible Power."

ENDING II

The doctor nodded.

"Wait a bit. I'm going over there." Sloane went crunching through the snow-crust.

The doctor stood gazing reflectively out at the diamond-morning, a triumph of winter, offered to the attention of those who love beauty.

The nurse came and told the doctor about Susy.

"She is conscious," she said. "Will be all right presently. She is asking for her little white shawl. I can't find it."

"Chilly?"

"Perhaps, maybe just a habit."

"Perhaps. She always has that thing over her shoulders. Go back and find something else for her until I come. I am waiting for Mr. Sloane."

The nurse obeyed, casting a puzzled glance at the doctor.

Sloane returned. He had a fluffy white mass over his arm. He was obviously agitated.

"What is it?" asked the doctor.

"Looks to me like a woman's shawl, found it beside the telephone."

The doctor paled. "That is Susy's shawl," he said slowly. "Have seen her wearing it all the time. The nurse has been here. She has come to and asked for it. I will take it in and see if she remembers."

Sloane was drinking more coffee in the kitchen when the doctor entered. "She is coming out all right," he said. "Strange what tremendous reserve strength there is sometimes in a little woman like that."

"Did she remember?"

"Of course not. She must never know where you found that shawl. She is cast on simple lines. Dangerous to snare them."

Sloane stared [in] an expression of horror. "How in Heaven's name do you account for it?"

"Don't account for it. This is not the first time for me. Of course you know as well as I do that there are other dimensions beside this in which we live and move and have our being. I believe that sometimes the partition walls are very thin for certain souls, perhaps transparent and there may be entrances for them under certain stress, of which you and I know nothing. That little woman in there had the almost invincible power of a great unselfish love last night. It certainly enabled her to go beyond our horizon view. That is all I can say. Bless her with her little white shawl."

"I too," said Sloane.

APPENDIX

Bibliography of Mary Wilkins Freeman's Works

SHORT FICTION

This complete listing of Freeman's adult short fiction, arranged alphabetically, includes several short sketches such as "After the Rain" and "Pastels in Prose" which
cannot properly be considered short stories; it likewise includes unfinished manuscripts. Publishing information given is for the collection if collected before 1930
(the year of Freeman's death) and for original publishing dates if not collected before
this date.

"About Hannah Stone," *Everybody's* 4 (Jan. 1901): 25–33.

"After the Rain," *Century* 45 (Dec. 1892): 271.

"Amanda and Love," *A New England Nun and Other Stories* (New York: Harper and Brothers, 1891), 288–304.

"Amanda Todd: The Friend of Cats," *The People of Our Neighborhood* (Philadelphia: Curtis Publishing Company, 1898), 75–90.

"Amarina's Roses," *The Fair Lavinia and Others* (New York: Harper and
Brothers, 1907), 43–83.

"The Amethyst Comb," *The Copy-Cat and Other Stories* (New York: Harper
and Brothers, 1914), 211–36.

"The Apple-Tree," *Six Trees* (New York: Harper and Brothers, 1903),
169–207.

"Arethusa," *Understudies* (New York: Harper and Brothers, 1901), 147–69.

"The Auction," *Woman's Home Companion* 36 (Oct. 1909): 7–8, 93.

"Away from Sunflower Ranch," *Boston Evening Transcript: The Holiday Transcript*, Dec. 1890, p. 4.

"The Balking of Christopher," *The Copy-Cat and Other Stories* (New York:
Harper and Brothers, 1914), 267–91.

"The Balsam Fir," *Six Trees* (New York: Harper and Brothers, 1903),
101–27.

"The Bar Light-House," *A Humble Romance and Other Stories* (New York: Harper and Brothers, 1887), 180–91.

"Betsey Somerset," *Harper's Bazar* 26 (18 Mar. 1893): 205–7.

"Big Sister Solly," *The Copy-Cat and Other Stories* (New York: Harper and Brothers, 1914), 107–35.

"Billy and Susy," *The Winning Lady and Others* (New York: Harper and Brothers, 1909), 103–22.

"The Blue Butterfly," *Woman's Home Companion* 40 (Jan. 1913): 3–4, 44.

"The Boomerang," *Pictorial Review* 18 (Mar. 1917): 22–24, 44.

"Both Cheeks," *Edgewater People* (New York: Harper and Brothers, 1918), 215–31.

"Bouncing Bet," *Understudies* (New York: Harper and Brothers, 1901), 99–119.

"Brakes and White Vi'lets," *A Humble Romance and Other Stories* (New York: Harper and Brothers, 1887), 107–17.

"The Bright Side," *Harper's Monthly* 146 (Apr. 1923): 630–44.

"The Brother," MS (c. 1927). (Cited in Foster, 213.)

"A Brotherhood of Three," *Harper's Weekly* 41 (18 Dec. 1897): 1248–50; also in *Illustrated London News* 111 (18 Dec. 1897): 879–81.

"The Buckley Lady," *Silence and Other Stories* (New York: Harper and Brothers, 1898), 55–110.

"The Butterfly," *The Givers* (New York: Harper and Brothers, 1904), 229–65.

"Calla-Lilies and Hannah," *A New England Nun and Other Stories* (New York: Harper and Brothers, 1891), 99–120.

"The Cat," *Understudies* (New York: Harper and Brothers, 1901), 3–16.

"Catherine Carr," *The Love of Parson Lord and Other Stories* (New York: Harper and Brothers, 1900), 143–81.

"The Cautious King, and the All-Round Wise Woman," *Harper's Weekly* 53 (26 June 1909): 22–24.

"The Chance of Araminta," *The Givers* (New York: Harper and Brothers, 1904), 192–228.

"The Christmas Ghost," *Everybody's* 3 (Dec. 1900): 512–20.

"Christmas Jenny," *A New England Nun and Other Stories* (New York: Harper and Brothers, 1891), 160–77.

"A Christmas Lady," *Ladies' Home Journal* 27 (Dec. 1909): 17–18.

"A Christmas Pastel/In Prose," *Boston Evening Transcript*, 19 Dec. 1891, p. 20.

"The Christmas Sing in Our Village," *The People of Our Neighborhood* (Philadelphia: Curtis Publishing Company, 1898), 149–61.

"A Church Mouse," *A New England Nun and Other Stories* (New York: Harper and Brothers, 1891), 407–26.

"Cinnamon Roses," *A Humble Romance and Other Stories* (New York: Harper and Brothers, 1887), 164–79.

"The Cloak Also," *Harper's Monthly* 134 (Mar. 1917): 545–55.

"The Cock of the Walk," *The Copy-Cat and Other Stories* (New York: Harper and Brothers, 1914), 33–54.

"A Conflict Ended," *A Humble Romance and Other Stories* (New York: Harper and Brothers, 1887), 382–98.

"A Conquest of Humility," *A Humble Romance and Other Stories* (New York: Harper and Brothers, 1887), 415–36.

"The Copy-Cat," *The Copy-Cat and Other Stories* (New York: Harper and Brothers, 1914), 1–31.

"Coronation" (previously titled "The Door Mat"). *The Copy-Cat and Other Stories* (New York: Harper and Brothers, 1914), 183–209.

"Criss-Cross," *Harper's Monthly* 129 (Aug. 1914): 360–72.

"Cyrus Emmett: The Unlucky Man," *The People of Our Neighborhood* (Philadelphia: Curtis Publishing Company, 1898), pp. 41–57.

"D. J.: A Christmas Story," *Mail and Express Illustrated Saturday Magazine* (New York) (5 Dec. 1903): 14–15, 22, 30; also in *Advance* 46 (17 Dec. 1903): 766–69.

"Daniel and Little Dan'l," *The Copy-Cat and Other Stories* (New York: Harper and Brothers, 1914), 83–106.

"Dear Annie," *The Copy-Cat and Other Stories* (New York: Harper and Brothers, 1914), 293–351.

"A Devotee of Art," *Harper's Bazar* 27 (27 Jan. 1894): 69–71.

"A Discovered Pearl," *A New England Nun and Other Stories* (New York: Harper and Brothers, 1891), 253–67.

"The Doctor's Horse," *Understudies* (New York: Harper and Brothers, 1901), 85–96.

"The Doll Lady," *Harper's Monthly* 124 (Jan. 1912): 279–90.

"Down the Road to the Emersons," *Romance* 12 (Nov. 1893): 3–24.

"An Easter-Card," *Everybody's* 4 (Apr. 1901), 372–77.

"Eglantina," *The Givers* (New York: Harper and Brothers, 1904), 93–131. Republished in *The Fair Lavinia and Others* (New York: Harper and Brothers, 1907), 87–108.

"Eliza Sam," *The Winning Lady and Others* (New York: Harper and Brothers, 1909), 281–303.

"The Elm-Tree," *Six Trees* (New York: Harper and Brothers, 1903), 1–40.

"Emancipation," *Harper's Monthly* 132 (Dec. 1915), 27–35.

"Emmy," *Century*, 41 (Feb. 1891), 499–506.

"Eunice and the Doll," *Boston Evening Transcript* 13 Dec. 1897, p. 8; 14 Dec. 1897, p. 10; also in *Pocket Magazine* 5 (Mar. 1898): 1–41; also in *Best Things from American Literature*, ed. Irving Bacheller (New York: The Christian Herald, 1899), 369–82.

"Evelina's Garden," *Silence and Other Stories* (New York: Harper and Brothers, 1898), 111–183.

"The Fair Lavinia," *The Fair Lavinia and Others* (New York: Harper and Brothers, 1907), 3–39.

"Far Away Job," *Woman's Home Companion* 36 (Dec. 1909): 6–7, 72–75.

"A Far-Away Melody," *A Humble Romance and Other Stories* (New York: Harper and Brothers, 1887), 208–18.

"The Fighting McLeans," *The Delineator* 75 (Feb. 1910): 113–14, 150–52.

"The Fire at Elm Grove," *Good Cheer* 4 (June, 1884): 5–6.

"Flora and Hannah," *The Winning Lady and Others* (New York: Harper and Brothers, 1909), 307–17.

"The Flowering Bush," *Edgewater People* (New York: Harper and Brothers, 1918), 101–27.

"For the Love of One's Self," *Harper's Monthly* 110 (Jan. 1905): 303–16.

"Friend of My Heart," *Good Housekeeping* 57 (Dec. 1913): 733–40.

"A Gala Dress," *A New England Nun and Other Stories* (New York: Harper and Brothers, 1891), 37–53.

"A Gatherer of Simples," *A Humble Romance and Other Stories* (New York: Harper and Brothers, 1887), 280–95.

"General: A Christmas Story," *10 Story Book* 1 (Jan. 1902): 10–15.

"Gentian," *A Humble Romance and Other Stories* (New York: Harper and Brothers, 1887), 250–265.

"A Gentle Ghost," *A New England Nun and Other Stories* (New York: Harper and Brothers, 1891), 234–52.

"The Gift of Love," *Woman's Home Companion* 33 (Dec. 1906): 21, 22, 73.

"The Givers" (previously entitled "The Revolt of Sophia Lane"), *The Givers* (New York: Harper and Brothers, 1904), 3–50.

"The Gold," *The Fair Lavinia and Others* (New York: Harper and Brothers, 1907), 231–54.

"The Gospel According to Joan," *The Best Stories of Mary E. Wilkins*, ed. Henry Wysham Lanier (New York: Harper and Brothers, 1927), 441–65.

"The Great Pine," *Six Trees* (New York: Harper and Brothers, 1903), 67–99.

"A Guest in Sodom," *Century* 83 (Jan. 1912): 343–51.

"The Hall Bedroom," *Collier's* 30 (28 Mar. 1903): 19, 22–23; also in *Short Story Classics (American)*, ed. William Patten (New York: P. F. Collier and Son, 1905), 4: 1231–57.

"The Happy Day," *McClure's* 21 (May 1903): 89–94.

"Her Christmas," *The Winning Lady and Others* (New York: Harper and Brothers, 1909), 209–40.

"The Home-Coming of Jessica," first printed in *Woman's Home Companion* (unlocated). Reprinted in *The Home-Coming of Jessica* (by Mary E. Wilkins); *An Idyl of Central Park* (by Brander Matthews); *The Romance of a Soul* (by Robert Grant) (New York: Crowell and Kirkpatrick, 1901), 3–17.

"An Honest Soul," *A Humble Romance and Other Stories* (New York: Harper and Brothers, 1887), 78–91.

"Honorable Tommy," *Woman's Home Companion* 43 (Dec. 1916): 15–16, 68.

"The Horn of Plenty," *Collier's* 48 (18 Nov. 1911): 22–23, 30, 32, 34, 36.

"How Charlotte Ellen Went Visiting," *Boston Evening Transcript*, 1 Nov. 1897, p. 10; 2 Nov. 1897, p. 8; also in *New York Ledger* 54 (14 May, 21 May 1898): 17–18 each issue.

"Humble Pie," *Independent* 57 (1 Sept. 1904): 477–84.

"A Humble Romance," *A Humble Romance and Other Stories* (New York: Harper and Brothers, 1887), 1–24.

"Hyacinthus," *Harper's Monthly* 109 (Aug. 1904): 447–58; also in *Quaint Courtships*, ed. William Dean Howells and Henry Mills Alden (London: Harper and Brothers, 1906), 75–107.

"I Am a Rebel," undated MS, privately owned. (Cited in Foster, 142–43.)

"In Butterfly Time," *A Humble Romance and Other Stories* (New York: Harper and Brothers, 1887), 315–29.

"An Independent Thinker," *A Humble Romance and Other Stories* (New York: Harper and Brothers, 1887), 296–314.

"An Innocent Gamester," *A New England Nun and Other Stories* (New York: Harper and Brothers, 1891), 363–83.

"The Jade Bracelet," *Forum* 59 (Apr. 1918): 429–40.

"The Jester," *The Golden Book* 7 (June 1928): 821–28.

"Johnny-In-The-Woods," *The Copy-Cat and Other Stories* (New York: Harper and Brothers, 1914), 55–82.

"Josiah's First Christmas," *Collier's* 44 (11 Dec. 1909): 9–10.

"Joy," *The Givers* (New York: Harper and Brothers, 1904), 132–55.

"The Joy of Youth," *The Winning Lady and Others* (New York: Harper and Brothers, 1909), 71–100.

"Julia—Her Thanksgiving," *Harper's Bazar* 43 (Nov. 1909): 1079–82.

"Juliza," *Two Tales* 1 (12 Mar. 1892): 1–14; also in *Romance* 10 (July 1893): 352–70.

"A Kitchen Colonel," *A New England Nun and Other Stories* (New York: Harper and Brothers, 1891), 427–47.

"The Last Gift," *The Givers* (New York: Harper and Brothers, 1918), 266–96.

"The Liar," *Edgewater People* (New York: Harper and Brothers, 1918), 153–85.

"Life Everlastin'," *A New England Nun and Other Stories* (New York: Harper and Brothers, 1891), 338–62.

"Little-Girl-Afraid-Of-a-Dog," *The Winning Lady and Others* (New York: Harper and Brothers, 1909), 35–68.

"The Little Green Door," *New York Times* 13–15 Apr. 1896, p. 9 each day; also in *Pocket Magazine* 3 (July 1896): 56–90; and in *New York Ledger* 52 (25 Apr. 1898): 16–17.

"Little Lucy Rose," *The Copy-Cat and Other Stories* (New York: Harper and Brothers, 1914), 137–62.

"The Little Maid at the Door," *Silence and Other Stories* (New York: Harper and Brothers, 1898), 225–54.

"Little Margaret Snell: The Village Runaway," *The People of Our Neighborhood* (Philadelphia: Curtis Publishing Company, 1898), 23–38.

"The Lombardy Poplar," *Six Trees* (New York: Harper and Brothers, 1903), 129–67.

"The Long Arm" (by Mary E. Wilkins and J. Edgar Chamberlin), *Pocket Magazine* 1 (Dec. 1895): 1–76; also in *The Long Arm and Other Detective Stories* (London: Chapman and Hall Limited, 1895), 1–66.

"The Lost Book," *Book Culture* 1 (Sept. 1899): 136.

"The Lost Dog," *Understudies* (New York: Harper and Brothers, 1901), 53–61.

"The Lost Ghost," *The Wind in the Rose-Bush and Other Stories of the Supernatural* (New York: Doubleday, Page and Co., 1903), 201–37.

"Louisa," *A New England Nun and Other Stories* (New York: Harper and Brothers, 1891), 384–406.

"The Love of Parson Lord," *The Love of Parson Lord and Other Stories* (New York: Harper and Brothers, 1900), 3–81.

"A Lover of Flowers," *A Humble Romance and Other Stories* (New York: Harper and Brothers, 1887), 192–207.

"Lucy," *The Givers* (New York: Harper and Brothers, 1904), 51–92.

"Luella Miller," *The Wind in the Rose-Bush and Other Stories of the Supernatural* (New York: Doubleday, Page and Co., 1903), 75–104.

"Lydia Hersey, of East Bridgewater," *Silence and Other Stories* (New York: Harper and Brothers, 1898), 255–80.

"Lydia Wheelock: The Good Woman," *The People of Our Neighborhood* (Philadelphia: Curtis Publishing Company, 1898), 91–109.

"A Mistaken Charity," *A Humble Romance and Other Stories* (New York: Harper and Brothers, 1887), 234–49.

"A Modern Dragon," *A Humble Romance and Other Stories* (New York: Harper and Brothers, 1887), 60–77.

"The Monkey," *Understudies* (New York: Harper and Brothers, 1901), 19–36.

"A Moral Exigency," *A Humble Romance and Other Stories* (New York: Harper and Brothers, 1887), 219–33.

"Morning-Glory," *Understudies* (New York: Harper and Brothers, 1901), 217–30.

"Mother-Wings," *Harper's Monthly* 144 (Dec. 1921): 90–103.

"Mountain-Laurel," *Understudies* (New York: Harper and Brothers, 1901), 173–90.

"Mrs. Sackett's Easter Bonnet," *Woman's Home Companion* 34 (Apr. 1907): 5–7.

"The Mystery of Miss Amidon," *Boston Evening Transcript*, 22 Dec. 1900, p. 18.

"Nanny and Martha Pepperill," *Harper's Bazar* 28 (14 Dec. 1895): 1021–23.

"A Narrow Escape/How Santa Claus Baffled the Mounted Police," *Detroit Sunday News*, 25 Dec. 1892, p. 12.

"A New England Nun," *A New England Nun and Other Stories* (New York: Harper and Brothers, 1891), 1–17.

"A New England Prophet," *Silence and Other Stories* (New York: Harper and Brothers, 1898), 184–224.

"A New-Year's Resolution," *The Winning Lady and Others* (New York: Harper and Brothers, 1909), 321–28.

"Noblesse," *The Copy-Cat and Other Stories* (New York: Harper and Brothers, 1914), 163–81.

"An Object of Love," *A Humble Romance and Other Stories* (New York: Harper and Brothers, 1887), 266–79.

"An Old Arithmetician," *A Humble Romance and Other Stories* (New York: Harper and Brothers, 1887), 368–81.

"Old Lady Pingree," *A Humble Romance and Other Stories* (New York: Harper and Brothers, 1887), 148–63.

"The Old Man of the Field," *Edgewater People* (New York: Harper and Brothers, 1918), 26–50.

"An Old Valentine," *The Home-Maker* 8 (Feb. 1890): 367–74; also in *Romance* 9 (Feb. 1893): 50–64.

"Old Woman Magoun," *The Winning Lady and Others* (New York: Harper and Brothers, 1909), 243–77.

"One," MS (c. 1928). (Cited in Foster, 213.)

"One Good Time," *The Love of Parson Lord and Other Stories* (New York: Harper and Brothers, 1900), 195–233.

"On the Walpole Road," *A Humble Romance and Other Stories* (New York: Harper and Brothers, 1887), 134–47.

"Other People's Cake," *Collier's* 42 (21 Nov. 1908): 14–15, 32, 34, 36–37.

"The Other Side," *Harper's Bazar* 24 (26 Dec. 1891): 993–95.

"The Outside of the House," *Edgewater People* (New York: Harper and Brothers, 1918), 128–52.

"The Parrot," *Understudies* (New York: Harper and Brothers, 1901), 65–81.

"Pastels in Prose," *Harper's* 86 (Dec. 1892): 147–48.

"A Patient Waiter," *A Humble Romance and Other Stories* (New York: Harper and Brothers, 1887), 399–414.

"Peony," *Understudies* (New York: Harper and Brothers, 1901), 193–213.

"Phebe Ann Little: The Neat Woman," *The People of Our Neighborhood* (Philadelphia: Curtis Publishing Company, 1898), 59–73.

"The Pink Shawls," *The Fair Lavinia and Others* (New York: Harper and Brothers, 1907), 111–42.

"A Poetess," *A New England Nun and Other Stories* (New York: Harper and Brothers, 1891), 140–59.

"The Poor Lady," *Woman's Home Companion* 38 (Oct. 1911): 7–8, 84–86; 38 (Nov. 1911): 17–18, 75–77; 38 (Dec. 1911): 23–24, 70; 39 (Jan. 1912): 25–26, 56; 39 (Feb. 1912): 23–24, 62–63; 39 (Mar. 1912): 20, 93–96; 39 (Apr. 1912): 23–24.

"A Pot of Gold," *A New England Nun and Other Stories* (New York: Harper and Brothers, 1891), 178–97.

"The Price She Paid," *Harper's Bazar* 21 (10 Mar. 1888): 158–59.

"Prince's-Feather," *Understudies* (New York: Harper and Brothers, 1901), 123–43.

"The Prism," *Century* 62 (July 1901): 469–74.

"The Prop," *Saturday Evening Post* 190 (5 Jan. 1918): 12–13, 109–10.

"A Protracted Meeting," *The Housewife* 6 (Feb. 1891): 6; 6 (Mar. 1891): 6.

"The Proud Lucinda," *Harper's Bazar* 24 (7 Feb. 1891): 101–3.

"The Pumpkin," *Harper's Bazar* 33 (24 Nov. 1900): 1863–71.

"A Quilting Bee in Our Village," *The People of Our Neighborhood* (Philadelphia: Curtis Publishing Company, 1898), 111–28.

"The Reign of the Doll," *The Givers* (New York: Harper and Brothers, 1904), 156–91.

"'A Retreat to the Goal,'" *Edgewater People* (New York: Harper and Brothers, 1918), 285–315.

"The Return," *Woman's Home Companion* 48 (Aug. 1921): 21–22, 83.

"The Revolt of 'Mother,'" *A New England Nun and Other Stories* (New York: Harper and Brothers, 1891), 448–68.

"The Ring with the Green Stone," *Edgewater People* (New York: Harper and Brothers, 1918), 261–84.

"Robins and Hammers," *A Humble Romance and Other Stories* (New York: Harper and Brothers, 1887), 118–33.

"The Rocket," undated MS; also entitled "One Old Lady." Manuscript and Archives Division, New York Public Library.

"Rosemary Marsh," *Harper's Bazar* 30 (11 Dec. 1897): 1026.

"A Rustic Comedy," *Ladies' Home Journal* 8 (Mar. 1891): 7–8.

"Santa Claus: Two Jack-Knives," *Springfield* (Mass.) *Sunday Republican*, 15 Dec. 1901, p. 24.

"Sarah Edgewater," *Edgewater People* (New York: Harper and Brothers, 1918), 3–25.

"The Saving of Hiram Sessions," *Pictorial Review* 16 (May 1915): 20–21, 70–72.

"The Scent of the Roses," *A New England Nun and Other Stories* (New York: Harper and Brothers, 1891), 198–214.

"The School-Teacher," *Harper's Bazar* 28 (6 Apr. 1895): 262.

"The School-Teacher's Story," *Romance* 13 (Feb. 1894): 5–18.

"The Secret," *The Fair Lavinia and Others* (New York: Harper and Brothers, 1907), 187–228.

"The Selfishness of Amelia Lamkin," *The Winning Lady and Others* (New York: Harper and Brothers, 1909), 125–72.

"Serena Ann: Her First Christmas Keeping," *Hartford Daily Courant*, 15 Dec. 1894, p. 10.

"Serena Ann's First Valentine," *Boston Evening Transcript*, 5 Feb. 1897, p. 9; also in *New York Ledger* 53 (13 Feb. 1897): 6–7; also in *The English Illustrated* 17 (June 1897): 235–42.

"The Shadow Family," *The Boston Sunday Budget*, 1 Jan. 1882 (unlocated).

"The Shadows on the Wall," *The Wind in the Rose-Bush and Other Stories of the Supernatural* (New York: Doubleday, Page and Company, 1903), 41–72.

"She Who Adorns Her Sister Adorns Herself," *Harper's Bazar* 38 (May 1904): 456–60.

"Silence," *Silence and Other Stories* (New York: Harper and Brothers, 1898), 1–54.

"Sister Liddy," *A New England Nun and Other Stories* (New York: Harper and Brothers, 1891), 81–98.

"A Slayer of Serpents," *Collier's* 44 (19 Mar. 1910): 16–17, 19, 36, 38.

"The Slip of the Leash," *Harper's Monthly* 109 (Oct. 1904): 668–75.

"The Soldier Man," *Edgewater People* (New York: Harper and Brothers, 1918), 232–60.

"A Solitary," *A New England Nun and Other Stories* (New York: Harper and Brothers, 1891), 215–33.

"Something on Her Mind," *Harper's Bazar* 46 (Dec. 1912): 607–8.

"Sonny," *Lippincott's* 47 (June 1891): 776–85; also in *Romance* 8 (Nov. 1892): 13–27.

"Sour Sweetings," *Edgewater People* (New York: Harper and Brothers, 1918), 186–214.

"The Southwest Chamber," *The Wind in the Rose-Bush and Other Stories of the Supernatural* (New York: Doubleday, Page and Company, 1903), 107–64.

"A Souvenir," *A Humble Romance and Other Stories* (New York: Harper and Brothers, 1887), 350–67.

"A Sparrow's Nest," *Good Cheer* 6 (Aug. 1887): 3–4.

"The Squirrel," *Understudies* (New York: Harper and Brothers, 1901), 39–50.

"Starlight," *Woman's Home Companion* 35 (Dec. 1908): 19–20, 74.

"The Steeple," *Hampton-Columbian* 27 (Oct. 1911): 412–20.

"The Stockwells' Apple-Paring Bee," *The People of Our Neighborhood* (Philadelphia: Curtis Publishing Company, 1898), 129–47.

"A Stolen Christmas," *A New England Nun and Other Stories* (New York: Harper and Brothers, 1891), 321–37.

"The Story of Little Mary Whitlow," *Lippincott's* 21 (May 1883): 500–504.

"A Stress of Conscience," *Harper's Bazar* 25 (25 June 1892): 518–19; also in *Illustrated London News* 100 (25 June 1892): 785–87.

"The Strike of Hannah," *Woman's Home Companion* 33 (Nov. 1906): 9–10, 50–52.

"A Study in China," *Harper's Bazar* 20 (5 Nov. 1887): 766–67.

"Susan: Her Neighbor's Story," *Harper's Bazar* 32 (23 Sept. 1899): 801, 804.

"Susan Jane's Valentine," *Harper's Bazar* 33 (17 Feb. 1900): 132–33.

"Sweet-Flowering Perennial," *Harper's Monthly* 131 (July 1915): 287–97.

"Sweet-Williams," *Harper's Bazar* 28 (25 May 1895): 418.

"A Symphony in Lavender," *A Humble Romance and Other Stories* (New York: Harper and Brothers, 1887), 37–48.

"Tall Jane," *St. Louis Republic* 25 Oct. 1891, p. 5; also in *Detroit Sunday News*, 25 Oct. 1891, p. 12.

"A Tardy Thanksgiving," *A Humble Romance and Other Stories* (New York: Harper and Brothers, 1887), 49–59.

"A Taste of Honey," *A Humble Romance and Other Stories* (New York: Harper and Brothers, 1887), 92–106.

"Thanksgiving Crossroads," *Woman's Home Companion* 44 (Nov. 1917): 13, 58, 60.

"A Thanksgiving Thief," *Ladies' Home Journal* 9 (Nov. 1892): 1–2.

"The Third Miss Merryweather," *Good Cheer* 3 (Sept. 1884): 7.

"The Three Old Sisters and the Old Beau," *The Love of Parson Lord and Other Stories* (New York: Harper and Brothers, 1900), 185–92.

"Timothy Sampson: The Wise Man," *The People of Our Neighborhood* (Philadelphia: Curtis Publishing Company, 1898), 1–21.

"A Tragedy from the Trivial," *Frank Leslie's Popular Monthly* 50 (Aug. 1900): 334–49; also in *Cornhill* 83, n.s. 10 (Jan. 1901): 63–79.

"The Travelling Sister," *The Winning Lady and Others* (New York: Harper and Brothers, 1909), 175–206.

"The Tree of Knowledge," *The Love of Parson Lord and Other Stories* (New York: Harper and Brothers, 1900), 85–140.

"The Twelfth Guest," *A New England Nun and Other Stories* (New York: Harper and Brothers, 1891), 54–80.

"Two for Peace," *Lippincott's* 68 (July 1901): 51–70.

"Two Friends," *Harper's Bazar* 20 (25 June 1887): 450–51.

"Two Old Lovers," *A Humble Romance and Other Stories* (New York: Harper and Brothers, 1887), 25–36.

"The Umbrella Man," *The Copy-Cat and Other Stories* (New York: Harper and Brothers, 1914), 237–66.

"Uncle Davy," *Detroit Sunday News*, 10 Jan. 1892, p. 10.

"The Underling," *The Fair Lavinia and Others* (New York: Harper and Brothers, 1907), 257–308.

"An Unlucky Christmas," *Harper's Bazar* 29 (12 Dec. 1896): 1037–39.

"An Unwilling Guest," *A Humble Romance and Other Stories* (New York: Harper and Brothers, 1887), 330–49.

"Up Primrose Hill," *A New England Nun and Other Stories* (New York: Harper and Brothers, 1891), 305–20.

"The Vacant Lot," *The Wind in the Rose-Bush and Other Stories of the Supernatural* (New York: Doubleday, Page and Company, 1903), 167–98.

"Value Received," *Edgewater People* (New York: Harper and Brothers, 1918), 74–100.

"A Village Lear," *A New England Nun and Other Stories* (New York: Harper and Brothers, 1891), 268–87.

"A Village Singer," *A New England Nun and Other Stories* (New York: Harper and Brothers, 1891), 18–36.

"The Voice of the Clock," *Edgewater People* (New York: Harper and Brothers, 1918), 51–73.

"A Wandering Samaritan," *Cosmopolitan* 2 (Sept. 1886): 28–33.
"A War-Time Dress," *Cosmopolitan* 25 (Aug. 1898): 403–16.
"A Wayfaring Couple," *A New England Nun and Other Stories* (New York: Harper and Brothers, 1891), 121–39.
"The Whist Players," *Century* 44 (Oct. 1892): 817.
"The White Birch," *Six Trees* (New York: Harper and Brothers, 1903), 41–65.
"The White Shawl," undated MS. Manuscript and Archives Division, New York Public Library.
"The Willow-Ware," *The Fair Lavinia and Others* (New York: Harper and Brothers, 1907), 145–83.
"The Wind in the Rose-Bush," *The Wind in the Rose-Bush and Other Stories of the Supernatural* (New York: Doubleday, Page and Company, 1903), 3–37.
"The Winning Lady," *The Winning Lady and Others* (New York: Harper and Brothers, 1909), 3–32.
"The Witch's Daughter," *Harper's Weekly* 54 (10 Dec. 1910): 17, 32.
"Wrong Side Out," *10 Story Book* 1 (July 1901): 10–16.

NOVELS, COLLECTIONS, PLAYS, FILMS

This list does not include recent collections of Freeman's works.

An Alabaster Box, [by Mary Wilkins Freeman and Florence Morse Kingsley]. New York: D. Appleton and Company, 1917.
An Alabaster Box. Directed by Chester Withey. Vitagraph Company of America motion picture production, 1917.
The Best Stories of Mary E. Wilkins, ed. Henry Wysham Lanier. New York: Harper and Brothers, 1927.
The Butterfly House. New York: Dodd, Mead and Company, 1912.
By the Light of the Soul. New York: Harper and Brothers, 1907.
The Copy-Cat and Other Stories. New York: Harper and Brothers, 1914.
The Debtor. New York: Harper and Brothers, 1905.
"Doc" Gordon. New York: Authors and Newspapers Association, 1906.
Edgewater People. New York: Harper and Brothers, 1918.
Eglantina: A Romantic Parlor Play. Ladies' Home Journal 27 (July 1910): 13–14, 38.
The Fair Lavinia and Others. New York: Harper and Brothers, 1907.
False Evidence (based on *Madelon*). Metro motion picture production, 1919.
Giles Corey, Yeoman: A Play. New York: Harper and Brothers, 1893.
The Givers. New York: Harper and Brothers, 1904.
The Heart's Highway, A Romance of Virginia in the Seventeenth Century. New York: Doubleday, Page and Company, 1900.

A *Humble Romance and Other Stories*. New York: Harper and Brothers, 1887.
The Jamesons. New York: Doubleday and McClure Company, 1899.
Jane Field. New York: Harper and Brothers, 1893.
Jerome, a Poor Man. New York: Harper and Brothers, 1897.
The Love of Parson Lord and Other Stories. New York: Harper and Brothers, 1900.
Madelon. New York: Harper and Brothers, 1896.
A New England Nun and Other Stories. New York: Harper and Brothers, 1891.
Pembroke. New York: Harper and Brothers, 1894.
The People of Our Neighborhood. Philadelphia: Curtis Publishing Company, 1898.
The Pilgrim's Progress. Adapted to a motion picture play by Mary E. Wilkins and William Dinwiddie. New York, 1915.
The Portion of Labor. New York: Harper and Brothers, 1901.
Red Robin, A New England Drama. Copyrighted in 1892 and 1893 but unlocated. (Cited in Kendrick, 455 n. 1.)
The Shoulders of Atlas. New York: Harper and Brothers, 1908.
Silence and Other Stories. New York: Harper and Brothers, 1898.
Six Trees. New York: Harper and Brothers, 1903.
Understudies. New York: Harper and Brothers, 1901.
The Whole Family: A Novel by Twelve Authors. Mary W. Freeman, William D. Howells, Henry James, et al. New York: Harper and Brothers, 1908.
The Wind in the Rose-Bush and Other Stories of the Supernatural. New York: Doubleday, Page and Company, 1903.
The Winning Lady and Others. New York: Harper and Brothers, 1909.
The Yates Pride: A Romance. New York: Harper and Brothers, 1912.

NONFICTION

"Emily Bronte and *Wuthering Heights*." In *The World's Great Woman Novelists*, edited by T. M. Parrott, 85–93. (Philadelphia: The Booklovers Library, 1901).
"The Girl Who Wants to Write: Things to Do and to Avoid," *Harper's Bazar* 47 (June 1913): 272.
"Good Wits, Pen and Paper." In *What Women Can Earn: Occupations of Women and Their Compensation*, edited by G. H. Dodge et al., 28–29. (New York: Frederick A. Stokes Co., 1899).
"He Does Not Want a Fool," *The Delineator* 72 (July 1908): 80, 135.
"How I Write My Novels: Twelve of America's Most Popular Authors Reveal the Secrets of Their Art," *New York Times*, 25 Oct. 1908, mag. sec., 3–4.

"If They Had a Million Dollars: What Nine Famous Women Would Do If a Fortune Were Theirs," *Ladies' Home Journal* 20 (Sept. 1903): 10.

"Introductory Sketch" in "Biographical Edition" of *Pembroke* (New York: Harper and Brothers, 1899).

"Mary E. Wilkins." In *My Maiden Effort: Being the Personal Confessions of Well-Known American Authors as to Their Literary Beginnings*, 265–67. (Garden City, N.Y.: Doubleday, Page and Company, 1921).

"Mary E. Wilkins Freeman: An Autobiography" in "Who's Who—and Why: Serious and Frivolous Facts About the Great and the Near Great." *The Saturday Evening Post* 190 (8 Dec. 1917): 25, 75.

"New England, 'Mother of America,'" *Country Life in America* 22 (July 1912): 27–32, 64–67.

"We Are With France." In *For France*, edited by Charles H. Towne, 336. (Garden City, N.Y.: Doubleday, Page and Company, 1917).

"A Woman's Tribute to Mr. Howells," *The Literary Digest* 44 (9 Mar. 1912): 485.